LOST IN THE LIGHT!

"Chris?" she called in a thin, frightened voice. Jennifer was still a good ten feet or more away, her ears full of shouting behind her and from the direction of the house, but Lialla must have heard something. Hell-Light was lapping at her feet, and Edrith yelled: "Lialla! Get back, it's spreading!"

"But I can hear him!" she shouted back, and, dropping to hands and knees, she vanished into the glowing mass . . .

D0801994

RU EMERSON

NIGHT·THREADS

BOOK THREE:
ONE LAND, ONE DUKE

ACE BOOKS, NEW YORK

This book is an Ace original edition,
and has never been previously published.

ONE LAND, ONE DUKE

An Ace Book / published by arrangement
with the author

PRINTING HISTORY
Ace edition / February 1992

ISBN: 0-441-58087-4

Ace Books are published by The Berkley Publishing Group,
200 Madison Avenue, New York, New York 10016.
The name "ACE" and the "A" logo
are trademarks belonging to Charter Communications, Inc.

PRINTED IN THE UNITED STATES OF AMERICA

10 9 8 7 6 5 4 3 2 1

For Doug
and
Patrick Rumrill,
best of all the Mongeese

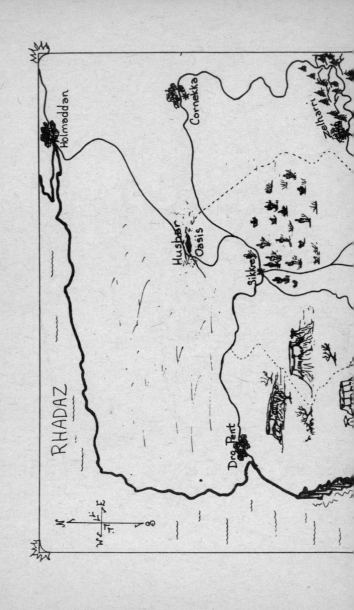

RHADAZ

Holmaddan

Cornekka

Zelharri

Husbar Oasis

Sikkre

Dro Pent

N
W E
S

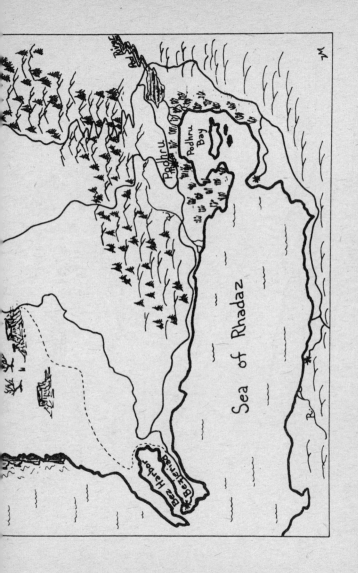

ONE LAND,
ONE DUKE

I

𝄢

THERE was fog this second day out of Bezjeriad; everything was damp, the air still, thick with the smells of salt, washed-up weed and small, very dead fish left by the last high tide. Enardi, who was familiar with spring fogs along the northern shores of the Sea of Rhadaz, suggested an early halt, so that the tent could be set up and the horses staked to a loose line before it became too dark to see anything. He had no arguments: His companions were one and all wet and chilled right to the bone.

An hour later, with the sun a mere haze of deep orange in thick gray, eight people huddled inside dark canvas walls over mugs of hot tea. "We can set a watch later, if you like," Enardi said finally. It was the first thing anyone had said in some time. "But I know this kind of night; there won't be any wind, the fog will double and with no stars or moon you can't see your thumb when it's rubbing at your nose. As still as it is, we'll hear any approach. But no one would be fool enough to attempt to ride through *that*, would they?" He gestured, a wave of his hand taking in the road, the rock-strewn land to both sides of it, the sea a half-mile of slope away, the fog that hid it all.

"You might be surprised," Jennifer said mildly. "We've some determined people after us just now; you'd do well to keep that in mind, since you've chosen to come with us." Enardi, his young face suddenly quite grave, nodded. "I tend to agree with you, though: We'll hear anyone trying to ride along the road long before we could possibly see them. Since we'll be able to hear just as well from inside the tent, I can't think why anyone should court pneumonia by walking around outside it."

"We'll hear anyone provided they come by horse," Robyn said. She shook her head. "I'm sorry I said that. God, I didn't need to think about that!"

"Well, don't then," Jennifer replied. "Think about what you're going to feed us instead, why don't you? But don't scare yourself conjuring up ugly scenes, either. If you're thinking about someone using magic to find us, well, think it through, Birdy, we can deal with that. We've done it enough times already, haven't we?" Robyn nodded rather reluctantly, but she looked considerably less unhappy as she drew the largest of the food bags across her shins and began rummaging inside. "I for one," Jennifer finished firmly, "am not going back outside until I thaw." She shivered down into her leather jacket. "And that may not be until tomorrow." She glanced over at Dahven, who sat cross-legged next to her, silently sipping his tea. He looked absolutely dreadful, damp hair plastered to his forehead, a drop of water formed on the end of his nose. She resisted the urge to remove the water drop and kept concerned remarks resolutely to herself; he wouldn't want to hear it, and he certainly didn't want anyone else to hear it, either. *If he hadn't insisted on riding all day,* she thought sourly. Getting angry wouldn't help, either; it only upset her stomach. Dahven could out-argue her, anyway, and he was at least as stubborn as she.

She didn't agree with him, but she *could* understand his problem; he didn't want anyone finding out where he had really been this past month. Didn't want them knowing that he'd been chained to the oar of a Lasanachi merchant ship, mistreated and beaten, until circumstances and luck had come together in Bez and frightened his owners into releasing him. By purest chance, Edrith had located the desperately ill and injured man and with Jennifer's help they'd gotten him into hiding before his brothers' men could take him.

Once she would have dismissed his attitude as macho posturing, but that wasn't all of it. *Why?* she asked herself. *Because you wouldn't ever fall for a macho posturer, or because you'd dump him if you found out that's what he was?* Or because she could sense the same reaction somewhere deep in her own guts? *I might do the same, if it were me. I'd want to bury it, pretend it never happened, just go on.*

She still felt vaguely guilty, somehow responsible for his enslavement. *I didn't want him to give us all his protective charms, even if I didn't have a reason for that. If he'd come with us*— Instead, they'd left Sikkre heading south across rough country for Bezjeriad, while Dahven went home all unaware to find his father awaiting him—with Lasanachi slave-buyers, and a bag of coin. *Robyn would probably say I'd had an Awful Warning that night.* Good old Robyn, with her Tarots, Wicca, tea leaves, I Ching—anything to give her a grip on the future. Birdy had always been so certain she had a sixth sense. Jennifer knew darned well she wasn't prescient, and even with all she'd seen lately, she still didn't believe in Sight, or Awful Warnings. It had been the desperation of new love and pure selfishness. *Well, don't be so hard on yourself, Cray,* she told herself. *After all, having a first schoolgirl crush at twenty-eight, and that after being torn from everything you'd struggled for in L.A., trading a law career for magic and two obnoxious young nobles—you did all right, girl.* Hell, she might have burst into tears or fainted; she considered this, considered Dahven's reaction to either, and grinned briefly. Fortunately for both of them, she'd been very calm and collected about the whole thing.

But I always have been good at that: Take charge, stay cool when it's blowing up all around me. At least, the insanity of love at first sight hadn't been one-sided; *that* would have been truly awful. Dahven had been thrown as off-balance by it as she. Maybe moreso, she thought dryly. According to various comments by Aletto, Edrith—Dahven himself—the man hadn't been quite as intent on his career to the exclusion of the opposite sex as she had.

Well, he was with her now, and she couldn't feel selfish about bullying him into coming to Podhru. The promise she'd extracted from him had probably saved his life. The damned idiot actually had thought of going back to Sikkre, alone, to browbeat his brothers into giving him back his Duchy, and here he still couldn't sit a horse for more than a few hours! *Is he really that dense, or is brother-love that strong? He has to know they have men out looking for him!* Men looking for "the traitor Dahven" probably weren't tracking him down to make certain he was eating right and taking his vitamins, and somehow Jennifer didn't think the twins would simply step aside if Dahven got close enough to ask them. More likely, they'd kill him in hopes it would seem he'd murdered his father and vanished. If they didn't kill him, they'd hand him over to the Emperor, unless they planned an end for their elder brother that was more devious and twisted than anything she could work out. Having met them, she didn't doubt they could devise such an end.

Look at him. What they've done to him. All of them. She could feel the muscles in her jaw tightening; forced herself to leave it, to relax. But before it gave her a headache. It was a no-win situation, at least for her: It made her fighting mad but there was no one to fight, and she couldn't fight with Dahven. She closed her eyes and turned her head slightly away from him. He looked so ill.

Just now, Aletto didn't look much better. None of them looked very good, really. The stay in Bezjeriad had given them a chance to relax. But the good food, warm bathing water, clean clothing, a real roof and real beds—hard to remember it was anything but a dream: Reality was wood smoke, a little warm water from one of Robyn's pots, a cloth to dab into it, soup made with dried vegetables and herbs, biscuits burned on one side. Men pursuing them, and ill will on all sides. Only Enardi was untouched by anything but the adventure of it, but then he knew nothing of privation, fear or pain. The rest of them knew all three only too well.

Aletto sat with his lame leg out straight; the bad shoulder was higher than the other and he rested his head on one hand, the way he did to keep it from being obvious that his head would loll to that side anyway. He spoke seldom just now and only in monosyllables; the slurring was noticeable only to one who knew what to listen for. Nothing could be done, though, about the acnelike scars that marred an otherwise attractive face.

In his case, it was very possibly a literal case of macho that kept him pushing so hard. Jennifer wished at the moment she had one of those magazine articles her secretary had photocopied and set on her chair, though Jan had never had reason to think her boss would need anything on the effect of partial paralysis, lack of male bonding activities and sterility on a man's behavior. *Good old Jan.* Jennifer swallowed around a sudden lump in her throat. *I hope they're taking good care of her, now that I'm gone.*

Well, it wasn't really her business anyway—Aletto was Robyn's to deal with, if she married him and had to provide him with heirs. Their problem. All the same, it must contribute to what made Aletto tick.

It was too bad she hadn't paid attention to something else

4

Jan had run by her, a while back, but then, who was to say that information about polio rehab would be useful here? She'd just have to rely on Robyn to slow Aletto down; difficult, since he'd discovered he actually could do things. Fortunately, he admitted now when he ached and wasn't so prickly about asking for help.

Of course, he couldn't be expected to show his weak side, considering all the years he and Lialla had lived with Jadek.

Lialla sat a little apart from the others, staring moodily at her feet. Jennifer considered asking her something—anything—to draw her out of it, then decided to leave it alone. Let Lialla work it out herself; Jennifer couldn't think of anything she could say that she hadn't already said, at some point or other. Lialla had worked so hard, so long, trying her damnedest to become a high-ranking Wielder—only a few days before, in Bez, she'd learned that Merrida had taught her everything wrong. Lialla had wanted a Silver or White sash as badly as Jennifer had wanted to make partner in three years. There didn't have to be a lot of logic on the side of that. And it was easy to say that in Lialla's place she'd be grateful to have the chance to undo the error and fix it; Lialla could only see the wasted years, all that time spent wading laboriously through skills that anyone with talent would have learned easily.

Leave it, she told herself. *It is not your problem. Lialla has to learn how to manage these things on her own; she's a grown woman.* Lialla wasn't talking about it, but that was her way of dealing with things—not dealing with them at all. Maddening. At least she'd stopped telling people she was going to give up Wielding entirely; apparently she and Aletto had had one of their shouting matches over *that* the first night out of Bez. *It's a good thing I didn't hear her, after everything I've done to encourage her to think about it, to find other ways to work it, I think I'd have killed her.* After all, the woman could—and did—use Thread during the day, she listened to it, she was willing to at least talk about the theory behind it. She no longer sounded like Merrida's parrot. She might actually have been starting to grow some backbone. *She might yet, if I don't strangle her out of sheer frustration,* Jennifer thought grimly.

She finished the now lukewarm tea. Awful stuff; Jennifer never had cared for any kind of tea, and the herbal ones were the absolute rock bottom. She would have to dig out her precious coffee beans, pot and roasting pan as soon as her feet thawed. Until she could actually feel all ten toes, she wasn't pulling them so much as an inch from Robyn's cook-fire.

Chris looked fine, but then—other than right after his rescue from the Cholani nomads, he always did. *I can't even remember what it feels like to be seventeen and totally resilient.* A whole, what, eleven years later? At the moment, Jennifer thought she felt more like a hundred. Chris was off in a huddle under one of the blue-lights with Enardi and Edrith—Ernie and Eddie, as he called them. They owed Enardi to Chris—most of those eager young Bez traders on their way to Podhru were Aletto's because of Chris. He fascinated young Rhadazi, and small wonder: They had never seen anyone with hair spiky on top, falling behind his ears to his collar, blue jeans and hightops. He walked with a spring that wasn't in their walk, and his style of dancing was both startling and astonishing. He wound the Rhadazi language into an amalgam of Los Angelese, mellow-speak, Val-slang, and—now that he had a better handle on it— something akin to rap. Jennifer had picked up a taste for reggae and rap both from Chris back in L.A. and thoroughly approved of it. Robyn made her laugh: The woman often as not sounded like a hippie in a time warp, and she hassled him constantly for murdering the language. Of course, Jennifer thought, you had to keep in mind that was how she and Chris showed love for each other.

She was glad Chris had made such good friends; he needed them, definitely needed people his own age to help him adjust to such a totally alien culture. Besides, Robyn was of necessity deeply involved in Aletto's well-being— above and beyond her affection for him. It left her son at something of a loose end. And this time, Robyn might well settle down for good and all with Aletto. Well, only look at what she'd gone through so far for him! Not only privation, which she had certainly known well enough between communes, food stamps and generally living at the bottom of the social ladder most of her adult life. But she'd also faced everything from loud arguments to physical danger, things Robyn had always done her best to avoid. She'd even dressed up in Bez to impress the sixty-year-old Zelharri merchants Robyn had called the nearest thing Rhadaz had to upper-middle-class Republicans, to help Aletto get financial backing. *Boy,* Jennifer thought irreverently, *it must be love.*

But Aletto must be genuinely fond of her: For a man who'd loathed shapeshifters all his life to accept such a thing in Robyn must have taken courage and love both.

Robyn was sitting cross-legged on one of the many carpets that lined the large tent—a gift from Enardi's father, together with the carpets, the three blue-lights that illuminated the interior, the pile of fat cushions stacked in one corner at the moment. She coughed, rubbed her nose on the back of her wrist and sniffed discreetly. The fire pit had been set right under the vent in the roof but the fog was so thick the smoke wasn't going even high enough to clear the top of the tent. It was giving her a headache, and the tea— a blend she'd got from Enardi's eldest sister Marseli, who ran a magic charm and herbalist's shop in central Bez— wasn't really helping, though it contained raspberry leaf and rosemary both. Nor was the mantra she'd chosen all those years ago, back in the commune where she'd had Chris.

Face it, she told herself gloomily. *It didn't work that well back then, either. Some people have what it takes to meditate and get something out of it. You, on the other hand—* Well, fortunately the commune hadn't gone macro at the time she gave birth to Chris. *I'm damned lucky the kid didn't come out brain dead, all the weed I smoked during labor. Man, I cannot believe the stupid things I did back then; obviously, God looks out for idiots and their kids.* Smoke. Robyn ran a hand through her long, straight blonde hair and bit back a sigh. Over a month since that horrid old woman had dragged the three of them and Jen's shiny new Honda from the Devil's Punchbowl road and into this place. *And me, with a two-plus pack a day habit. God, what a way to quit.* She still had three cigarettes left, but no way to ever get more. She'd smoked the last two furtively, half at a time. And then put up with Chris's looks—*Darned rotten kid, him and all the rest of them. I mean, there's things in the market that smell twenty times worse than a cigarette!* Maybe it was guilt that took the pleasure from smoking them—all of them looking at her, her feeling somehow like a kid who got into grandpa's Camels to sneak out behind the barn. They tasted absolutely rotten. It was too much to hope for that she might be losing her taste for them; it was just too bad she wasn't losing the need as quickly. *God. They were something to do with my hands, something to fiddle with or drag on while I thought about what I was going to say—something that went with, oh, Jesus, don't think about a good bottle of California burgundy, either.*

Not even a whole one: just enough to blur the edges on reality; that would be lovely. She sighed. *Forget it.* Wine was available. But not to her. She'd promised herself. Because Aletto shared that with her—not an addiction. *I'm no wino, I'm not an alky. I could've given it up any time, if I'd wanted to. Aletto says he could, and I believe it.* All the same, he had a—all right, call it a *problem* to equal hers. A taste for wine and the oblivion it brought—from money or man problems in her case, physical pain in his. But Jen and Chris had always protected her; thanks to Aletto's uncle, he had such a rep as a useless, crippled drunk, he didn't dare drink above a cupful in public. Unfortunately, like Robyn, he wasn't altogether certain he could stop at that. In his case, people would be watching every swallow he took, and so, while he'd let them press the stuff on him, he actually tasted hardly any wine at all the entire time in Bezjeriad. And she'd done the same. *Moral support.* So far as she knew, he now actually had not drunk wine since the night in Sikkre, when they'd escaped Dahven's father.

The night I killed a man. Robyn let her eyes close briefly. The night she'd given up trying to pretend she could cope; Chris had tried to shine her on, but Aletto had understood. The rest of the night, thank God, had been a complete blur, and now she couldn't even recall if Aletto'd had any of that bottle after all.

So damned, horribly unfair, that of the three Angelenos, she should develop a murderous alter ego, the woman afraid of the least height should assume the form of a monstrous bird that could kill—had killed once already. *I never hurt anyone in my life, not even under provocation.* Chris—she'd instilled a belief in nonviolence in the boy from the first, and to her knowledge he'd never sought a fight. But he was practical, more practical than she: He was able to accept the need to defend himself, and he didn't agonize it later. Jennifer was probably even more pragmatic about such things than Chris; Robyn suspected her younger sister knew about the fight in Bezjeriad, down by the docks, where the Sikkreni had been stabbed. *I remember what she said, though: Them or me and it's them every time.* Jen knew herself; she probably *could* kill to protect herself and never look back on it. *I wish I could be like that—now that I have to. I wonder if I ever will.*

She rubbed her nose again. The headache was growing worse, even though the smoke was no thicker. She hated to ask Jennifer for one of her precious aspirins, she so seldom took such things. But the others weren't going to want to put this fire out once her pan of biscuits was cooked and the soup hot. Come to that, she didn't want it out either: Her back was cold and she could feel the damp seeping through the carpet under her backside. With the fire, the inside temperature was bearable; eventually, the heat would work its way into the corners—probably in time to make it too hot for sleeping. Without the fire, though, the inside air would be just like that outside—foggy-cold and miserably damp. She herself could feel ancient ankle sprains and the ten-year-old break in her arm when it was fog-cold; Aletto felt things like that much more. He wouldn't be able to get himself upright in the morning. Robyn checked her biscuits.

Aletto must really be feeling the damp. But she knew better than to mention that tonight; he was tired and out of patience. And she knew he was trying to keep up a front around Enardi.

I wish he wouldn't, Robyn thought unhappily. But macho stupidity seemed to translate as well here as in her own world. And it wasn't only Aletto, just look at Dahven! A woman would never half-kill herself trying to pretend she was fine—not just so no one would feel sorry for her! Robyn stirred her soup, sniffed it gingerly, and felt for the seasoning packet she'd made up before they left Bez: salt, dried peppers, cumin or something very similar. She poured some into her cupped palm, dumped it into the pot. They'd be lucky if Dahven didn't have some kind of relapse back into whatever flu-thing he'd had. He looked half dead at the moment, but try and talk him off that horse this afternoon and into the wagon, oh no! And then she'd actually heard him arguing with Jennifer that he ought to turn around and ride off for Sikkre. As if he would have made it halfway to the Bez gates!

Women had more brains than that, Robyn thought firmly. She eyed her younger sister covertly from under her spill of blonde bangs. Most women did. Jennifer was capable of the same kind of behavior, but then, she hadn't ever depended on men—emotionally, financially, any way. She'd taken charge of her life early and kept hold of the reins, putting herself through college, then through law school, pulling herself up by her own bootstraps, living and working in *that* kind of—as Robyn saw it—man's world. Well, men still held the best positions, and male stiff-upper-lip behavior was expected to be the norm. *I couldn't do that,* Robyn thought. Fortunately, she'd never had to. Jen managed it very competently.

Just as well. Merrida had dropped them in this world so hard Robyn still felt the emotional bruises. They'd needed someone strong to take over and run things. Aletto hadn't any idea what they should do, where they should go. Jen took charge and probably kept them all alive.

Give it a rest, girl, she told herself. *All this junk is bad for your digestive juices, and you're gonna burn the soup.* She gave the pot another stir, checked her biscuits and pulled them away from the fire. "All right, folks, get it while it's hot."

It must have been midnight; Chris didn't bother digging under a snug sleeve and the blanket he'd thrown over his shoulders to check his watch. It was definitely late, anyway. He and the guys were on fire-watch for a little longer. Enardi had just crawled over to add wood to the fire and balance some more of the damp stuff near enough to the heat to dry it, not near enough for it to catch and start the carpets smoldering. Unfortunately, the stuff wasn't really that dry when it went onto the fire and the tent interior was a little too cool for comfort.

Chris had been trying to write out rap lyrics and not getting very far: Too dark and too cold, and for some reason the shift into Rhadazi wasn't obvious to his brain until he tried making it rhyme. And it was a little embarrassing, doing it with Ernie and Eddie sitting there; he'd have liked a little time to polish what he was doing, at least the first tries.

It was a lot harder than he'd have thought, back home.

Edrith was fiddling with the blue-light, trying to get a little more illumination out of it. Chris stretched his legs, flexed his fingers. They were stiff and cold; the tips of his ears felt like ice. Probably they could wake Jen up before much longer and let her take over the fire-watch. The fog was at least as thick as Ernie had predicted, though; thick enough that they didn't really have to worry about anyone riding up and grabbing them in the middle of the night. Even paranoid ol' Lialla wasn't staying awake to listen for sounds of pursuit.

He cast a guilty glance in her direction. That wasn't exactly fair—or nice. Lialla had taken some serious crap off her stepfather, and he was such a total jerk, she had every right to be paranoid about him. Besides, it wasn't as though the guy hadn't been doing his best to grab them all. And the stories he'd spread about them—! *Boy, I'd be pissed if I was her and someone told the world my brother killed this fat, middle-aged guy so I wouldn't have to marry him and my brother and I could keep sleeping together. Jeez, what a jerk.*

It was a wonder those two ever made it past the gates of Duke's Fort, they had started out so damned unworldly. Fortunately, they had some good people with them. His mom really had done a lot to straighten Aletto out, and Jen had got Lialla past yelling about how you couldn't do all this stuff with Night-Thread; dumb, because Jen could, and here she'd never been trained in magic. Now—you could actually talk to Aletto, and he was growing muscles. Starting to use his brains. At one point Chris had wondered if the guy had any. Lialla—well, she was still fairly weird and hard to talk to, but some of that was shyness.

All the same, Aletto had shown a normal interest in the opposite sex—once he'd had the chance. Lialla didn't. And particularly in the day or so since Dahven joined them, she'd gone even quieter than usual. Maybe she really had liked the guy, or she just wanted what she couldn't have; some girls were like that. Another thought hit him. *Jeez, I wonder if she's gay, or something?* Of course, it might not be the big deal it was where he came from, but wouldn't it be grim if on top of everything else Li had a thing for *Jen*? Jen was pretty broad-minded, of course, but it wasn't like she was likely to ever have a thing for other girls, not with the way she felt about Dahven.

At least Lialla wasn't fighting with everyone right now; Chris had absolutely hated listening to her and Jennifer go at each other. And Aletto went longer between fits of sulking, and now you had a pretty good idea what would set the guy off. He was less sensitive about his limp and about magic—probably because he could see it worked, when it wasn't that old bat Merrida trying to use the stuff.

Learning how to take care of himself in a fight had done the most for the nera-Duke's ego, Chris thought. He was extremely proud of himself for introducing them to staff fighting—it worked, and Aletto had proven he could not only absorb what he was taught, he could think up his own maneuvers and improvise in need. *Those guys of his uncle's had to have been major impressed, and I'll bet ol' Jadek's chewing nails,* he thought in satisfaction.

They had better get back to practice, though. Aletto was pretty stiff, but they needed to reinforce the moves. And then there was Ernie to get in shape before something else hit them. He was glad for the guy's company, but a little concerned that he might not be up to this; Ernie hadn't struck him, back in Bez, as anything but an easygoing party dude: Dad's money and all that. Well—they'd just have to see.

Edrith gave the light one last fiddle and dropped back down cross-legged next to him. "Not very bright, but the best I could do," he whispered. "These aren't strong ones."

"It's all right," Chris assured him. "My hands're too cold to write any longer, anyway. Listen, though, I can watch the fire until it's time to get Jen up if you're tired." Edrith shook his head. "You?" Enardi, who had just come back from the fire, rubbed his hands across the thick rug under them.

"Me what? Oh—no, I'm all right."

Chris glanced over at the sleepers. His mother was a still, faintly snoring shape next to Aletto, who was moving restlessly but apparently not being kept awake by the low conversation across the tent from him. Jen and Dahven hadn't moved in what seemed hours. Lialla—well, she'd sat up a while back but she seemed to be asleep once more. "Well, then, tell me more about those two ships, okay?"

Enardi shifted, trying to get comfortable, finally dragged a pillow over and sat on it. "I miss couches more than I would have thought possible, you know? And chairs."

"Yeah, I know," Chris said. "Body wasn't meant to sit around like this. Those ships, though. You're sure they came from the east, and not from straight across the sea?"

"The Lasanachi come from somewhere out that way." Enardi waved a hand in what he thought might be a westerly direction. "Until they came up the south coast, these guys'd never even heard of Lasanachi. Besides, the Mer Khani brought goods they'd traded for down the south coast; things father's trading company brings into Bez."

"Mer Khani," Chris echoed. "Is that what they call themselves, or how it sounded to you?" Enardi shrugged. "And they came—?"

"Around the point of the southern continent," Enardi filled in patiently and for perhaps the fifth or sixth time as Chris paused expectantly. "Because they actually live somewhere across the east mountain barrier. But not next to it, on their own seacoast. So it's a very long journey just to reach the mountains and they are impassible most of the year. According to the Mer Khani, the journey around the southern point isn't pleasant, either," he added thoughtfully. "Just easier than the land route."

"You met them, though." Chris thought a moment, then shifted with a little difficulty to English. "Did they ever speak to each other in a language that sounded anything like what I'm saying right now?" Enardi's brows drew together; Chris translated into Rhadazi. His friend shook his head.

"I can't say. Their language was foreign, of course. But it's been so long since I saw them—well, perhaps, a little."

"Well—all right." It was so *damned* tantalizing, the possibility of American ships in Rhadaz! And if Ernie's information was right, this really *had* to be the west coast, the big water out there the Pacific. But then Ernie had paid so little attention, it was too long for him to remember much, and there were all these things that didn't track. He should be able to pick up more information in Podhru, if there was time. And Ernie had said one of the ships might have gone there. They'd been worried about the weather south, worried about the return journey, might have simply gone back home without journeying to the Emperor's city.

Mer Khani—God, it *had* to be a corruption of American!

It was truly frustrating: All this time, asking as many questions as he could, and Chris still had no idea where they could possibly be in relation to where they *had* been. The terrain south of Sikkre was enough like the Palmdale area north of L.A., but outline maps of Rhadaz looked more like Spain and the Mediterranean—except it wasn't mountainous enough. Chris had put in enough hard work on geography the past year to know such things. And the distances were all wrong. The language didn't sound like anything Chris knew but if this was the L.A. Basin, then why was there a sea about where the Mexican border should be—and did that make the Rhadazi American Indians?

Couldn't be. So maybe all the stuff about alternate universes really was just fiction. But then, why would they have a Cortez, a Nero, a Charlemagne? That carried coincidence a little far.

Yeah, you're hoping you can learn enough to somehow get yourself back home, right, guy? Chris demanded of himself. *Good luck, all right?* Well, but it might work that way, and besides, it would be neat to know, try and figure out where things had branched to make a world like this one. Figure out how magic got into it, how come there wasn't any major technology.

Probably he'd have the rest of his life to figure it out, the way Jen said—God, there was a depressing thought. Much as he liked these guys, he'd trade them both for the CD player he'd left behind, for an afternoon at the movies, for a really rad skateboard or even a bucket of Kentucky Fried Chicken. And a girl to share it with. *Yeah, like maybe Jessica Morrow from English, with those legs and the outrageous short skirts . . . oh, man?* Girls here: The ones he'd met in Bez dressed in wads of material and were pretty much off limits except to talk to a little bit. They were nice enough, but they didn't smell quite right—different perfumes or shampoos or whatever. And then there was that innkeeper's daughter up in Sikkre, the one Dahven'd kidded him about. Wow. Chris wasn't certain he was ready for anything *that* hot.

But it was going to be pretty depressing if a guy had to pass on just—*nice* girls unless he got married. *So ask. But not so you sound like a total nerd.* Bad enough Jen had been there when Merrida announced he was a virgin; it wasn't the kind of thing you exactly wanted spread around. He cast one more wary glance across the fire to assure himself Robyn was still asleep, then he dropped down onto his elbows and leaned toward Edrith. "Hey, listen. I got this dumb question, okay?" He could feel his ears growing warm. "Um, like, girls."

"Girls?" Edrith shook his head. "What about girls?"

"Well, you know—" Chris spread his hands rather help-lessly. "Okay, where I come from, it's okay if a guy goes out with a girl, just the two of them, go do stuff together, kiss and all that." He swallowed; amazing how warm it had become in here, the past few moments.

To his relief, neither of them seemed to think the subject odd and when Edrith laughed it didn't seem to be *at* him for bringing up embarrassing stuff. "It's pretty much an ac-cording to your class matter—wouldn't you say, Ernie?" En-ardi nodded. "You remember the party in Bez—there were girls like Ernie's sisters, music, food. I doubt it would be possible to just go somewhere by yourself with a girl of that class." Enardi shook his head. "People like me, at least in Sikkre, have a little more freedom about such things, even the women. People like Aletto have less." He shrugged. "I don't know if that's what you wanted to know—"

"It's what I suspected," Chris said gloomily. "No dates—no taking a girl somewhere—"

"Oh, that's not so, really: In Sikkre, there are festivals and parties, sometimes there will be some kind of celebra-tion when a caravan comes in, and there's music, good food and ale, dancing. And it's acceptable to go with either a crowd, or just one other person—even alone."

"And even dance with girls there?" Chris asked. He shook his head. "Without—I'm not saying this very well, I guess—say, there was a caravaner girl just standing around, you could go up and talk to her without her parents getting pissed?"

"Probably. Caravaner women particularly have consid-erable rights of their own, even the unwed ones." Edrith tipped his head on one side to consider his friend thought-fully. He grinned and looked rather embarrassed himself suddenly. "I remember now; something Jen said to Lialla. About not sleeping with men before life-bonding? That holds true more for women like Lialla, who are expected to keep blood lines pure, not for the rest of us."

"Um, swell," Chris mumbled.

Edrith dug under his shirt and held up a hollow wooden ball on a leather thong; Chris had seen it before and pre-sumed it to be the local equivalent of a crucifix, if he'd thought about it at all. "Most girls insist you protect them from babies, of course. Perhaps we should get you one of these." He held it out; Chris, now red to the ears and very grateful for the dimness of the blue-light, touched it, sniffed cautiously. It smelled green, odd—not unpleasant. "Charm," Edrith said briefly as he stuffed it back under his shirt. "One like this is pretty inexpensive, keeps you safe for three moon-seasons. Someone like Dahven can afford to buy the silver armband that's effective for a year."

"Well, yeah, okay," Chris said. "Just—wanted to get the ground rules straight, you know? I mean, I like hanging out with girls, and I'm sure not ready to marry one at seventeen."

"Sensible of you," Enardi said. "If I had life-mated at seventeen, I could never have come with you to Podhru. There's time for that, but later."

"Oh, you could've come to Podhru with us," Edrith informed him cheerfully. "But you'd have had to act like your father. If we have a little time, like we did in Bez, we can have some *real* fun in the Emperor's city. I've never been there, but I know some who have. And even if the Festival of Numbers isn't started yet, there will be lots of other things going on." He tapped Chris's wrist. "Is it possibly time to get Jen up? I'm quite honestly freezing; we don't get fog like this in Sikkre."

Chris slid his arm out of the sleeve, twisted it around so blue light hit the dial. *Conserve the battery, leave the little light button alone.* "Close enough. Hey. Thanks for the information. You know how mom is, scared somebody's parents are going to murder me if I so much as look at their daughter."

"We'll keep you un-murdered, I promise," Edrith assured him.

"Great. Let's crawl in, then; it's Jen's turn and I'm tired all of a sudden." But once he was curled up in his blankets, he found himself wakeful. *Never did ask about the gay thing,* he realized. *Oh, well, the other was tough enough. And should I care what Lialla likes?*

It just seemed unfair, if that was her problem. Poor old Lialla. He had thought she was pretty stuck-up until the afternoon she healed the physical damage the Cholani had inflicted on him. And told him something about living with Jadek, the way he'd knocked her around. She hadn't had to do that; it took guts and he admired her for it. She'd been trying to make him feel a little less ashamed for having been kidnapped and beaten, and she'd succeeded. She was as old as Jen, maybe older, but she was awfully young for her years and, like his mom, she needed someone to lean on. Most of her life she hadn't had anyone—well, she had someone now.

2

𝐙

THE fog was thicker than ever the next morning; by midday, they could see sun—a pale yellow ball wreathed in cloud—but the cloud cover never lifted enough to allow them to make any speed along the road. During the middle hours, they all rode, at a walk, but late in the afternoon, Chris and Enardi dismounted and walked ahead of the others. Not only was visibility down to the point where Jennifer could no longer tell what was on either side of the narrow road, but the road itself had deteriorated from the already dreadful mess it had been.

Aletto rode close to Robyn, as he usually did, but he had been quiet most of the day, and now he sat the horse in discomfort. He'd pulled the hood low over his forehead so no one else could see the set of his mouth, the line between his brows. Robyn gave him both aspirin she'd reluctantly accepted from Jen the night before for her headache and never swallowed. The nera-Duke must have felt as awful as he looked; he took them without a word of protest and drank both down with a swallow from her water bottle.

Robyn chose her words with care as she capped the bottle and hung it from one of the numerous hooks on the saddlebow. "How much farther, do you think?" For a moment, she was afraid he'd ignore her, or glare at her for asking a stupid question, the way her men usually did. Aletto stared over his horse's ears for several moments, finally shrugged.

"Not very, I hope. But I don't know how we're supposed to decide where to stop." He wrinkled his nose. "Those tablets have an awful taste."

"I know. Do they help?"

"I suppose—times like this, it seems they take forever, though." He cast her a very brief smile. "I've been so wrapped up in myself I've forgotten you. Are you all right?"

Robyn shifted her weight cautiously. "I really hate being wet and cold, but—yeah, I'm fine." She caught her breath in a faint little gasp as Chris suddenly came back between them. He caught hold of both bridles. "Don't do that, kid, you scared me!"

"Hey, sorry. Next time I'll lay down a couple lines on the way back, so you know it's me, all right?" He grinned self-consciously and shifted into a clipped, rhythmic cadence. "Like, 'I'm your main M.C., rappin' down the roadway, tellin' you to hang close, everything be okay.' " He tilted his head back to give her a broad, exceedingly smug flash of teeth. Robyn ran a hand across her forehead and closed her eyes.

"God. I swear you sound *proud* of yourself. What the hell was that?"

"You're kidding. Where you been the last couple years you never heard rap?"

"And why would I have listened to rap?"

Chris chuckled. "Yeah, I forget, it doesn't get air time on your golden moldies stations. Think of it as the logical successor to all those weird rhymes Bob Dylan used to do, okay?"

"Words fail me."

"Sure, mom."

"You're right, they don't. That was *bad*, kid."

"Well—hey," Chris said rather defensively. "I only just got started, and I rap better in English. Besides, with no kind of sound system—you know I'm gonna have to teach one of the guys to do backbeat for me? Listen, though. What I was trying to tell you, the road seems to be clear, but the fog isn't going to. But Ernie says that unless he's like totally confused, we aren't too far from a good place to set the tent up, trees for shelter, running water, all that. Sound all right to you?"

"Lead me to it," Robyn said.

"Yeah, me too." Chris let go the reins and turned away to head back to the front. "I hate it when I can't even figure out where the sun *is*, and there's water running down the back of my neck." He vanished in mist before he'd taken five steps, his voice coming back to them as a low, disembodied sound. "One of you ease back a little, tell the others, will you? I *really* don't want to yell in this. It's creepy."

"Never mind." Jennifer's voice came from somewhere behind Robyn. "We heard. Get back up there and find this campsite, will you? And see if you can't find a hot tub while you're at it."

"I wish."

"Work on the rap, kid; it's a start but it needs help."

"Tell *me*." Silence descended, except for the occasional creak of harness or the crack of a metal-shod wagon wheel against stone. Edrith was driving the wagon—or, rather, holding the loose reins while the mule followed Robyn's and Aletto's horses—and mumbling softly to himself. Jennifer drew her horse back a pace or two from the wagon, and then a little more; the possibility of a collision at this speed might have once sounded like a joke to a woman used to fifty-five miles per hour on the freeway, but she didn't want to be on the horse that slammed into the back of that wagon, if Edrith stopped suddenly. *My luck, I'd go right off and break something*, she thought gloomily. Accordingly to Neri, some things couldn't be healed instantly—like broken bones.

Dahven had stayed so far to the rear that for one terrible moment she wondered if he'd simply turned and left while he had the opportunity, while her attention was diverted. But he was there after all, farther back than he had been, bundled in a thick cloak and hood from Chris's things, hunched over the saddle. He started when Jennifer touched his arm.

"Not far," she said softly.

He nodded, stifled a cough. "Good." They rode in silence for some moments. "There was fog like this, a few days, out at sea. It's—I don't like it."

"No," Jennifer said quietly. "I wouldn't like it either."

Another silence. He touched her knee and when she looked up, he gave her a brief smile. "Thank you."

"For what?" She shook her head but he merely shrugged. "For not asking any more than you want to tell me? Or not judging you, thinking less of you because you find the fog unnerving? You have cause, and I wouldn't judge you."

"People do," he said after a moment. "Judge others, that is. When something terrible happens. I remember one of my father's men who'd gone through something rather nasty, I was young enough, I don't remember what, just something to do with one of Father's sorcerers, it was hushed up. The man was—sick, I guess—for a time, no one saw him except the healer and his assistant. I remember thinking it odd, because when he came back into service he didn't really look so different—thinner, perhaps, like he'd been ill. For a while he joined Father's market guard, but he left almost at once, left Sikkre entirely, I think. I remember when he was still in the halls, how people—other guards and servants—stared at him all the time. Wondering what had *really* happened, how he felt. Or they'd ask him what happened—questions people don't have a right to ask each other, but they'd ask because they were curious and they thought that gave them a right to know. I didn't think that then, of course; I didn't realize what it was until—well, you know. But I remember the look on his face when I asked.'' He glanced at her. "He—froze. And then he—went on talking, just as though I hadn't said anything.'' He slammed one hand against the saddlebow; the horse was apparently too damp and miserable to pay any attention. "I understand better now, better than I wish I did. I couldn't stand it if anyone else knew, I'd feel Aletto's eyes on me whenever my back was turned, I'd feel all of them wondering.'' He was silent for a moment. "I suppose it's stupid to feel so—part of me feels shamed and dirty and—oh, I don't know.''

It must be the fog, Jennifer thought, the fact that he couldn't see her face clearly, that she couldn't see his, that let him speak freely for the first time. She opened her mouth, closed it again in sudden panic. *God, he needs real help, and all I have to offer him is pop psychology from Jan's magazines and TV programs about rape victims!* But she had to say something; any moment now, he'd begin to wonder if he hadn't gone too far. Confessed more weakness than she could accept. Another moment, and she would lose any chance she had to at least try and help him talk it out. "Ashamed? Because you didn't somehow know not to go home, because you didn't somehow know in advance what your father was capable of? Because you weren't stronger than a shipful of armed Lasanachi used to brutalizing other men? Or because you can't just put it behind you and pretend it never happened? Nothing so terrible has ever happened to me, Dahven, so I only know what I've read or seen of other people's experiences in my own world. No one survives being victimized, brutalized, without bearing some kind of emotional scars. Scars don't fade overnight, but usually they fade in time. Maybe it's harder for someone who was always in charge of his life, to suddenly be at the mercy of others, to carry the guilt that you should have somehow done something to avoid it. Everyone feels that guilt; at least, that's what I'm told, and I believe it. I would feel that, in your place. It wasn't your fault! Believe that!''

''I—that's not really it. It's—somehow, I feel almost as though it were someone else.'' His voice was a hoarse whisper. ''As though I were pretending it had been me, to gain sympathy. But I'm not like that!''

''I know that,'' Jennifer said rather tartly. ''Think, though: to stay up all night, ride home, be carried off by slavers, chained to an oar, beaten—and then, after a month—sorry, a moon-season—you get thrown ashore in the dregs of Bezjeriad, lightheaded with fever and half-drowned, bargaining for food and shelter in a filthy hut from a man who'd steal your boots once you passed out. That's so—so alien to anything you've ever experienced, why shouldn't it seem like a nightmare after too much to drink? We haven't that much background in common, Dahven, but I had a very regulated, patterned life. If anything like that had happened to me, right now I'd begin to wonder if I hadn't made it up, or maybe that it had happened to someone else and I was pretending it had been me, instead. Or that I was blowing things out of proportion, pretending it was worse than it really is. I'd be afraid anyone I told would think I was trying for sympathy by acting sick, hurt—spooked by it all after it was physically over.'' Jennifer waited. Dahven finally nodded, one barely discernible motion of his hooded head. ''You're not making it up; I know better. I—was there, remember?'' He nodded again. ''It happened, it's over, but it's not going to let go of you right away. I know all that. I understand it. And I know that when anything so awful happens, you can't possibly return to normal the next day.''

''You can't—''

''I can. In my own world, there are men who killed in a war twenty years ago and still have nightmares of what they did; raped women who live with guilt, with a horror of all men for the rest of their lives. I'm not trying to say you'll carry this with you so long; not many do, and you're

21

stronger and more sensible than most people I know. But right now, you have every right to be unnerved by fog—or anything else. It's not stupid, it's human.''

He considered this. Finally shook his head, looked up the road—the little he could see of it—and sighed, deeply. ''I don't feel in control of my life.''

''You are. Everyone has setbacks.''

''Setbacks.'' Dahven gave a snort of laughter. ''If I were truly in control of my life, I'd be on my way to Sikkre right now, I'm no asset to Aletto or to you, just another body to protect if Jadek sets another trap. You'd be better without me, and I could remove one of the matters gnawing at my guts—I could deal with my brothers and maybe even discover what really happened to my father.''

Jennifer sighed. ''I thought we'd decided to bury this particular discussion. Dahven, you couldn't possibly have ridden from Bez to Sikkre as sick as you were; you still couldn't. You don't seem to understand; your brothers are calling you traitor and I'd swear by anything you like the men he's sent to capture you don't care what shape you're in when they deliver you.''

''They wouldn't dare—''

''Oh, no?'' Jennifer shifted in the saddle so she could look at him; a swift snatch of her hand pulled the hood off his tousled hair. ''You weren't there, when they jumped us in the desert. You weren't in any shape to pay attention when they came down on us south of the Bez docks.''

''I heard some of the rumors from that man—Dowbri, Enardi's wedded brother.''

''One of them I knew from your father's hospitality; he was the wizard's guardsman. He didn't like you much.''

''Mmmm—big man, ugly eyes, bent nose? Snake's personal man, Vikkin. No, he and I never got on. My brothers sent *him*?'' He scowled down at his hands, across the horse's ears. ''To bring me back?''

''He didn't say anything about alive, either,'' Jennifer replied dryly. He didn't answer; he was clearly considering this new—and not very pleasant—news. ''Look, just weigh it, will you? Think about how simple things would be for your brothers if you really were dead. You should have been, of course; the idea as I understand it was that the Lasanachi would keep you in chains until you died—which wouldn't be that long. They were supposed to.''

"Three years," Dahven whispered.

"But the Lasanachi panicked and set you loose."

"I was already ill, I think; I remember being unlocked, shoved into the few clothes they'd taken from me, into my boots because those hurt my feet; my feet were so swollen from sitting on the benches to row." His low voice trailed off. Jennifer fought a shiver and waited. "Why did they panic? No one frightens Lasanachi."

"Perhaps they'd wondered all along why anyone would sell them a Duke's son. And then word came that your father was dead, you missing—they thought they were being somehow set up."

"Set—? You're not making sense. Or I'm not understanding."

"Sorry. What if they believed you had been sold to them so that later it could be brought out this had been done? What they do is illegal, isn't it—buying Rhadazi men? So they do it very quietly. And now it comes out that they have bought the Thukar's son, and you're in dreadful condition. The Lasanachi either think you'll be held up to public scrutiny as you are—or perhaps as a dead victim of the dread rowing ships. Might that not be an excuse for the Emperor to declare war against them?"

"Shesseran wouldn't—"

"Not from what I've heard of him. Perhaps they don't realize that. I don't think they do, as quickly as they dumped you overboard."

Dahven rubbed his chin thoughtfully. "It's insane enough to be logical—to a Lasanachi."

"Fortunately, since it meant they would get rid of the evidence and run for open sea. But of course, that wasn't what your brothers planned, just what the Lasanachi thought had been planned. No one knew where you were except your brothers and your father. Officially, the story is that your father tried to disinherit you and you killed him in the quarrel, only to discover he'd taken the precaution of writing you out of his will."

"And people really *believe* this?"

"More importantly, who would bother to question the story? No one has, because it *looks* all right: Your father is dead and everyone knows you argued, there is a will giving Sikkre to your brothers. And your brothers have been sending out companies of guards to track you down—their traitor brother—and bring you to justice. It should be enough to keep the Emperor from worrying about their part in matters, and I've heard often enough that he doesn't want to know how things are run so long as they're run smoothly."

"There's something in that," Dahven admitted.

"Stay with me, then. There is no reason for them to let you stay alive—you could be a focal point for rebellion, if people in Sikkre thought you'd do a better job of being Duke than your brothers."

"That's true. And they wouldn't want me to tell anyone what *really* happened—would they?" Dahven considered this and shook his head. "It sounds just fine, until I realize it's my *brothers* we're talking about! You've seen them!"

"They don't look capable of working up the energy to kill and sort out such a plot," Jennifer agreed. "Then again, perhaps your father set it all up, not realizing they wouldn't wait for him to die naturally. It wouldn't be the first time a father underestimated his children. And murderers don't have to look like thugs. Your brothers struck me as self-centered; people like that can justify removing anyone who stands between them and what they want, and they seldom worry about it later. All that matters is what they want, and getting it." Silence. "Think about it, why don't you? About what you'd be getting into if you turned around and went home right now? About honestly whether you're ready to deal with it?"

Dahven spread his hands in a wide shrug. "I said I wouldn't just leave; I swore, remember? I don't swear to things lightly. I will think about it, if you like. I just—" He bent over the saddlebow, coughing. "That. I'm not well, I'm not at all strong, and we both know it. I'd hate it if someone got hurt trying to shield me. I don't think I can protect myself just now."

"Don't worry about that," Jennifer replied mildly. "We seem to be doing all right so far. Besides, you're stronger than you were the other day; you won't be sick for long."

"I also haven't any weapons," Dahven grumbled.

"Talk to Aletto; he has a sword he bought in Sikkre."

"I saw it." The thought didn't seem to cheer him. "I suppose I'd feel better with it strapped to the horse, though."

Jennifer nodded and edged her bo a little forward in the straps that held it high on the horse's side, under her knee.

"I know that feeling; I don't let this out of reach anymore." She bit back a smile at the very dubious look he gave it. Probably it was the same look she'd given Chris's six-foot-long wooden stick when he'd tried to assure her she could flatten a trained swordsman with it. Well, Dahven would get a chance to find out soon enough. He leaned over to touch her shoulder and pointed forward.

"Look—I think I can see a little. The wagon's pulling off."

Jennifer sighed. "I hear running water, don't I? I think we've found the local KOA—sorry, Dahven. Enardi's camping site."

The least breeze began to blow in from the water not long after they stopped; not enough to lower the temperature further, it did disperse the fog and by the time Robyn went out to wash her face after dinner, there were stars directly overhead. On her way back, she passed Enardi on his way out to keep the first watch. She shivered and murmured, "Better you than me," as she went around him. He laughed quietly and replied, "It's not so bad now the fog's off." Robyn shook her head in obvious disbelief and hurried back inside. The main problem, she decided as she dropped down next to the fire, was her feet: She simply couldn't get comfortable in either the long wraps Aletto wore under his boots or in the knitted stockings Chris had found for her in the Bez market. The former itched and worked down around her heels and toes, leaving her insteps bare and forming blisters around her ankles or the ball of her foot; the latter were clearly an early attempt at stretchy fabric and not too good at it. After the first few minutes, there wasn't any more give or stretch, and the socks slithered down her legs and began edging into her tennies again. Which left her, effectively, with one pair of good American-made cotton and nylon socks that at the moment were sloppy wet from the day's ride. Her toes felt like blocks of ice.

Fortunately, once the food was cooked and eaten, she was done for the night. Chris and Edrith were beginning to wash up when she came back in. She settled down next to Aletto, pulled off her shoes and set them as near the fire as she dared, tucked chilled feet under his legs. He leaned back to catch hold of one of the many small carpets covering the bare ground and wrapped it around her lower legs and feet, then pulled her against him. Robyn rubbed the soles of her feet against the harsh rug fabric until the friction warmed them a little, wrapped her arm around his waist and closed her eyes. Things could have been worse. Much worse.

Outside, Enardi was watching the road for signs of pursuit from Bez, now three days behind them. But they hadn't made very good time, what with his father's wagon and the weather. This particular spot was only a day and a few hours from the Zelharri and Sikkreni guardsmen rumored to have been turning the Bez market inside out for the heir to either Duchy. For the first time, Enardi thought seriously about such a pursuit and it left a very uncomfortable feeling in the pit of his stomach. *I could have been with friends I've known all my life, drinking in one of the taverns, even listening to Father gossip with his old friends—and instead I chose this?*

But having talked with nera-Duke Aletto, with his Robyn—a sweet, quiet woman who reminded him of his own mother, what he remembered of her—with clever, crisp Jennifer, how could he have chosen otherwise? And Chris—Enardi found it difficult to think of a time before Chris, who turned everything upside down with his oddly cut hair, his outland clothing, the rhythmic and sometimes downright odd way he spoke Rhadazi, all the exotic words he threw into a conversation. Chris made everything in Bezjeriad seem so dull and ordinary, even though Enardi had once asked for nothing but the ordinary in his life—a career either in his father's shops, eventually perhaps his own trading company or his own share of Fedthyr's far-flung company. Now, he didn't know what he wanted. More than he had. To go places with Chris and Edrith, with all of them.

Chris called him Ernie. Enardi like that; he liked Edrith—or, as Chris called *him*, Eddie—the Sikkreni who candidly admitted he'd spent most of his youth stealing for a living but who now was one of Aletto's company. Who already spoke a lot like Chris: Enardi was shy about trying to talk that way—yet.

He looked up as someone moved the flap aside and came outside. It was Lialla. She was so quiet, so self-effacing—so *medium*, with her brown hair, dark eyes, the dusty-looking Wielder Blacks that tended to fade into the background anyway, he sometimes forgot Lialla was with them. She seldom said anything, except to Jennifer or Aletto and at first he thought she was making certain they remembered she was noble; then he thought she was just unfriendly. When he'd said something to Chris, though, his outland friend had shaken his head. "She's had a hard time lately, and she's the quiet kind. You're just used to Lasinay." Enardi grinned. His youngest sister could talk anyone half to death; by comparison, anyone else might seem too quiet.

He stepped into the open as Lialla came toward him, adjusting her loose scarves. One had wrapped itself around the long staff she kept with her at all times—a bo, Chris called it. A fighting stick. Enardi wondered how good a stick could be for fighting. Chris and Eddie had promised he'd have a chance to find out, though, as soon as they had a few hours during the day to show him.

"Enardi? I'll take over," she said as she came up to him. "You'd better go in and thaw; they've decided to keep the watches short. And Robyn's talking about letting the fire die down because of the wind." Long speech for Lialla; as unexpected as the smile she offered him.

"The wind won't last to middle night; I'll tell her. If you're sure—"

"We all share guard, even Aletto. Go on, Robyn's got tea brewing." Enardi headed quickly and gratefully for shelter.

The smile slid from Lialla's face and her too-thin shoulders sagged. Everything was so wrong! Oh, Aletto had genuine support now. He even had something of a following, not just the few people here with him. Gyrdan, their father's old Captain of the Guard, was supposed to meet them in Podhru with more of Amarni's men. After this truly hectic past few days, a few of the Zelharri merchants who'd left Sehfi when Jadek took over Duke's Fort were talking about following Aletto back to Sehfi, and more were willing to at least finance him in exchange for considerations for their children. There was supposedly a delegation of those young people—representing most of the major expatriate Sehfi merchants—on its way to Podhru by sea right now.

It still wasn't enough; she could tell Aletto was worried about things, but he wouldn't talk to *her*; he fretted to Robyn, talked policy with Jennifer, strategy with Dahven, fighting style with Chris. . . . *I'm useless,* she thought bitterly. *He used to talk to me about things, until he found people who knew more than I do—and that wasn't very difficult, was it? I don't know policy or strategy—I can fight but not very well, and that leaves only magic.* But it hurt to think about the magic. All those years she'd dreamed of gaining a White or Silver sash, all the effort, hours—years she'd put into Wielding, and for what? So a brash outlander could come in and Wield rings around her, so a filthy old Bez Wielder could have the pleasure of telling her just how badly Merrida had mistaught her. That everything she'd learned was wrong. Gods knew it had hurt badly enough, all the years she'd believed that the old woman had been trying to din magic into an over-thick skull. To have to start over again—it scarcely helped at all to know she'd learned more in an hour from that disgusting old man than in all her years under Merrida. For that matter, she had learned more from Jen—*Jen,* a scant moon-season and a half in Rhadaz from her strange, outland world, where according to her there was no working magic at all. *It's so unfair!* Lialla thought miserably. She wanted nothing more than to climb in a hole and hide forever. Let Aletto do as he wanted, or as he must—she hadn't the heart for it.

Besides, she thought even more miserably, *what will come of it all at the end? Jadek still holds Duke's Fort, the Emperor has done nothing but try to sort out who murdered Carolan. Whatever support Aletto gets from merchants and soldiers, it won't matter. Jadek has a full Triad, he has Duke's Fort—he has Mother and Mother's pregnant with his child. He's going to win again, like he always has.*

Chris came out some time later to relieve her. "Quiet?" he asked. Lialla shrugged.

"There were deer a while back, coming down to drink."

"It's warm inside, Ernie convinced mom to leave the fire burning, and there's some tea left if you want it." He gripped her shoulder. "You better have some; you're cold right through that black thing."

Lialla swallowed around a sudden, enormous lump. Chris was being particularly nice to her lately—the way he ordinarily could be, thoughtful and a little bossy—except he didn't try to tease her the way he did Robyn. Maybe he just had to be nice to someone, Lialla thought; after all, his

28

mother spent most of her free time with Aletto these days. Whatever his reasons, she wasn't used to it and particularly when she was tired, or down like she was this night, it threatened to make her cry. She merely nodded, not trusting her voice, and went.

Chris walked out into the road and stood a while, listening. He couldn't even hear a mouse at the moment, and the way the wind had died down, he was sure he'd hear anything big long before he could see it. He shoved the bulky cloak back across his shoulders and shifted his grip on the bo. He had an idea for a new set of maneuvers to work out before he tried it on Eddie, and he needed to run through the most basic moves—it had after all been almost a month since he'd originally worked them out—so he could start teaching Ernie how to take care of himself.

In spite of himself, and the deadly seriousness of the situation, Chris grinned. It was really going to be something, teaching a sweet guy like Ernie how to bash heads. At least as fun as trying to teach his mom. Well—the grin faded. Maybe it would be funny in retrospect. Years from now. If he lived to enjoy the joke.

3

ROBYN was out at sunrise, hanging clean, wet socks and still-damp jeans across bushes. "You people can do what you want," she said as she came back inside. "I'm not leaving here while my stuff is wet. We're in a hurry, fine, but we're not in such a hurry we all have to catch pneumonia because of fog-damp pants and grubby socks, right?"

"No argument, ma," Chris assured her. "We need a workout, and I went over the map with Ernie last night. He says—you tell them, okay?"

Enardi held up one of Chris's yellow-pad maps. "There's another stream, about here, not too far away; it's a good place to stop the night. We could reach it by early afternoon if we left here within the hour, but that also means we could spend the morning here. The stream ahead is big enough for proper-sized fish.''

"I'd like fish," Robyn said. "But I never could catch them and we don't have any gear, do we?''

"I brought some in the wagon," Enardi said. "In case I came on with you. I haven't fished since I was a small boy but I'm—I *used* to be good at it." He tapped the paper. "About the same distance on, we could reach it easily the night after, there's an inn my father recommends.''

"Inn," Aletto said gloomily.

"It's very clean," Enardi assured him anxiously. "Father says the woman who owns it is outlander. He says you can always tell, though, because everything is so clean. The food is different, and there are separate sleeping rooms, with doors that can be barred.''

"If it's called The Lion, I've heard of it," Dahven said absently. He was running a finger along the edge of Aletto's sword and shaking his head. "It has a repute as *safe* lodgings.''

Aletto shook his head. "Safe," he said even more gloomily. "The inn in Sikkre was supposed to be safe, too.'' Lialla, who was spreading damp black scarves next to Robyn's wet socks, turned to scowl at him, and Dahven gave him a very faint, sardonic smile.

"Ah. But that *was* a safe inn; caravaners have used it for a good many years, and all one ever has to worry about ordinarily is the innkeep's long nose. Unfortunately, no inn in Sikkre is proof against the Thukar. Don't look like that, Aletto; I know all too well what my father was like, remember?''

Aletto shook his head and spread his hands in mute apology. "Three more nights. With good fortune, anyway. But with men behind us, and possibly men coming overland to cut us off. And didn't I hear something in Bez about a Spectral Host somewhere above the Coastal road?''

"Spectral—?" Enardi looked at Aletto in amused disbelief. "I know who told you that, it was old Chuffles—Casimaffi, or maybe his brother, they're both terrified of the roads and they both tell anyone who'll listen about bandits and ghosts and the villagers that they say used to pick caravans clean, until the Emperor put a stop to it. But that was

30

years and years ago, back when the Feuds nearly destroyed Podhru. Besides, if people thought the roads safe, quite possibly they wouldn't bother with ships and Casimaffi would lose business. He thinks like that.'' He chuckled. "Spectral Hosts.'' The laughter faded when he turned to look at Chris. ''No, truly. It must be a jest, one in poor taste, I admit, but a jest nonetheless. After all, my eldest brother has ridden to Sikkre a hundred times and seen nothing but a dull, dry road and other travelers. He's taken this road to Podhru with Father, too—a few times. I promise you, no one has ever told me of a Spectral Host.''

"Which only means they didn't see one,'' Aletto said. "I might have laughed once, too, but we crossed the path of one between Duke's Fort and Sikkre. We were fortunate; we only lost a horse to it. Next time it might be one of us.''

Enardi gazed at him for some moments, finally shook his head. "Spectral Host,'' he mumbled. "But—they only hunt at night, isn't that so? If we travel during the day, as my father always has, why, then we're safe, aren't we?''

"Who can tell?'' Lialla demanded generally. "Everyone *says* they hunt at night and in the next breath says they don't exist.''

"Oh, they exist,'' Dahven said mildly. "The caravaners meet up with them now and again; it's one reason that north trail between Zelharri and the Hushar Oasis is so rarely traveled. I agree that might have been part of the overall plan to get Aletto where they wanted him, waiting for Casimaffi's ship. You'd think of it as just one more reason not to ride to Podhru, one less obstacle to face. All the same, Aletto, why didn't you tell me?''

Aletto shrugged. "I forgot. There were other things to think about in Sikkre, if you recall.''

"True enough, my friend. You'll have to tell me when we get the chance, though. Caravaners have been known to stretch a tale for better effect, and I've often wondered if some of the things you hear about a Spectral Host aren't the result of too much wine, not enough sleep, maybe lack of water. The desert does odd things to your mind.''

"Not *that* odd,'' Jennifer said firmly. "I wish you hadn't brought them up, I'd managed to forget them. Now—oh, hell. Are they truly only night hunters, or are we going to get into 'they say' and 'people think'? Rumor I don't need.'' Dahven shrugged.

"Rumor is all I can offer you, I'm afraid."

Lialla drained her tea and refilled the collapsible leather cup. "I personally care only about stopping one. But the caravaners must have some idea of how to avoid them or how to deal with them. Do you know anything about that?" Dahven shrugged again.

"N-no. Then again, I *think* I might have asked that once, or maybe someone just said. Unfortunately, I probably wasn't in the best condition to remember which, or what answer I got." He cast her an apologetic grin. "Late hours, some inn or other, *you* know—"

Lialla sighed. "Not really, but I can imagine. I suspect we're fortunate you recall anything at all."

"Well, it wasn't anything I expected to *need* to know," he said huffily.

There was a cool silence. "I've heard things," Edrith said cautiously. He was tugging at his hair, Chris-like, and scowling fiercely at the ground before him. The others waited. He finally shook his head. "Can't remember just now, it's been a long time and it didn't seem so important then. Let me think about it."

"Neri didn't say anything?" Lialla asked Jennifer.

"I made the mistake of asking about ghost camels and he was a lot of help. Just laughed rather nastily, said if we came up with anything useful to let him know."

Lialla snorted. "Stubborn, arrogant old Wielder—"

"All of that," Jennifer agreed.

"If I get like that in my old age—"

"One of us will kick you," Jennifer said cheerfully as she hesitated. "And remind you about Neri."

Lialla laughed briefly. "That's if I live so long," she said. The thought sobered her. "Or if I even bother to Wield at all—"

She stopped as Jennifer's hand closed around her wrist, hard. "Don't, all right? Just—don't. Not now."

"I agree." Aletto got to his feet. "Well—has something been decided about today? Robyn?"

She glanced skyward. "If it keeps warming up the way it feels, everything—including my jeans—should be dry by midday."

"All right. And Enardi, that gives us enough time to reach this place you want to reach?" Enardi nodded.

"Even if the fog comes back."

Aletto considered this, nodded once. "Well, then. We'll stay here until midday." He sounded a little self-conscious, still, making such a direct statement, and after a moment, he qualified it. "Is that all right? I need to move around, stretch. I'd like to take a walk, maybe practice with the staff a while."

"That was going to be *my* suggestion," Chris said. "Ernie needs to learn the basics, in case anyone finds us out here, and we're all pretty soft from time off in town. It's too new a skill to get away with that, and I bet most of the guys after us know about it now. Which means we don't have total surprise on our side any more. Which means we need to be good, and fast. If we're both of those things, we'll have the edge that—you know, even if they know what we're using, knowing it's one thing, actually fighting it is another." He looked up at Robyn. "And mom, you *gotta* start getting serious with it, you know? You can whack someone with the bo and lay them out, without killing them, if you know how to control it. You can't say that for other kinds of fighting." *You can't say that for a large, black bird with murderous intent,* his eyes said.

Robyn looked back down at him; she'd gone rather pale but her voice was steady when she finally spoke. "Point taken, kid. I'll try, all right?"

"All I ask, mom. Hey, Eddie, let's take the soft city kid with us, see if we can't find a nice piece of wood for him."

"Yah," Edrith said. "He gets to shape it himself, I did everyone's last time and it was too hard on my hands."

Chris jumped to his feet. "So? Maybe I'm trying to keep you from poking them in other people's pockets."

Edrith snorted. "When have I done that since I met you?"

"Sure, right," Chris laughed. "Ruined your life, didn't I?"

"Changed it," Edrith grumbled, but he didn't sound that unhappy. "Jeez, you know? Enardi, let's go find you a young ash." The three went off toward the upper bank of the stream.

Chris turned before they'd gone very far. "Aletto, you know what you need to do to get ready for a workout. Mom, you're going with him, right? Meet back here, say, half an hour?"

"Who knows?" Robyn replied tartly. "I haven't worn a watch in twenty-some years." Chris grinned at her and waved a dismissive hand; his other arm fell across Enardi's shoulder as they walked off.

Jennifer laughed quietly as the three vanished into a stand of young trees and brush. "Portrait of a man torn. Ernie looks like he suddenly can't decide if he really wants this." She shook her head. "I wonder if he's done anything physical in his life."

Aletto shook his own head. "Considering his class and where he grew up, I doubt it. A wealthy merchant's son wouldn't learn weaponry as a matter of course; the Duke's personal armed guards usually come from among the poorer sorts."

"What else is new?" Robyn demanded generally. When Aletto looked at her, though, she merely shrugged and motioned him to go on.

"He wouldn't have had to shift his father's stock, either; Fedthyr has men in the harbor, men on his ships." Dahven gazed thoughtfully after the now vanished boys. "He looks soft. Mentally and physically. It's a hard combination to break."

Aletto nodded. "I know. All too well. Probably he's in no better shape than—well, than I am. Was," he amended as Robyn nudged him.

"You're not in bad shape at all these days," she said. "Except that you've pushed a few times when you should've taken it easy. Come on, let's go walk, get the kinks out of my legs. That kid of mine is going to put me through it this morning, I can just tell."

Jennifer spread her feet apart and bent over, hands kneading the small of her back. "He'll probably be too busy beating poor Ernie into shape, but I wouldn't count on that. Robyn, where did you ever get a son with so much energy?"

"God knows, he didn't get it from me. See you in a little bit, kiddo. Don't mangle anything."

"You know me better than that, Birdy." Jennifer stretched her neck side to side, rubbed her chin against the tee-shirt and tossed her hair back. She came up, red-faced, to find Dahven gazing down the road after his friend.

"I would never have thought it possible. You're all good for him, I can see that. But she particularly is, isn't she?"

Jennifer bent to one side and then the other, hands still working the muscles over her kidneys. Nothing felt hot or tight. She brought one arm up and bent sideways with it. "I think so. He needed someone who could accept him, handicap and all. Most people—I have to admit I'm one of them—don't know where to look when they first come up against someone like Aletto. Robyn's so matter-of-fact about things like that. I don't know how far we would have gotten after—after you left us, if it hadn't been for Robyn convincing him to try what he's doing now."

"I'm glad to see he's trying. I knew him before it happened, of course—before he got the fever. That changed him more than his father's death." Dahven pulled himself to his feet. "Why are you doing this?"

Jennifer bent forward once more. "The stretchout? You've probably had the sword training Aletto didn't get, right?" She looked up. He nodded. "How did it feel the day after, when you first began, remember that?" He cast his eyes up and she grinned through a spill of dark curls. "This gets the muscles warmed up, so you avoid some of the misery the next morning. If you run like I do, helps you avoid turning an ankle or tearing a muscle."

"Oh."

"Don't sound so doubtful. You probably don't run—?"

"Run? To get away from my tutors a few times—"

Jennifer laughed briefly. "I think you're feeling better, if you're up to a bad joke like that. Maybe up to a workout?" He considered this, nodded. "It's probably a good idea, get back into things a little at a time, ease yourself back into good fighting trim."

"You think I was *in* good fighting trim?"

"I think so, even if you were only fighting off women." She grinned as he averted his eyes.

"Your world must be odder than Father's wizard ever reported it, that *women* say such things." But he was smiling back at her.

"Sorry. I'm used to saying what's on my mind. Will you listen if I tell you—or Chris does—that you've had enough?"

Now he looked truly embarrassed. "Like I did yesterday?"

"Like yesterday. You *did* get off the horse by yourself before you fell off," Jennifer said. "All right, here, get your feet apart, like I have, start loosening your back up."

When Chris came back, Dahven was holding Jennifer's

feet while she did sit-ups. "Hey, awright!" he said cheerfully. "You going to give it a try?"

Dahven looked up and shrugged. "I'm not certain how good I'll be just now. But I'll try this new thing of yours; the only alternative is that ghastly sword. Do you know, I still find it hard to believe anyone would have wasted coin on that sword!"

Chris laughed. "Well, we did, and yeah, it's pretty rotten, wouldn't cut butter if you heated it first. But hey, we never intended to *use* the thing, not even for cutting butter, you know? I mean, Aletto doesn't know any more about swords than I do."

"If you'd needed it—"

"Hey, we didn't, we had a couple to wear so no one would mess with us. Besides, it's like I told all these guys when we started with the staff, the bo: Your old man's hired men and Jadek's guys know how to use swords, right? They've done it for years, probably started when they were kids, and now they get *paid* to use them and be good at it. Aletto probably ought to know how to swing one, just because he's a Duke, but he wasn't gonna pick it up overnight, any more than I was. This other thing, though." He held up the six-foot, well-polished and now darkened by sweat staff. "It's not just a toy, you know. And especially at first, none of the guys after us—your Sikkreni or Jadek's men—had ever seen anything like it, so they couldn't figure how to fight it." He turned it end for end, planted one rounded tip in the road and leaned into it. "Well, most of them know about it now, I'll bet, but we've gotten better, too. So it's still damned hard to fight—either defensively or aggressively. Because it's hard to figure where it's coming from, you don't move it like you would a sword. Particularly if you're good with a sword, it's gonna screw up your game, fighting something that different. That's logical, isn't it?"

Dahven considered this as he took Jennifer's place and she held his ankles. "Very logical. But it doesn't seem sensible. After all, I know most of my father's—of the Sikkreni guard." He closed his eyes, set his jaw and pulled himself slowly into a curl over his bent knees.

"Yeah, well, I know some of 'em too, now," Chris said. "The hard way, you know?" He watched Dahven's progress critically, finally nodded. "Doing great, guy, don't start with too many of those unless your gut muscles are really tight.

Jen, you can tell, keep an eye on him, right? And get him on pushups, why don't you?'' He turned to gaze over his shoulder, toward the stand of woods where Edrith and Enardi were just emerging. Enardi looked even more doubtful than he had going in, but he had a six-foot length of de-branched staff in his left hand and he was listening to Edrith; Edrith was speaking in a low voice, too low for Jennifer to catch what he was saying, but his hands were sketching out the basics he and Chris had taught them all. *Lift with your legs, not your arms; keep your grip at shoulder width, your hands relaxed.* ''Jeez,'' Chris muttered under his breath, ''the guy looks more spooked than mom.''

''He's no pacifist, this is just very new to him,'' Jennifer replied as quietly.

''Yeah, I know. I won't push him too hard, before you say it. But I—hey, what's that?'' Chris turned slightly so he was staring down the road. ''Jeez,'' he added in a much louder voice. ''Something's up; when's the last time you saw mom run like that?''

Jennifer leaped to her feet. ''You're not kidding, Chris. Something's wrong, and where's Aletto?'' Dahven was leaning on her shoulder, looking where she pointed. Robyn came sprinting into their midst moments later, red-faced and gasping.

''I—God, time out—men—'' She shook her head and pointed back the way she'd come. ''Men coming—''

Lialla pushed forward and caught Robyn's elbow; Robyn leaned against her briefly. ''Aletto? Where's my brother?''

''Th—there. They aren't—that close. He—told me to run, he'd get off the road if he had to—''

''It's all right, I see him,'' Dahven said. Jennifer turned her attention briefly back to the road, then looked away. Aletto was running, or attempting to. It made her hurt all over to watch him. ''Robyn, how many, could you tell?''

''Twelve, maybe fourteen,'' Robyn replied breathily. She took the cup of water Chris handed her and drained it. ''God. Thanks, kid. I didn't think I'd make it back. My stomach feels like I swallowed a balloon, ooh, it hurts.''

''Yeah, what happens when you get soft, ma.'' Robyn scowled at him and flicked drops of water in his direction. Aletto came staggering into their midst moments later and she handed her son the cup back before helping the nera-

Duke edge down. He let his head drop into his hands; he was whooping for air.

"Fill that, kid, make yourself useful. Aletto—?"

He shook his head. "Fine." He clearly wasn't, though he was getting his breath back.

Robyn looked up. "Dahven, I think they're all from Sikkre."

"Fourteen," Aletto agreed. "All Sikkreni." From the look on his face, Dahven had already done the math and come up with very mismatched odds. His shoulders sagged and he offered Jennifer a small smile that didn't reach his eyes. Aletto broke the silence once more. "Robyn, please, go get my bo, bring it to me. Get your own," he added crisply as she hesitated. "Go. I promise, I'm fine, just hurry, will you?"

"Aletto," Dahven began. Aletto made a chopping motion with his hand, then held it out.

"Don't say it, make yourself useful and help me up, why don't you?"

"I have to say it, it won't go away if I don't, you know." The two men were nearly of a height. Dahven scowled at Aletto, who scowled right back, unintimidated. "I'll go with them, quietly. I can't imperil all of you, Aletto. I intended to return to Sikkre anyway, to deal with my brothers. And I know all the guardsmen who served my father—"

"Do you really?" Jennifer demanded crisply. "You might be surprised." She had her own staff now and was running it between her hands.

"Eight to fourteen," Chris said in the brief silence. "I'd call that bad odds for *them*."

Robyn handed Aletto his bo. "Chris? Where are the boys?"

He shot her an incredulous look. "You kidding? Ernie's back in the woods with Eddie; Eddie can come around behind those guys if we need him to and he's got Ernie to help him make noises like a handful of brutes with broadswords. You gonna hold onto that thing and look like you mean to use it, or you gonna go hang out with Ernie?"

"Chris," Dahven began. Chris turned to scowl at him and he sighed heavily. "In the first place, I won't be in any danger with Sikkreni guardsmen. In the second, that's your *mother* you're putting into peril—"

"An old bat named Merrida did that before I did," Chris

replied flatly. "And I *really* think you need to check these guys out before you decide you have it figured, you know?"

"Just don't promise them anything," Jennifer said. "That, and reserve judgment. Please."

Dahven sighed again. "I keep promising you these things, as if I had good sense—oh, all right. But it doesn't seem to work both ways."

"How?" Jennifer demanded.

"I'm supposed to stay safe, but *you*—"

"There isn't any safe around here.'

"Nonsense," Dahven replied sharply. "But I suppose it won't do me any good to ask you to stay behind me for once, out of danger—"

"It just might get you a black eye," Jennifer snapped. "Haven't you got that straight, yet? Look," she added in a softer voice, "I appreciate the thought. This isn't the place for chivalry, and I don't need or want it." Silence. "Aletto, are you going to want a horse—?"

"No. I'm fine on my feet. Besides," he added as the first Sikkreni guardsmen appeared over a low rise in the road, "there isn't time for that now. Dahven, my good friend, please do what Jen suggests. At least until you've seen and heard for yourself."

Dahven shook his head dubiously but he walked over to the tree where he'd leaned the resheathed sword. He drew the blade, placed it upright against the trunk, leaned against the tree and began loosening the straps that would hold the sword-belt to his body. Aletto had tightened them down for his own much narrower chest and tightened them again when he hung the weapon from his saddle. Jennifer cast him one last anxious glance, but even to her concerned eye, Dahven looked supremely relaxed. Certainly no one would have thought him barely recovered from the ordeal he'd been through. She turned away from him to face the oncoming riders, rested one end of the bo on the road and braced her feet apart.

The horsemen checked briefly when they saw six people in the middle of the road, making no attempt to conceal themselves: Aletto standing mid-road, bo held in rest position across his thighs; Jennifer just behind his right shoulder, Lialla at his left and Robyn a little back and between them. Chris had taken a position to the left, where the horsemen might try to spread off the road into open grass;

Dahven was not far behind him, leaning against his tree, legs crossed at the ankle, his hands busy with a stiff buckle. The men came on then, stopping only just short of Aletto. The nera-Duke changed his grip on the bo, from the resting position to a ready one. Robyn took an involuntary step back, but only one; she braced the end of her bo against the road, free end up and pointed at the nearest of the riders. Except for the creak and jingle of harness, the thud of hooves on the hard-packed road, it was quiet for some moments.

"Can we help you?" Jennifer asked. One of the men nudged his mount to the fore and glared at her, then down at Aletto, over their heads.

"Help us," he spat. "If that is a joke, it's a very poor one."

"Don't pick on the woman, Firsi," Dahven said mildly. "Not good manners."

There was another, rather ugly silence. "You," Firsi said venomously. "All the time you have wasted, all you have done, traitor—"

"I?" Dahven loosened the strap and held up the buckle to study it. "I cannot think why you call me a traitor since to my understanding that calls for a treasonous act, and I assure you I have committed none."

"Only caused the death of Lord Dahmec—"

"Bosh," Dahven replied flatly. "And you know as much, Firsi. You must be aware I was not even within the city walls when my father died."

"The Thukars told us that would be your defense."

"I have no need of a defense, having done no wrong. My brothers, on the other hand, have a good deal to answer for."

"And who will bring them to account?" someone well back in the milling riders shouted.

"Hey, dude," Chris turned to Dahven. "You get the feeling these jerks don't like you very much? Maybe don't think you should make it home alive?"

"I begin to dislike the tone of the conversation," Dahven replied cheerfully. (Jennifer found herself wishing she dared take her eyes from the mounted men to glance at him; she could have sworn by his voice that he was smiling.) "And I wonder why it is, Firsi. I had thought us on terms of acceptance, if not friends."

"You," Firsi said, so softly Jennifer had to listen hard to hear what he said. "Is there a man serving the Thukars who would name you friend? Look at him, at the look on his face," he demanded of the man next to him. "He does not understand. Oh, no! He has money, power, the right to pick and choose which market disputes to settle, so that the merchants call him a good administrator and treat us as they would jackals! A man with everything, and yet he took his father's life! Lord Dahven—the traitor Dahven—with his pretty face, and a manner pleasing to women. Innkeeper's daughters and barefoot market bawds adore him, and he denies none of them." His voice trailed away; his mouth was set, his eyes dark with loathing. *He's trying to gross me out, as Chris would say,* Jennifer decided. She wouldn't give him the satisfaction.

"Whoa, wait, time out," Chris said, and he was trying hard not to laugh. "Let me get this straight. All this traitor stuff, that's just the bullshit on top, isn't it? I think you want to kill this guy because the girls like him better than they like you, and that has to be the stupidest thing I ever heard!" It was the kind of thing Chris had seen first-hand in his own high school—and it had to have hit home, judging from the look Firsi turned on him.

"It is not your business, outlander."

"Yeah? People try to kill me, it makes things my business. I guess with *your* pretty face and your totally charming manner, it isn't easy to figure why girls would like him better, though."

Firsi's mouth twitched. "It is easy for such a man to win the attentions of women, and the praise of their fathers. Since he did not collect taxes, or arrest wrongdoers—oh, no! Men like us are always given the dirty tasks."

"Yeah," Chris jeered. "Bet you get paid for it, too."

Firsi glared down at the outlander, then drew himself up straight and glared over him at Dahven, who was still fiddling with leather straps and, to all appearances, disinterested in the quarrel, or the presence of his brothers' men. "Their honors the Thukars have sent us to return you to Sikkre. Alive, if possible."

Chris laughed. "I am so sure."

"In all honesty," Firsi went on stiffly, "their honors have more than once expressed aloud distress that such a dreadful affair—a family matter—should become public, that the

41

name of their brother should be spread through Rhadaz as a father-murderer, or that the Emperor should hear of it—"

"Nonsense," Dahven said. "Shesseran heard of Father's death no doubt within hours of the occurrence—long days before I heard of it, I assure you."

"Assure us of anything you wish, for all I care," Firsi replied even more stiffly. "I care only that we have at last found you, I have myself wasted a full moon-season at the search and have already encountered these persons entirely too many times." A sweep of his hand took in Chris, Robyn, Jennifer. His eyes fixed on Aletto. "*This* time, nera-Duke, you will come with us. Your uncle has offered a princely sum for your capture and the Lady Lialla's." Aletto brought his chin up and said nothing. Lialla, not far behind him, folded her arms across her chest and stared coldly from under her black scarves.

"Oh, sure." Chris took a step to the left edge of the road, to block the horseman trying to edge behind him. "Maybe if you get enough reward for that kind of dirty work, you can just buy a girl or two—preferably one with crummy vision and lousy taste." The Sikkreni leaned forward; his nearest companion laid hold of his shoulder and kept him in place.

"Firsi, can't you see he's a green boy, trying to provoke the fight? But there is also a reward for *you*," he said pointedly. "And it is enough to repay us for the trouble we've been caused, finding you. As for you, traitor, we've heard all the stories put about Sikkre's market by your common friends. Unfortunately for you, the stories don't make as much sense as the truth does."

"Which, according to my brothers and to you," Dahven returned smoothly, "is that I murdered my father so I could become Duke years before my time and offer the Duchy as a marriage portion to a certain lady." He loosened a buckle, snugged it down again by feel; his eyes remained on the horsemen.

"That is what you did—"

"Or at least what you and my brothers hope everyone will believe. Jennifer," he added lightly, "I owe you an apology, my lady love, for doubting your reading of my brother's men."

"Accepted," she replied in kind. Firsi shifted his glare

to her; she gave him a chill look. "I remember you," she said, and clipped her words. "From an encounter in the desert, south of Sikkre. You must have learned nothing, to come in search of another fight."

Firsi shifted and this time evaded his companion's arm, edged his horse forward a pace. As he passed Aletto, the nera-Duke took one step back to keep from being boxed in; Robyn backed with him and Lialla moved to one side. Jennifer set her teeth as the sin-Duchess started fingering Thread, began humming Puccini under her breath to counter the discomfort. "You, woman. You caused a good deal of trouble in Sikkre, beginning with the wizard Snake's death. I will take considerable pleasure in handing you to Lord Jadek personally."

She bared her teeth at him. "You sound pretty damned brave up there. Climb off that damned horse and see how far you get."

"Firsi, don't—!" one of his company began, but the man had already thrown one leg across the horse and dropped to the ground. Jennifer's bo caught him under the chin; his teeth slammed together with a loud click. He reeled back into the horse and fell. Jennifer shoved the horse back with one extended swing of the staff and leaped over the unconscious Firsi to snap a strike at the man who'd ridden up behind him. He ducked and snatched at the end of the bo; the other end came around and cracked across the back of his neck. He caught hold of his horse's mane two-handed, but slid slowly down the animal's back and onto the road not far from Firsi. Jennifer jumped aside, cast one quick glance over her shoulder. "Dahven?" she demanded; she had to shout over men yelling, Chris snapping loud, rhythmic insults at the two men riding for him, over what sounded like an army in the brush on the other side of the road, Robyn's startled shriek as Aletto leaped forward to press an advantage. "Dahven, damnit, where are you?"

"Right here!" He was shouting from somewhere behind her, but a moment later he was a reassuring presence on her right side.

"Don't get too close," she warned him and he laughed. "The way you're using that thing? Are you mad?" He had the sword out and up, and as she watched for the next opening in the milling mass of horsemen, Dahven took two long strides, passed Aletto and caught one of the Sikkreni guardsmen by the open throat of his leather overshirt, hauling him from the saddle and forehead-first into the pommel of the dull sword. Before the next man could press past the riderless horse and attack, Dahven had the fallen man's sword and kicked the worthless one behind him. He grinned up at his new opponent. "Eprian, you and I have fought for practice, are you certain you want to try it for blood?" Eprian apparently didn't; he dragged his horse back and began edging around to try and catch Chris—who was busy with a man afoot. Jennifer waited until the guardsman had his full attention on her nephew, then came up under him as she had the first man; he ducked sharply, only to catch the polished end of the bo under his ear. The horse, startled, took off down the road and the man toppled from it some distance away.

Suddenly it was all over; Lialla leaned against Robyn, eyes closed, making rope from Thread. Aletto was moving from Sikkreni to Sikkreni, watching expressionlessly as the three-strand plaited stuff wound itself around wrists and ankles and knotted tightly. Chris stood guard over the three men he'd dispatched, bo at the ready. Edrith came out of the woods, bo trailing behind him, and placed himself next to Aletto. Dahven, sword in hand, came back to where Jennifer waited, standing over the still-unconscious Firsi. "I fear I owe you a second apology," Dahven said. "But I think you *must* be mad, talking like that to a man as angry as he was."

Jennifer laughed; Firsi groaned. "I'm no madder than you, and not half as crazy as Chris. Did you *hear* him? I was simply getting this one angry enough to do something stupid, and he did. And I didn't walk into the middle of the whole pack of them to pick up a new sword the way *you* did."

"Yeah, that was pretty nifty," Chris said. "I really like your style, reminds me of that guy in the movies—whatsisname, you know, Jen, played privateers and Robin Hood and all. I am *really* impressed, I thought that kind of fighting was *only* in old movies."

"You have to ignore them," Lialla said faintly. She'd finished making rope and was leaning on Robyn, who wrapped both arms around her. "They use these *words*—"

"Ah, but I know what movies are," Dahven said cheerfully. "Jennifer told me." He sobered. "What are we going

44

to do with them?'' He gestured. ''We can't simply leave them like this, can we?''

''I would certainly like that,'' Jennifer said flatly. She sighed. ''A three-strand rope unfortunately won't keep them here for very long. But we haven't much of the real stuff, have we, Edrith?''

''No—but Dahven's right, we can't leave them helpless. Why do I think this sounds familiar?'' he added plaintively. ''I have a suggestion this time, however.'' He knelt next to Firsi and tugged at the man's hair. ''I know you heard that; you were making enough noise a moment or so ago, and you don't breathe like an unconscious man. I would like to propose a truce.''

Firsi gazed at him for some moments, finally shrugged. ''I've seen you, and your accent is Sikkreni. I cannot place you.''

''That isn't important,'' Edrith said. ''Listening is. Even you must have reasoned by now that you aren't able to beat us by force. You must also realize that once we've gone on, you will be behind us. I have seen maps and spoken to men who know this road well; there simply is no way you could get around us to set an ambush. Which means if you persist in following you will yourself be walking into an ambush, because we will certainly be watching for you from now on. And if you come against us by force, you'll only gain another bruise or two to go with the previous ones. A sensible man would give it up.''

''He's right, you know,'' Dahven said mildly. ''You've lost any surprise you might have had; even catching us short, you got nowhere. And next time, my friend, *I* won't be so trusting of your good will. And,'' he grinned widely and held up the sword he'd taken, ''next time I'll have a proper piece of Sikkreni steel in my hand, and I do swear, Firsi, if you so much as come near us again, I'll run you through where your heart should be. Go back to Sikkre, tell my brothers you couldn't find me.'' The smile faded. ''Better still, give them a message: Tell them I'll come back at a time *I* choose. And we will talk.'' He turned and walked away; Jennifer went with him.

Enardi was behind the tent, hastily and sloppily loading bags into the wagon. He was pale and looked very frightened. ''Jen? Is it over? Eddie said it was all right to come out of hiding but not to let them see me. Is this okay?''

"Everything's under control," she assured him. "Here, I'll start rolling the blankets. Stay back here; no one will see you. That was very sensible of Edrith."

"He said in case the Emperor came down on Dahven, it might be better if no one knew I was part of it; there might be sanctions against Father." He shoved a pack under the seat, hesitated. "Did I do all right?"

"That was you making all that noise in the woods?" Jennifer asked. He nodded. "You distracted them; it sounded like we'd brought a whole army with us."

"That was Chris's idea," Enardi admitted. "Since I didn't know how to fight yet. It was a movie, he said—a play of sorts, about a thief who thought other thieves were after him, so he pretended to be many different men, all armed and deadly." He grinned rather abashedly. "Chris also said the thief ran when it seemed to him that his scheme failed and that I was to remember that, too."

"God," Jennifer said devoutly.

Enardi paused, hands full of Robyn's pots. "It *was* all right, really?"

"It was all right. Chris's mind—well, get on with it. Dahven, how do you feel about saddling horses?"

4

༄

THEY were on the road within the hour. Lialla—who had stood silent among the fallen Sikkreni guardsmen while the others finished packing and while Edrith dealt with fourteen pairs of boots and fourteen horses—took the reins of her mount from Robyn and stepped across to look down at Firsi, who glared up at her. "The ropes will hold another hour or so, then dissolve. You'll find your boots a ways up the bank of the stream; they haven't been damaged. Nor have your horses."

"You'll find *them* a short distance back down the road," Edrith said, "the way you came."

"If you're sensible, you will continue that way your-selves," Dahven said. "But next time we meet, Firsi—" The man mumbled something Jennifer couldn't quite catch; Dahven laughed, and one of the lower-ranked men said, "By all the little warm sand gods, Firsi, let it go!"

"Yes, Firsi, let it go," Dahven said evenly. "And take a message back to Sikkre. Tell my brothers I send my love. They want to see me again, and soon? They will, I promise you. And in case they prefer I not return at all—however they intend that to happen—well, tell them they won't be rid of me so easily." He wheeled the horse around and set off down the road at a canter. Aletto followed, Robyn at his side, Lialla at his other side and a little behind him; Chris and Edrith took up the rear, which blocked the guardsmen's view of the wagon and its driver. Jennifer stayed behind for a moment until the captain of the Sikkreni looked at her; he was reluctant to meet her eyes—something to do with being beaten twice, she thought. By anyone.

"You and I had best *not* meet again in the near future," she said flatly. "For your own sake. If we do, it'll be be-cause you're still after him. It's possible he still holds a little trust in his brothers and doubts you'd murder him at their asking. Don't even bother to deny that's what you intend. Next time I swear I'll kill you. Don't dare to doubt I'm capable."

She was about to ride away when he finally answered her. "I don't doubt that. Two of the men here with me had sand in their boots a few days back—Bez sand. I wonder you'd dare pretend you never saw them before."

Jennifer shrugged. "It was dark on that beach."

"You killed their captain."

"To save my own life. And Dahven's." Silence. "And you know it. Another thing: I don't want him for Sikkre— I can see you don't believe me. But he wants what is right-fully his, and I'll do everything I can to see he regains it. Don't get between me and mine, as the man in Bez tried to do. You'll live longer." And then she did turn and ride away. Her back prickled; the men behind her were very quiet. She was glad when the slight grade in the road crested and she was out of their sight.

The others rode close to the wagon, except for Edrith who'd gone back the other way with a long lead line of horses; Jennifer momentarily worried about him. But if there

47

had been other Sikkreni with the company of fourteen, surely they'd have come in to rescue their friends at once. And Edrith was no fool; he'd avoid the Sikkreni on his way back up the road. She drew a deep breath, her first in some time. Once again they'd come through against uneven odds; it surely couldn't last. *Unless,* she thought dryly, *Dahven's brothers fired everyone with brains when they took over.*

Fortunately the mule was used to following the road and the horses, because Enardi was holding the reins but not actually doing anything with them; Jennifer thought he looked absolutely ill, and he had stuffed both hands between his knees. They still shook. She opened her mouth, but shut it again without saying anything. Enardi was enough like Chris that he wouldn't want her calling attention to him just now.

Chris was watching him too, she noticed; after a few moments, he and Edrith began talking as though nothing were wrong with their shaken, too-pale friend. Eventually Enardi chuckled at something Chris said—rather raggedly, but he was coming out of it. Jennifer edged her horse forward, to where Dahven was riding. His face was blotchily red across the cheekbones, and sweat beaded his upper lip. "All right?" she asked.

"Of course." He considered this gravely, shook his head. "Actually, no."

"I'm sorry," Jennifer said. "That was a truly stupid thing to ask."

"I didn't exert that much, you know." He glanced at her sideways. "Just got myself a decent sword." He grinned impudently and she laughed. "I truly must find out where Aletto bought that wretched blade, and see that the merchant goes into another business. He shouldn't be selling swords like that; someone might actually try to use one."

"It wasn't so bad," Jennifer said. Dahven stared at her. "The hilt didn't break. It served its purpose."

"Funny woman. The steel itself couldn't cut a line in sand." They rode in companionable silence for a while. "I actually thought I had to shield you from Firsi. Did you leave anything of him just now?"

Jennifer grinned. "Unfortunately. I'm sorry I threatened you with violence earlier. Oh, I understand your reasoning, but I can't agree with it. All the same, you didn't know I could take care of myself. So—sorry."

"You've done nothing else since I met you."

"All the same. Enough men where I lived try to coddle their women—mostly as a means of keeping them second-class citizens, and keeping them from doing things. I have a low burning point on the subject—just so you know."

"Now I know."

"I don't say it isn't confusing; not everyone wants as much independence as I do. You have only to look at Robyn."

Dahven turned in the saddle and did. "Well—yes. But some people aren't fighters by nature, are they? She isn't the only one, though; your young friends will have quite a task teaching Enardi."

"God," Jennifer groaned. "I was worried about bringing him in the first place—you know, worst-case scenario, he dies, Fedthyr boycotts Aletto, we all wind up eating cactus in the desert south of Sikkre." Dahven laughed, shook his head. "It hadn't even occurred to me he'd be so shaken by a fairly minor fight. But we've grown so used to violence; even Robyn wasn't as upset as she'd have been once. That's terrible."

"You aren't deliberately seeking it, you know." Dahven touched her hand. She captured it and held it against her knee.

"We could have refused to help Aletto—"

"I doubt you would have."

"God," Jennifer said once more and ran a hand through her hair. "Probably not. But even Chris, with all his books and his games for some kind of reference, didn't realize how bad it might get."

"Nor did I," Dahven replied gloomily. "And I surely had more reason to be aware, knowing my brothers, my father—" He straightened, shifted in the saddle and went on in a determined change of subject. "How long have you been fighting with that long staff?"

She thought about this. "Thirty—forty days? About that. Since a day or two after we left Sikkre, when Chris started training us—"

"You're not serious."

"Don't look so awed. Chris was trying to tell you in his own inimitable way; it's done with leverage and a few very basic moves. That's why Aletto can use it so well, why I can. And like Chris said, it's different enough to catch a swordsman off balance—a good one expects certain counters to what he's doing, and the oddness of the weapon throws him.''

"I saw as much. All the same, you show talent at it—besides the willingness to fight. That's uncommon.''

"What—among women?''

He shook his head; apparently the sarcasm didn't register. "That, of course. But nearly a fourth of my father's guard—and I'll wager Jadek's guard, too—can use weapons but only as a game. I would hate to depend on some of them to guard my back in a real fight.''

"They looked all right coming up to you.''

Dahven snorted. "Deehar's and Dayher's men? They aren't even good in a pack, or hadn't you noticed?''

"It had occurred to me. But your back is safe here,'' Jennifer said gravely.

"I think so. I like the way your Chris thinks.''

"Thank you.'' Chris had come up behind them, unnoticed by either. "Still want to learn bo?'' Dahven nodded, and with more enthusiasm than he had the first time. "Good. Poor old Ernie's gonna be tough to show anything; I thought he was gonna lose it back there when the scene got real on him. But you should do just fine.''

"I'll trade you lessons, sword for bo,'' Dahven suggested, but Chris was already shaking his head.

"There's no way I'm gonna *ever* use a sword, all right? I mean, I don't even carry a pocket knife, all they're ever good for is I cut myself and a sword is a *lot* longer than a pocket knife. Besides, I'm specializing, once we get Aletto home, I'm gonna open my own shop, charge through the nose for lessons. Tell you what, though: Aletto really needs to know how to swing a sword; why don't you show *him* how?''

Dahven spread his hands wide. "Because I don't think he'd accept the offer. You've been with him a while; you know how he takes anything like that.''

"Well, but maybe not,'' Chris said. "I mean, when we first met up with him, you couldn't talk to him about almost anything, he'd get snooty and offended and stomp off. Mom figured out how to handle him, of course, but she's got a gift or something, she can handle anyone. You just have to figure out what his problem is and work around it, like when we were out in the desert, remember, Jen? The night we had that wall of stickers and no water?'' She nodded. ''And he was a, like, genuine hurting frog and chewing on anyone who so much as looked at him. I think Lialla was about ready to stuff him in with the cactus and leave him there. So anyway, Eddie and I talked about how we felt like crap, just between ourselves, you know, except loud enough he could hear us. So he finally figured he wasn't the only softie paying for not being in good shape.''

''I hope some of that made sense to you,'' Jennifer told Dahven. ''I can only assure you it wouldn't have made much more sense in our own language, even if you were another Angeleno.''

''I caught the intention, if not the exact sense, thank you.''

''Hey,'' Chris demanded. ''Am I being double-teamed, or what?''

Jennifer laughed. ''Get used to it, kid.''

''Not likely. No, anyway, what I think is, you ask Aletto why doesn't he practice sword with you, that you're so out of shape or whatever that you really need to go back to the easy stuff and work up. That way you don't have to bring up that he's never done it, and he doesn't have to admit to it—with Aletto that could be half your battle right there.''

''It's not far off, either,'' Dahven replied gloomily. ''*I* haven't had occasion to use a sword since my last weapons tutor gave up on me.''

''Yeah, well, you could've fooled me,'' Chris said. ''And probably you could've fooled the other guy, too—you know, the one back there who traded a sword for a headache? But hey, you got style.'' He glanced over his shoulder. ''So, anyway, how far we going?''

''You guys were the ones with the map,'' Jennifer said. ''And the built-in good campsite for tonight.''

''Right. Before the goon squad hit us, though.''

Dahven shifted. ''We have no reason to go farther than that, do we?''

''Don't know,'' Chris said. ''Those guys: I didn't recognize any of them from our last bash.'' He grinned; Jennifer groaned. ''But the source is the same, right? The last ones weren't all that bright.''

''These don't seem to be either,'' Jennifer said. She couldn't see any point in mentioning the ones who'd been in Bez.

"They aren't," Dahven said flatly. "If Firsi comes after us, he won't have much difficulty catching us, no matter where we stop for the night—thanks to that wagon."

"I know." Chris nodded. "Try and talk Aletto and mom out of it, though."

"Why don't we wait and see what Edrith has to say when he gets back?" Jennifer asked.

Chris sighed. "Eddie," he reminded her in an exasperated voice. "I mean, really. You know?" He drew back on the reins, slowing his horse so the wagon could catch up to him. Dahven shook his head in mild bewilderment.

"I mean, you know," he echoed. "Is this some kind of invocation?" Jennifer laughed.

"Wait'll he starts trying to teach you the hip hop," she said. "And no, it's not another kind of fighting." Dahven merely shook his head.

Edrith showed up well over an hour later, by Jennifer's watch—long enough that Chris was getting noticeably worried about him. "Yo, guy," he called out as Edrith came riding up behind them. "I was beginning to think you'd fallen in the surf."

Edrith rolled his eyes. "Sure you did. You knew I had to go around those guys."

"So, how long could that take?"

"Well, if *some* of us were smart enough, they'd realize I stopped and snuck in close to listen to them for a little, see what they were planning. You know?" He would possibly have gone on in the same vein, but Lialla came up on his other side and tugged at his sleeve.

"The rope—it was holding?"

"When I left them. That was a while ago, though. But that isn't the important part. As soon as they get loose, they're sending a couple of men after the horses, and coming right on up the road behind us."

Lialla's face was very pale against the Wielder Blacks. "That still should give us—Jen? How long, do you think?"

For answer, Jennifer slid from her horse and closed her eyes. She finally shrugged. "I can tell they're back there, a number of them, not going anywhere. That's about all, just now. All the same, two men walking back for the horses— Eddie, how far did you take them?"

"Not far enough," he said gloomily.

"That isn't exactly specific. An hour by foot? Two?"

"Maybe an hour. But Firsi was saying something about the two he sent being messengers and if they are, then it wouldn't be nearly that long."

"You didn't recognize them?" Dahven asked. Edrith shrugged.

"I know the Thukar has always kept a few runner-messengers; that's common knowledge. *You* didn't recognize them?"

"They're outside the market," Dahven said. "And Father kept a number of men I didn't really know. They were all familiar, you know—I'd seen the faces—"

"Is this important?" Lialla asked impatiently.

"It isn't," Chris said. "You're right, Li, we need to boogie, like now."

"Whatever that is, we'd better do it, if it means moving fast," Dahven said. "That wagon—well, it can't be helped."

"It's my father's," Enardi put in tentatively. "I told him I'd take care of it—"

"It's cool," Chris assured him. "Let's get going and everything'll be fine, all right?" From the look on Enardi's face, he didn't believe a word of it.

They took an hour stop at the site Enardi had suggested for the night's camp—to rest the horses and the mule, to eat a cold lunch, and to give Jennifer a chance to try and find their pursuers. She found them, apparently still not moving, but she still wasn't able to tell anything else. "Sorry, folks," she said finally to the rather anxious group around her. "I don't know anything else to try. So far as I can tell they haven't got the horses yet."

"I thought you could tell the difference," Lialla began.

"Well, I can, usually," Jennifer said stiffly. "This time, I can't. Let me go at it again, after dark."

"They're probably all carrying good market charms," Dahven put in quickly, before Lialla could say anything else. She looked at him with unfriendly eyes, then turned away. Dahven cast his own up.

"It's possible," Jennifer conceded. "It could be running water; Neri said it's been known to affect Thread. It's harder to Wield in full daylight."

"Hey, does it matter?" Chris asked. "We know they're

back there and Eddie says they're on us. So we find some place we can hide and either let them slide on by, or some place we can hang out and jump 'em *real* good this time. Ernie, you got any ideas at all what it's like ahead of us?''

The Bezanti shook his head. ''Other than what I said this morning.''

''It's rough country,'' Dahven said.

''I can see that,'' Chris said sarcastically.

''There's a pass of sorts, cliff running down to the water, then gradual slope cut by dry washes, a lot of rock.'' Dahven cast Chris a withering look. ''It's a hot, dry area, and not that many years ago said to be controlled by two villages back in the hills. Not that much was ever shipped by road, even a reign or two ago, but for a long time little or nothing got through.''

''Bandits?'' Chris asked. ''Oh, great.''

''Snake country and bandits,'' Robyn muttered; she looked even more unhappy than Lialla did.

''No, it's all right, they're long gone,'' Enardi assured her. ''Shesseran XII finally sent in almost an army; there hasn't been anyone living near the road in at least fifty years, until you get near the inn.''

''We can't make the inn tonight?'' Lialla asked him. Enardi shook his head.

''Then we'd better decide, now,'' Aletto said. ''They'll expect to find us here, and there isn't any place around here to hide.''

''Not all of us,'' Chris agreed. ''And personally, I don't feel it's a good idea to just sit here and wait for them.''

Aletto nodded. ''Bad idea.'' He looked at Dahven. ''You seem to know more about the road around here than anyone else. What do you think?''

''I don't really *know* it,'' Dahven said. ''Not from my own experience. I talk to caravaners, that's all.''

Aletto considered this; Dahven waited him out—unwilling, Jennifer thought, to let Aletto lean on him. ''Well, then.'' At the same time, Aletto looked uncomfortable with making the final decision. *Life as usual,* she thought sourly. Except that Lialla, for once, was staying entirely out of it. Well, that was just fine; the last thing they needed just now was another screaming fight between Lialla and her brother. Aletto squared his shoulders, gave Dahven a faint, rather embarrassed smile. ''I think we should go now, as quickly as we can, find some place to get ourselves completely off the road and out of sight before dark. What we find might decide whether we hide or we fight.'' He spoiled the effect by adding, ''Don't you think?''

Dahven spread his hands. ''Don't ask me. It's your decision, after all.''

''I—'' Aletto looked briefly angry; he considered this then, and nodded. ''This time, at least. We'll go, then.''

''Well, yeah,'' Chris said slowly. ''I got only one comment, though. I mean, if we hide and let them go past us, that puts them ahead of us. Do we *really* want those guys ahead of us? Logically, even if they're as dumb as they come across, they're gonna eventually figure out that's what we did, and that lets them pick the ambush. I say we break heads.'' Robyn, who was breaking up a crumbling cheese and spreading it on dry, flat bread Edrith handed her, made a faint, wordless protest. ''Sorry, ma. But I am totally *bored* with these guys, and I'm ready to pull someone's card. You know? Someone in that pack of geeks is gonna get lucky and do one of us down, and then I'm really gonna be pissed, because we just let 'em keep coming until they did. You don't want them in your face either, mom, do you?''

''You've made your point,'' Robyn said flatly. ''At least, I think you have; either my grip on the language is slipping or—''

''Chill out, mom,'' Chris said as she hesitated, but he was grinning. Robyn took a swing at him, and missed his ear.

''Chill yourself, brat. Shut up and eat, so we can get out of here, before they catch up with us right here. *I'd* be pretty bored with that.''

The sun was sliding behind a brush-covered ledge when the wagon stalled. Chris swore under his breath, leaped down to grab the mule before it could drag its burden any farther. Edrith and Dahven were already down behind the wagon, inspecting the problem. Edrith shook his head. ''It's going to be a job, but I think we can get it free without damaging anything.''

''How bad?'' Enardi asked anxiously. He slewed around on the high seat, peering back across the loosely piled goods they'd thrown in all anyhow hours before.

''Wheel's caught.''

"You could just back it—" Aletto began.

"We can *try*," Edrith said. He was squatted before the wheel now, scowling at it and the stones blocking it. "It was bound to happen," he added gloomily. "This wretched road might have been made for wagons once but now—" He bent forward, caught hold of the wheel, leaned back to call up to Enardi, "Set the brake, and Chris, don't you dare let go of that animal, it's my hands down here, and I'm rather fond of them." He started nervously as cloth brushed across his back; Lialla came up to crouch beside him.

"What's happened?" she asked brusquely. He shrugged.

"The wheel slipped down, wedged between two rocks; another came down off them or from above something and that's what has it pinned."

"It wasn't—set that way," she went on, more tentatively.

"I doubt anyone could have planned anything like this. Why?" For answer, Lialla shook her head and got back to her feet.

"What next?" she asked generally.

"With luck, we lift it out and everything's fine," Edrith said. He sighed. "Until the next time—probably the next five times, between now and full dark. Ernie, I really do think we're going to have to leave the wagon."

The Bezanti was already shaking his head. "I can't do that. My father—"

"Would surely prefer you alive to you dead and the wagon returned in one piece, don't you think?" Jennifer demanded acerbically. She remained on her horse and was now standing in the stirrups to better see around them. Enardi looked at her unhappily but his mouth was set in a stubborn line. "You won't be abandoning it, you know; we can hide it off the road, we have one spare horse so you won't have to ride the mule, and we can divide the things in the wagon. And then you can retrieve it on your way home. Don't—" She held up a hand as he would have spoken. "Just think about it while we get the damned thing free, why don't you?"

Chris nodded. "Mom, you're better at animals than I am; why don't you hold this stupid mule, so I can get back there and help with the lifting?" He looked back down the road. "It's starting to get dark, you guys, let's do it."

It took what seemed like forever. By the time Jennifer, Aletto and Lialla had shifted the tent, the packs, the blankets and the spare horse gear as far forward as possible, the last yellow glow of sunset was gone from the horizon. By the time Edrith had found an angle from which he could work to pry the fallen rock out of its tightly wedged position over the wheel, so he, Chris and Aletto could lift the back corner and Robyn could lead the mule a few paces on, the only color left in the sky was deep blue and the gray of a few clouds drifting in from the west on a rising wind. Enardi eyed these anxiously; Jennifer caught the look on his drawn face as she straightened with the last armful of blankets she was tossing toward the back of the wagon. "What? You see something?" She turned. "Dahven, anything?"

Dahven, who had reluctantly allowed himself to be persuaded to stay mounted and serve as rear guard, shook his head. She could barely make out the movement, near as he was; apparently aware of this, he added aloud, "No horses, no riders."

"When the clouds come in like that," Enardi said, "it means rain. A lot of it. Before morning." Jennifer glared down at him.

"You scared hell out of me for a rainstorm?"

"You haven't been in one along the inner sea," he replied rather defensively.

"Hey, you guys, can we continue this later?" Chris demanded. "If this thing's ready to move on, anyway."

"Ready as it's going to get," Edrith replied shortly, around the finger he was sucking. He'd pinched it just as they freed the wheel and it was hurting him. Aletto clapped his shoulder as he walked along the side of the wagon to join Robyn. He peered ahead and sighed.

"We'll need to put one or two afoot, out front."

"Great," Lialla muttered. "That should slow us."

Enardi, hunched on the wagon seat, looked so unhappy, Jennifer felt rather sorry for him—except that it was his stubbornness that had landed them in such a spot in the first place. They'd been trying to talk him into leaving the wagon behind for the better part of two days, since the road had gotten so bad—even Aletto, who had been the most pleased to have it, had suggested since leaving Firsi that they might be better off without it.

"It's all right," Aletto said—probably as much to ease Enardi's embarrassment as Lialla's nerves. "Even without your father's wagon, we couldn't ride fast through here after dark; we'd lose half the horses in no time. If those men are behind us, they'll have the same problem.''

"Good thinking," Chris said. Enardi sighed.

"If we can find a place where the wagon won't be visible from the road, I'll leave it.''

"We'll worry about that later," Chris said firmly. "Right now, let's just go.''

At full dark, Aletto called a brief halt. "Someone break out the blue-lights, so we can see something up here.''

"If anyone can find them after the way the box got loaded," Robyn added sourly. Jennifer dismounted and climbed into the back.

"I had my hands on just about everything here. I saw them—hang on.''

"As if we had a choice," Robyn retorted, even more sourly.

"Just—hang on," Jennifer said. Her voice was muffled by the sides of the wagon box and the bag she was digging through. "I felt them—no, damn. Not that one." Her head popped up briefly. "Dahven, what's the word back there?''

"No word," he said. His voice sounded strained.

"You all right?''

"Don't worry about me; find the blue-lights.''

"I'm working on it," Jennifer snapped. A moment later, she came up with a pair of them. "Here. God knows where the third is; two had better do us." Robyn, her eyes angry, came back to grab them and marched back to the front, where she handed one to Aletto. "Get the mule moving; the rest of you go on. Dahven, stay back with me, will you?''

"What—?" Lialla began.

"Nothing," Jennifer interrupted her sharply. "I can't work Thread from horseback, remember? Will you please stay with the wagon?" Lialla, her face a pale and unreadable blotch in windblown black scarves, rode on in stiff-backed silence. Dahven rode up and reined in. Jennifer looked up at him. "Well?''

"I said nothing," he replied. "Is something wrong?''

"I don't know." She sighed. "I'm snarling, aren't I? Everyone wants to *argue*; it drives me frantic. I don't know if anything's wrong, but somehow it doesn't feel right—oh, hell, that doesn't make any sense. I want to check it but I'm not going to stand back here in a Thread-trance by myself.''

"You certainly aren't," Dahven said vigorously. "Do what you have to. Shall I stay up here, or is there something I can do to help?"

In spite of herself, Jennifer laughed quietly. "Don't sound so meek; it doesn't suit you. Stay where you are and keep that damned beast still; for once I'm going to lean on you." She let him take her reins, caught hold of his knee to steady herself and closed her eyes.

Thread wanted to evade her at first—too many thoughts cluttering her mind, too much going on. Hard to concentrate. Finally she let go of Dahven's leg, sat in the road and began simply breathing: count of three, in; count of three, out. She was only vaguely aware of Dahven drawing the horses away from her. The Thread she wanted—red, thick stuff, and that yellow Neri had shown her, both caught up together, twisted together into a temporary, doubly thick rope. The Sikkreni *were* following them: fourteen men on horses. They weren't as far away as she would have liked, but the bicolored twist of Thread let her judge distance much better than the red alone ever had. It would take a hard burst of speed for the guardsmen to take them tonight, and they weren't taking the chance of riding that hard. She suspected they had a lead man riding or walking ahead also.

But they weren't her main concern—there was something, or someone, else. A familiar sensation of being—watched? Was Jadek once again readying a Light spell? But he was easy to stop, if that was all—at least, if he hadn't already located them exactly. "Dahven," she said urgently.

"Jennifer?"

"Hum. Or sing. Don't stop." With her fingers woven in the stuff of night, she could sense his surprise and confusion, but after a moment, he began singing, softly, something that might have been one of those he'd sung for her before. "It blocks a Triad," she added; it was awkward, trying to speak with so many sensations vibrating her fingertips.

Jadek. It wasn't Jadek, *or* his Triad. Or any of the odd magic that had come from the Thukar's tower, neither Light nor Thread. Something—Dahven's singing somehow made her certain of that, something it blocked or changed in her perception.

Something else, then. But there was no sign of habitation for miles about; if there had once been bandits along this road, villages like the English coastal ones of her own world a hundred or so years earlier—wreckers, who lived by attacking merchants and taking their goods—there was no such village now. Not within her grasp. Far up the road, a faint jangle on the edge of her ability to sense, something that might have been Enardi's inn, run by an outland woman.

Something that caused unease and yet left no trace in Thread—Jennifer leaped to her feet, snatched the reins from Dahven's hand and threw herself into the saddle. The others were already a distance ahead, the blue-lights scarcely visible; the wind had picked up and what stars there might have been were muffled behind thick clouds. She brought the horse around and urged it forward at the best speed she dared, clutching two-handed at its mane for balance while she tested the ground with Thread. She couldn't keep that up for long; it would make her physically ill. But—

"What?" Dahven was at her side, hand outstretched to catch her when she swayed in the saddle. She let go of the Thread, shook her head to try and clear it, not too successfully.

"There's—I think maybe Casimaffi didn't lie, I think there's a Host, not far ahead. Something familiar about the feel of things." She swallowed, grimaced at the taste of bile. "God, we really needed this. Chris! Birdy!"

The wind was rising, making it increasingly hard to be heard. But Robyn's hearing was phenomenal; the wagon came to a halt, shifted on the uneven surface and slid sideways. Chris, with a blistering oath, threw himself from his horse and slammed his back into it. "Jeez, was that really necessary?" he demanded breathlessly. "Eddie, damnit, give me a hand with this thing, will you? Aunt Jen—"

"Can it, kid," she snapped as she came up even with the back of the wagon bed. "I think there's a Host out there"—she waved a hand—"ahead of us, somewhere." She took the reins to Dahven's horse as he jumped down to help lift the back of the wagon clear of disaster. He staggered back into his mount when they set it down, swore breathlessly.

"Hey, don't try for a relapse, we got this under control, dude," Chris said. "You better keep a hand on Jen and an eye out for funny lights, you know?"

"Got it," Dahven said. He was a little slow in remounting, but his face was so grim, even in the faint light, that Jennifer prudently said nothing. "I know about the lights."

Lialla materialized from somewhere on the other side of the wagon. "I don't suppose you remembered anything about stopping them," she began.

"I've been trying to think." He drew a little away from them all, set his elbows on the saddlebow and let his head fall into his hands. "One of the caravaners, coming across the north way from Dro Pent three summers ago. Something about—that wasn't it, either."

"I'll watch for lights," Jennifer said as Chris and Edrith guided the back of the wagon over another rough spot. "You think."

Moments later, the mule stopped, and absolutely refused to go on. When he did move, it was to plunge sideways half a dozen steps before he froze once more. The wagon lurched, and something cracked loudly. There was a very uncomfortable silence, which Enardi finally broke. "All right," he said. "Chris, help me unfasten him; we can pull the wagon over—"

"Absolutely not!" Lialla said sharply. "Didn't you hear what Jen said? There's a Spectral—"

"I heard!" Enardi snapped back. His voice was nearly as high and shaky as hers by now. "I—he won't go! And even if he did, the wagon can't! Didn't you hear that? It was the wheel or the axle; it can't go anywhere like that, can it? We have to unload it, we gotta get it off the road, get out of here—"

"The damned mule won't go!" Lialla shouted.

"It might if it's unhitched!" Enardi yelled. "If not, I'll turn it loose!"

"Hey, chill *out*!" Chris's bellow cut across both now very shrill voices. "Ernie, you know the harness better than anyone else; go unhook it, then leave the stupid thing with Mom and come help us divide the stuff in the back. We can worry later about who carries what, right?"

"I'll—" Aletto began. Chris cut him off.

"You come help us figure out what's back here and get it on the horses so we can go, will you?" To his credit, Aletto left the mule in Robyn's hands and came back at once. "Jen, you're watching, right? Li, you'd better stay on the horse, get up front. I'll call you back when we've got stuff for you to carry."

"I—" For one moment, Chris thought Lialla might argue

61

with him. From the anger in that one word, Lialla thought so, too. She turned then, rode on past Robyn and drew in, a dark shadow in mid-road, only the movement of scarves in the stiff breeze marking who and where she was. Robyn, motionless as the mule, was barely visible at all.

Chris and Edrith were in the bed of the wagon, Chris checking ties, hurriedly stuffing loose items into bags, handing things to Edrith to fasten onto first Chris's horse, then his own. Aletto, seated cross-legged up front, was locating items that had rolled under the seat and into the corners, by feel, and passing them to Chris. He swore hard as he felt along the rough boards and ran a splinter under his thumbnail. "That's it."

"It's good enough," Chris said. "Jen?"

"Still nothing."

"Look, are you certain—?"

"I'm not certain of anything, kid, I just know what it felt like, and you're the one who said he'd rather be overcautious than dead."

"What I said was—never mind," Chris said stiffly. "That damned mule moving yet?"

"One step into me," Robyn said. "I think it scared him as much as it did me; he did a little dance sideways but now he won't go again."

"Swell," Chris muttered. "All right, the wagon's empty. Can we get a couple of us under the back end? Ernie, maybe you can pull, help us get it off the road? Personally, I'd like to leave it here but I guess it wouldn't slow those guys down and it isn't mine."

"I—I—" Enardi seemed incapable of anything but a high-pitched, faint stutter, and after a moment, he gave that up.

"It's all cool, guy," Chris assured him. "No one's really gonna get us, right?"

"Light!" Lialla shouted.

5

❧

"THERE is not!" Robyn's voice soared above Lialla's, drowning whatever else the woman said. Aletto caught her arm, then both shoulders and pulled her close; he said something against her hair no one else could hear.

Lialla was standing in her stirrups, staring intently north from the road. "I saw a light up there! And I don't sense anything human anywhere near it; that means a Host! And it means one any time now! Let's get away from here, get the rest of the things out of that wagon—"

"They're out," Chris yelled. "Ernie, pull, damnit! We gotta get this thing off the road—"

"Leave it," Dahven said curtly. He drew his horse back from the wagon, looked at Jennifer. A faint breeze lifted the hair from her forehead and moved clouds away from the moon. Her face was pale in the sudden light. "Get off your horse, lead it past," he told her. "If it's a Host, you don't want to be trapped back here, or between the wagon and the drop."

"You don't either, Dahven!"

"I'll come in a minute. I remember something, I think, someone from Gray Fisher's told me."

Jennifer shook her head. "You *think*?" Without turning away from him, she shouted, "Chris, get the wagon off the road, fast! Lialla—"

"I'm watching," she yelled back. "Aletto, remember last time, get back on your horse!"

"I—Robyn—" Jennifer heard that much of his spluttering reply, his voice tense with irritation and worry, equally mixed.

"That was my fault last time," Robyn said sharply. "Aletto, I'm all right, see? Where's the reins—thanks."

Worry about one thing at a time, Jennifer told herself. "Dahven, look," she said. "I've seen a Host in action.

Trust me, this is not the time to be fiddling with possibilities! Let's get away from here—''

''And if it follows us?'' Dahven looked past her; Jennifer heard the wagon creak ominously, heard Chris swear furiously as something crashed down, hard. Robyn for once didn't say anything; from the sounds of it she had her hands full with her horse and the mule.

''What if—well, but, they don't do that,'' Jennifer retorted. And, in a smaller voice, ''Do they?'' Dahven shrugged.

''How would *I* know? I was told a Host hunts in one locale, but it can be a damned large locale; what if we're just on the edge of that? And what if it's really true that a Host doesn't quit without taking a life, once it's scented its quarry?'' He waited. Jennifer folded her arms across her chest, as much to fight a sudden chill as for effect, and met his eyes squarely. Behind her, Lialla said, ''Nothing yet—'' and Chris, his voice tense with the effort of shoving at the wagon, grunted, ''Maybe it was a star, a low one?''

''Inside the line of hills?'' Lialla demanded sarcastically. ''I'm going a few paces down the road; maybe I can see farther up that way.''

''Suit yourself,'' Chris mumbled; only Jennifer heard him—and Edrith, who bit back an explosive snort of laughter. Dahven was still watching her, waiting her out.

''I can't convince you, can I?'' she asked finally. He shook his head. ''I don't like it.''

''Who does?'' He glanced behind her. ''Wagon's moving.''

''Good,'' Jennifer said calmly. ''Then you won't be difficult about my sticking with you—''

He shook his head. ''I won't waste the time right now.'' He glanced in Lialla's direction, bent down to check the surface of the road, walked back a few paces. Jennifer dismounted, took the reins to his horse and led the two a short distance away. Dahven straightened, fought a cough, cleared his throat noisily and held out a hand. ''Your staff—the bo. Let me have it.'' She fumbled it loose from its place along the horse's side and pressed the end into his palm. ''Thank you. Damn, I'd give a lot for light.''

''Light. Maybe I can manage a little.''

The horses were nervous, but not unduly so; they stood still when she twisted the ends of the reins together and set them on the road, put her foot over them. The handbag was

64

in its usual place, fastened to the saddlebow; she had followed habit, fortunately, and hooked the little flashlight back on the keychain that was in turn attached to the shoulder strap. She shoved the switch forward with her thumb, flashed the light onto the track. It was weaker than it had been the night they'd lost Chris in the desert; slightly yellow now, but still functioning. Dahven glanced at it in momentary surprise, then turned his attention to the figure he was scratching in the dust. She trained the pool of light there, squatting down to give him the best intensity, recapturing the reins from under her high-top.

"It's a set of four looped circles," Dahven mumbled. "Once it's done, I erase all the inside lines, then do another one in the middle." He cast her an apologetic grin, teeth flashing in the yellowish light. "It's what I remember. There's more; maybe the drawing will remind me."

"I hope you have the time," Jennifer began; she came half upright to glance nervously at the slope north of the road. Dahven made a vexed little sound and she brought the light back into place. "Sorry. Chris? That wagon—"

"Almost," he panted. "Eddie, can you hold the weight while I get my back into this? Ernie, are you pulling?"

The response was so high, breathless and shrill Jennifer would never have known it for Enardi's. "I'm—I'm—I'm—!"

"Hey, guy!" Chris drew a deep breath and somehow managed to sound reassuring. "No big deal, right? Let's just get this wagon out of the way so your old man doesn't ground you for the next year and a half, right? It's cool, Ernie, trust me, c'mon, now." The strain of the lift showed in his voice; the wagon creaked and something hit the road with a clank. "Damn—okay, you guys, let's move it." Jennifer glanced over her shoulder to see the wagon move in a series of uneven jerks; it came to rest most of the way out of the two dusty ruts that separated the road from the surrounding land, and the back corner went down lower than it should have.

"Damn, we lost the whole wheel," Edrith said feelingly.

Chris groaned. "I know; it bounced off my foot, I think I broke a toe. Ernie, you all right up there?" Silence. "Ernie?"

"Light!" Lialla's shrill cry brought them up short.

"I see it," Robyn shouted. "North—it just went out, no, there it is again—!"

"Watch for me," Dahven told Jennifer tersely. "Steady the light."

"Got it." She came up onto one knee, peering up the now blue-white lit, brushy hillside. Somewhere along the line, they had left the steep cliffs behind; here the land sloped up into rounded hills. There were narrow gullies and washes everywhere, most only visible as lines, making the terrain extremely treacherous. All the same, the riders who bore down on them were moving at a very fast trot.

An awkward trot. Jennifer squinted, shook her head, could make no sense of what she saw until Chris laughed rather wildly. "Oh, *man?* First camels and now *donkeys?* Gimme a break!"

"Watch yourself!" Robyn screamed at him. Jennifer tensed, eyes fixed on the riders. Her thigh muscles were already beginning to cramp but she was afraid to move, afraid movement might shift the flashlight from Dahven's drawing at a critical moment.

There were seven of them: short, dark and very wild-looking men whose legs dangled almost to the ground on either side of the sturdy little long-eared donkeys. Instead of cutlasses, most of them carried long, broad-bladed knives. "Try to hold steady!" Dahven yelled.

"Trying!" she shouted back. "They're going east of the wagon—gone past!" She could hear the clatter of small hooves across rock farther along the road, could smell what she would have sworn was stale sweat, woodfire smoke. They passed close enough for her to see the nearest man's oily curls, the unshaven face and thick moustache, a gleam of teeth—the shining lines spreading out from the long knife edge where it had been recently honed. At the same time, unnervingly, she saw Robyn and Aletto on the other side of him—through him. The bright, intent eyes were wide open but seemed fixed on a point just in front of the donkey's ears. They bounced down the slope toward the sea—and simply vanished. Silence, except for someone's whistling pant, and the scratch of Jennifer's bo in the dirt as Dahven drew his figure.

"Geeks on donkeys." Chris was still giggling. "What, are they filming a remake of *The Corsican Brothers* out here?"

"Can it, kid!" Robyn snapped. "And pay attention, all right?"

"Hey, just trying to lighten things up, okay?" He was

still laughing when Aletto pointed downhill and said, "There—light!"

"Got it," Lialla replied tensely. "Everyone pay attention!"

Edrith slid along the side of the wagon, heading toward her. "Anyone see Enardi?"

Chris stopped laughing. "Not—oh, jeez. That didn't get him, did it?" He started up the road, stopped as Robyn shrieked in sudden surprise. The riders were maybe twenty feet away, coming up the slope fast, straight for her. Aletto grabbed his reins and hers, kicked his horse hard. It bolted down the road, hers of necessity following. Lialla followed; Chris grabbed Edrith and rolled him away from the front of the wagon. Both fell.

"Done," Dahven said. He stood, bent over coughing, but waved her off when she came toward him. "No—stay there, keep the—damn!—the horses back." He drew a wheezing breath, shook his head, coughed again.

"Two more times," Lialla warned as she rode back toward them. She dragged the nervous horse to a halt and stood in the stirrups to peer up the slope. "They split up last time, remember?"

"Who wouldn't?" Chris retorted. "Mom?"

"Coming. Oh, God." Robyn was panting. "Is it there?"

"I'll tell you," Lialla said grimly. "What are you doing back there, Jen?"

"Trying something; don't distract us," Jennifer replied.

"Oh, God," Robyn said again. "I swear I heard horses coming up the road, just now. Let—shut up, everyone, and let me listen, will you?"

Momentary silence. Jennifer reached into Thread and caught hold of the red: familiar and easy to work. She detached herself almost at once. "New trouble, folks. Enough horses that it has to be Firsi and his friends."

"Light," Lialla said tensely.

"See them," Chris said.

"Dahven," Jennifer said anxiously. He was still staring at his handiwork—something that looked like concentric four-leaf clovers to her—and mumbling to himself. "Dahven!"

"I heard." He drew a deep breath, coughed a little, mumbled something under his breath. Finally took up the bo again, glanced uphill and drew a line that cut through the inner and outer figures, pointing the way he'd looked.

"I don't know. It's supposed to somehow block them. Doesn't look like much, does it?"

"No," Jennifer agreed. She stuffed the flashlight in her jacket pocket, bent her knees slightly, came up onto the balls of her feet, ready to dodge an attack. The Host came across the road at a different angle—almost paralleling the road, west to east. Two of the riders missed the back corner of the wagon by inches; a third came down between Robyn and Lialla; the rest split around Dahven and his drawn figure. Jennifer, behind him, had her hands momentarily full with hysterical horses. "I think I'll kill you!" she shouted at him. "Trusting that thing like that!"

He turned to grin at her; his forehead was damp. "I didn't; I couldn't move. It *did* work." He came over and took the horses from her. "I'm only sorry I don't know a way to unmake a Host—but this will help, won't it?"

"Final time," Lialla said. Apparently she hadn't heard them, or the words hadn't registered in all the excitement. "If we can evade them this time—"

"Up north, you said they don't go away until they kill something," Chris said pointedly.

"I didn't," Lialla snarled back. "I said four times, if you can avoid them, that's it. Light—watch yourselves!"

"Look out!" Robyn was pointing back down the road. A slight rise had hidden the riders until just now; moon shone on metal—protective plates on leather armor and drawn swords. Fourteen men checked at the top of the hill. Firsi or someone else saw those they pursued and shouted, "There!" A loud, rough cheer greeted this; men urged milling horses forward.

Dahven thrust the bo into Jennifer's hands and pulled himself into the saddle, drawing the sword that hung from the saddlebow. The already frightened horse stood on its hind legs and swung in a half-circle. With an oath, he brought it back around and down onto all fours, coming back to face south just as the Host came into sight for the fourth and final time.

Firsi and his men saw it at the same moment; men shouted, swore, dragged horses back and around. The Host was coming at the same swift trot but time around it seemed to somehow slow—as though giving her more time to fear it, Jennifer thought rather wildly. She threw herself onto the horse, laid the bo across her thighs and tried to still her own nerves so the poor animal didn't have those to cope with as well. The donkey-riders were splitting up. Firsi and two of the Sikkreni were almost upon them, unable to control their panicked mounts and shoved forward by the men behind them. Dahven drew his horse off to the north side of the road and swore hotly. Firsi came to a halt right on top of the carefully drawn figure; his sword was up and out.

Dahven cast a quick glance at Jennifer, at the approaching Host, at Firsi, whose attention was all for him. "Get back!" Jennifer followed his glance, dropped the bo and somehow forced her mount around and down off the road toward the water. She felt the wind of the passing rider and smelled dust and grubby donkey. Fortunately for her, the other riders had gone the other way; she was shaking too much to avoid anything else. *Save it,* she ordered herself. But now the horse refused, utterly, to cooperate and she came close to being thrown. A shrill, terrified cry; she glanced up as the donkey-rider passed over the spot where she'd been, over the destroyed sketch, and over Firsi.

Someone grabbed the reins, jerking them from her hands, yanking down hard. The horse snorted, stopped; Chris's voice was overly loud against her left ear and it echoed oddly. "Hey, lady! I said get off that thing, okay?"

"Okay," Jennifer said. She wrapped both arms around the thick neck, forced her right leg over the unfamiliar pile of things tied behind her, slid to the ground.

"Here," Chris said. He shoved the bo upright between her and the saddle, wrapped her left hand around it. "I've got the brainless wonder tied off to a rock; he won't pull anything now."

"Bets?" Jennifer asked, rather breathlessly. She turned, weight against the saddle, bo dug in to help her balance. Chris patted her shoulder.

Dahven sat his horse in the road, talking to the two men who'd ridden out ahead of the others with Firsi; she couldn't hear what any of them said, but moments later, the Sikkreni turned and rode back to join their companions, and all thirteen went back down the road.

There was no sign of Firsi or of his horse. Dahven jumped from his horse and squatted in the middle of the road, peering at what was left of his sign; Jennifer took a couple of deep breaths to clear her mind and went to join him. The flashlight, fortunately, hadn't fallen from her pocket. It was perhaps a little dimmer. She flashed it over the ground once, thumbed it off. "It's too bad; if he hadn't erased that, he might have been all right," Dahven said. He didn't sound very sorry. "They may come after us again, but I doubt it. Firsi had some kind of grudge; I don't fully understand that thinking."

"No." Jennifer laughed faintly. "It's a self-eliminating sport."

"Mmmm?"

"Joke. Never mind." She stood, turned. "Everyone all right over there?"

"Counting heads," Robyn replied. Her voice was still trembly.

"Can't find Ernie," Chris said. "He didn't—"

"No," Edrith said flatly. "They didn't go anywhere near the tongue of the wagon, did they? He was right there, and I never saw any of them near him." He added, rather defensively, "I was watching out for him the best I could." He went forward, vanished around the empty wagon. "It drops off here pretty suddenly; couldn't see that before the moon came out. Chris, you got that blue-light?"

"Not *on* me, jeez, you know?"

"Here." Lialla came forward on foot, blue light seeping between her hands. "You think he's—?"

"Could be," Edrith said. He took the light and vanished momentarily. "Got him!" The voice was muffled, even when Jennifer came up to the front edge of the wagon, where it tilted forward and slightly down. Another step or two and the entire wheel would have been in the rocky little defile that had been almost invisible earlier. Even now, with full moonlight on them, Edrith was a dark, vague blue-lit movement in a darker hole. "He doesn't look very good. Lialla, I think you and Jen better both come down and look at him—here, wait," he added as he looked up. Blue light cast strange shadows up his face, changing it to a stranger's. "Let me climb up first; there isn't very much room down here."

Jennifer let him hold the blue-light while she edged cautiously down the first few steps, then took it to hold for Lialla. It took them several moments to work their way down to the fallen Enardi, who lay on his back, one leg bent under him. Lialla edged around to his right and down below where he lay, then came back up so she could ease herself down onto her knees. Jennifer crouched next to him. "All right, we're here," she called up. "Everyone shut up, please, so I can concentrate on what I'm doing, will you?"

Lialla had already shifted into Thread-awareness; in the narrow cleft it was even more disconcerting and uncomfortable to deal with, and humming was only a partial help. Fortunately, the sin-Duchess withdrew into the normal almost immediately. "I don't think he came down on his head; I should be able to see—you know. This shoulder"—she pointed, not quite touching it—"is dislocated."

"Fine," Jennifer replied tightly. It really wasn't better than it had been at the beginning, living another's pain when she must think, deal with that pain and heal it. "That can be fixed without much trouble." She gazed down through a maze of Thread, heightened awareness showing the tangle of purple knotted nearer Lialla than her—shoulder, surely. Bruising everywhere—easily recognizable by the way it pulsed. The color lower, near where she crouched, was ruddy, frayed ends everywhere. She brought her hands down close to the damage, felt heat, fragments of Thread drifting loose. "Break," she announced briefly. It was hard, nearly impossible, talking from the midst of Thread; one of the things that never seemed to get any easier. She dragged herself free, ran both hands through her hair and looked down at the boy. Sighed heavily. When she glanced up, Lialla was watching her anxiously.

"Can you fix it?"

Jennifer shrugged. "Not really. Neri showed me a couple of things but he didn't figure on any of us falling ten feet to rocks. I don't think there's anything that works on a break, unless you know of something." Lialla chewed one knuckle and sighed. "What I thought." She shifted her weight cautiously and tilted her head back. "Chris. He's out cold, broken leg, dislocated shoulder. Probably a royal headache when he comes to, but no cracked skull."

"Small favors," Chris said. "How the hell do we get him out of there?"

Jennifer considered this briefly. Met Lialla's eyes. The sin-Duchess was still chewing on her knuckle. "Are you going to help me with this, Lialla?" she asked crisply.

"I—"

"If we hurry up, we can probably get that shoulder back where it belongs before everything in there swells up and it becomes a serious job. We can probably spare the poor boy a lot of hell. But if you don't want to—"

"Stop it," Lialla said sharply. She shoved scarves out of the way, shoved the sleeves of her black shirt up to the elbows and nodded. "I'll do what I can—what I have to."

The shoulder had swelled enough that Lialla had to deal with that before they could do anything else; Jennifer had seen a dislocation reset once and was braced for an ugly time of it. Lialla, who hadn't, set her jaw and stuck with it but was nearly sick after. She crawled away for several moments, came back pale and shaking, but set her lips in a tight line once more and did what Jennifer said.

"Chris?" she called up. "Need a couple pieces of straight something to brace this leg; do it, all right?"

It was Edrith who peered over the edge. "Already working on it."

"Good. Keep everyone back, will you? I don't want any rocks coming down on *my* head."

"Did that, too."

Jennifer let her head fall forward and reached up to rub the back of her neck. The muscles felt like a solid sheet of wood. She began humming under her breath—something by Liszt, she thought, hard to remember such details at the moment. Lialla was dealing with Enardi's bruises. *Doing a good job of it, too,* Jennifer thought. *I wish she'd realize that. Before she drives us all nuts.*

6

CHRIS leaned over the edge some time later, to ask anxiously, "Hey, is he all right?"

Jennifer had to try twice to form the thought and get it out; working with Thread in such a cramped space seemed to be affecting her mind. "I think he will be. Are you people going to come up with a couple boards so we can secure his leg and get him out of this hole?"

"Eddie's working on that. Aletto and Dahven are trying to do something about the wheel. I don't know how we're going to transport him—"

"Save it, okay, kid?" Jennifer let her head fall back so she could look up at him. Chris was shadow against the night sky; she could see blue light moving somewhere behind him. She ran a hand through her hair, blotted her forehead with the backs of her fingers. "Look, I know you're worried about him, but one thing at a time, do you mind?"

"I don't mind," Chris said gloomily. "His old man's going to kill me—"

"Save that, too. The last thing you have time for right now is a major guilt trip, agreed?"

"Major guilt trip," Chris echoed. "Hey, who you been hanging out with? Your Rhadazi sounds really rad!" Jennifer laughed, shook her head.

"All right. If you were trying to ease the tension down here, you helped a little. Now scram, go find something useful to do, all right? Perhaps come up with a system of padding to keep this poor child off the bottom of the wagon so he doesn't die every time it hits a hole."

"That's presuming the noble boy wonders can fix the damned thing. And if you're real nice to me, I won't tell Ernie what you called him," Chris warned as he got to his knees. "Poor child; rully."

"That's *boys* wonder, Mr. Grammar," Jennifer replied. "Scram, will you?"

"I—wait. Got the boards you wanted." Chris turned his head and Jennifer lost a few words. "—Whoa, guy, what'd you do, make a box?"

"Best way to transport a break on such a road."

"No, it's not," Chris replied gloomily. "Life Flight's a *lot* better. Never mind, tell you later. Hand that over; you're better on your feet than I am so you drop in, I'll pass it down, and you can hand it on to Jen."

"Chris?" Jennifer called up. "Stretcher of some kind, maybe one of the thickest blankets, a couple of the long ropes? Fix it and get it down here. I hate to manhandle him out of here like that, but I don't think we'll have any choice."

"Get the leg packed good; I think I can keep him out," Lialla said tersely. "Tell Robyn to dig out the sleeping draught Marseli gave us."

Jennifer turned to look down at her. "How do you plan on keeping him unconscious?"

"What Neri showed me, for calming? If you tighten it enough, it puts you out cold." Lialla smoothed hair back from the boy's forehead. "It did for me, anyway; it's worth a try, isn't it?"

"It certainly is," Jennifer said vigorously. "Do it. I'll— here comes Eddie; watch out for loose rock."

"The *boys* wonder have the wheel faked somehow," Chris called down.

"Swell. One thing at a time, remember?"

Chris sighed rather dramatically, then said, as though to a small child or the mentally halt: "You get Ernie in the sling. We will pull on the ropes. Is that all right?"

It was a mess, working in the enclosed little space, fighting the triple thickness of reinforced blanket under Enardi, making certain the ropes were straight, that nothing had looped or bunched so that it would come loose when the boy was off the ground. Lialla was visibly trembling with the effort of gripping Thread; Jennifer felt ill from his residual pain, from the external jolt of Thread and the shuddering vibration of Lialla's Wielding. Even with Edrith and Chris pulling steadily, there seemed to be a lot of dead weight on her arms. Shoulder height; and then she was on her knees, on her feet, pressing above her head with arms that ached and trembled. Suddenly, he was gone beyond reach; Jennifer sagged, then fell to her knees and rested her

74

forehead against a braced hand. Lialla's hand gripped her wrist.

"Are you all right?"

"God, no, I think I'm dead," Jennifer replied breathily.

"He's out; they have him," Lialla said. "We'd better go. You can rest in the wagon with him."

Jennifer nodded, managed to slow her breath from a thin, rapid pant to something nearer normal. "Yeah. Go ahead, I'm right behind you." She caught Lialla's arm as the other woman turned away. "Before we go, though: just so you know. You did great."

"Think so?" It was hard to tell the other woman's expression with only a faint blue light for illumination; Lialla shrugged finally.

"You did great. That kid will thank you for what you did. I'm just doing it now. Don't beat on yourself so much, Lialla. You're turning into a damned fine Wielder, and you're good under pressure. Now, let's get out of here."

The wagon had been pulled back onto the road, beyond the mess of holes, fissures and cuts that had damaged it earlier; the mule was in place once more, and Edrith held the reins. Lialla knelt halfway back in the flat bed, but as Jennifer and Dahven came up, she edged back and over the tailgate. Chris handed her the reins to her horse. Aletto was restowing goods that had been piled all anyhow on the horses back in the wagon, stuffing the last blankets along one side. He went back to squat by the wheel and waved a hand. Edrith urged the mule forward several cautious, slow paces, then brought him to a halt. Aletto shook his head, sighed, used the side of the wagon to pull himself back to his feet.

"It seems all right. We'd better have a walker out front, all the same; it won't take any abuse, and I don't know if we can tie it back together again if it breaks a second time."

"Let's not try and find out, shall we?" Lialla said tiredly. She gestured. "If only for Enardi's sake. Jennifer—? Oh, there you are."

"Right here."

"Good. Why don't you ride in the wagon first? Edrith will have his hands full with the mule and the road."

Edrith shook his head. "I can—"

"It's all right, Eddie," Jennifer assured him. "I think I'd fall right off the horse at the moment and the kid really needs a full-time watcher. I'll keep an eye on him; you drive.''

Robyn came back past the wagon and handed her a water bottle. "I mixed that powder of Marseli's in here, I don't know how well it dissolved, though, so you'd better shake it up before you pour it down him." She hesitated. "I don't suppose I have to warn you to make sure he's really awake before you do that?''

"Thanks, Birdy. I remember about that part, and I sure didn't go to all that trouble fixing him up only to choke him. How much powder did you put in?''

"According to what Marseli's instructions said, that thins it out a lot, so you'll have to get as much as you can down him, but I bet he'll need the water anyway.''

"I'd think so.''

"I'm taking the first walk," Robyn announced generally. "And I'd like to start right now, if we're ready.''

"Yeah, me, too," Chris said feelingly. "Let's go find this poor guy some help, and let's get out of here. Place is giving me the creeps.''

It was a long, extremely slow night. Enardi woke bewildered and disoriented, and in considerable pain; he drank down the liquid obediently, however, and about the time Jennifer was beginning to wonder if the powder had been defective, old, or simply mislabeled, he fell asleep. He remained asleep for most of the rest of the night, but he slept restlessly.

They stopped on the crest of a hill to let Jennifer and Lialla change places, to let Chris take over for Robyn, and to give Edrith a chance to walk up and down and stretch out his legs, because he refused to give up the reins. "I'm fine, and I know how to guide a wagon. Besides, Fedthyr's mule and I are used to each other; that's important right now.''

Jennifer groaned as she pulled herself into the saddle. Dahven leaned over to touch her knee. "Are you all right?''

"Yeah. Bored with having a bruised backside." She ran a hand over her eyes, fought a yawn and smiled at him. "How are you holding up?''

"Just now, all right," he said in a low voice, even though Aletto had already dropped back to keep a rear guard, and the wagon had moved on.

Still worried about it—but I'd swear he doesn't sound

quite as defensive, she thought. Aloud, she only said, "Good. Then, if you don't mind, stay here and keep me awake, will you?"

They made one more stop, near dawn, where a stream crossed the road, and someone had dammed off a section on the oceanward side for watering animals. Jennifer climbed back into the wagon to check Enardi and to let Lialla get down and walk around. In the early, gray light, the sin-Duchess looked ghastly: She was paler than normal, her eyes barely open, and her mouth drooped like an old woman's. She refused Aletto's offer of assistance, but didn't object when Jennifer held out a steadying hand as she climbed over the side rail, onto and down the wheel. "He didn't look good; I used the Thread again," she said faintly.

"I know. Felt it."

"Sorry—"

"Don't be. I can deal with that; Enardi doesn't need that kind of pain." Jennifer looked down at the woman in Wielder Novice Blacks in concern; Lialla was still clinging to the wheel, swaying ever so slightly. "You should maybe get some sleep, Lialla. I can ride alongside and watch him; there's room enough up by the seat for you to curl up."

"Thanks. I'll be all right. Get some fresh water; maybe that'll help." She managed a faint smile as she stepped back from the wagon.

Jennifer watched her walk away. She shifted. Chris was approaching, bo in hand. "Hey, kid, how much farther to that inn?"

"Another couple of miles? The way the mileage on this map seems to work, I'd say we'll be there in time for breakfast, if the road doesn't get any worse." He sagged into his bo, straightened again and buried a yawn in the elbow of his shirt. "How's Ernie doing?"

"Sleeping."

"Yeah—well, okay. You think he'll be all right? I mean, his leg—" Chris drew a deep breath and used it to steady his voice. "I mean, if he comes out of this with a limp, like one leg shorter than the other? Jeez, I think I'd die if that—"

Jennifer shook her head, silencing him. He looked up at her, his face mirroring his misery. "We'll get him a good healer, Chris. I can't promise what you fear won't happen, but I don't think it's likely."

"A halfway decent healer will be able to put that right in no time," Dahven said. "And he's not a small child, so it's most unlikely he'll heal wrong."

"Better not be just saying that to make me feel better," Chris said darkly. Dahven shook his head and Jennifer held up a hand.

"This is me, remember, kid? The woman who never gave you a sugar-coated lie? Why would I start now?"

"Yeah—well. I guess." Chris looked over the side of the wagon. "Jeez, it makes me sick, seeing him like that. I wish I'd known before we left Bez—hell, I don't know." He folded his arms on the top board and let his chin rest on them. "I guess in a way, this is better. You know?" He glanced up at Jennifer. "We couldn't take him the rest of the way with us, not if he's gonna be that scared all the time. It's dangerous for everyone and it isn't fair to him, is it? How'd *you* like it if you got stuck in the middle of a mess like this and found out even *mom* was braver than you are?" He sighed, let his arms fall. "But I would hate to have been the guy to tell him he'd have to stay in Podhru while we went on; he'd have felt like the biggest jerk ever. He probably will anyway; he's a kind of sensitive guy, you know?" Chris sighed again. "We were going to have such a blast in Podhru. Oh, well. Here comes Lialla. Want me to hold the horses while you two go get water, do whatever else you gotta?"

Jennifer slid to the ground and handed over the reins, waited for Lialla to come up, then wrapped an arm around Dahven's waist under his cloak. He threw the fabric over her shoulders and led her along the streambed. Cold, fresh water helped a little; she drank from cupped hands, blotted her fingers on closed eyelids, splashed a little on her cheeks and on the back of her neck, shivered as a thin trickle ran down her back. Dahven drank, stood and drew her back against him, wrapping his arms around her waist; she folded the cloak across her chest, rubbed her head against his shoulder. "Think I'll hold onto you for a while," she said. "You're warm."

"All right."

"What did those men say to you back there? After Firsi—went?"

He was silent for so long she began to wonder if she'd offended him. Finally he shrugged, tightened his grip on her momentarily, then released her, taking hold of her hand instead. "Let's walk, a little. What they said? I asked them what my brothers hoped to accomplish. No one would come out and say, but I begin to believe you. That the twins would sleep easier if I were not around to embarrass them." He sighed, deeply, and was quiet for a long time. "I don't think, at this point, any of those men would object to killing every one of us. They lost face, you know that, don't you?"

"I know it," Jennifer said.

"It doesn't seem real, does it?"

"No. I should be as frightened as poor young Enardi right now, and I just don't feel it."

"*You* shouldn't be. Unlike Enardi, you can at least defend yourself."

Jennifer looked up at him. "You don't do too badly yourself, you know."

"You're good at that—"

"Mmmm?"

"—Patting people on the head, making them feel like something worthwhile."

Jennifer stopped, kept her grip on his hand so he must stop also. "I don't lie to people, you know," she said in mild exasperation. "I point out things they don't see, is all. Lialla really *is* cool in a crisis, as long as it isn't an immediate threat by her uncle against her or Aletto. Robyn's a good, sweet woman who can do wonders with the kind of crap food you have when there's no fridge and no gas stove—never mind, I'll explain later. You"—she leveled a finger at his nose—"are a good man to whom dreadful things have happened. You're capable of coming back from that, and you're better suited to rule Sikkre than a pair like your twin younger brothers. All right?"

He caught hold of the finger, kissed it and began walking again, back toward the wagon. "No. Because you don't lie doesn't mean you see everything as it is."

"You honestly think Deehar and Dayher deserve Sikkre?"

"Of course not."

"Well, then."

He laughed shortly. "It's not exactly that easy, you know!"

"Of course not," she replied, consciously mimicking him. "That doesn't matter. It shouldn't."

He stopped short, took hold of her shoulders and gave her a gentle shake; his eyes were darkly angry, his mouth hard. "By every god the Emperor holds dear, what do you want of me?"

"I want?" Jennifer brought her arms up inside his grip and shoved, pushing his hands away. "I want you, nothing else. It's what you want that should matter! And you want Sikkre—"

"I don't! Let them have the damned Dukedom!"

"Oh, yes?" Jennifer said in a low intense voice. "Is this the same man who was ready to ride from Bez to the Thukar's palace and demand his rightful place back?"

"I was sick, I had fever! I was babbling and deranged. I've come to my senses since then."

"Dahven—damnit!" Jennifer ran a hand through her hair. Down by the wagon, Chris yelled for them, and she turned to shout back, "Coming!" Turning back, she wrapped both hands in the long hair at the back of his neck and kissed him, hard. "I'm not going to let you give up on yourself, do you hear me? I'm not!" She let go of his hair and turned to start down the road. Silence. He caught up with her, stepping in her path, and wrapped a long arm around her shoulders.

"I don't think anyone's ever done such a fine job of turning a kiss into a curse-word," he said conversationally. "I think it may be a form of bad luck." His free hand slipped under her chin and brought it up. "Can't have bad luck like that haunting us," he said softly, and set a very gentle kiss on her lips. "Better," he said finally, even more softly.

"Cheater," Jennifer whispered. Her knees were trying to buckle and her face was flushed. "You didn't win the damned argument like that," she added, but the anger was gone from her voice. He laughed and lightly touched his lips to hers again before releasing her.

"Stubborn woman." He glanced over his shoulder. "I fear Chris is about to come fetch us." He laid a finger on the corner of her mouth. "Later?"

"Shhhh," she said, and caught it in her teeth. "You're right; here he comes."

"Hey, boys and girls, your timing's a bit off, you know?"

"One more word," Jennifer warned him. Chris merely laughed, shook his head and went back to take his place in front of the mule. Jennifer pulled herself into the saddle and tried to put the past few minutes out of mind. She was only partly successful.

* * *

The inn was a two-story affair, whitewashed, thick walls with dark timbers, shuttered windows with small diamond-shaped panes of glass, a steep, shingled roof. A low hedge separated the inn and its yards from the road; there were flower gardens everywhere. It reminded Jennifer of pictures of English cottages; it looked rather strange set down on the dry California high-desert-looking Rhadazi coast. Robyn handed her reins to Chris and stopped to sniff flowers.

"They really are roses! And marigolds! And—"

"They can't smell half as good as what's coming from the window there," Chris said patiently. "Let's get ourselves in, shall we, ma? I'll come back out and smell flowers with you after breakfast."

"Yeah—well." Robyn shook herself, smiled at the garden and permitted Chris to draw her away.

The inn-yard was full, the main room crowded. After a very brief argument, Aletto agreed that he, Robyn and Dahven would wait in a shaded corner of the yard with Enardi and the wagon, that Chris would accompany them as far as the door but remain outside, in case of difficulties, while Jennifer, Edrith and Lialla went in. The innkeep was a cheerfully large, gray-haired woman who seemed to be everywhere at once: overseeing the serving of food and drink at half a dozen long tables, stopping to talk with guests or laughing at someone's shouted remark. She came across at once when she saw them hovering uncertainly in the doorway. "Always plenty of room, you know! Are you in need of a meal or—a private room? Two!" She did a rapid calculation on her fingers, lips moving soundlessly and quick, curious eyes studying Jennifer's clothing and hair before she nodded emphatically. "I've two parties moving on as soon as they've eaten. It's not ordinarily so popular here, you know! I've the Emperor's Festival to thank for this—daresay he'll want a tithe because of it; well, I won't grudge him. Here—you fellows move down a bit, you've got the entire bench to yourselves, give these ladies a place to sit." She shooed Lialla to a seat, beckoned for one of her servers. "Son, bring a pot of tea for these folk, will you?"

Jennifer leaned over to speak near the woman's ear. "Can I talk with you privately? About—arrangements? And we have a bit of a problem—"

To her credit, the woman simply turned, still talking a mile a minute, and motioned for her to follow. Jennifer glanced at Edrith, faintly gestured toward the bench with her head. He sat down next to Lialla; Jennifer hurried to catch up with the inkeep.

They went through a heavy, dark door into what was clearly the woman's private quarters. "Problem, I think you said? What sort?"

"We've an injured young man with us. He fell, broke his leg. We need a healer."

"There's a local man," the innkeep said. "Not as good as he presumes himself, but capable of handling a broken bone. You want two private rooms—what, one for yourself and the Wielder, another for the injured lad and the one out front?"

Jennifer ran a hand through her hair, encountered knots and cautiously pulled her fingers free. "That's part of the problem. There are more of us—four others, two men, another boy, a woman. We need privacy—" *God, what have we gotten ourselves into here?* she wondered suddenly.

"Privacy—not an easy thing to attain in a place like mine, but not impossible." She considered the younger woman, rather thoughtfully tipped her head to one side and announced, "You're outlander."

Jennifer started—looked guilty, probably, she thought. Too late to worry about it now, though. "I am," she said. "I'm Jennifer Cray."

"Jennifer," the woman said slowly. "That's English, or American. Isn't it?"

"American."

The woman paused, then shifted—laboriously—into English. "I'm Caroline Ellaway. Caro, actually. From Newmarket, that's near Cambridge, north of London."

"Los Angeles, California," Jennifer said rather dazedly.

"When?" Caro Ellaway asked eagerly. "You must be recent, those are blue denims, aren't they? Haven't seen such pants in so long—"

"All of—God," Jennifer said and ran a hand into her hair again, forgetting it was still all snarls. "A month and a half, maybe? I've lost track. You?"

"Easy. It was June 22, 1972. We were fooling about with solstice and ley lines, pretending in quite serious fashion to be a coven. Everything went odd and I came around in an England that wasn't mine."

"We'll have to talk; you'll have to talk with my sister," Jennifer said. "But in the meantime—"

"You have an injured boy. We'll get him in here, if you

don't object—it's easier than attempting my stairs. And your other people, if they'd like a meal first?''

"Well—" Jennifer sighed. "That's the part that's a problem. The people out there—at least two of them—we'd rather keep their presence here something of a secret. If it's a problem," she went on hurriedly, "tell me, now, and we'll just go on toward Podhru—"

"Nonsense," the older woman said warmly. "I keep four private rooms on the upper floor, and they're seldom ever in use. Even with the crowds I've had lately, I can offer you a choice: adjoining or facing across the hallway. So long as you're not consorting with murderers, thieves and road agents, and so long as you intend to pay for the rooms, I don't much care who you have in them. Is that fair?''

"More than fair," Jennifer assured her. "Let me go out and let them know it's all right. When I come back, we can settle cost and getting Enardi in.''

7

LATER, Jennifer found it hard to remember anything of that morning: She was so tired that the simplest tasks, such as getting her handbag untied from the horse, seemed overwhelming. Lialla was only in marginally better shape.

Fortunately, Robyn was little the worse for wear, despite spending a large portion of the night on her feet, leading the mule, and she took charge, managing to get Aletto and Dahven shepherded into one of the two private rooms unnoticed by the remaining guests—most of whom were anyway still in the common room. Edrith and Chris brought the wagon across the courtyard as near the back as possible and the innkeep's son found a heavy wooden storm shutter in the feed room to slide under Enardi's blanket sling so he could be transported. Under Robyn's supervision, they got the boy into the innkeep's personal room—an enormous, whitewashed chamber that combined the functions of sitting room, winter cooking area, kitchen and bedroom—and settled as comfortably as possible.

Jennifer managed to get herself into the cheerful, sunny kitchen without actually tripping over anything, and she knelt on the edge of Enardi's bedding, trying to remember why she was there. She started as Robyn bent down to wrap an arm around her shoulders and give her a gentle shake. "Lady, you look like hell; why don't you give it up? Go on upstairs, take first pick of the beds in the girls' room and zee out?"

"I need to—I'm all right."

"You and Lialla both, I don't think." Robyn gave her another shake. "If I didn't have a hand on you right now, you'd fall over on your backside. The lady here is sending her daughter for the healer, the boys are eating—"

"Surprise, surprise."

"Yeah, really. The guys are tucked in and you've been up all night."

"So've you, Birdy."

"I didn't do anything at all like what you did. I just walked and rode, remember? I seem to remember you involved in that mess with the Sikkreni guards and D—whatsisname," she added in a cautiously lowered voice. "Not to mention crawling around the bottom of that ghastly hole patching up Fedthyr's kid."

"Really, Birdy—"

"Jen, do us all a favor, will you? I can handle this." Silence. "I can always tell when you're really tired, girl; you forget that anyone else can take care of things."

Jennifer managed a weak smile, spoiled it with a yawn. "Yeah, I do sometimes, don't I?"

"Sometimes." Robyn snorted. "Look, I'm fine. I can stick with poor little Ernie so he doesn't wake up in strange surroundings and panic. The boys can spell me if I start to do a fade and have to crash, fair enough? Besides, I really want to talk to the innkeep—Caro?" Jennifer nodded. "When she gets done feeding the crowd out front, we're going to compare notes."

"God." Jennifer stifled a yawn, rubbed her eyes. "If you're really sure—"

"G'wan, shoo," Robyn said good-naturedly. "Take Lialla with you before she disgraces us all, falling asleep in public. If we need either of you, you'll only be upstairs and down that hallway, after all."

"Yeah. Guess you're right."

"Go make sure the boyfriend's tucked in."

"Oh. Really cute, Birdy."

"Yeah, he sure is," Robyn said with a wicked grin, deliberately misunderstanding. "Been meaning to tell you, you sure can pick them. How'd Lialla ever let something that yummy get away?" Jennifer made a face at her, staggered to her feet and went in search of Lialla. The sin-Duchess was still sitting at the now otherwise empty table, elbows propped on the cloth-covered surface, hands wrapped around an empty tea mug. She blinked as Jennifer touched her arm, simply nodded when the other woman suggested going upstairs, apparently too tired for once to argue.

The room the three women were to share was small but had neat—whitewashed walls and scrubbed board floors, dark blue cloth curtains. There was a bench near the door, several pegs set in the wall above that. The remainder of the room was taken up by two wide beds. Lialla closed the door behind them, fingered the bolt momentarily, then shook her head. "No, better not. I remembered," she mumbled. "Robyn."

"Lock it," Jennifer said. "We'll sleep better, and Birdy can knock if she wants in." She threaded her way between the beds and briefly leaned out. The ground was some distance below—too far for anyone to simply jump up and catch the sill; the roof she remembered as quite steep and it overhung the window by at least a foot. There were no trees anywhere along this shaded side of the building, no built-in holds for a climber. The windows were small-paned and swung out from the center; someone had hooked them against dark shutters which had in turn been latched against the outer wall. A light, pleasant breeze lifted the hair from her forehead. Jennifer paused, hand on one of the windows; she glanced down once again and withdrew into the room. Lialla sat on the edge of one bed, blinking and rubbing the bridge of her nose. "Lialla, do you mind if I just pull this curtain across and leave the window as it is? The curtain won't keep out much of the daylight—"

Lialla sighed, edged back onto the bed and drew her feet up so she was curled against the whitewashed wall. "Leave the window open; it's going to get warm later and I hate sleeping in a stuffy room. My eyelids will handle the daylight." She let them close and drew a deep breath, letting it out as a long contented sigh. "Wonderful. A genuine bed. I don't think I much care for sleeping alongside the road; makes my bones ache."

"Me, too. Why I stayed in the big city when I grew up, where camping out isn't something you *have* to do." Jennifer sat on the edge of the other bed to untie her hightops, shoved them off with her toes and tossed her leather jacket across her feet. It took a couple of minutes to get settled, to find a pillow in the stack of at least a dozen that wasn't too high. She came up onto one elbow. "Lialla?" she said softly. No answer. Jennifer sighed, lay back down and closed her eyes.

The bedding smelled faintly of lemon. *What a change from that inn in Sikkre,* she thought happily. It was her last conscious thought for some time.

She came awake when Robyn tapped on the door; it took her several moments to realize what the sound was and then to work out what to do about it. She padded across cool boards to slide the latch. Robyn edged into the room, pressed the door silently shut behind her and after a glance at the sleeping Lialla, kept her voice very low. "Sorry to drag you up, kiddo."

"S'okay. Sorry it took so long—"

"Don't worry about it, I knew you'd be asleep but I thought you'd want to know right away that Ernie's going to be all right. Figured while I was up here, I'd go ahead and shed this jacket; it's getting warm downstairs."

Jennifer rubbed her eyes. "Thanks, glad you told me. Is the healer still down there?"

"Nope, checked the kid out, did his leg, left some foul-smelling ooze to rub into it the next couple days—hard to believe anything that smells that gruesome would heal anything—and then he split, I guess he and Caro don't get on."

"Oh. I'd kind of hoped I'd be able to watch what he did."

"Just as well you didn't come down; he was pretty snotty about Wielders. Some kind of professional jealousy, I guess; doesn't think anybody but a certified healer should be allowed to fix things." Robyn cast up her eyes. "You'd probably have smacked him one. I was ready to half a dozen times before we got rid of him. Anyway, that's a minor hassle; main thing is, kid'll be back on his feet in about a week."

"Great. Must be good goo. What time's it?"

"Which one of us wears a watch, kiddo?" But when Jennifer fumbled with her shirt cuff to expose the watch face, Robyn clapped her own hand over the fingers and shook her head. "Doesn't matter, does it? It isn't time for you to be on your feet yet. Lock the door behind me and grab another hour or so."

"Mmm. Take you up on that. You and the innkeep getting along okay?"

"Terrific."

"Tell her the room is lovely and the pillows smell wonderful." Robyn nodded, dumped her jacket on the corner of Lialla's bed—the sin-Duchess hadn't even stirred—and went back out. Jennifer shoved the bolt across and fell back onto the bed. It was warm enough in the room that she no longer needed the leather jacket for cold toes: She shoved it aside with her feet, pulled her legs up so she could tug the socks off. A light breeze flared the curtain, spilling light into the room, but no sun. *North facing?* she wondered. North or west, anyway. Probably meant the guys' room faced south, like Caro's private room—or east—which meant they were probably roasting in there. *Too bad.* She settled her shoulders and fell asleep once more.

It was noticeably warmer when she woke the second time, and now when wind puffed the curtains, a band of sun lay across the floor. Lialla still slept. Jennifer slipped bare feet into her high-tops, gave her scalp a vigorous massage with her fingertips to fluff up curl, and straightened her shirt. *I must look like hell*, she thought. *Tough.* She debated waking Lialla, at least so she could relock the door, finally decided against it. The woman needed the sleep, and surely no one was going to be wandering the hall looking for rooms to walk into.

The common room was deserted, except for a skinny, blonde-braided girl of perhaps twelve or thirteen who was scrubbing one of the table tops. She glanced up as Jennifer came down the stairs, eyed the outlander jeans and shoes with evident interest, dropped her rag back in the bucket and came across the room. "My mother said to go on through to the kitchen. I'll take you."

"Thanks. I'm Jennifer, by the way. Or Jen, if that's easier."

"Jennifer. My mother had a sister named that, when she

was an outlander. That was before we were born, of course. She named me Vanessa but everyone calls me Niss.''

"Niss. I'm glad to meet you.'' The girl smiled rather shyly, held the swinging door to let Jennifer through and went back to her scrubbing.

The kitchen was cool now, a breeze blowing through the lower half of an open door that faced south and out a wide pair of windows on the east side. A pool of sun lay across the floor at the base of the half-door, but was not enough to heat the room. Robyn sat on a thickly cushioned, low sofa watching the innkeep scrubbing vegetables. She waved a hand as Jennifer came in, and Caro stopped her work long enough to turn and cast her a warm smile.

"The boy was awake a little while ago,'' she said as Jennifer went over to check him. The rough board sling around Enardi's leg had been removed and replaced with a set of dark gray padded reinforcements that ran the length of his leg and others that went around to hold them in place. "Menij gave me a box of powders for him, though; they're to keep him sleeping as much as possible while the healing works.''

"Wish they'd had something like this Menij back home,'' Robyn said. "Remember when I broke my arm and had to wear a cast for what seemed like forever? Caro says this takes maybe a week, depending on how thick the bone and how major the break.''

"Yes, well, you wouldn't have wanted *Menij*,'' Caro said flatly. She scrubbed rather violently at a thick tuber that might have been sweet potato or yam and tossed it in the pot. Water splashed the table and she swept it onto the floor with the side of her hand. "He's a right old bastard, Menij, so set in his ways he might well be made of granite.''

"Ernie will be all right, won't he?'' Jennifer asked rather anxiously. "If we need to employ another healer—''

"You wouldn't find another this side of central Podhru; this is unfortunately the old man's territory. He did a good job on the boy; you can't fault him when the healing's a straightforward matter.'' She sighed. "It's a personal thing, as you'll have no doubt guessed: My eldest son sickened not long after we bought this inn—years now. Menij was difficult about the curing of him; he claimed Richard had been dabbling in some sort of magic that was restricted, but he never did come right out and say as much, and I was new enough to Rhadaz I didn't realize how serious it was.

Rather as though he were—oh, where I'm from, as if Richard were colored and trying to pass for white. Or as if he'd been falsely accused of that, but of course how do you prove it, and in the meantime the damage has been done. The pity of it was, of course, that Richard had no interest in any kind of magic, Rhadazi or other, but by the time I realized what Menij was doing, how serious he was about his feelings— the man was utterly scandalized—it was too late for anyone else to help my son, and he died.''

"Good Lord," Jennifer said. "How awful for you."

"Well, it was. Never mind that, it's past. I use city healers now rather than Menij, whenever I can; find a way to transport the younger children and myself or send them in to Podhru with Colin—he's my next eldest, nearly grown now." She shook herself, tossed the last vegetables in the pot and massaged the back of her neck. "There. There'll be a roast for tonight, and the soup is shellfish. It used to be quite an experience, trying to cook English here, and at first there were complaints, I had to bring in someone who could feed the locals so they'd not take their business elsewhere."

"I'd think it would be pretty difficult," Robyn said, "finding supplies. Spices and so on."

"Well, it's fairly basic cookery that I do, of course."

The top half of the dutch door opened and Chris came in, closely followed by Edrith. "Whoa, it smells really good out there. When's dinner?"

Caro laughed and shook her head. "Hours yet. But there's bread and cold meat from yesterday in the larder, for sandwiches. Wait and I'll get it."

"I can get it," Robyn said as she got to her feet. "I'm not being much use, and that's *my* hollow leg, after all." She jerked a thumb in Chris's direction.

"Larder's dug out under the floor—see the ring just below the window?"

"I got it," Chris said and pulled up the trap door. Robyn snagged hold of his sleeve before he could descend the steps into barely blue-lit darkness.

"You stay up here, kid."

"What, you don't trust me? I won't fall—"

"You falling is the least of my worries. Trusting you around food, though—"

"To your right as you reach the floor," Caro called out.

"Shelf is at about shoulder level; it's all together in a large basket."

"Found it." Robyn's voice came up faintly from below. She shivered as she came back into the kitchen. "Brrr! Chilly down there!"

"It stays a constant ten centigrade; certainly feels cold after afternoon temperatures in this room."

"Too bad there aren't refrigerators," Chris said, and sighed. "Or Cokes, or—"

"I understand there *are* ice houses farther north," Caro said. "You know how that's done, of course: ice blocks cut up in winter, buried underground or under straw in thick-walled stone houses? Just as efficient."

"Yeah," Chris said gloomily. "Nothing good to keep cold, though." He held up a hand. "Please don't tell me you get used to it, okay?"

"I wouldn't dream of it. You can't think how badly I still miss ice cream, even after all these years."

"Well, you could make that, couldn't you?" Chris demanded. "I mean, a hand-crank ice cream maker—isn't that kind of like a cream churn or something? And you pack it around with salt and stuff, it's not like you'd need electricity or a freezer, you'd just have to eat it all right away."

Caro shook her head and laughed. "Well, I suppose I could! If I knew how one went together. It's quite frustrating, you know: So many things that just—aren't."

"Tell *me*," Chris muttered feelingly.

The older woman indicated the tub of vegetables. "Why don't you and—Eddie, isn't it?—why don't you two run these out to the outside kitchen and hang them from the heavy chain over the fire, while I put a pair of sandwiches together?"

"Gotta deal," Chris said. "You're all right, you know?"

Enardi woke an hour or so later. Robyn gave him a drink of cool water, assured him his father's wagon was intact and the mule in good health, that no one was angry at him for having fallen and delayed them, then prepared one of the sleeping powders. The Bezanti fell asleep again almost at once without having been very awake to begin with. Jennifer went up to check on Lialla; someone had taken her a bucket of cool washing water and cloths and also a tray with herb tea and thin cookies. The sin-Duchess looked pale and drawn still but awake enough to come downstairs. Jennifer led her along the passage in the other direction from the way they'd ascended earlier in the day and pointed. "Down and to the right; you have to go outside along the edge of the herb garden. In the first door you find, that's the innkeep's private living quarters. She thought it might be better for us to use this way, stay out of the common room and out of sight."

"I think I'd prefer that," Lialla said. She rubbed a hand over her eyes. "Aletto—?"

"Came out of the fellows' room just as I was on my way to wake you up; I sent him that way a few minutes ago. There should be a regular hot dinner shortly."

"Good. I can't think how I worked up an appetite just sleeping, but food sounds good at the moment."

"Smells good, too—at least," Jennifer qualified, "it does to us. It's English—outlander—but very plain. Meat and potatoes kind of stuff."

"I can eat just about anything," Lialla assured her. She started down the hall, turned back, a finger against her lips. "I forgot Enardi."

"He's fine. Still sleeping."

"Poor boy." Lialla sighed. "I worried about him from the first. I—he's simply not going to be able to go any farther with us, Jen, even if he heals in time. But what if he insists? What are we going to do about him? Or what if Chris insists on him staying with us?"

"Chris won't, trust me. I don't think Enardi will insist either, not after last night. If you get a chance, say something to Aletto, why don't you? See if he can't come up with an idea; he's pretty good at that. Enardi tried, after all, poor kid. Really, we owe it to him to let him off the hook without shaming him."

Lialla nodded. "He's going to feel that anyway; there has to be a way to make it a little easier on him. I'll think about it, too." She laughed faintly. "Odd. I'd thought, when we started, that neither of us would be able to manage this. Me or Aletto, I mean. It was—we had to try, simply had to get out of there, but we didn't dare think beyond just escaping Duke's Fort, really. And then, Carolan, and Aletto getting hurt. I just did what I had to do, I didn't think there was anything special or difficult about that, not at the time. Now I wonder how we ever managed, whether I'd have the nerve to attempt that escape again, knowing what I know now about life outside the Fort." She paused to consider this, shook her head. "Don't think I'm trying to say we're better than Enardi, or braver, or more clever. We had reasons for what we did, life-and-death reasons—not just going along for the company and the adventure of it, like he did. It's rather surprising, though, to realize we're both tougher than either of us thought we were.''

"I keep telling you, Lialla, don't sell yourself short," Jennifer said mildly. "But you yourself told me back at the beginning that you were strong-minded."

"Stubborn would have been a truer word for it," Lialla replied with an abashed grin.

Jennifer laughed. "Men are strong leaders, women pushy and arrogant."

"What?"

"Bad back-home joke. Nobody laughs there, either. Nobody female—female with a brain—anyway. Go on down, why don't you? I want to get my socks so I can rinse them out, I won't be long." Lialla nodded, disappeared down the narrow back stair. Jennifer heard the door close behind her moments later. She went back to their room, hesitated with her hand on the knob, finally let go of it and went across the hall to tap on the opposite door.

It opened the least cautious bit. "Who?" She wouldn't have recognized the voice; it was a harsh whisper.

"Dahven?" she asked in a very low voice. He stepped back into the room, taking the door with him. She went in, closing it behind her.

"Just being cautious," he said. "Chris was up a short while ago, said the innkeep's eldest son is a bit too curious about us for his tastes."

"I imagine that's all it is. His mother's English, after all—outlander like us but from the eastern continent instead of the western."

"Oh." He considered that momentarily, finally shrugged. "One day you must draw me a map. I fear we Rhadazi are not any too knowledgeable of what the rest of our world looks like."

"Chris can do that; ask him when there's time."

"If." He sighed. "I'm sorry. I promised I wouldn't do that, didn't I?"

"I don't remember if you did or not, but I'd as soon you didn't." Jennifer moved across the room and wrapped her arms around him, leaned her cheek against his shirt to listen to the deep, steady heartbeat. "I have enough doubts of my own without doubling the load, thank you."

"I'd never know it." His arm went around her shoulders very briefly; he squeezed hard and let her go. "Aletto went downstairs; is that a good idea?" She nodded. "You're certain?"

She smiled and tugged the door open. "There's going to be food shortly; you need to eat. And I do know it's not a very good idea for the two of us to stay here much longer. I'm having a very hard time keeping my hands off you."

Dahven laughed quietly, followed her into the hall and pulled her close with a possessive arm across her shoulders as they walked toward the back stair. "You don't have to do that."

"What—keep my hands off you? If you recall, we're both sharing rooms with several other people. You might not care if someone walks in on you at a—call it personal moment. I care."

"Since you mention it—"

"*And,*" Jennifer overrode him, "since I don't know anything about Rhadazi personal relationships, I think it might be a good idea for me to find out what the ground rules are here." She drew a steadying breath; this kind of conversation always *had* thrown her back home, and the fact that she cared deeply about the outcome this time only seemed to make it harder. "I—what I'm saying, I guess, is that we have to seriously talk."

He slowed, pulled back a little to look down at her. "Talk? Ground rules? Relationships?"

Jennifer stopped at the head of the stairs, glanced over her shoulder to make certain the hallway was still empty, and nodded. "All of that. Where I come from, until fairly recently, it was highly immoral and damned near criminal for women to sleep with men outside of marriage. Now it's not as terrible as that, at least as far as a woman's reputation is concerned, but now it's dangerous because there are diseases, and some can be fatal."

"You don't think *I*—" Dahven began rather huffily. She laid a hand across his lips.

"I think we need to talk." She started down the stairs, bringing him perforce with her. "Believe this, please: I am absolutely *not* inferring anything personal about you. I'm not trying to insult you. Despite the fact that I'm here, this place and time, I'm a twentieth-century Los Angeles woman, and I'm being careful the way I've had to learn to be. I don't want to wind up pregnant or with something there's no cure for—the former is easy enough to prevent if you know how but the latter is a very real possibility. The chance of dying of casual sex has made most of us pretty choosey, and damned cautious. Beyond that, I sure as hell don't want to wind up burned at the stake or stuffed in a gunny sack and dumped in the river to drown because I fooled around without the piece of paper.''

He was silent a moment, finally pulled her to a halt once again at the foot of the steps. "You *do* use the strangest words." He touched the end of her nose. "And you've gone pink.''

"Well, I'm sorry, it embarrasses me. That's partly cultural and partly my upbringing.''

"Oh.'' He leaned against the wall, paused to consider this. Jennifer became aware she was holding her breath and tried to let it out quietly. Her face felt red and she wondered if anything could possibly be worth the bother of bringing all this up. *One of the reasons I never bothered dating much after I got into college, after all. Bet Birdy never had that kind of hang-up, she's so relaxed about things like this.* Dahven shifted his shoulders and finally shrugged. "The Holmaddi might drown their women for—fooling around? What a phrase for it!'' He considered this. "Well, they might do such a thing if they had the river for it. Rhadazi women by and large do as they please. Marriage—is that what you mean by piece of paper?'' She nodded, detached herself from his arm and leaned back against the wall, arms folded. "Marriage is a contract used by the nobility, by and large, to seal transfer of property or hereditary rights. There are short-term contracts for those who wish them; there are also religious contracts but I know less about them, having never bothered with any of the numerous religions available in Sikkre's markets. The merchant class is a fairly recent thing, actually; the current Shesseran's grandfather began encouraging open markets and it's improved ever since.''

"I know something about it; I spent a lot of time recently among the middle class in Bez.''

"Well, they've also adapted to the idea of long-term marriage contracts—as a control for inheritance of property and wealth.''

"It's the rule rather than the exception where I'm from—at least,'' Jennifer qualified honestly, "the idea of life contracts; they seldom last so long in reality. Fooling around isn't considered proper.''

"I think you must be trying to clarify things," Dahven complained mildly. "I'm not certain you're making sense, though. Never mind, since we're both here."

"I agree. Go on."

"Since we are talking about me, it must be obvious to you that marriage is not requisite for a person of my class before casual—um, encounters. Fooling around. If you remember Father's reaction, you'll also have gathered that some people think it should be." He studied his fingers. "Most Sikkreni women prefer not to become pregnant from fooling around. I wear a silver market preventive charm, an arm band—I *wore* one," he corrected himself expressionlessly, but the light went out of his eyes. "Until my recent sea voyage, when it was taken from me. I can obtain another. I assure you," he added even more expressionlessly, "that I have never given any of my women anything unwanted."

Jennifer took hold of his hands and gave them a shake, and when he looked at her, brought them to her lips. "You've covered the ground rules and answered my questions; that's all I wanted. Thanks." He managed a smile but still looked slightly affronted. She sighed very faintly. "Dahven, honestly, I wasn't trying to insult you. If I were a Rhadazi, I'd probably have known all that; I wouldn't have had to ask." He nodded. "Well, I'm not, and I'm a firm believer in safe sex, so I asked. So shoot me."

"Safe? That sounds very dull."

She laughed, wrapped an arm around his waist and drew him outside. "Oh, yeah? Dull, huh? We'll just see about that."

There were horses and several wagons in the courtyard, just beyond the inn's herb garden, but no people in sight. They could hear the buzz of conversation from the open windows of the common room.

It was nearly dark in the garden; a blue light hanging near the dutch door did little to improve visibility along the footpath. Dahven swept Jennifer's hair aside as they reached the stone step and kissed the back of her neck. She shivered and whispered, "I'll get you for that." He laughed; she eluded his hand and stepped into the crowded kitchen.

Enardi had been propped up a little and watched the room through half-open eyes. Robyn and Aletto were a huddle near the unlit, enormous stone fireplace. Edrith, Lialla and

95

one of the innkeep's several sons were sitting at one end of the long table, talking. Caro herself was nowhere in sight. Jennifer closed her eyes briefly; Chris was showing Niss how to moonwalk.

He stopped short as soon as he saw Jennifer. "Hey, you know what? Besides making dynamite sandwiches, the lovely lady has pulled down a ton of answers for me." He turned back to Niss. "You try that for a little bit, all right? And then I'll help you if you need it. All right?"

"All right!" the girl replied with enthusiasm. "You know?"

Dahven chuckled, let himself down onto the end of the bench and pulled Jennifer onto his lap. Chris raised his eyebrows; she swatted at his near hand. "Cut it out, Chris, I don't need a den mother and we have all four feet on the floor."

"I don't think." Chris settled on the corner of the table. Caro hurried in from the outer room, stopped short to stare at her youngest, shook her head and cast up her eyes, then went on through the dutch door to the outside kitchen. She came back moments later, her eldest son following with a large kettle. An imperious gesture brought Niss into the common room behind her. Chris shook his head. "I feel kinda bad, watching them running around like that, you know? And just sitting in here. But she said they do it all the time without outside help, and like mom reminded me, it would be really major stupid to hang out in public and get spotted by the wrong people."

"Caro's right and so's Birdy, you stay put," Jennifer ordered. "Tell me some of this stuff you've worked out."

"Well—she's English, you know?"

"I heard her talk; of course she's English."

"I mean, our English, like, the same world as us and not another alternate. Because as far as I can tell, everything seems to track right up until she popped through—1972, she said, Midsummer. Funny thing: As far as she and I could figure it, there wasn't any of this weird time-shift thing like that goofy wizard, whatsisname, was talking about. I'd really like to track that down, but—well, anyway.

"She and mom get on just great, you know? All this witch stuff—sorry, mom threatens me every time I call it that 'cause she says witch is the natural earth and herbal lore, not fortune telling and other supernatural garbage."

"I know that; why are you telling me?" Jennifer asked. Chris shook his head.

"I'm just reminding myself so mom doesn't have to jump down my throat when I screw it up, you know? Anyway, Caro had I Ching coins, too, and she says she still does tea leaves, can you believe it? She said a bunch of them were playing around with Druid stuff, something about ley lines, Midsummer, some kind of thing out of an old book, and blam! the sky fell on her and she woke up here—well, in England but *this* world's England. Weird place, she says. Her trip was because of what they were fiddling with, apparently. Like, it was all that, she didn't get snagged on by an old bat like Merrida or whoever grabbed that wizard—Snake, right? I don't know if that would make it better or worse, knowing you'd done it to yourself. Well, anyway, she says there's magic in the *here* England, but it's not like the Rhadazi kinds: There's less of it, and it's more like what you'd expect of a parallel to our world." He stared into space, marshalling his thoughts, shifted his weight, leaned forward momentarily to wink at Enardi, who gave him a rather wan smile in return. "Okay. I really was right about place, anyway. Remember I said I thought we had to have come down roughly where we left? Well, we did."

Jennifer stared at him in disbelief, finally shook her head. "No way, Chris. If this is Palmdale, what's the big saltwater pond out there?"

"Everything else tracks, Jen. Listen, okay? Apparently there are some other splits 'way early on—climate and geology and like that. The river that comes down into Podhru is the same as the Colorado, except something shifted, earthquakes or just a different something. It empties in about where the Colorado would—what, it's around Baja, right?"

"Can't be."

"Sure it can. Because if you go on to the south side of the sea, the western end of it, there's the Baja Peninsula, and on down Mexico and Central America, and around the Cape down there you come out in the Atlantic and go on up the other coast and then on over to Europe."

"Doesn't make sense, Chris. There should be—what about Chumash Indians, Diggers—for that matter, what about the Hopi or the Navajo?"

"*I* don't know," he replied in mild irritation. "For that kind of thing I think I need to find a Rhadazi local who's gone on history, or maybe some books. God," he added gloomily. "You were going to work out reading lessons for me; bet you haven't had time to think about that either, have you?"

"We'll get to it, kid, promise."

"Yeah, terrific, if I live so long. Anyway, that stuff I don't know, and neither does she. The land masses and all that—Caro knows more about them because she decided after a couple of weeks or so that the new England wasn't exactly New and Improved—kind of like I'd feel, I guess, if we'd come out in something like Los Angeles, except outdated and not really. She said she wound up marrying some British ship's captain and eventually got here—goofy relationship if you ask me, he shows up every few years or something and she just goes on her way in between. Oh, well; his ship is a steamship, by the way."

"Steam. Really. So do you have dates?"

"More or less." He scratched his head. "Not like, it's June fourteenth or something, or an exact year. It's strange, not really what I'd figured at all. I mean, it isn't just one split or two, it's all kinds of them."

Jennifer waited. "Well? Like?"

"Mmmm? Oh. I was just thinking how good that food she took through smells; I wonder when we get to eat. Um, for one thing, Isabella and her old man didn't win the war in Spain in 1492—the Moors did. Remember back a long time ago, that oasis, when Aletto and I were comparing names, Cortez? There was a Cortez but it can't have been the same guy, do you think? Anyway, these guys here, the Rhadazi, their umpty-great-granddaddies were some of the refugees after the Moors overran Spain: I guess they're some Spanish, Portuguese, other types from that end of Europe. And until, like, twenty or thirty years ago, they were pretty damn well sealed off from the rest of the world, by their own choice—like the Chinese."

Jennifer considered this in silence for some moments. "It helps make sense out of one thing. If this is a nation of uprooted Europeans and they've been kept from outside contact. Everyone I've seen thus far has been white."

"Hey! You know?" Chris slapped one hand on the table. "For a guy from L.A., it's odd *I* didn't notice that myself. Some darker than others, but basically Caucasians, yeah. All the same—yeah, I guess if there *had* been Indians around here, after a few hundred years, would they blend in?"

"How would I know? I'm a lawyer, not a geneticist. I do

know there are fairly dark types in southern Europe, and there might have been a few Jews; weren't there still Jews in Spain?''

"Ask *me*," Chris said sourly. "But that's *our* Spain, not this one, you know? I don't know if there were any blacks in that end of the world in our world, either.''

They both looked at Dahven, who'd been following the conversation with visible difficulty. "I truly don't understand what you're talking about,'' he said. "Black men, though: I've seen one or two. On—on ship.''

"Oh.'' Chris shifted his feet and looked suddenly very uncomfortable. "Um, anyway. Pretty weird, all of it, don't you think?''

Caro Ellaway came back through the kitchen a short time later, the empty kettle in one hand. She paused on the threshold, looked around the room and nodded in satisfaction. "Colin's taking care of the commerce for me tonight, not that there's much. I could use a pair of strong arms to carry this pot back in here, once I've filled it.''

Chris, who'd been sitting and talking with Enardi, leaped to his feet. "Volunteer right here, ma'am.''

"Ma'am,'' she scoffed, and tugged at the long hair on his neck. "You make me sound old; my *mother* was ma'am!'' She picked up the kettle and stuffed the handle into his hands. "What, pray tell, was that strange thing you were teaching my daughter?''

"Dance,'' Chris replied promptly.

"Mercy. If that's what's come of dance, then what's music like these days?''

Robyn sat up and shook her head. "You *don't* want to know.'' Chris overrode her.

"Hey, funny you should ask. Once I get a little food in me, maybe we can show you.''

The evening passed quickly and pleasantly. Enardi stayed awake long enough to eat a little and to serve as Chris's "backbeat,'' using his palms against the wall. A noticeably self-conscious Edrith made what Robyn called "disgusting spitting noises.'' Chris himself was fairly self-conscious about rapping for such a large and "adult'' audience (as he called it; it was Jennifer's private opinion that Robyn was more of an inhibiting factor).

The Rhadazi—Aletto, Lialla, Dahven, Caro Ellaway's son

and daughter—looked rather bewildered. "Emcee?" Aletto asked finally. "Deejay?"

"Never mind," Robyn told him firmly. "There are no words."

Chris waved a hand. "The M.C. tells the story, the D.J. makes the music behind him, usually out of other music, but since we're a little low-tech here, we're doing it this way." Aletto continued to look at him in mild confusion, and Chris added: "Your music all has to be sung or played right now, you don't have any way to save it on a machine to play any time you want, right? That's what Eddie would do, if you had machines like that, he'd be laying down music behind my line of rap. Make better sense now?"

"A little," Aletto admitted. "It's very different from Jen's music."

"Sure is," Chris said. "She goes for that opera stuff."

"This—rap? You use it to tell a story?"

Chris shrugged. "This time I did; it felt like the easiest way to start. You know, figure out what you want to say, the rhymes come down for it pretty easy." Robyn opened her mouth, closed it again and shook her head. "I swear, mom, it's like some of the early Dylan you used to listen to, it tells a story, always rhymes at the ends of the lines except there's no rules about how long the lines are. And a lot of rap is protest music, except instead of antiwar stuff, it's antipoverty and antidrug and stuff. I don't see how *you* can object to that."

"Well, I'm impressed," Jennifer said. "But opera's narrative, too, you know."

"Opera's hairball," Chris said flatly. "Far's the rap goes—well, it's a start. And I still think it's pretty hokey, but I'll get there."

"I don't doubt it."

"Yeah. Not in front of a bunch of grown-ups, though: I felt like the kid who gets hauled out to play the piano at family parties."

"Yeah?" Robyn demanded. "How would you know about things like that, kid? I never did that to you, and anyway, there's only me and Jen who could."

"Hey. I watch TV, I got friends who got stuck doing that. Major uncool, you know?" Robyn threw up her hands and sighed.

"It sounds quite complicated," Caro said. "You must have been practicing for quite some time."

"Not really. After all, it's a fairly recent thing—well, it *was*," Chris corrected himself gloomily. "Probably by now it's totally out and whatever's new—well, I'll never know, so who cares? But doing rap is like the Bojutsu, the martial arts stuff. That takes years to get really great at, but if you got nothing else to occupy your time—like TV and books and things—and if you need it, you get so you can use it." He went over to settle next to Enardi and Edrith; the three went into a huddle. "We need some more lines, guys; you two gotta help."

"I think it's going to be two of you coming up with them," Robyn said. "Enardi needs another of his powders." Enardi sighed, but made no additional protest; he still looked very weak and it had to be some measure of how he felt that he hadn't asked all evening about his father's wagon or the mule.

The innkeep and her elder son traded off serving the guests in the common room, so one or the other could remain in the family private quarters. Colin Ellaway was a year or two younger than Chris but seemed older, or at least more quietly self-possessed. Jennifer couldn't decide if he was shy, taciturn—or if he didn't like outlanders in general or them in particular. Maybe it was simply the way his eyes were set, or that he'd inherited his father's mouth, nothing to do with how he felt. After a large and wonderful dinner—it seemed as though it had been years since she'd had roast beef—and two glasses of an excellent pale, dry wine, she decided she simply didn't care what the boy's problem was.

Aletto and Robyn shared a glass of the wine; Jennifer could see Lialla sipping at hers and trying not to watch the two of them, knowing Aletto would be aware of her concern and be offended by it. Well, Lialla had cause for concern, Jennifer thought. At least, if her brother was anything like Robyn, who'd for years now been unable—or unwilling—to set her glass aside until the wine bottle was empty. After a sip or two each, however, Robyn got up and brought the half-empty glass over to the table and set it down, out of reach, returning to Aletto with a piece of some kind of mostly sugar confection. *Good idea,* Jennifer thought comfortably. The candy had to be utterly incompatible with wine.

She was tired, but pleasantly so, content to lean back against Dahven and listen while Chris, Caro Ellaway and

Robyn talked. At some point she must have nodded off; she lost track of the conversation and regained it when Dahven gave her a little shake. "You asleep?" he asked in an undertone.

"Mmm-mmm. Resting my eyes."

"Sure you are."

"Testing the insides of my eyelids for holes."

"What?"

"Never mind. I'd better get up, go upstairs before I fall over and embarrass myself. How strong was that wine, anyway?"

"Not very," Dahven said. "I'm quite out of practice and I barely felt a cup of it."

Jennifer yawned. "Ooh. S'cuse me. I've never been *in* practice, and I had two. Better drink some water before I crawl in, or I'll have the headache from hell." She dragged herself to her feet; Robyn looked up at her. "I'm slowing the party down; sorry, folks. Going to bed, all right?"

"I won't be far behind you," Robyn said. She rubbed her eyes. "Unlike some people, I didn't get a nap today and it's been a pretty long one. Caro, should one of us stay down here with Enardi?"

"Ernie," Chris corrected her in some exasperation. "And I can stay with him if you think someone needs to—"

Caro Ellaway shook her head. "Don't you worry about Ernie; he'll be just fine. I sleep on the fold-down over by the door"—she gestured with her head toward the now nearly silent common room—"so I'll hear if he needs anything. The powder he got for tonight should keep him asleep until midmorning, though."

8

DAHVEN stopped at the head of the stairs and wrapped both arms around Jennifer's shoulders; long fingers massaged the base of her neck and she leaned her forehead into his breastbone. "Lovely man," she murmured into his shirt. "I'll give you an hour to stop that."

He held her a little away. "Couldn't hear that."

"Never mind, wasn't important. Do some more."

"Your muscles feel like metal wheelbands."

"I know it." She let her eyes close and sagged face first against his chest once more; it might have been moments or hours when footsteps came thumping up the last several stairs and a rather high, huffy voice said, "Ex*cuse* me!"

"Sorry," Dahven said mildly. "Didn't see you."

"I notice," Lialla replied. Jennifer felt the sin-Duchess press by them and heard the door open and close a moment later. She brought her head up and reluctantly opened her eyes; Dahven was gazing up the hallway, forehead puckered.

"I don't believe she cares much for me, and I can't think why that should be."

Jennifer laughed quietly. "She *was* supposed to have married you, wasn't she?"

"Well—but that was never even formally decided, and surely she was relieved rather than otherwise." He considered this. "Well?"

"Maybe it's just the idea of the thing. I'll bet we looked pretty comfortable together just now." She smothered a yawn. "I'm sorry, Dahven, I'd stay right here the rest of the night and let you rub my muscles into putty but I'm going to fall asleep any minute now."

"Mmm. Come to think, I'm sleepy myself." He left one arm across her shoulders and started slowly along the hallway. "It's a pity—"

"It's just as well," Jennifer interrupted, as firmly as she could manage. "We're each sharing a room, remember?"

"As if I could forget," he said gloomily. Jennifer laughed and tugged on his hair.

"Besides, you're about to fall asleep and so am I; one or the other of us would wind up terribly offended."

"I doubt that." He stopped in the hall between the two rooms, let go of her shoulders and touched her cheek lightly with one finger. "Ground rules," he said finally.

"Ground rules," Jennifer repeated when he seemed to have difficulty going on.

"So you know. The offer of half of Sikkre—if I had it, the offer would be genuine. But I don't come to you with less than a life contract. Just—so you know."

"I'd been presumptuous enough to assume that was your intention, as opposed to a one-night stand. That's not important just now, truly." He raised his eyebrows and she laughed sleepily. "Dahven, I'm not after you for wealth or for half of Sikkre—and *not* because you don't have it back yet."

"Yet."

"Shhh. Don't say it like that; that's not important just now, either. That comes with the next set of ground rules—including the one where I refuse, absolutely and even for you, to play Mrs. Thukar if it means sitting in that tower room and spinning wool all day while you run the Duchy." He shook his head and she laughed again. "Never mind. I don't think I'd have even brought that up if I weren't dizzy from all the wine. But I'm quite seriously falling asleep on my feet; think how silly we'd both feel if Chris found us sprawled unconscious and snoring all over the hall."

"If Aletto did," Dahven said. He smiled, then chuckled at the thought.

"Let's not find out." She straightened up, ran her fingers into the long hair at the back of his head and kissed his cheek. "Good night. Get some sleep."

It was very dark and quiet in the small room, only the faint reflection of a blue-light from somewhere in the court-yard far below showing against the curtain—not enough to illuminate her way across to the bed. Lialla was invisible in the dark, her breathing scarcely to be heard. Someone down in the common room laughed raucously, then was abruptly silent. Jennifer bent forward and felt her way across the floor, banged a finger back the wrong way against the foot-board. She swore silently, stuck the throbbing digit in her mouth and scrabbled along the footboard with her other hand; she sat on the edge of the soft mattress and scooted along it to the head, where she removed her high-tops and jeans. It seemed almost too much trouble to unbutton the chambray shirt, tired as she was, but the mere thought of waking to the scratchy and not very clean cotton decided her. The sore finger made her even more clumsy than the combination of wine and exhaustion, but it was finally off. She shivered a little in her tee-shirt, slid under the comfort and between lemon-scented sheets. They weren't as silky as the ones Fedthyr had provided but they felt absolutely wonderful against her bare legs. The comfort itself was thick and would probably be too warm, once she settled in. She edged the covers over her shoulders, worked out of the tee-shirt and dumped it on the floor with her other outer clothes.

She heard Robyn come in a short while later; by then, she was too tired to respond when her sister sat on the edge of the bed and whispered: "Jen? You still awake?" A breath or two later, she wasn't anyway.

Something had her shoulder: Something was clamped down hard, pinching skin and bruising the muscle under, digging into the joint. Jennifer moaned, tried to pull free. What seemed a very great distance away, someone was calling her name, urgently: "Jen? Jen! Oh, Jennifer, damnit, wake up!"

Wake up? I'm not asleep, she thought fuzzily and tried to shut the voice out. It moved to her other ear and now something had her other shoulder, too. *Hands.* "Birdy?" she mumbled. "Birdy, don't—"

"Jen, not so loud, shhh!" It *was* Robyn's voice, a shrill, frightened whisper; Robyn's hands hauling her partway up and trying to shake her. "Jen, damnit, there's someone outside, trying to get in here."

"Mmmm—lock the door, then," Jennifer muttered. Her fingers dragged at the sheets and comfort, trying to pull them back around overly cool shoulders. "Birdy, c'mon, leggo, I'm cold and tired."

"Oh, God," Robyn whispered devoutly. She let go so abruptly that Jennifer's head fell back into the pillows, hard. The bed jounced uncomfortably as Robyn scrambled over the side. Jennifer frowned; why didn't she simply fix the bolt and shut up so her sister could get back to sleep? *Tired,* she thought and began to drift toward sleep once more. Robyn's words caught her fading attention. "Lialla, please wake up. I—someone's outside, in the yard, I can hear them, and Jen isn't waking up."

"Mmm—what?" Lialla sounded sharply awake; Robyn shushed her rather frantically. "What's wrong with her?" Lialla went on in a much less carrying voice. Jennifer felt her stomach shift rather alarmingly as her bed rocked and hands efficiently stripped the covers from her shoulders. The air in the room was cool, the cotton bra and briefs no protection against the chill.

"Cut it out, Birdy," she mumbled, and reached for covers. They were down around her knees—too far to grab.

"Tired," she whispered, and wrapped both arms around her in a vain attempt to stay warm.

"Jen, it's Lialla. Wake up, there's a problem."

Too much trouble to make words. Jennifer shook her head the least bit and let sleep catch hold of her again.

"I told you, I can't wake her," Robyn whispered anxiously. "I—did you drink much of that wine?"

"A very little; I seldom do, and I prefer something fruitier. Why—did you?"

"One swallow, just to be polite. Jen did, though. I think—"

"Wait. You think that woman drugged us—?"

"Not—I don't know. Listen, though!" Jennifer swam momentarily nearer consciousness, and found herself listening. All she could hear at first was her own heart thudding much too rapidly, Robyn's ragged breathing. "I don't think Caro, but I think someone could have."

"I don't feel particularly drugged," Lialla said quietly. "But maybe a swallow or so wouldn't be enough. She doesn't ordinarily sleep this hard, does she?"

"Jen? Never!" Robyn's voice moved away, the bed frame creaked and the mattress swayed a little.

"Don't push the curtain aside!" Lialla hissed.

"I'm not, I'm—I can't hear anything out there now. Wait. Come here," Robyn whispered. The bed shifted again; the weight was gone. Jennifer shivered and tried to ease her upper body down under the covers. They were both over by the window; she could hear them, couldn't seem to make herself want to open her eyes. *Tired*, she thought. There was a long moment when she heard and felt nothing. Then Robyn's hands had her again; Robyn dragged her up into a sitting position. "Jennifer, damnit, there are men out there. They're after us! Wake up!"

"Slap her," Lialla ordered curtly. "Or pour water over her. We need her."

"Don't," Jennifer whispered. Robyn's hand patted her face back and forth, tentative little slaps. Jennifer caught hold of the hand finally, forced her eyes open. Robyn gazed at her anxiously. "I'm awake, Birdy, cut it out."

"You're not. I'm going to get the water—"

"No." Jennifer forced her hands up, tugged hard at her hair and bit one thumb. "No, don't, help me out, I'll do it." Robyn got her off the side of the bed. "The guys—"

"Oh, God," Robyn said.

106

"Don't—" It was nearly impossible to think. Jennifer clutched at the footboard, dragged herself to her feet. "Don't panic. You hear better than I do; check the door. If—all right. If there's no one out there, go warn them."

"Hurry!" Lialla hissed. She turned from the window briefly. "There's nothing in this room to make rope, is there?"

"No. Your bo's by the door," Jennifer said. "With mine. I'll get it." She staggered as she let go of the footboard, reeled into the wall, hard, and sat down cross-legged on the chilly floor. The bench next to the door seemed a mile away, but Robyn was already gone, the door closing quietly behind her. Jennifer swore under her breath, fought her way onto hands and knees and crawled the short distance, grabbed at the metal bowl and pulled it toward her. It caught on something, rocked, and came down across the back of her neck, the bowl itself dealing a ringing blow to the back of her head, ice-cold water pouring across her scalp and down over her shoulders and chest.

She caught her breath in a faint shriek, which brought a wordless protest from Lialla. "Oh, Lord, I think I've killed myself," she chattered, but the cold cut through the drugged thick feeling. She sat up, hands chafing her upper arms rapidly, eyes properly open for the first time. "Who's out there?" she whispered, but Lialla had already shifted into Thread and didn't hear her.

Backlash vibrated through her, the last straw to an already distressed stomach. Jennifer hastily clawed for the metal water bowl and was violently ill in it.

She came back upright shivering even harder, dizzy, her stomach still threatening to go out from under her again—but awake now and fighting mad. "The one night I strip down to my underwear and we have company. Right. Someone's going to pay for this." She got to her feet cautiously, clutched along the wall until she found both her bo and Lialla's where they'd been leaned against the wall with their personal bags, used them for balance as she felt her way across to the pile of clothes and fished out her tee-shirt. The sin-Duchess's fingers closed around the staff as Jennifer shoved it across her knees; she was still deep in Thread-awareness. Jennifer gritted her teeth and began singing— Beethoven, the Choral from the Ninth Symphony. German was a good language to sound angry in, she thought. She shifted the bo to her left hand, felt for her jeans with the right.

Too late. The curtain flared; a hand came across the sill and wrapped around the fluttering blue cloth, yanking it loose and letting it drop to the floor. The shadowy silhouette of a man filled the window; Jennifer tugged the hem of the tee-shirt as far down as it would go and backed away bare-legged and barefoot, bo trailing beside her. As she passed the end of the two beds, she shifted it to a proper two-hand grip. *I sure hope Birdy got across the hall all right, and I hope she plans on staying,* she thought. *Because that door's about to get locked, I'm not up for a two-front attack.*

She doubted that she was capable of defending against a one-front attack at the moment and momentarily wished she'd been able to snatch up her jeans. The tee-shirt didn't cover anything but her chest and shoulders; bare legs left her feeling uncomfortably vulnerable. Her head pounded and her stomach was still queasy: hung over, possibly. But on two glasses of wine, with a meal? Maybe it *had* been drugged.

Lialla abruptly abandoned Thread and jerked her feet onto the bed, caught up her bo and scrambled back over the footboard to the floor. She touched Jennifer's shoulder, put her mouth near the other woman's ear. "Are you going to be all right?" she whispered.

"I'm fine," Jennifer replied in kind. Lialla gave her a dubious glance but didn't bother to dispute what was obviously untrue. Jennifer backed toward the door, freed a hand to slide the bolt into place, moved back to Lialla's side. Both women jumped as something slammed into the door, hard, and the man in the window was suddenly over the sill and into the room; another filled the opening behind him. There didn't seem to be any need for quiet any longer; dark as the room was, the night sky was bright with moon and the men could certainly see *her*, all white shirt, pale arms and legs. Lialla couldn't have heard anything less than a shout, with all the noise out in the hallway, anyhow. "Move over, give us both some room!" Lialla backed off a pace, lost her footing and nearly fell. Jennifer crouched down, then came back to her feet as the first man stepped past the end of the bed. Whatever he held deflected the blow she intended for his middle—something wooden by the sound of it. She let the deflection give her momentum, then brought the bo back around. He parried that one also but the staff bounced off the footboard of the bed and caught him a ringing crack on the arm. Probably right on the elbow, judging by his reaction: With a loud howl of pain, he collapsed to his knees, curled protectively around the arm. The weapon clattered to the floor and rolled away. A glint of metal gave away its position; Jennifer snatched at it and dragged it toward her.

Something cold and sharp sliced across her fingertips and she hissed, then swore as she felt blood coursing down her palm and over her wrist. She dropped the weapon, snagged it across the floor with the end of the bo and picked it up with more caution. It was a short, thick length of wood, about three feet long, with a knife bound into the end. Throwing spear. A damned sharp one, too. "Li! Watch yourself, they've got something new for weapons!"

"See it. What's wrong with the floor over here? It's slick and awful!" Lialla said angrily. She moved away, along the wall, climbed onto the end of the bed and worked her way to the head. The second man seemed to be having a little trouble getting into the room, or perhaps he was trying to let his eyes adjust to darker surroundings, or to figure out what was wrong with his cursing, huddled companion. Lialla brought her bo down with a hard snap of the wrists and caught him across the back of the head. He slid down, caught momentarily across the sill, fell back out of sight. Someone below him shouted a warning; someone else was yelling furiously from down in the yard.

There were people out in the hallway shouting, too: Jennifer couldn't decide who they were—guests, more of Jadek's men or the Thukars', possibly even their own people, trying to get in. Whoever it was, was going to have to wait. Three men piled into the room in rapid succession, filling the window, the narrow space between the two beds. Lialla caught one a hard crack across the shoulder, hit the man just behind him a glancing blow. He pivoted, caught the staff and tore it from her hands, slammed the end into the wall. Lialla yelped, scuttled down the length of the bed and dropped over the footboard, ducking out of sight. The man came cautiously around the corner, edging around his fallen companion only to trip over the man who was still curled around his arm, rocking and moaning. Jennifer took two steps to her left; the bo tip caught against rough wall, jarring her hands. One more man in the window, foot on the sill, hesitating. Sensible of him, Jennifer thought grimly.

The little room had been crowded enough with only three women in it. Now—well, she wasn't moving any more than she had to; that was courting a fall.

Too bad she and Lialla were separated; there wasn't much she could do about it, though. She glanced nervously along the wall to her right as something hit the door, hard, and she briefly could see light along the upper edge. That bolt might be strong, but she didn't think the door itself or the frame could take much of that kind of abuse. "God," she muttered to herself, "what a way to go!"

Someone edged around the first man she'd hit—possibly the one Lialla had just clobbered. He threw himself at her, coming in hard, fast and sideways, leading with his right shoulder and a massive upper arm, sweeping the tip of her bo around with him. His weight slammed her arms into the wall, trapping the staff between them. Her shoulders hit hard, momentarily went numb. *Not like this*, she thought desperately, but there was no shoving him back—he was easily half again her size and he had the leverage the way he leaned into her. But his feet were well away from the wall; he wasn't ready when she folded at the knees and dropped, taking the bo with her. The wall must have been rough-finished plaster; the tee-shirt caught on it, sliding up to her shoulder blades, and it felt like she had scraped all the skin from her back.

No room to maneuver the bo; the end was braced in the corner, anyway. She scooted sideways on her backside, trying to free it; the guard swore and brought his foot down in an attempt to pin it and her hand. She scooted again, rattling her teeth, nearly lost her balance entirely when she came down on the end of the throwing spear. *I can't stick someone again, I can't, not now, I'll lose it again!* she thought desperately. But the moment's delay had cost her; the guard had the bo flat on the floor under his boot and only a quick jerk and a palmful of splinters from a rough board saved the fingers. Jennifer brought her knees up, cautiously fished the spear from under her and forced herself to wrap two badly hurting hands around the haft.

Lialla yelled something just then, a wild curse that rose to a piercing, furious shriek. The guard was distracted—just enough. Jennifer scrambled away under him, and when he turned back, she reversed the spear, slammed the wooden end into his temple and brought it down across the back of his neck as hard as she could. For one horribly long moment, he stared right into her eyes; his lids fluttered then and he fell jarringly into the floor, Jennifer's bo trapped under him.

"Oh, *shit*!" she shouted furiously.

"Jen, are you on your feet?" Lialla screamed at her. "Get—the—door!"

"Are you crazy?"

"Get it! That's my brother out there, can't you hear him?" Her voice went up into a shriek as the guard who'd been poised on the windowsill threw himself into the room and onto the bed. "Get the damn door, do it!"

"All right, I heard you!" Jennifer bellowed. She shook out her left hand, gnawed at the palm to see if she couldn't free some of the embedded bits of floorboard, pressed the spear against the wall for balance and, with a wary glance at the man she'd just hit, another for the one who'd brought in the ugly little weapon she now held, she edged her feet toward the door.

It was too damned dark, even with the curtain gone—even with moonlight bathing the side of the inn and coming through the empty window opening. She could make out where Lialla was—all that movement on the far corner of the bed, the sin-Duchess and at least one of their assailants. Two down that Jen personally knew of, one Lialla had hit earlier. *How damn many of them made it in here?* she wondered. But it *was* Aletto out there, and as she reached for the bolt, she could hear Dahven shouting her name.

A hard hand clamped on her shoulder, spinning her around, tearing her fingers from the piece of metal. They went numb. Jennifer's head cracked into the wall; she swore, blinked rapidly to clear tears of pain from her eyes. For a frightening moment, she couldn't see anything but a swimming, shadowy shape and wondered if she'd hit her head hard enough to blind herself. The shape stabilized; the hand released her shoulder to take a grip in her hair. "Drop that, or I'll break your neck," he ordered. When she didn't move, he tightened his grip, dragging her off balance. "Drop it."

"It's—it's caught," she managed.

"Caught? In what?" He laughed grimly. "Caught in your breeks?"

"My watchband—a wristband," she finished in a shrill voice that didn't sound at all like hers. The grip on her hair eased slightly. "The end ran under the band, let me work it loose—"

"Tell me another one."

"I'm telling the truth," Jennifer replied faintly. She tightened her fingers around the wood, shook her arm in a sharp downward series of jerks, as if trying to release something stuck inside the watchband. There was pandemonium in the hall, something struck the door hard, and now she could hear Chris shouting in a full fury. The guard ignored it; he wasn't taking his eyes off her for a moment. She couldn't make herself let go of the spear, her last possible defense against him. Anything, she thought desperately, any delay. But any moment now, he might simply grab her wrist, realize he was being had, squeeze until she had to let go. She shook her arm down again, harder this time, made the spear clatter against the wall.

Someone hit the door again; wood cracked but still held. Lialla shrieked and was answered by the high, familiar shrilling of a giant hunting bird beyond the window. Someone below bellowed out a warning; a terrified howl just outside the room distracted the men inside. The grip on Jennifer's hair released slightly; she set her jaw and reversed the spear with her fingers, tightened her hand on it once more and jabbed, hard. The tip struck something metal, bounced, slid over the slick surface with a screech that made her fillings ache before it went in. The guard let go of her, clapped both hands around his thigh, staggered back a pace; the spear tore from shaking hands, haft bobbing. Jennifer swallowed bile, stared at it in horrified fascination. *Oh, no.* It had barely cut him; she could see most of the metal blade, a gleam of steel against his dark trousers in the line of light that came through the half-ruined door. It hadn't stopped him and, worse, now he had the spear.

Jennifer braced both hands against the wall in an effort to steady herself, swallowed desperately and, as the guard yanked at the haft, she tried to throw herself sideways, toward the door. He was there before her, bracing his body against the wood. She stopped short, clutching at the wall for balance; he shouted to those behind him: "Will you get hold of that female back there so we can get out of here? It's only two women, after all!"

Jennifer laughed breathily. "Trying to reassure yourself?"

He didn't take his eyes from her as someone behind him yelled back, "There's a bird, a shapeshifter outside the window!"

"Never mind the shifter, that's why we've got two archers in the yard, remember? Hurry, will you? You get the sin-Duchess under control, I'll bring this one."

"Like hell you will," Jennifer said flatly. *The bo,* she thought suddenly. It was just behind her; he hadn't touched it and the one who'd knocked it out of her hand—he'd crawled away sometime after this other one came in. She edged herself back a pace, dropped down to one knee and fumbled around as wide an area as she could, without letting go the wall; she doubted she could regain her feet without it. The guard shifted his weight and she thought he might lunge after her. The door shuddered as someone hit it, hard; he rebraced his legs and edged his shoulder back into the wood.

The bo was reassuringly hard and familiar; her left hand closed around it. Her cut fingertips stung; she set the end against the floor, used the staff to haul herself up, then swung it up, cocked her wrists and slammed it down. It cracked against one of his shins, hard enough to shake her grip. He roared with pain and fury, drew the leg up, hopping for balance, and fell against the door once more. As he hunched over, Jennifer threw herself at the bolt and actually got her fingers on it. Searing pain ran like fire from her left wrist all the way up her arm. She staggered back several paces, fell into the wall and slid down it, staring in shocked, sickened disbelief at her shoulder. The wooden shaft of the throwing spear lay across the backs of her fingers, the end pressing against her outflung leg. Most of the wickedly sharp blade was buried in her shoulder. There was blood everywhere. *My blood. That's my blood,* she thought faintly.

The room spun sickeningly, tunneled down to nothing. The unbearable shouting and pounding stayed with her only an agonized breath longer.

Terrible, throbbing pain brought her back to consciousness moments later. She was half-sitting, held up by the wall and her outflung legs. The door stood ajar, spilling light and more noise into the room. There seemed to be bodies everywhere. *Including mine,* she thought dizzily. *Why can't I just pass out and stay out?* Her eyes sagged closed. *God. Hurts. I think I'm going to be sick if it gets any worse. Don't you dare be sick, Cray. Don't dare—*

"Jennifer?" Dahven's voice. She managed to open her

eyes once more. He knelt before her, hands hovering but well away from her arm; his face was very white in the light someone had brought in.

"Don't—touch," she whispered.

"You're bleeding; we've got to get that out, get it stopped."

"No. Please, no. Hurts."

"I know, my love." He rose partway, turning to look around them urgently, then stripped off his shirt and hesitated, as though uncertain where to press it. Jennifer let her head back against the wall and tried to breathe so nothing moved.

"Oh, jeez!" Chris's voice slammed through her; she winced and bit her lips not to cry out as the spear shifted slightly.

"Don't," Dahven urged in a low voice. "Don't. Find Lialla, hurry."

"Jeez—right."

"Jennifer." Dahven's voice was still low; she wondered if he thought it sounded soothing. Because all she could hear was fear.

You can be strong for Dahven, she reminded herself, and for a confused moment she thought they were back in Bezjeriad, Dahven the ill, thin, tormented huddle of a man in that dreadful little shack, herself kneeling next to him, reassuring him. "It's all right," she whispered. "Don't worry, Dahven."

"Of course not." His fingers were cool against her cheek; they trembled, steadied again. She tried to bring her right hand up to cover his but it fell back into her lap. "You'll be fine. Once we get that out." He cautiously slid his hand between the spear haft and her hand, edged shirt fabric between the two and let the haft down again to hold it in place.

Everything shifted alarmingly and briefly faded. When she opened her eyes once more, he had his shirt worked up her arm to the elbow. The pressure was pure misery; she had to bite her lip not to tell him so. *He's trying to stop it bleeding. God, what a hope.* She was aware of the rough wall against scraped and bruised shoulders, of the fiery agony that was her left shoulder, of pressure against the inside of her left knee. The rucked-up tee-shirt and ruined underwear seemed very unimportant at the moment, in comparison. She laughed very faintly, rather breathily. "Guess if I had to ruin something, better my skivvies than my jeans, huh?''

"Jen? Oh, God," Robyn said and dropped down hard enough to shake the floor boards under her. Jennifer took her lips carefully between her teeth, forced her eyes partway open. Robyn's face shone with perspiration and she was trembling. She drew a deep breath, forced herself back to her feet and leaned against the ruined door frame to shout into the hall, "Caro! Caro, we need something for bandaging, *fast*!"

"No," Jennifer whispered. "Thread—" She tried to bring herself to look at her arm again and couldn't. It didn't surprise her that she couldn't shift into awareness of Thread, either. It did come as a shock that the pain was so much worse than what she'd felt when healing Aletto's arm. There was a difference after all. She felt consciousness slipping away once again, and let the darkness take her.

9

THREAD-VIBRATION woke her. Lialla was kneeling next to her, weaving the fingers of her right hand apparently through plain air, while the left shifted very lightly up and down Jennifer's arm. The overall pain had lessened, she thought; the bleeding had definitely slowed. Immediate pressure was going to make her sick, if she couldn't deal with Lialla's touch, careful as it was. She had one brief glimpse of the spear on the floor between her knee and Lialla's, the entire tip a dark, rusty red. It lay in a frighteningly large puddle, very dark against pale floorboards. Jennifer swallowed, forced her eyes away.

Dahven had eased her away from the wall at some point and put himself on her right side for support, his left hand lightly rubbing her neck and holding her hair out of the way. His right fingers were threaded through hers. She gave them a squeeze and he managed a smile when she looked up at him. But his eyes were dark with worry and he looked as sick as she felt. "It's all right," she assured him—or tried to. Her voice was a harsh, dry whisper that didn't sound very convincing.

"I tried to tell him as much," Lialla said stiffly. "It's a cut—"

"A cut!" he protested.

"All right, it's a nasty one, it's long and deep, but it's a cut all the same. Even I can deal with a cut," Lialla added; she ran the fingers of her weaving hand through her hair and sighed in exasperation. "If you want to do something useful, keep quiet until I'm done, will you? I'm deathly tired and, quite honestly, this kind of thing is difficult enough for me when I'm fully awake and not trying to do it around a lot of people. You keep talking to me, and it breaks my concentration. Things take longer. Jen might not want that."

"Sorry," Dahven said stiffly, and shut his mouth hard. Lialla ignored him, closing her eyes and sifting through Thread once more. The stuff wrapped around Jennifer like a swirl of thick jelly, swaying her back and forth; she set her jaw and tried to think of a piece of music—any piece. Pain, Thread and nausea were effectively blocking her brain at the moment; she finally tightened her grip on Dahven's fingers, and when he bent his head close to her face, she murmured, "Sing to me. Something, anything." He cast a doubtful look at the top of Lialla's bowed head. "It's all right; that won't interrupt her. What she's doing is making me ill. Help me take my mind off it. Anything. Please."

He must have had as much difficulty as she in gathering scattered wits; he finally began humming something that might have been one of the Childe ballads she'd sung to him, back in that Red Hawk caravan—perhaps one of his own that was similar. Her throat was too dry to hum with him; she concentrated on the sound, on anticipating what the next notes would be. It was enough to partially block what Lialla was doing; the nausea faded.

The arm throbbed dreadfully—more than she could block with only music—and she was still uncomfortably aware of blood trickling down her forearm. She was caught up in the picture once again, thrown back into the moment when there had been blood everywhere, her arm laid open from wrist to shoulder, the spear haft balanced almost delicately against the backs of her fingers. She clenched her teeth, swore under her breath. *Dear God, no, stop it.* Dahven's fingers tightened on hers, reflexively; she could feel his worried gaze on her face and he stopped singing. Thread jostled her, sickeningly, but for once she welcomed it: It shattered the nightmare vision. She opened her eyes, whispered, "Go on. Please." He nodded, began to sing again. Thread faded. Lialla's fingers came down on her shoulder then, perhaps with light intent, but it felt like a brick. Jennifer sagged and everything faded.

She wasn't certain she'd actually passed out, or lost only a moment or two. When she opened her eyes, however, Lialla was sitting back on her heels, eyes closed, breathing rather heavily. Jennifer set her teeth, flexed her fingers cautiously. It hurt, all the way into her shoulder and back again. But the fingers moved; her thumb folded over the way it should, even though the movement set everything throbbing wildly. After that, she decided not to attempt bending her elbow just yet. After one hesitant look at it, she decided she wouldn't do that again, either: There was blood everywhere, dried in dark patches on her forearm; creased in her knuckles—still dripping from the slashed sleeve of her ruined tee-shirt.

Lialla looked abnormally white and perilously near tears; she dragged herself to her feet and walked out of the room before Jennifer could so much as try to thank her. Caro Ellaway, radiating calm and efficiency, settled down in the same place with a tray that held a large bowl of water, a pile of washing cloths, a steaming cup of something that smelled like herbs and lemon, a clay mug with beads of sweat on the side. Caro put the tray beside her and held the clay mug to Jennifer's lips. "It's only water," she said. "But your sister said you prefer it for drinking, and she found your aspirins. I've two, will that be enough?" Jennifer nodded. "Good. I did bring tea, in case you'd like that. It's plain herb, no sleeping powders."

"All right," Jennifer managed.

"Well, I suppose it might not have occurred to you, not the way you look just now. All the same, I'd want to know, and I didn't want you wondering about it, or being afraid to take anything." She handed Dahven the water mug, wrung out wet cloths and began carefully sponging down the left arm. The water was cool, the woman's touch light and gentle. It hurt, but not as much as Lialla's healing had. "I'm sure you don't feel much like having me do this," Caro went on. "But once we get you cleaned up and out of those bloody things, you'll feel better."

Jennifer nodded, let Dahven give her another sip of water. "I—yeah. Didn't think I'd get that sick, seeing blood."

"I don't wonder, when it's yours. You're fortunate to have had a Wielder who could deal with it."

"I know." *I could have bled to death,* Jennifer thought bleakly. "But I think I ruined my shirt. The rest—when they're gone, I don't have any others."

"I know, it took me years to adapt to what the locals wear for underpants. But don't worry about it," Caro said. She wrung out another cloth and set it aside, brought the bowl where she could immerse Jennifer's fingers in the water. "It's only blood, after all, not ink or acid. With so many boys I'm quite good at getting blood from clothes. And I've a spare nightshirt you can put on for now, if you like." She turned her head, found Robyn sitting cross-legged against the wall, chin resting on her knees; she was staring across the room at one of the bound men, or possibly through him. "Birdy, dear, why don't you get those men to do something useful, like get the rest of those brutes out of this room so we can get your poor sister into bed? Help them shoo everyone else out, too, why don't you, dear?" She turned back and gave Dahven a determined look. "That really does include you, you know."

"He doesn't go," Jennifer said faintly but as firmly as she could manage.

"I'm not leaving," Dahven said at the same moment.

Caro laughed and shook her head. "Well—if you're *both* going to be that way about it. And I suppose there isn't much of you left to the imagination anyway, is there, young woman?"

Jennifer refused to allow them to cut the tee-shirt off her; Robyn lost her temper. "Don't be stupid, Jen, it's only a damned shirt, after all!"

"It's only *my* damned shirt," Jennifer pointed out. "And you put one more hole in it, it'll come out of your hide."

"Stubborn, arbitrary, dumb," Robyn began. Dahven shifted ominously; Jennifer tightened her grip on his hand and he stayed put and quiet. Robyn scowled at him, turned the scowl on her sister. "You break that thing open again, trying to salvage a tee-shirt—"

"It's *my* material possession," Jennifer said flatly. "And I bought it because I liked it, all right? If you're not going to be helpful, go find Lialla and compare notes on how stubborn and dumb I am.''

"That's not fair," Robyn said.

"I'm not feeling fair, damnit. Either help or split, got it?''

Robyn's eyes narrowed; her mouth twisted then and she nodded. "Hell. It's your damn arm, after all. I hear one bitch or moan out of you, though—''

Jennifer sighed, loudly exasperated. "Shut up and get it off, all right?'' It cost her, despite the extreme care the two women used in working it off her right arm, over her head, stretching the ripped sleeve even wider to ease it over her left arm without touching it.

Dahven shifted so he could brace her from behind while they worked the shirt off, holding her up as Caro dropped a very loose, lightweight thing like a cotton shift over her head, and Robyn eased off the remainder of her underthings under cover of the nightshift. She managed a smile, blotted her sister's forehead. "Hey. Just like the beach; remember how good I was at changing into a bikini under my coverup?''

Jennifer forced the corners of her mouth up. "Modesty preserved.'' She didn't much care at the moment; Dahven probably didn't either. Caro still looked vaguely scandalized by his presence, though, and the remark was Birdy's way of apologizing for her earlier anger. Dahven edged himself partway up and pulled her to her feet. She leaned against him, breathing hard, eyes closed, finally managed a faint nod. "Don't try to carry me, I can use my feet if you can hold me up.''

He pushed away from the wall, wrapped an arm around her waist. Robyn darted around them to pull the comfort and sheet down; somehow Jennifer wound up under them. Dahven sat rather heavily on the end of the bed, hand wrapped around the footboard. Caro edged past him to lay a hand against Jennifer's cheek, then smoothed a wrung-out cloth across her forehead. Jennifer managed a smile. "Thanks. I'm sorry about the fuss—''

"We'll worry about all that much later," Caro said very firmly. Her eyes were anxious, though. "Are you going to be all right in here? I hate to shift you any farther, but—''

"I'll be right here with her," Dahven said. "Robyn—?''

"She's already gone across to the other room.'' Caro leaned over and gave the cool cloth a final smoothing.

"Don't you worry about anything, Jennifer, you just sleep. Everything is all quite under control." She went out, taking the lamp with her, pulling what was left of the door into place. Jennifer could see light all along the latch side and across the top; then Dahven's hunched-over form came between her and the light. She reached up to adjust the damp cloth so it lay across her eyes, and let sleep take her.

When she woke, the inn was quiet once more. The room was very dark: By that and the stuffy feel of the air, someone had locked the shutters.

Dahven was a still weight on the wall side of the bed; he'd fallen asleep on top of the comfort.

The arm was hurting her rather badly; she thought that was probably what had wakened her. It lay outside the comfort, across her chest. Her fingers felt like balloons and the back side of her elbow, of her shoulder, ached from the weight of the arm itself. "I can't take this," she whispered. Faint as the sound must have been, Dahven stirred and groaned; his hand stole across the pillow to touch her cheek.

"Jen?"

"I'm sorry. Go back to sleep."

"S'all right. What—" he coughed heavily. "Damn, sorry. What can I get you? Do you need Lialla again?"

"No—" Jennifer considered this. "I think she's done all she could manage. She—I know she tried, she probably kept me from bleeding to death. It's—I wish I knew what time it is. Oh, God, I just remembered, my watch—"

"The time piece? It's all right. Chris found it on the floor; the band was cut through. I think he's still got it."

"Damn—oh, just that I can't tell—"

"It's late," he offered.

"I guess it doesn't matter. I'm going to have to try and finish the job myself. Right now it would be a lot easier if it was still night."

He shifted onto one elbow. "I don't know what I can do to help—"

"I don't either," Jennifer said. "Be there when I finish."

Thread didn't want to respond; she had to pinch one earlobe with her good hand to force herself awake and aware enough to concentrate on access. It was even more difficult to locate the healing stuff, and in the end she had to utilize the same red Thread she'd used on Aletto's arm. Not as effective or as quick to work as the yellow Neri had shown

120

her, but she hadn't the physical strength to Wield that, even if she'd been able to separate it from the rest. The arm itself—she flinched away from it twice before she was able to disassociate herself from it. *Not mine,* she told herself. *It could be anyone's arm. Just a cut, like Lialla said. Any cut.*

It might still scar. She put that thought out of her mind, fought to concentrate on laying more Thread over what Lialla had already done. She did good work, she thought dispassionately; it hadn't been enough, but what was there had been neatly done. Probably a combination of exhaustion on Lialla's part and fear of causing pain. *I hope she doesn't realize what I've done. Anyone else might handle it all right, but she'd be right back in the dumps again.* Well, that wasn't her problem just now.

It was even more difficult separating herself from Thread once she was done; the wrench left her shaking and nearly ill again. She swallowed an evil taste, experimentally flexed her fingers. Stiff. Still swollen. Sore, but not as painful as they'd been moments before. She drew a deep breath and let it out in a rather shaky sigh, gripped the fingers that lay against her right arm. "Lord, that's better." She turned her head and squinted, trying to see him. The room was too dark for more than shadow and outline. "Are you all right?"

"Of course," he began, spoiled it with a cough. "Tired."

"That's all? You'd tell me, wouldn't you?"

"I—"

"Never mind," she said. "Save you having to lie. What happened?"

He shifted so his cheek rested against her shoulder. "A lot happened—too much. The wine was tampered with; at least, we presume the wine, since you and I, and Edrith, drank the most of it. Chris said he had a swallow of it; I know Aletto and your sister scarcely touched it. Chris woke immediately when he heard Robyn at the door; a moment later there was a hellish din in this room and that got me on my feet. Chris had to roll Edrith onto the floor and Aletto wasn't too steady. Robyn wasn't making a lot of sense until someone came through our window and hit Aletto between the shoulders."

"He wasn't hurt—?"

"Mad clear through; probably that helped get him on his feet right. Chris had his weapon by then, he was the only one who'd had sense enough to keep his handy last night. My sword was hanging on one of the pegs, under half a dozen things, I think I nearly died twice before I got it loose." He laughed faintly. "I don't care much for that kind of fighting—dark room, not enough room for my feet, a madly aching head. All the same, we finally took care of the men who'd come in after us, and Chris saw three or four riding away. There was still an uproar over here."

"I know about that part. Who were they?"

"No one's for certain," Dahven said. "Hired, Aletto thinks, and I agree. Probably bought on Podhru's docks. One or more of them might have been among the common room guests yesterday; anyone might presume we'd stay here overnight, coming from Bez overland. It wouldn't be too difficult to discover the innkeep had private guests, even if she didn't tell anyone. Or her children might have mentioned us—they do the serving, of course."

"God," Jennifer said quietly. "Surely she wouldn't have—!"

"No? Because she's outlander also?"

"I—no. Your father's wizard was outland, remember; it doesn't automatically make us friends or allies. I just can't see it, though."

"She has several children and no future for any of them but this inn."

"God." Jennifer was silent for a long moment. "I can't recall for certain; I think she drank as much of that wine as I did, though." She shook her head impatiently, dislodging the still damp cloth. "Leave it for now."

"All right. Whoever paid those men was down in the courtyard; they were the ones who rode off when they realized it wasn't going to work. Chris thought they were clad like guards but he couldn't make out colors."

"Stupid. Attacking an inn like this. What did they think it was going to get them?"

Dahven managed a faint, humorless chuckle. "If we'd all drunk as much of that wine as you and I did, they might well have ridden away with unconscious prisoners, leaving behind two empty rooms and a very puzzled innkeeper."

"Or two rooms of dead guests," Jennifer said. Her mouth had gone dry.

"Or some of each." Dahven sighed quietly, fought a cough. "If it was my brothers, using that kind of violence against all of us so they can deal with me—"

"Don't," she urged and gripped his fingers, hard. "Please. Not just now, I don't think I can handle that argument again."

"They nearly killed you! Do you think I can take that?"

"They didn't."

"Not for lack of trying. I—all right, leave it, we're quarreling to no point and there's a more important problem: Three dead men and six prisoners, plus an innful of witnesses to an outrageous breach of law. The innkeep has to send for the Andar Perighan guard, and there are going to be questions."

"Questions. Oh, God. What do we tell them?"

"Not the truth, at least, not all of it. Aletto killed a nobleman, his uncle may not have signed a warrant but the Emperor might choose not to ignore such a murder."

"I know, Lialla tried to explain. They'd keep him; it's the last thing we can afford." Jennifer sighed. "He'll have to hide, and so will you."

"No—"

She brought up her good hand to lay across his cheek; it was too warm. "Don't. Not now. Please. How long do you think we'll have?"

"I don't know, but probably less than a day."

"If we just left—"

"Very bad mistake, believe me. It would raise suspicion of *us*. We don't need the Emperor's guard out looking for us also."

Silence. Jennifer tried to gather scattered wits enough to think. Ugly situation; all they'd needed. "I don't think sneaking off is an option, anyway. We can't leave Enardi behind, particularly not after this." She considered this, shook her head. "God, poor kid. I surely hope he slept through it all."

"I think someone said—gods, I can't remember. The eldest boy said, just before he and Chris tore into each other."

"Oh, Lord." Jennifer drew a deep breath, let it out in a sigh. "Don't tell me, I don't think I can handle any more right now."

"No." Dahven turned his head away and coughed.

"I don't think I'll be able to ride anywhere tomorrow. I think if I tried to sit up right now, I'd throw up or pass out. I lost blood and Thread doesn't replace it. But after what I've heard, I'd just as soon glue myself together the hard way as have that healer Menij. He'd probably consider *me* some kind of heretic and let me die."

"I wish I could say I have a plan," Dahven said vexedly. He coughed again and when he went on his voice sounded too thin. "I'm supposed to be good at them. I—to be honest, I'm too tired to care."

"Oh, Lord. Tell me—swear to me you weren't hurt?"

"I promise you were the only one of us hurt, except for a few bruises, and Aletto had a nosebleed from when he fell." He yawned again. "Maybe if I sleep on it, an idea will come."

"Sounds good," Jennifer murmured. It felt good to close her eyes, to let her head roll to the right so her cheek rested against his hair. *Tell him to get under the comfort,* she thought. *After all, he's dressed, I'm covered, there's the sheet—* As if anyone cared, as if either of them were capable of doing anything more than holding hands right now.

He drew a deep, shuddering breath, let it out as a very faint snore. Sleeping already. He was doing it all wrong—out of necessity, she knew. Still, a man just over the fever he'd had shouldn't be riding long hours, worrying constantly, exposed to chills—fighting for his life. If he fell ill again, out here, with only that healer Menij to care for him! *I can't take this,* she thought suddenly. The hand resting against Dahven's shoulder was shaking; she freed it with extreme caution and he sighed in his sleep, rolled away from her. She wrapped the arm around her ribs, accidentally knocked cut and scabbed fingers against her forearm. Blood, pain, violence and death—she suddenly wanted nothing so desperately as to be home again, where pain was a stress headache, violence something on television. "Oh, *God*," she moved her lips soundlessly, and turned her head away so Dahven wouldn't hear her cry.

He was gone when she woke again—to a cool room, sun pooled on the floor under the edge of a dark blue curtain that looked as though someone had jerry-rigged it back in place. The door was slightly ajar; she could hear familiar voices out in the hall or possibly in the room across it. She shifted, managed to roll onto her right arm and edge up on her elbow. The room tilted rather alarmingly and she groaned, let herself down again.

She heard rather than saw the door creak open. "Jen?" Robyn's tentative voice.

"Mmmm—yeah, that's me, isn't it?"

"Most of you. Got some warm bread and things for you if you think you can handle them. Caro made you and Ernie chicken broth this morning and she said she'd add veggies to it later if you kept the liquid down." Robyn came across to sit on the edge of the other bed. "You feel any better, kiddo?"

"Sure. That's not too difficult, though. Last night was pretty ugly."

"Tell me." Robyn shook her head. "Listen, if you do feel better, we'd probably better get some food down you and like that. Caro sent Colin into Podhru for guard to deal with those guys that jumped us last night. I guess she had to—"

"Dahven explained; she's right. We don't want to look like we're the bad guys."

"Yeah. Suppose so." Robyn pushed to her feet.

"How are you holding up?" Jennifer asked her. "I thought I heard you out there, last night—"

"You did. I got really pissed, it just happened. Can you believe one of those guys shooting arrows into a room when he couldn't even see what he was hitting? One jammed in the end of Chris's bo, and that was all it took. Look, let's not talk about it, why don't I go get you something, all right? Unless you're up to going down—"

"Don't think I'll even try; sitting up was a big enough thrill. Besides, I don't think this thing of Caro's is decent wear for mixed company, and I feel damned flimsy without my underwear."

Robyn laughed, paused in the doorway. "I'll see if your stuff isn't maybe dry, it came pretty clean. Caro's down there right now trying to darn the holes in your tee-shirt."

"You're kidding."

"You made enough of a fuss over it last night, she figured it was important. Besides, she knows how it feels, having real clothes start to wear out."

"I'll really owe her for that one."

"I told her that. She says you can pay her by eating what she's fixed." Jennifer let her eyes close, heard Robyn's retreating footsteps. All right, she thought tiredly. How *are* we going to deal with a suspicious pack of guards?

Instead of Robyn, Chris came in with a large, steaming mug and a wedge of bread. "Mom says she's gonna get your skivvies spread out in the sun. Think she wanted me out of the kitchen anyway, so she could apologize to Caro.'' He settled on the edge of the bed. ''This all right, or am I joggling you too much? Cause you look like you're gonna need help sitting up.''

''You're joggling but that's all right. Yeah, I can use an arm.'' She took a sip of the broth. Chicken, and very plain, not even peppered. Bland, but probably all her stomach would accept anyway. ''Why apologize?''

Chris looked uncomfortable. ''Oh. Well. After everything last night, I got sort of pissed off and when Colin started yelling about us busting up his mom's inn, I blew. Well, really,'' he added huffily. ''We didn't *ask* those guys in, and it wasn't like any of them got hurt, and there was Mom all white and staggery, Aletto bleeding all over himself and then you—'' Chris swallowed, tore off a bite-sized bit of bread and fed it to her. ''Hey, that was just bad, lady. Don't do that to me again, will you?''

''Try not,'' Jennifer said rather shortly. It was hard, even with his arm around her shoulders, keeping herself upright. There were filmy edges to everything.

''Well, anyway, I already talked to the guy this morning and we got it square between *us*. He doesn't think we did that stuff on purpose and I guess I don't really think any of them got bought off to dump downers in the wine.'' Chris separated more bread for her and brought the mug to her lips again. ''Boy, I'm sure glad I don't do wine.''

''You didn't drink any?''

''Well—a swallow of Eddie's, so he wouldn't think I'm totally strange, it's not like back home, you know, people don't have the same attitude and a guy my age can hit the bars and stuff.'' He handed her bread. ''So even Eddie thinks I'm kind of weird on the subject. But I really don't like drinking around mom when she's trying to quit. You know?''

''I know. Has to be hard for her.''

''Well, Aletto's helping, they're kind of propping each other up. You sure that's enough?'' he added anxiously when she held up a hand to block the mug.

''Sure. Let me down, okay?'' She felt absolutely limp once he got her flat again. Chris set the mug on the floor, pinched off another corner of the bread and ate it himself.

''You'd better sleep some more,'' he mumbled around the mouthful.

"I'm all right now. Tell me things."

"Yeah, well." He finished the bread, chewed and swallowed, nodded. "The inn's pretty emptied out, everyone trying to pass on getting involved, I guess. Mom apologized to Caro for that while she was getting the soup for you, Caro said never mind, she'd be full up the next few nights, local people coming in to find out what happened. Caro didn't wake up until someone out in the courtyard by the barns started yelling when mom dropped on him; I guess she had a pretty good slug of that wine, too. Ernie didn't even know until this morning that anything had happened. Which is good. Mom was totally embarrassed but I don't think anyone caught on what went on outside, it was pretty dark and even with those guys howling at the tops of their lungs about a shapeshifter, no one really saw her. Which is good, too.

"Aletto's nose was a mess but he let Lialla fix it, and Eddie had a godawful headache when he woke up. Dahven—wow. You know, I am really almost tempted to make him the trade, sword for bo? The guy's got style."

"He was all right, wasn't he?"

"Hung over from whatever went in the wine. Pretty dead tired, too, he's across the hall sound asleep. He didn't get cut up or anything, though."

"He said as much, but I wasn't sure."

"Yeah. He's the kind of guy who'd tell you he's fine and then fall apart on you. Nice, though, I like him."

Jennifer grinned faintly. "Yeah. Me, too."

"Well, I noticed," her nephew said dryly. "Listen, though: The city guard's probably going to be here any time now. And we don't want them figuring out it's us, do we? So if you're up to listening, I think I've got a plan."

Jennifer settled herself a little more comfortably and nodded. "Talk."

Chris talked. It was a little complex and turned on her, mostly. "Aletto and Lialla are the most obvious of us, and probably my description's out there, too. You know, the clothes and the hair, I stand out. But you—you're pretty ordinary-sized and all, mostly it's all the curly hair, right? So Caro's got a scarf to hide that. And what we can do, is right where your forehead is, I can trim my hair, some off the back, you've got tape, we'll make it like you've got a few dark blonde, straight bangs."

"Let me think." Jennifer considered this. "There's holes."

"Yeah, well, we aren't the only outlanders in Rhadaz, and Caro says she gets them in here because everyone knows she's outlander. We push for mistaken identity, right?"

"I—well . . ."

"And you stay flat and look pale and weak, they won't bug you too much. Caro says the city guard can be pretty obnoxious but they wouldn't get tough on a wounded woman." He glanced at her arm. "And if we wrap that back up, so no one can tell Li worked on it—" He shrugged. "We really don't have a lot of options, if we're gonna keep the noble boys wonder—remembered, see?—keep the guys out of the clink."

"I'm not the best actress around," Jennifer said dubiously.

"Around here, you just might be. Tell me where your big bag is, okay?"

She napped again after Chris left, and woke feeling a little less desperately unnerved, perhaps even a little hungry. Caro and Robyn came in to check on her, and Caro went in search of more soup, some drinking water while Robyn searched out Jennifer's handbag, then unfolded a long piece of badly stained cloth. "Chris sent this up, with his love," Robyn said. A piece of cut hair, about an inch long and enough to cover part of Jen's forehead, lay on the fabric. Robyn dug up the roll of clear tape, tore off a length and gingerly affixed the hair to it, then to her sister's brow. "Caro's got a dark brown scarf, make you look really pale. Not that you need it much."

"Yeah. Feel pale."

"This rag didn't come all the way clean; we'll wrap your arm in it."

"Carefully, all right?"

Robyn sat up, tilted her head to one side. "Sure. Quickly, though. I think we have company coming." She moved over to the window, put the curtain aside and glanced out. "Wow. Flash and dazzle uniforms and there must be twenty of them." She came back, sat on the other bed and looked at her sister anxiously. "They look awfully damned official. Kiddo, can you handle this?"

Jennifer sighed. "I don't have much choice now, do I?

See if you can't get a little of the soup down me before they come rousting in here, will you?"

10

✦

SHE could hear them down in the courtyard, a clatter of horses and plenty of metal harness. She concentrated on drinking soup, leaving Robyn to wad damp, flat hair back in a makeshift knot before wrapping the whole in a scarf, bandana style. Robyn fiddled with the taped hair on Jennifer's forehead, sat back to look at the effect and whistled. "Wow. That really changes you. Don't move around very much; I didn't have any way to pin your hair up, and it could fall down."

"Don't think I'll be moving very much." Jennifer handed her the soup mug and set her jaw. "Get that grubby-looking thing around my arm before I lose my nerve, will you?"

"Yeah." Robyn glanced nervously over her shoulder and began winding the long strip of fabric down her sister's arm. She tucked the ends under, pressed Jennifer's thumb over that and put the arm flat against her side. "I know I don't have to tell you not to move that, right?"

"Don't even—" Jennifer looked up as the door creaked; Dahven, plainly clad in brown roughspun breeches and shirt, a darker long vest, heavy boots much too large for him, came across the room to sit on the other bed. His hair was parted and flattened with water, tied across the ears with a dark band of fabric that looked like the one Colin wore. "What are you doing in here?" she hissed. "They're already here, they'll catch you!"

"Leave it," Robyn said tersely. "It was Chris's notion, those guys are bound to wonder why you had two rooms and all that damage, aren't they? Edrith is down talking to them right now. He's your cousin by marriage, Gemric, by the way—"

"I'll never remember that," Jennifer said and clutched at her hair. Robyn lightly slapped the hand away.

129

"Your cousin, you can remember that, can't you? This is your husband, he's a fairly prosperous farmer from the northern part of Andar Perigha, and you don't have to call him anything but sweetie, do you?"

"Oh, God, Birdy, this isn't going to work—"

"Of course it is. Take a deep breath, slow down. You've got a few minutes, Caro's delaying them as much as possible. You came south to see the Festival and to visit with the outlander running this inn; you'd heard there was one." Robyn looked down at her and nodded. "You can do it, you're good at this, remember? Didn't you tell me being a trial lawyer was half acting?"

"Yeah, but, I never got a chance to do it for real—!"

"You acted in high school. *I* can't do it, we all know that, you're stuck. Don't think about anything but these guys and the ones who jumped you, all right? Don't try anything fancy, just remember who you are, who this is. Don't sass the guards, they apparently don't like that."

"Don't mouth the cops," Jennifer said faintly.

"Don't bug the fuzz," Robyn replied and managed a grin. "Look, I'm gone, Caro's letting me hang out in one of the rooms at the end; Chris is keeping Aletto and Li company down in the larder. There's a thought, isn't it?" Robyn hesitated, bent swiftly and kissed Jennifer's cheek. "You can do it, kiddo. Go for it, all right?"

Dahven watched her go. Jennifer turned to look at him. "I'm not leaving you," he said, before she could say anything.

"They'll know you—"

"How?" he asked reasonably. "Chris and I talked it over. No one has any kind of likeness of me, none of the Emperor's guard is likely to have seen me in years. They'll see a peasant farmer in his clean best, a man worried about his outlander wife. Nothing more. More suspicious if I wasn't here, and Edrith looks much too young for you to have wed."

"I don't—" Jennifer began. A hard tap against the door sill interrupted her; a moment later, without invitation, three men in red and gold uniform were inside the room.

Arrogant wasn't the word for them, Jennifer later decided. They were also sharp, full of questions, suspicious. It made her extremely nervous, but it also settled her mind and she maintained the part Chris and Robyn had created for her. It wasn't difficult at all for her to appear weak and hurt. Dahven spoke only when addressed, and slowly, his words very basic and accented. He kept his eyes on her as much as possible, and radiated worry.

She had to credit Chris; it wouldn't have occurred to her anyone would wonder about three or four people having private rooms. Here it really did seem to be the exception rather than the rule for anyone to utilize them. She sighed, let her eyes close when the master guard asked her yet again. "I can't sleep around strangers, that's dangerous in my world. And—" she cast Dahven a very wan smile—"we only married a little while ago, we wanted privacy. His cousin—I could hardly ask him to sleep among all those strange men, and he'd drunk a lot of wine. I asked the innkeep if we could have a separate room for him." She turned the smile on the master guard and sighed faintly. "I didn't see anything wrong in it." They questioned her closely about the attack itself. "I was asleep, I don't really know much, and I found it hard to understand them. It's not my language, you know. I think they wanted someone else—someone called me Duchess."

"Duchess," one of the men repeated. He exchanged a glance with the others but didn't volunteer any information. "Any other names that you heard?"

For one moment, she half considered giving them Jadek's, or one of the twins' names, but decided not to try it. Better to let the guard think she knew nothing else; mention such names and they might decide she warranted more questioning and she didn't think she could dissemble indefinitely. And it made her terribly nervous, Dahven sitting right under their noses. "I'm sorry," she whispered. "It was all so quick, and then when I tried to get away, and the one man cut my arm—I can't remember anything else."

"Sirs, my wife is in pain," Dahven put in quietly.

"Yes. Of course." The men moved to the end of the beds, conferred in very low voices. Finally the master guard looked at both of them. "You still intend on the Festival?"

"We hope to," Jennifer said. "If we have enough money left."

"The innkeep told your cousin she'd pay for the local healer," the guard said. He glanced at Dahven. "The men who attacked you. Who used a blade against them?"

"I—" Dahven blinked. "I carry a knife, of course. I may have cut one or more, I don't recall."

"You served a term of guard?"

"Not yet."

"Your cousin has served?"

"No. The farm is new, we're both required to work it."

"I see." The master guard eyed him thoughtfully; Jennifer felt her stomach contract. But he finally nodded. "One of the dead bore a purse, much too fine a fabric to belong to one of his class; it held twenty silver ceris. Either he stole it, or it was paid him in exchange for an attack against an outlander woman and those with her." He was silent again, turned on Jennifer suddenly. "Have you heard the name Aletto?" She gazed up at him—she hoped blankly—and shook her head. "Lialla? Sin-Duchess Lialla?"

"I don't think—no," she said doubtfully. "Sin-Duchess. That might have been what someone said last night."

"You're a lone outlander?" She nodded. "We won't trouble you more, just now. If you remember anything else, send word to the city guard, the innkeep will know how to reach us." He folded his arms and drew himself up to full, impressive, height. "The Emperor does not permit such lawless behavior. It seems unlikely the men below initiated the attack—they ordinarily wouldn't leave the city walls, nor even the dock area, certainly not to travel half a day's hard ride to this inn. For simple robbery? It's ridiculous." He glared down at her. *Right*, Jennifer thought. *I agree, but that doesn't make it my fault I got jumped, does it?* She let her eyes close again, sighed faintly. Dahven's fingers trembled against her cheek. She heard the clomp of heavy feet across the floorboards, heard the door swing shut behind the guards. She forced one eye open; Dahven's finger slipped down to her lips and she nodded. It was an old trick, probably one they knew, too: Leave someone outside the door to listen.

"You're all right?" Dahven asked finally; he maintained the accent, she noticed.

"All right," she agreed. "I'd like something to drink, though. Water, tea—" Her eyes went to the door, and he nodded.

"I'll go, get something from the innkeep." He got to his feet, went to the door and pulled it open. He turned back, then. "No one," he said in a low voice. "Wait—" He vanished into the hall, came back a moment later. "Nor across in the other room. You still want—?"

"No." Jennifer shook her head, drew a shuddering breath

and held out her right hand. "Don't go, they don't need another look at you, and—I need you."

The smile he gave her had all the warmth and charm of the very first one, back in his father's tower and it went through her with the same warm shock. "I like being needed," he said, and came back across the room.

They heard men riding off some time later; Dahven wanted to look, Jennifer wouldn't let him. "I don't care if you'd normally be curious about them, if you were some dirt farmer. Please don't." She shifted cautiously; he finally nodded, shed Colin's enormous boots and edged past her so he could settle on top of the comfort on her right side. "If they're suspicious, I don't want to know yet; if not, if it's all right down there—we'll find out soon enough."

"Too soon, probably," Dahven grumbled, but he was smiling when he edged up onto one elbow. He touched her forehead lightly, brushed at the hair Robyn had taped there. "I prefer your real hair."

Jennifer managed a smile; she was terribly tired, all at once. "I owe Chris, you know what that must have cost him?"

"I was there when Robyn cut it. It didn't show much, she gave him a terrible time about it, but she was very careful when it came time to actually take any." He leaned forward, touched his lips against her cheek. "You're much too pale."

"I feel pale. I'm sorry, Dahven—"

"Why? Sleep some more, you need it."

"Not until we hear something from downstairs," Jennifer began. Quick, heavy footsteps in the hall silenced her; Dahven clutched her fingers anxiously. Chris and Edrith pushed into the room a moment later, though, and Jennifer could tell at once by the look on her nephew's face that they'd pulled it off.

Chris was laughing excitedly; his eyes were a little too bright. "Oh, man? They bought it, you know?"

"No. Tell me." Jennifer let Dahven edge her partway back up, let him and Edrith stuff several pillows behind her so she could hold her own cup and drink the leftover water Robyn had brought earlier.

Chris sat hard on the edge of the spare bed, ran a surreptitious hand over his eyes and under his nose. "Hey, you're the one who sold them, lady."

"They talked to the innkeep and her son," Edrith said. "And I thought they'd never be done asking me questions. I told them I have nightmares, loud ones, that was why I had the separate room and you two didn't want me in with you, even with the two beds. I guess that was all right. They finally gave up and went to work on Ernie, but he didn't know anything because he was full of sleeping stuff and he kept dozing off on them. They gave up on him, and I thought they were getting upset—they say that isn't good, city guard isn't like other guard and I explained about the broken leg, about the stuff he's taking to keep him quiet so it can heal. Some of them went off to poke around the common room and talk to anyone who was still about; some went on out to the horse barn to talk to prisoners and look over the bodies. And then the big fellow with all the officer markings on his jacket picked two of his followers and went up the stairs to talk to you: I don't think I even *breathed* until they came back down without either one of you." He looked across to Dahven. "They didn't recognize you?"

"How?" Dahven asked simply.

Chris shrugged. "I heard someone say there were descriptions of you, Aletto and Lialla. Not that you look much like you did the first time I met you, right now. Anyway, they finally came back down and I could hear them up in the kitchen, laying down the law to Caro about sending someone for them if you remembered anything, if other outlanders showed up, particularly if they were in the company of any member of the Rhadazi upper class. I'm glad I wasn't in on that, I was getting pissed at the guy's tone of voice, but Caro just took it and said she'd be glad to."

"This isn't a democracy, Chris," Jennifer said.

"Tell me it isn't."

"Keep that in mind, or you're going to get yourself in hot water."

"Yeah. Eddie'll have to keep me on a short leash in Podhru, I guess." Chris sighed. "Getting in might be a problem, though, you know? I can probably slide by with Eddie, if we're careful and I flatten my hair down, get back into those gruesome gray britches I had to buy in Bez."

"And keep your mouth shut," Edrith put in genially.

Chris sighed again. "Just reminding you."

"Jen, you can pass just like you are, and Dahven looks all right—well, not all right, but not like himself, which is all we need. Aletto, though—"

"The walls aren't any tighter than Sikkre's," Dahven said. "It won't be hard to get him in after dark, particularly if there's a place for him to hide."

"Supposed to be," Edrith said. "Gyrdan is meeting us—Lord Evany's, isn't it?"

Dahven considered this, finally nodded. "It seems a lifetime ago and I didn't give any of it much thought then. Now—I never met this Evany, I hope Gyr chose well."

"Aletto likes him," Chris put in. "Not that he's seen the guy in years, and I'm not totally sure he can pick people."

Dahven smiled. "I should resent that, but I take your point. He still operates on old memories and too much trust." The smile slipped. "But who'd have thought, that night in the Purple Fingers, how badly things would turn out?"

"Don't," Jennifer said firmly. She held the water cup out so Edrith could take it, caught hold of Dahven's hand with her freed fingers. "We've still come out ahead. Not as ahead as I'd have liked this time," she added as the three stared at her. "But we're all alive, three of them are dead. And we apparently convinced the Emperor's guard it was mistaken identity."

"Yeah," Chris said. "Maybe even got them wondering who's hiring thugs to attack outlanders who might be traveling with some guy named Aletto? Could that hurt?"

"Don't know," Jennifer said. She let her eyes close. "I think after all that, though, I'm going to take a nap. I've earned it."

"Earned," Chris said. He laughed suddenly; Jennifer looked at him as he got to his feet and dug inside his shirt. "Reminded me; lookit. When those guys left? They left this behind—it's part of the money one of those thugs had on him, it's to repay you for the healer to fix your arm, and for the rooms here until you're well enough to leave. If I hadn't heard that snotty-voiced guy talking to Caro about it, honestly, I'd never have believed it." He flipped the bag up and caught it; it jingled. "This is half. Mom was trying to argue with Caro about it, how she ought to take it all because of the damage and the hassle. You know how mom is. She lost, like she usually does, though. Caro took half a dozen ceris and jammed this down my shirt." He shrugged. "What could I do? I said thanks, like you're supposed to, she calmed down—and I guess that's it." Edrith tugged at his arm and got him moving toward the door. "Oh, and no one's really going to send for that old jerk that did Ernie's leg, so you don't have to worry about that, all right?''

"They'd better not," Jennifer warned him as he closed the door behind them. She heard Edrith's voice but couldn't make out the words; Chris laughed and she heard them running down the hall. "I can't stand it," she murmured. "All that energy, it's indecent." She turned her head, tugged at Dahven's shirt and kissed the corner of his mouth. "So is falling asleep on you but I don't think I have much choice."

He pressed the scarf back from her forehead. "Sleep. We'll have time."

"We'd better," she whispered. She wasn't certain he heard that. He settled down next to her, fingers twined in hers. His breathing slowed almost at once. She found it comforting, listening to him, feeling the slow, deep pulse where his hand rested against her throat. She shifted cautiously, easing her left arm against her side, wondered briefly if she could get the cloth off it. It was loose, lightweight and dry; still too much of a weight. *Leave it,* she decided finally. *It'll keep the afternoon breeze off the thing, that might feel worse. They might come back, too—* But that was nothing to think about right now. *Think about something nice,* she ordered herself. *Something pleasant.* She smiled, settled her face against Dahven's. *Or someone.*

It was two days before she could stand on her own, another before she managed to make it down the back stairs to Caro Ellaway's sitting room. Once there, she sank gratefully into the large chair piled with cushions Caro had set up for her. Dahven got her settled before he went in search of Aletto and Jennifer suddenly realized she'd seen neither the nera-Duke nor his sister since the attack. Robyn wasn't anywhere in sight either, though she'd been in and out of the room Jennifer and Dahven had taken by default—with food and water, with gossip Caro picked up in the common room and passed on.

She felt weak, half sick from the effort it had taken to get herself down the flight of stairs. Nervous. *God, if I've totally lost my nerve,* she thought. *I can't. Even if the Emperor stepped in right now, I can't believe it would mean the end of the danger to Aletto. Or to Dahven.* But just now, she couldn't imagine herself picking up a weapon and using it on anyone, not even to defend herself. She managed a smile for Caro, who brought her toast and a cup of herb tea. "I'm so sorry for all the trouble," she began. The Englishwoman shook her head.

"How were you to know someone would actually try to murder you under my roof?"

"I should have—"

"Nonsense," the other woman said warmly. "Drink your tea while it's still hot, get some of that bread down you. Your young man looks much better," she added. It was a clear change of subject. Jennifer let the matter drop, obediently sipped tea. "He looked dreadful that night—mostly worry for you, I daresay."

"He was ill in Bez," Jennifer admitted.

"I don't doubt that. Well, he's spent enough of his time with you that he's caught up on sleep, that'll help." She glanced out toward the horse barn. "Your sister's out there, seeing to the horses, she and Chris took young Ernie with them."

"He's not walking on that leg—" Jennifer began. She shook her head then. "Never mind. I forget this isn't home, he'd be off it for months there."

"I still forget," Caro said. "Now and again. Gives me a jolt; you'd think all these years would be enough for me to fully adjust. The other boy—he's a little older than that, though, isn't he? He and the Wielder are staying upstairs, in the private room. Out of sight. In case, you know."

"I know." Jennifer set the cup aside, nibbled at a piece of toast. It was cold and dry, and she suffered a momentary pang: hot toast, smeared with melted butter and jam. "How is he taking the delay, or have you talked to him?"

"A little. He's not saying much, neither of them is. He's not dealing at all well with your injury."

Jennifer sighed. "I'd better talk to him. Maybe we can go on in another day or so—"

"Oh," Caro said as she refilled Jennifer's cup and set a small pot of honey next to it, "it's not the delay. Hard as your young man's had it, you being cut up like that, the other boy's taking it worse."

When Dahven came back, Jennifer edged herself out of the chair and to her feet unaided, though she scattered cushions all around. She needed both hands on the table to hold herself steady, at least until she'd taken several deep breaths. "No, don't," she said as he came forward. "Let me, I have to know how far off I still am, don't I?" She turned to the innkeep, who was also hovering anxiously, and managed to balance on one hand, so she could hold out the other. "Caro, I'll be back down for dinner—I think I will," she qualified.

"At least you're honest," the woman said doubtfully. "You have enough brain to know not to push, I won't fuss at you."

"Good. All right, Dahven," she added, and pivoted carefully. "Take me back up." Once they were outside, she drew him to a halt against the warm wall, let her head fall back and her eyes close. "The sun feels absolutely wonderful. Maybe I'll come sit out here tomorrow morning, before it gets too hot. Right now I'd better get flat again." She was quiet while they climbed the stairs, but once they reached the repaired door to the private room she stopped. "I'd like to talk to Aletto."

"I'll bring him, once you're settled."

"No. I'm all right, and this will be better anyway." Dahven gave her a sidelong look, but he didn't argue for once, merely tapped at the door and waited for the sound of the bolt being drawn. Lialla stared at them expressionlessly, stepped back from the door and closed it behind them.

Aletto sat on the room's only chair—a long bench that had been fastened to the wall under the window. He glanced at his visitors, turned back to stare out the window. Jennifer caught hold of the footboard of the nearest bed, eased away from Dahven's arm and let herself down. There was a long, not particularly comfortable silence. "Are you all right?" Aletto asked finally. He wouldn't look at her.

"I'm better," Jennifer said honestly. "I'll be fine, it's just taking longer than I'd have thought. I'm sorry to have delayed you; if that's worrying you, you should go on perhaps. Dahven can—"

"Gods of my fathers," Aletto said softly. He slammed one fist against the windowledge and spun around. "You could have died!" Lialla, a shadow in the corner, made a faint, protesting little sound, and her brother shook his head. "I'm sorry, Li; it's true, she could have died before you got to her. I—" He turned back to the window and drove both hands through his hair, let his face down into them. "When we talked that night in Duke's Fort, Li, remember? It seemed so simple, didn't it? For the first time in a long time I could see everything clearly. I should have made you go,

I should never have listened when you persuaded me to come with you.''

"Where would I have gone without you?'' Lialla replied. Her voice was dry and tremulous, as though she'd been crying. "To Shesseran? To the Thukar? Aletto, Jadek would have killed you if I'd gone!''

"That was only my life,'' Aletto mumbled.

"Please,'' Jennifer said quietly. "Don't, either of you. I'm not up to this and you're just making yourselves miserable. Aletto, damnit, it isn't your fault this happened.'' She held out her left arm. Aletto glanced at it, at the long, darkly red line that ran up from her wrist and vanished under the neatly mended tee-shirt sleeve. He shuddered, let his eyes close. "Look, I think I can follow the argument, I've heard enough variations on it over the years. You have the right to run your own life but not to jeopardize anyone else's, isn't that it? Aletto, you're a Duke's son. Your father made decisions probably every day of his life that at least altered other peoples' lives. As for me—who knows? If Merrida hadn't dragged us here, maybe I'd have been run over in a crosswalk, or shot from a passing car, or murdered by someone breaking into my apartment. And no one made me stay with you, did they? It might not have been easy, but I could have walked away from Merrida back in Zelharri. I could have stayed in Sikkre, or in Bez. I gathered what I could of your side of the argument, Merrida's, Lialla's—even your uncle's, if you recall. I *chose* your side, Aletto.'' He glanced at her, looked away again. "Don't tear yourself apart like this, I knew the risks. I chose to accept them.'' Silence. Jennifer sighed, pushed herself one-armed to her feet and held onto the footboard. "We all did. Look, if you're examining your motives, that's fine. Don't back out now, though, if you're only doing it because of anyone else. Personally, I feel like I have an interest in seeing your uncle out of Duke's Fort at this point. And I'm going to be a little irked if you take that away from me because you're afraid I'll get hurt.''

Silence again. Dahven came across and wrapped an arm around her waist, got her as far as the door when Aletto sat up and pounded a fist against the windowsill once more—not as hard, this time. "It's that,'' he said finally. "It's more, too. They had archers out in the courtyard—''

"I remember now. Robyn knows that, doesn't she?'' He nodded. "What did she have to say?''

"I don't know; we haven't talked about it."

"Talk about it. She might surprise you. Don't sell her short, though, Aletto. Birdy's tougher than she looks, sometimes. And she feels pretty strongly about seeing you back where you belong."

"I know," he whispered.

"Well, then. They shifted the odds, turned violent on us when we weren't ready. Next time, we will be." *God*, she thought in sudden despair, *if he knew how I really felt, right now.* "And think about this: The city guard knows that someone's paying and arming men in an attempt to kill you."

"Jadek wouldn't be stupid enough to let something like that be traced back to him," Lialla said harshly.

"No? He's getting frustrated, and when people get like that, they sometimes make dumb mistakes. But the guards I talked to aren't dumb; even if they can't get names and information out of the prisoners they took back with them, they're going to be able to add things up." Silence. Jennifer let Dahven prop her against the wall while he got the door open; she concentrated on keeping her knees from buckling until he could get a supporting arm around her again. "Don't sit in here feeling guilty, or feeling sorry for yourself," she said finally. "I'm responsible for myself; that's whether I'm helping you or on my own somewhere. We all are; don't insult our intelligence by presuming anything else. Why don't you do something worthwhile instead? Figure out how to let young Enardi down once we get into Podhru, so he doesn't feel completely useless when we leave him behind."

"If we go on," Aletto said, but he didn't sound as ghastly as he had when she first came into the room.

Lialla followed them into the hall, one hand holding the door closed behind her. Jennifer managed a wan smile. "I never got a chance to thank you for what you did—"

"It wasn't enough, though, was it? I—felt you Wielding, later."

"It wasn't complete. It was enough, you dealt with the worst of it. Without that, I really might have bled to death; I certainly wouldn't have been able to finish what you started."

"I should have—" Lialla turned on her heel and went back into the room, closing the door behind her. The bolt slid across a moment later.

Dahven got her across the hallway and into the second

room. The last few steps to the bed seemed to take forever; Jennifer sat hard, sagged over her knees. "That wasn't fun," she managed finally. "And I was afraid she'd know I'd had to do a patch job on her work, that she'd take it like that."

"It's not your problem," Dahven said indignantly.

"No. Not entirely." She sighed and eased down onto her back, let Dahven smooth the comfort over her knees. "All the same, I've done a lot to get that woman's confidence up, and I hate to think I destroyed all that good work overnight." She flexed her fingers. "God. I think it's finally quit hurting when I do that."

"If it hurts, don't do it," he began.

Jennifer laughed faintly. "And you a swordsman! You follow your own advice, all the time, right?"

He bent down to touch her cheek. "I'm reminded by that; I promised Chris an exchange of lessons."

"Lord," Jennifer said devoutly. "He'll cut himself, he always does."

"He won't. He doesn't get anything sharp to swing at *me* until he learns the basic moves. Here, I've set the water where you can reach it. Want me to pour some for you?" She nodded. "I'll come back to see if you still feel like going down for evening meal."

"I will," she said.

He laughed. "You sound it."

"I will. Go, before Chris comes in here and starts saying smart things."

11

T HE third night after the attack, Jennifer came down for dinner with everyone else. Caro fussed over her good-naturedly on her way through to the common room with a pot of stewed chicken, sent Colin back to feed all of them. Aletto finished his in record time, ignored the cup of wine at his elbow, and cleared his throat. "I want to settle things, now, tonight." Lialla set her cup aside and leaned past Chris to look at him anxiously. Aletto ignored her. Robyn took hold of his fingers and he squeezed hers before releasing them. There was a rather uncomfortable silence. Aletto fetched a sigh. "About going on. After this last attack, I don't feel I have the right to simply assume anyone goes with me." He looked around the room, then fixed his eyes on the table in front of him. "In all honesty, at this moment, I can't be certain I have the courage to continue."

"You can't just quit," Lialla urged him in a low, desperate voice. "You can't! Do you think it would make any difference to our uncle? After all this time?" Silence. Aletto continued to gaze at the table before him. Lialla leaped to her feet and came around to lay a hand on his arm. "Aletto, what would you do? Where would you go?"

He shrugged, spread his hands. "I don't know. If I went far enough—"

"Where? Outside Rhadaz? He can't let you live anywhere within her borders, you know that!"

"Your sister's right," Jennifer said.

"I don't know that I intend to give in," Aletto said softly.

"*You* can't stop him alone," Robyn said. She sounded near tears. Aletto shook his head.

"Perhaps I can. Perhaps if I spoke with him, face to face. Perhaps he would see reason—"

"You don't believe that," Lialla protested faintly. "He'd never hear you. He'd simply lock you away, or kill you, you *know* that!"

"I don't. He's lost face and he resents that. But that doesn't necessarily mean there's no way but confrontation, or violence, to win, does it? Even so, that's only my life, if I'm wrong, or if he takes me. Now—" He looked around the room again. "We had luck, the other night. Even so, those men were dockside thugs, the sort who'd murder anyone—all of us—without compunction." Aletto sighed heavily. "Don't you understand what I'm trying to say? It was hard enough, accepting that you'd come with me, Lialla, knowing that any violence our uncle aimed at me might take you also."

Lialla snorted. "It was *my* decision, *my* choice! Do you forget what he did—?"

"Do you think it made anything better, running from him?"

"Yes!" Lialla shouted. She glanced over her shoulder

toward the common room door and lowered her voice. "Aletto, by every god there is, are you forgetting Carolan?"

"Hey, Lialla," Chris said disgustedly. "Chill out, all right? Let him yap, maybe he'll just run down after a while if you don't keep feeding him lines. The dude's on a guilt trip, he's forgetting everything including his brains. If he still has any." Aletto slewed around, his eyes narrowed. Chris jumped to his feet and came around the table, sent Aletto's empty plate flying, and leaned back against the table. Robyn swore in a low voice, grabbed the heavy dish before it hit the floor and called her son a rude name. He ignored her, and so did Aletto. "Jeez," Chris said even more disgustedly. "No, don't start on me, I'm not your sister or your girlfriend, all right? I've put up with enough of this Hamlet act the past couple-three days, it's totally boring." He folded his arms, glared Robyn into silence when she would have spoken, waited until he was certain Aletto wasn't going to say anything. "You know," he said finally, and in a much milder tone, "for a guy who's got great potential, you can be so damned dumb."

"Chris," Robyn protested.

"Chill out, ma, all right?"

"I don't think I have to take this from you," Aletto said evenly.

"Just bet you don't," Chris replied. "Look. There are some things that you start and you don't—*not* finish them. Like walking a rope across a canyon, you can't get halfway across, say, 'Oops, not what I wanted to do after all,' and just step off the damned thing! Not only is that what you're trying to do, you're trying to tell the rest of us to jump, too. Li's right; if your uncle had those goons hired to take us on here, then he's way beyond reason. He's not only lost face, he's past quitting anywhere short of taking you out. That's killing you, dead, in case you don't understand plain language."

"That doesn't follow," Lialla began.

"Oh, hell. It sure does. Those guards weren't too pleased about the whole mess here, were they? I could tell that; they don't expect this kind of stuff, they have laws against it, and people can't get away with mayhem. Your Emperor obviously draws the line at murder—I'm glad, you know? After everything we've gone through, I was frankly beginning to wonder if there *was* a line. But the thing is, Jadek has absolutely nothing to lose and everything to gain by taking us *all* out—before we decide it's getting too rough and we should rat on him. Or before the guard decides to pull us in and get information out of us, and I'd be willing to bet they don't take it easy on witnesses or victims they think are holding out on them. You really think if you just go home and say, 'Whoa, guy, bad joke, I quit, okay?' that he'd pat you on the head and—''

"Of course not!" Aletto said angrily. Both his hands were wrapped around the edge of the table and the knuckles were white.

"Or that he'd let the rest of us be? When every last one of us has bumped heads with his guys at least once? When any one of us could drop a dime on him—inform on him? Dumb, guy, really dumb!" Chris said. Aletto glared at him. "Look. You want to take a poll? Fine. I for one am thoroughly pissed, this dude Jadek has tugged on my chain once too often. Personally I intend to be there when someone pulls his card, and I wouldn't mind right now if it was me. In fact, way I feel at this moment, I'd prefer it."

"Chris," Robyn said faintly. He ignored her, and after a moment she turned from him to reach for Aletto's hands. "I'm not leaving you," she said flatly. "Or letting you go on without me. I'm afraid, I'll admit that. I'd be afraid anyway, wherever I was. I'd be more afraid without you, for you and for me, and you know I wouldn't be safer anywhere else, away from you." She looked up at Lialla, who shrugged.

"I knew it wouldn't be pleasant or easy when we left Duke's Fort. Aletto—don't *ever* suggest that to me again. Ever."

"I agree," Edrith said. 'I didn't have to leave Sikkre. I did, I'm here, and I'm not going back with things half settled. I'm not backing out on you, either."

Dahven laughed. "Aletto, you're not trying to back out on *our* agreement, are you? I can't deal with my brothers on my own, you know. Keep in mind, though, it might have been my kin who hired those men, not yours." He shook his head and the laughter faded out of his eyes. "We have a bargain, we shook on it just outside Bez, and I believe my advocate witnessed that, didn't you?" he added lightly as he touched Jennifer's arm.

Jennifer was silent. Dahven looked at her for a long moment; the smile left his face and his hand dropped away from her. "You know, Aletto," she said finally, "I am so angry right now, I don't know if I can speak straight. I don't know which I resent more: that you don't seem to have paid the least attention to anything I said this afternoon, or that you seem to think we're all a pack of feeble, witless—where do you get off?'' she demanded furiously. ''There isn't one of us here, Birdy included, who can't take care of him or herself! Who can't make a decision, and hasn't already done so! You think we're so brain-dead we'd have to wait for you to tell us it's dangerous and we should go away?'' She paused. Aletto stared at her, jaw sagging. She leveled a finger at him. ''One—more—word! Like that crap you just laid on us! Ever! And I'll personally flatten you!'' She paused again; Aletto was clearly stunned past words. ''Chris is right, so is your sister. You made a decision, the kind that you can't back out of without lethal repercussions. Not just for you, for everyone connected with you. I think we *do* need to talk. But that's talk, work out what we're going to do next. How we're going to get into Podhru, what happens there, where we go from there. How we get into Duke's Fort, for that matter, without mayhem and murder along the way. I think we've had enough breast-beating.'' She shook her head. ''Damnit, I was the one who took the spear and lost the blood—because I was outnumbered and stupid both, by the way, not because I can't take care of myself. I *can* take care of myself, and damnit, *I'm* not ready to quit! I agree with Chris, I want to be there when your uncle gets taken down, however you eventually deal with him. I want to be part of it, whatever happens. Don't you dare think you're taking that from me, after all this time.'' Silence. ''And just as one final matter,'' she added in an only slightly milder tone, ''don't you dare try anything like that on your sister again, either. She's too nice a woman to tell you so, but I'm not. She's risked her life for you, just smuggling you out of Duke's Fort. You've got some nerve trying to just cancel all of that out by quitting.''

''I—'' Aletto got that much out, fell silent. He toyed with the wine cup, finally pushed it away. ''I'm sorry—''

''Don't do that,'' Chris said in exasperation.

''Sorry for bringing it up at all. I won't again, if that's how you all feel.'' He glanced around the room, managed a faint, rueful smile. ''Thank you.''

The outburst put a damper on the rest of the early evening. Aletto finally took Robyn when it got dark and went for a long walk. When they returned, the tension had eased, and Aletto himself looked less embarrassed. Chris helped; he'd been trying to teach Lialla checkers with Caro's handmade board and after a silent, stiff beginning to the first game, he reduced her to giggles half a dozen times with his running commentary and outrageous attempts at cheating. Jennifer finally took up a position behind the sin-Duchess's shoulder and started coaching her; Chris deliberately upended the board when he had only one piece left. "Earthquake! Game called on account of earthquake!" Lialla scooped up a handful of checkers and tossed them at him; when Aletto came over to see what was going on, she dropped one down the back of his shirt.

"It's one of *their* games," she told him after Robyn retrieved the wooden piece. "Don't let them talk you into it, it's maddening."

"Yeah," Chris retorted. "Wait'll I put together a Monopoly board. It's not only maddening, it takes *hours*."

Jennifer laughed. "If I catch you making Monopoly, Chris, it'll be game called on account of mangled kid."

"Hey, just because I always creamed *you* at it," he replied cheerfully. "I thought all you lawyers were money-grubbing capitalists, you know? So, anyway," he added generally, pivoting on one heel to take in the entire room. "When is Gyrdan expecting us in Podhru—like, how much longer before he starts figuring we aren't going to show?"

Aletto shrugged and considered this. "I don't know. There wasn't any fixed day for us to meet; he intended to search out Father's men who would go back to Zelharri with me. We're to meet at Lord Evany's, remember?" Chris nodded. "I should think that Gyr keeps touch with Evany."

"Logical," Chris agreed. Robyn smiled at him, visibly relieved that he wasn't picking up the quarrel once more, and dropped back into her chair. Not, Jennifer thought, that he was likely to, so long as Aletto didn't pick up his earlier plaint again: Chris usually blew once, hard, and that was it. "Now. As far as getting all of us into the City. Jen, you kept my Samson locks, right?"

"The cut bit of hair? I intend to frame it," she replied seriously. Chris tossed her a startled glance, then laughed.

"Bit? Felt like half the stuff off my neck, I can feel the breeze back there, you know?"

"Poor Chris. It's *really* obvious."

"Yeah, why don't you write a poem: *Ode to a Sacrifice*?"

"Poetry's your line, kid. Yeah, I kept the fake bangs. Figured the city guard might just be keeping an eye out for us, after all the excitement out here. And I told them we still wanted to come into Podhru. They might get suspicious if we didn't, especially after they left behind money to cover our unexpected expenses. They looked like the kind of guys that might keep track of things like that, too."

"That's three of you—four of you, then," Chris said. "You and Dahven, Ernie and Eddie, right? Because they think Ernie's with you, right? And the wagon. Rest of us— mom and I and Li should be able to manage, my hair's long enough right now it doesn't spike too well, and I bet I can plaster it down with your hand lotion or something and tie a band around it, wear local clothes—yeah, I know, and keep my big mouth shut." He looked over at Robyn. "Mom, there's enough blondes around you don't stand out that much, especially when you wear that long black thing."

"I have the new dress from Bez."

"Better yet. Let Li do something with your hair."

"Which just leaves us two," Lialla said with a sidelong look in Aletto's direction.

"Leaves Aletto," Chris said. "In that thing you're wearing, with your hair back like that, I swear you could pass for my kid sister, you know?"

"Thanks," Lialla said and she gave him a genuinely pleased smile. "I should stick with Aletto, though. How do we get *him* past the guard? They aren't supposed to keep a tight check on the gates—I doubt we constitute a large enough emergency, the attack here or just me and Aletto— that there would be a gate guard. But they'll be all over the city. And Aletto's—pretty visible."

"Not as much as he was back in Sikkre, though. I don't know, Li. You *could* stay with Aletto," Chris said. "I'm thinking, though, that if Mom had on that thing she got in Bez, and she stayed with him—I mean, think about it. Anyone who has his description has yours; the two of you together, both about the same size and all—someone might put it together and realize who you are. They might not expect him to be half of a pair that one of looks like a prosperous Bezanti merchant."

"I didn't think of that," Lialla said slowly. "But—"

"I—um," Enardi put in diffidently. "I have an idea. If I

went in first? I could find my sister, some of the others who came here by ship. Bring them back out with me? A real wagonful of people, going out for a picnic. You see, if there were enough of us going out, who would ever notice there were one or two more coming back in?'' He looked anxiously from Aletto to Chris, to Edrith and back again. ''You have Bez-cut clothing, haven't you? So, who would even wonder?''

''That's good, that's very good,'' Chris applauded silently. Enardi flushed, turned his attention back to Aletto, who frowned in concentration. The nera-Duke finally nodded.

''It's a good thought, and it could work. If you were caught, though—''

''Oh, well,'' Enardi said rather casually. Jennifer bent down to hide a smile. He sounded very much like Chris at the moment. ''The city guard *will* be everywhere, particularly with the Emperor's Festival so near and so many people in the streets. I've often been in Podhru before, though, so I know what the guards and the streets are like. But the city guard doesn't ordinarily bother people who are minding their own business and behaving themselves. In normal circumstances they'd never search a wagonload of Bezanti merchants.''

''If they saw someone or something suspicious, if they caught me in your company,'' Aletto said tentatively. Enardi shook his head.

''They would probably take you, if they somehow found out who you were. They would do that anyway, wouldn't they?''

Aletto waved that aside. ''But you—''

''Oh.'' Enardi considered this, finally shook his head again. ''No, I don't think they would do more than caution me, and really, against what? Carrying other Bezanti around Podhru? If told them that was what I thought you were, you see—and if you were clad as a Bezanti and had said you were . . . After all, I couldn't know better, could I? Even my *father* doesn't know everyone in Bez. If I said you'd told me you were so-and-so's son or cousin from another part of Bez, they wouldn't find it odd. I'd believe it.'' Aletto continued to look at him unhappily, and Enardi shook his head once more. ''I see your point. But the guard doesn't—not everyone—Chris, you tell him, I don't think it's making sense.''

"It's all that stuff the old man put on your leg, got into your brains," Chris said equably. He turned to Aletto. "I think what he's trying to say is that most people haven't been living the good life like we have—hiding from everyone in the world, and for good reason because they really are out to kill us. People ordinarily aren't suspicious of everything, the way we have to be. That about it, Ernie?" The Bezanti nodded. "Even these city cops—okay, if we slunk in looking dicey, they'd probably grab us just because they're paid to do that, and to be suspicious. But unless they're really fascist about it, they aren't likely to harass ordinary-looking kids like Ernie who are doing ordinary things, not causing trouble or anything. Offhand, I'd be willing to bet that in a well-behaved town like Colin says Podhru is, the guard don't ordinarily suspect everyone of furtive and nasty motives, because they never see that kind of thing."

"Fascist?" Enardi asked.

"Tell you later. Anyway, that's what you meant, right?"

"That was it. People like me don't ordinarily expect that a companion isn't what he says. So why would we doubt you, and why would the guard doubt us? Normally, I mean? Besides, no one ever bothers people like me in Podhru," Enardi went on. "My father's wealthy."

Robyn laughed. "He's right, Aletto; unless people are *really* different here, no one's going to risk offending old money. You'd probably be safer with them than with anyone else."

"You, though," he said rather anxiously.

Robyn shrugged. "Chris may be right, about how we should pair up. But we'll sort it out, maybe once we get close, it'll be easier to figure what to do. Does anyone know where we find this Evany?"

"I have the street name," Aletto said doubtfully. "And Gyr said he's in the old section, north of the civil buildings."

Robyn pulled out a chair and dropped into it. She picked up the wine cup Aletto had left earlier, frowned at it, set it aside, got back to her feet and touched Aletto's cheek. "Look, I gotta crash, it's been a long day and that walk did me in." He nodded, brought her fingers to his lips and let them go. Robyn slowed as she passed Jennifer, bent down to mutter, "Actually, I just think I'd better get away from

149

that wine. You wouldn't happen to have a stick of gum, would you? Anything to put a different taste in my mouth?''

Jennifer shook her head. ''Sorry, Birdy. Wait, though— Caro has some mint in a pot. Just outside the door, I think, I smelled it when I came downstairs.''

Robyn wrinkled her nose, finally nodded. ''Yeah, anything. Just outside, huh? I'll look for it. God.'' She glanced wistfully at the wine cup, turned away from it. ''God, right now, I'd—This is getting ugly.''

''I—oh, Robyn. I won't say I know.''

''No, I don't think you do. Don't say sorry, either, all right?''

''What was all that about?'' Dahven asked as Robyn left.

''Mmm? Oh.'' Jennifer caught hold of his hand and leaned into it. ''Frustration, mostly.'' She smiled up at him. ''You know anything about that?''

''A little,'' he admitted cheerfully. ''Not as much as I would if things weren't *quite* so active around us, though.''

She tugged at his arm and murmured against his ear, ''Wait until I feel better.'' He laughed, very quietly.

''Wait until I do.''

Lialla was already gone and so was Edrith; Colin had gone back into the common room. Jennifer yawned and let Dahven pull her to her feet as Chris closed the short distance between them and shook his head. ''Hey, lady,'' he said very quietly. ''You two mind sticking around for a few minutes? I think Ernie's gonna need a little support, you know?''

''I don't—oh.'' Jennifer nodded. Enardi had set his jaw and was studying Aletto, who was tracing patterns on the edge of the table and clearly considering the problem of getting them safely into—and through—the Emperor's city.

The Bezanti shook himself, nodded and cleared his throat. ''Um—sir? Aletto? I need to speak to you—if you don't mind.''

It was probably one thing more than Aletto needed on such a night. But he handled the matter with understanding and tact, reminding Jennifer of the morning they'd found Chris on the road south to Bez, and a tired, nervous and worried Aletto still managed to create a very positive impression on the merchants who'd rescued her nephew from his kidnappers. *Poor Aletto*, Jennifer thought. *I wonder if it'll ever come naturally to him, or if he's always going to have that nagging suspicion that he's faking everyone?*

Enardi was nervously plaiting his fingers. "It's—sir, I can't go any farther with you. I thought—when we left Bez, I never thought—" He shook his head, somehow forced his hands to be still, though he still looked very strained. "I'm not any use, sir. I see you all, doing what you've done against men and shades and—and I can't do any of that. I'm just—I'm simply terrified, it makes me ill. I'm very sorry," he finished in a low voice.

"You don't need to be sorry," Aletto said quietly. "You heard what I said—all that arguing, earlier. Of all of us, I should have best known my uncle, what he might do. I'd spent enough time thinking of little else, those last months in Duke's Fort—when I wasn't drinking," he added. Enardi glanced at him and looked uncomfortable; Aletto waved a hand when the boy would have spoken. "Never mind, that isn't important. If I'd known—if any of us had known what to expect ahead of time, perhaps none of us would be here. If anyone had told me I'd be able to stand on my feet and face armed men, be able to fight them, I'd have laughed. That kind of nerve—in my case, it simply happened when I needed it. Because I haven't really had the opportunity to think about it, maybe. I doubt anyone has it simply for wanting it. Maybe in my case it was there because it's my need, my Dukedom." He paused to consider this, shrugged. "*Not* having it doesn't make you less of a person, or a man, than I am, though. What I've done since leaving Sikkre isn't a talent, or anything to envy, it's merely the ability to stop thinking and try to kill before you're killed. If you think otherwise, consider those who fight us, the Sikkreni who came after us, the men who attacked this inn. Men paid to fight and kill: armsmen who should be trained to keep order or defend Rhadaz against outside attack, men who instead tried to kill the Thukar's true heir, to murder all of us. And the others—common dock thugs. Enardi, anyone with no imagination or sense of right can kill another. Anyone who has no honor for human life can utilize magic to kill, the way my uncle has."

"I still—" Enardi began hesitantly. He fell silent when Aletto waved his hand again.

"No. Listen, please. When you asked to come with us, I agreed—not because I thought there was danger and we'd need another fighter; not as part of a personal guard for me or my sister. Believe me, if I'd properly thought matters out, I'd never have agreed to your presence, I'd have suggested you return to Bez—but only so you could take a ship and safely meet us in Podhru. Because I do have a purpose for your presence here.''

He was quiet until Enardi looked up. ''Sir?''

''Your father and men like him have no personal interests outside Bezjeriad, I know that; I accept that they will give me only financial aid. Just as your sister Biyallan and people like her haven't money of their own yet, but are willing to give me themselves, their talents, their skills in Sehfi, once Zelharri is mine.

''I need more, though: I need someone who knows these people, who can tell me whom to trust. Which of those who come now to join me will work hard, which of them is only along for a chance at quick profit. Someone who can help sort through the welter of possibilities for the Zelharri marketplace, who can deal with the paperwork and politics here in Podhru, who understands money, people—'' Aletto spread his hands wide. ''I know less about these things than I do about—about the Emperor's latest religion, or about women's fashion.''

Enardi was staring at him, open-mouthed. He pulled himself together with a visible effort. ''And you think I—? Sir, you scarcely know me! You don't know—I've never—!''

''I listened to you in Fedthyr's house, don't you remember? When you and Chris brought friends to that party the first night? And I remember a long conversation between you, your sister and your father during the gathering later, when he and several of those who knew my father met to agree upon financial backing. You possibly haven't had much opportunity in Bez to utilize your knowledge, since your father is still very much in control of his trading house. All the same, I believe you have that talent.'' Silence. He looked up to find Enardi still staring at him, and now looking nervous. ''Understand this: I'm not simply trying to let you down. I have a very real need for someone I can trust in Podhru, someone who isn't simply looking for profit to be channeled back from Zelharri to another duchy. I know the Sehfi market is in terrible condition, but I don't know what to do about it. You do.'' He smiled—his politician's smile, Jennifer thought; but Enardi was caught now, and he smiled back. ''And I hope you won't refuse me. I need you, Enardi.''

"I—well, then." Enardi spread his hands wide and sighed. "I won't refuse you, sir. I hope I won't fail you."

"You won't," Aletto said.

They left the inn two mornings later, Jennifer bundled into an old dress of Caro Ellaway's and her brown scarf, her left arm resting in a physically unnecessary but visually useful dark sling, Chris's hair plastered to her forehead under a new piece of tape. The tape itched; her shoulder still itched, and she was cross because of the early hour, too nervous to have eaten anything before they left. Robyn had promised to search out the bag with her coffee supplies and had forgotten about it until too late; Jennifer had to stay completely away from her sister until the irritation wore off.

If Jennifer was unrecognizable, Robyn was nearly so: She wore the dress Aletto had bought for her in Bez, mauve like the one Enardi's sister had lent her but of a heavier fabric, more suitable for public wear. It was wider in the skirts, too, making it easier for Robyn to ride in it without the material rucking up around her legs. She wore a pair of lightweight slippers, not very suitable for horseback, but Chris wouldn't let her keep her sneakers on even partway to the city gates, and he'd packed them in the bottom of the Nike bag, which in turn had been wound in two silkcloth blankets and buried under a pile of things beneath the wagon seat. Robyn's long, straight, center-parted hair, normally one of her most visible features, had been pulled back off her forehead to the top of her head and worked into three looped braids. It looked darker and it changed the line of her face with her full brow and her ears visible.

Aletto had a shirt and overshirt purchased for him in Bez, which he wore under Enardi's short cloak—a garment visibly, expensively Bezanti. The britches were very plain and ordinary, the tattered hems hidden inside his boots. The cloak covered the difference in his shoulders, though that was far less noticeable than it had been when Jennifer had first met the nera-Duke weeks before.

Chris's high-tops and jeans were buried in the bottom of the Nike bag; he wore instead the things they'd bought for him in Sikkre—and Enardi's boots, since he had no shoes but the high-tops, and Enardi was settled into the driver's seat, bare feet tucked under a pile of blankets. Like Robyn,

Chris had changed his hair: He'd rinsed it in cold sage tea at Caro Ellaway's suggestion, and that had darkened it from blond to a dull, ashy brown; he'd then used some of Jennifer's dwindling supply of hand lotion to plaster the top of it flat, side-parting it and tying the long nape stuff back the way Colin did his. A borrowed band tied below his left ear completed the change. His beard was coming in light and uneven but it was enough to alter the line of his jaw. Jennifer hadn't recognized him at all when she first saw him, until he came close. The walk was unmistakable, even though the too-small boots pinched his feet and took some of the swing out of his step. Horseback—no one would know him.

Dahven dressed again as he had when the guard came out to the inn, and he sat on the wagon seat next to Jennifer. Edrith, who like Enardi hadn't needed to do anything about his appearance, sat just behind her on a stack of bags and rugs.

Lialla, after considerable argument, had taken Chris's suggestion; she'd shed the Wielder Blacks and, dressed in a bright blouse and the wide breeches, her hair pulled back in a ribbon-trimmed plait, rode at his side. She really did look like she might be his sister—certainly no more than a year or so older than Chris, if not his twin—and as they rode along the broad, well-paved and tree-lined road toward the city gates, Chris had her laughing and kidding him right back.

Colin had come with them, a pile of his mother's bags and baskets in the back of the wagon—partly, as he said, because he needed to replenish certain things anyway; partly to help with the overall innocent appearance of their party, if necessary. And so he could reclaim his clothing and his mother's, once they all reached Lord Evany's and were off the streets.

Jennifer tried to put everything else—including a still near-overwhelming desire for a cup of hot, strong coffee—out of her mind as they neared Podhru. *Remember who you are, what you are,* she told herself for what was surely the twentieth time. *Who he is.* Dahven—*my farmer husband,* she reminded herself—had an arm around her shoulders; he squeezed briefly as he felt her tense up. She gave him a smile, leaned into his arm and let her eyes close for a moment.

They stopped a ways on, several miles from the inn but still short of the now visible city wall and its east gate.

Aletto and Robyn drew off to one side, Robyn dismounting so she could take the bundle Enardi put in her hands. Colin jumped down from the wagon and indicated a knoll just north of the road. "It's a good place to picnic; people often do. Particularly when it's not overly warm like this morning."

Enardi leaned over the side of the wagon. "I'll come back as quickly as I can. Don't any of you go from this place, will you?"

"Unless we have to," Aletto said. He looked uncertain, all at once. Robyn glanced up at him anxiously, at Enardi. Over at Chris. She managed a smile.

"It's cool, folks, we'll be fine. Ernie, just don't forget where this place is, that's all." She turned away to lead her horse off the road and the two men followed; Enardi got the mule moving. Jennifer turned away as the wagon jolted forward once again. Chris looked rather grim as he kneed his horse forward; with an almost visible effort, then, he turned to Lialla, grinned and tugged at the thick braid that lay between her shoulder blades. Whatever he said brought an outraged gasp from her; then she giggled and smacked his hand.

A much too short while later, they passed through the east gates and into the crowded streets of Podhru.

12

T HE streets were what Jennifer would have expected and had not previously seen anywhere in Rhadaz: Very medieval-looking, they were narrow, surrounded by the high, stone walls of buildings and ramparts, and extremely crowded. Her eyes were assaulted by a bewildering array of goods, pack and riding animals of a variety of colors and types, pulled, pushed or ridden by an equally wide variety of people—everything from nomadic types swathed to the eyes in unrelieved black to brightly clad caravaners recognizeable by the family crests borne prominently on shoulders or wide-brimmed hats, every possible type and size between. Except, she corrected herself, that she still had yet to see anyone Oriental, black—American Indian. Even in her small Wyoming hometown, twenty-plus years earlier, there had been a Korean family, and of course Indians. Especially after so many years in Los Angeles, it felt damned odd.

Unlike Bezjeriad, where the market was a well-ordered system of shops and a gridwork of streets, or Sikkre, where the market was large and sprawling but centralized, in Podhru there were sellers everywhere—shops side by side with inns or eating houses, with temples, homes and stables. There were also makeshift stands selling everything from costly-looking jewelry to food and drink, jutting into the already too narrow streets. It was nearly impossible to make sense of, and the wild variety of scents—human, animal, edibles—left her reeling, while the tightness of remaining traveling space and the number of people all around her would have choked her with claustrophobia, if she'd allowed herself to think about that.

In an effort to avoid thinking about how many obstacles were now between her and the relatively open roadway, she turned to Edrith, who was kneeling just behind her. "Tell me things," she said. "Like, why the people with the real shops allow anyone to set up business in front of them like that?"

"They don't," Edrith said. "But as I understand it, so long as the portable stands remain portable—they have to be gone by sundown and can't return until after sunrise—and so long as they leave a proper width for customers to reach the shops, so long as the owners of those shops can't prove they're being blocked or their custom is being diverted, they can't stop people from setting up in the street—isn't that right, Ernie?"

"About," Enardi replied tersely. He had his hands full at the moment with the wagon and a rather balky mule.

"This is fairly recent," Dahven said. It was the first thing he'd said all morning, and it occurred to Jennifer that he sounded nervous. "There used to be only shops, none of this additional—and there wasn't half the custom in the streets the last time I was here, I don't think."

"This is partly the upcoming Festival," Edrith reminded him. "But so much business is a recent thing, since the current Emperor reopened trade with the outside. They say it made an astonishing change in the markets everywhere; that was well before I was born, of course, but one of my mother's men used to work aboard a merchanter between Dro Pent and Podhru, and he said he could remember when there was a winter palace here, several temples on the great island, and of course a clerks' building. Little else in the new part of the city, and the old he said was a smelly collection of mud huts that made him glad to return to Sikkre, where the dirt is at least dry.''

"He'd never know it now," Enardi said. He edged the mule into a side street and breathed a faint sigh of relief when this proved to be much less crowded than the one they'd just left. "There are new temples every year, most of the mud huts are long since gone. And the clerks' building—my father says he can recall when it was the size of my sister Marseli's shop. Now it covers a space twice as great as our entire house and grounds, and there are four floors.''

"Long live the civil service," Jennifer said dryly. She swallowed as the sun vanished; the street that was less crowded was also narrower, the buildings closer together and taller. "Um. We know where we are, right?''

"Of course," Edrith replied at once.

"Ah. And we know where we're going, is that right?''

"Of course. Street of the Blind Muse.''

"And we know right where that is, do we?''

Edrith sighed. "This line of questioning has a purpose?''

"Pay no attention, buddy," Chris said from not far behind them. "Jen, chill out, okay?''

Jennifer slewed around to glare at him. "Watch your language," she said crisply. "Slang isn't permitted just now, remember? And I know all about the gas-station syndrome—''

"Who," Chris demanded in a low, aggrieved voice, "is using funny words *now*?''

"I'm an outlander, remember? I've been with certain to-be-unnamed males, whose initials are Chris Cray, who ran me all over East L.A. in my nice new Honda because he wouldn't pull into a gas station and get directions for downtown Azusa. That happens here, I'm *not* going to be a happy camper, got it?'' Silence. Chris made a face at her. "Excuse," Jennifer added sweetly, "the outlander words; I know a nice, quiet local boy like you doesn't understand them. You gentlemen keep in mind I'm a wounded woman who doesn't want to be lost in an unfamiliar city if asking directions from a local will get her where she's supposed to be.''

"God," Chris muttered feelingly. Lialla touched his arm, shook her head, and he subsided but Jennifer could feel his eyes on her back for some time after she turned around on the seat again. *Tough*, she thought. *I don't care how bad I bruised his teenage American macho bump of so-called direction. I know what he's like, and the way the rest of these guys are acting, I don't think it's a cultural thing.* She tried not to look nervous as Enardi turned right, left, left again, and let the mule walk along a dark street that smelled faintly of salt water. If push came to shove, she'd get down off the damned wagon and find someone to ask herself.

They got their first check a few minutes later, as the street opened out to a long, high, unfeatured wall on their left (the north side, Jennifer thought, but found it difficult with the sun almost directly overhead to be certain of that) and the bay on their right. There were men in pale yellow spread across the pavement, redirecting traffic around a small, dark stone building, an enormous crowd of silent, head-scarved onlookers and water everywhere. "Oh, god of small coppers," Enardi swore mildly, "it's a temple washing. They won't let us through while that's in progress."

There was room for foot traffic and horses to turn, not for the wagon; Edrith jumped down and spoke to one of the yellow-robed priests, who finally was persuaded to help clear a little room among the watchers so the wagon could be moved back and forth until Enardi could edge it into an alleyway at the end of the wall. It was just barely wide enough for the wagon. One of the wheels scraped wall as they entered the narrow passageway; Jennifer clenched her teeth and closed her eyes. She opened them a few moments later; the wagon had taken several turns and suddenly everything was different: There were a series of low stair-stepping walls on their right, strong-scented hedges on the left, no other people in sight. Enardi drew the mule to a halt as they came around another bend to confront a radiating network of streets, at least five different possibilities, none marked as far as she could see. Enardi came partway off the seat, looked around, glanced at the sky, nodded and headed the wagon down one narrow way that looked no more likely than any of the rest of them. Jennifer opened her mouth, closed it again without saying anything. Dahven turned to look at her.

"Are you all right?"

"I'm fine," she said rather shortly.

"You're certain?"

"Of course."

"Everything's all right, isn't it?" Lialla asked. Apparently she'd seen the brief conversation but hadn't heard any of it. Jennifer glanced over her shoulder.

"Why ask *me*?" she demanded. "I'm only along for the ride."

"You can see outer walls from here, if you raise up a little," Edrith said huffily. "We aren't *lost*."

"Of course not."

"How could we possibly get lost in Podhru?" Edrith asked. Jennifer sighed heavily; the Sikkreni scowled at her but let the matter drop.

The heat was growing by the moment; the sun reached zenith and began edging west. By the time they could make out shadow sufficiently to tell direction by it, even Chris had to admit they probably weren't going to find the Street of the Blind Muse on their own. That they had no idea where they were in relationship to it, the gate they had come through early in the day, or even to the temple they'd passed hours before. By Jennifer's count, they'd had at least a glimpse of Podhru's bay twenty or more times. They'd smelled more dead fish than she cared to think had ever lived, and there'd been other, less pleasant odors.

When the two men in plain, dark blue uniform came walking around the end of another of the endless, featureless walls, Jennifer stirred, ready to jump down and accost them herself, if need be. Dahven got a grip on her elbow, minutely shook his head, leaned over to touch Enardi's arm. The Bezanti sighed faintly but obediently waved an arm to catch the guards' attention, drew the mule to a halt and waited for them to come up. Jennifer cast a warning glance back at Chris, who touched Lialla's knee and winked at her. The sin-Duchess gave him a smile in reply; she looked too pale and very nervous. *Keep quiet back there,* Jennifer thought; she leaned into Dahven's arm, cautiously shifted her left onto her lap, grateful all at once for the sling: The jolting ride through rough-cobbled streets was making it ache in earnest.

The guards were both young, probably not any older than

Chris, slender in new-looking blue uniforms, unmarked except for a small copper pin at the throat. Both wore belts that held a short wooden club and a narrow blade—something longer than a dagger, shorter than a sword. One also had a number of rope lengths hanging from a leather strap attached to the belt. *Low-tech handcuffs,* Jennifer thought, and shifted her glance at once. The very thought made her nervous, and she wondered whether they'd expect that; whether an ordinary Rhadazi woman would be nervous around armed city guards. *But you're an outlander, one who was wounded only a few days ago, in mistake for someone else,* she reminded herself firmly, and leaned into Dahven's side. *You have every right to be shaky, even around what Robyn would call the local fuzz.* Around anyone with a sharp blade. She forced her eyes away from the weapons belts and studied the two men: One was fairly dark, what she was beginning to think of as the typical Rhadazi—medium height, compact body, hair as dark a brown as Lialla's, brown eyes, swarthy complexion. His companion was perhaps a little taller and more slender, slightly paler against a reddish brown moustache and dark red hair. "Sirs?" Enardi said when they came around the mule to look at the wagon and its contents. It didn't ease Jennifer's nerves at all to hear the unusually deferential tone the boy used.

Or the slightly arrogant voice of the dark-haired guard. "Young sir? You appear lost."

"I fear so." Enardi smiled, spread his arms in a broad shrug. "I've come from Bez on my father's business, he sent me to finalize a contract for wool—"

"Yes," the dark guard broke in impatiently. "What business do you seek, have you a name?"

"Sirs, Kamahl, he's from Bez years since, a shop among the weavers in the Street of the Blind Muse." Enardi's smile became rueful. "I've not visited Kamahl in perhaps three years, and my elder brother always found the shop. The way I know, that he used to take—well, there was a temple washing."

"There were several today." The red-haired guard sounded just as impatient. The heat, Jennifer told herself. Maybe she'd sound like that, too, if she had to patrol the narrow, airless streets in this town.

"I was forced to turn north, and so lost my way. If you could give me proper directions—"

The guards looked at each other appraisingly and didn't

respond right away; Jennifer's stomach dropped and her mouth went suddenly dry. But the redhead shrugged, looked back the way they had come, shrugged again. "There aren't any good directions. The street comes to a dead end four separate times that I know of, against new buildings. And it's not the only street that does in that sector. But the Street of the Blind Muse isn't very far; we can take you partway. Far enough to point you where you should be.''

Enardi inclined his head and picked up the reins. "That's extremely kind of you, sirs.''

"It's what we're paid for," the dark man replied and he sounded rather huffy about it. Jennifer glanced nervously at Enardi, who seemed momentarily at a loss for anything to say and finally decided to say nothing. The guard glanced across Enardi to look at her. "The lady looks unwell," he said accusingly.

"An injury," Jennifer managed, adding, "sirs," when the man's eyebrows went up. "I can rest when we've reached Kamahl's shop.''

"Sirs, my wife is tired and hot," Dahven put in quietly, when the guard gave no sign of moving. "We spoke with city guard some days ago, when this"—he indicated Jennifer's wrapped arm—"occurred.''

"City guard—what name?" the dark man demanded.

"They gave me none, sirs. Red and gold uniform.''

The dark guard gave his companion a look Jennifer couldn't begin to fathom; the redhead tugged at his moustache, finally nodded and took hold of the mule's harness. "Apologies, lady," he said, and gave her a smile that would have been almost friendly, if it had reached his eyes. Those were still chill and appraising, or so she thought. "It is our business to make certain such matters aren't left unreported in city walls.''

She nodded, swallowed past a dry throat. "Of course, sirs.''

"Since the matter has already been reported and dealt with, we won't delay you any more." He started back up the street, turning the way he and his companion guard had just come. Jennifer sighed and leaned against Dahven. She could feel sweat trickling down her ribs. *Waste of the antiperspirant I put on this morning.* Dahven's arm was across her shoulders; the hand that rested against the base of her throat trembled. Behind them, Chris and Lialla were extremely quiet, and if not for the sound of hooves against large paving brick, she wouldn't have been certain the two were still there.

They went slowly, since the two men who led them were afoot. Another of those radiating intersections, and then another. Jennifer tried not to look anxious, however she felt, tried not to watch the guard lest they catch her at it and take offense.

Something simply felt wrong. *Thread*, she thought. Would either of these men know, if she attempted to Wield right now? She finally decided not, as they passed through a widening in the street that held a well and a pool, where three women were washing clothes. Lialla would know; Jennifer hoped she'd have the sense to keep quiet. She tried to shift: nothing.

After three attempts, she swore under her breath and gave it up. Something *was* wrong; unlike those times when she'd been too tired or hurting too badly, even when she was riding that wretched horse—she could sense it out there. See it, hear it, however faintly; almost touch it. *Almost*. There was something between her and Thread.

Sweat beaded on her forehead; she wondered how much longer the tape would hold Chris's bangs against so much moisture. *Something there.* It could be some block set by the Emperor, or one of his religions, to keep magic from being utilized in Podhru. But if so, why hadn't anyone told her? *Damn unlikely,* Jennifer thought. *Those two*—She shifted, sitting as straight as possible so she could whisper against Dahven's ear. "Problem," she said softly. "I can't touch Thread. The guard—"

Dahven's arm stiffened around her; he made no other sign she'd spoken. She glanced at him sidelong; he was studying the two. "Different uniform," he murmured finally. "I don't know it, means nothing, haven't been here in a long time." He fell silent.

"I'm blocked," she said and bit back anything else; her whisper didn't want to stay under control. One of the guards glanced back at them as they crossed through yet another of the radiating intersections, bearing left this time. Jennifer managed a faint smile, winced as the wagon jolted across a drainage cut. The red-haired guard smiled in reply, said something to his companion. The second man turned briefly to say, "Not far now." Jennifer smiled at him, too, then

162

bent forward to let her head fall on her hand. She sighed, heavily, felt Dahven's arm tighten on her waist.

Edrith was behind her, a silent presence still kneeling just behind the bench seat, where he could look between her and Enardi. She let her right arm fall, brought it close across her body and worked it under the layers of brown cloth to poke the Sikkreni in the side. He jerked, caught hold of the bench and then her fingers, leaned forward as though looking around. "What?" he breathed against her ear.

"Something wrong—"

"I thought so. They don't feel right. You know—?"

"No," Jennifer admitted. "You be ready to run."

She'd feared argument from him; he scratched his chin, gave her the least of nods. "Of course. Get help."

"Chris," she went on anxiously, and with a nervous look from under her eyebrows at the two guards.

"I'll get Chris and Lialla out," he assured her. The dark guard glanced around; Edrith yawned hugely and sat back on his heels, dropping out of sight. Jennifer sighed, leaned into Dahven once more.

I can't take this, she thought miserably. *More fighting? Knives, blades—I can't do it.*

They took another turn, into a narrow street so high-walled the sky was a slender ribbon of blue far overhead. There were paving stones missing here; the mule stumbled in the gloom and Enardi swore as the wagon creaked ominously. "Sirs," he began anxiously. "If there is another way, my wagon won't take this mistreatment." The guard ignored him. Enardi pulled the mule to a halt. "Sirs," he said, a little louder. His voice echoed; he looked around nervously. There were no windows here, only a few doors and those in disrepair. The walls were solid, dark stone and Jennifer would have sworn the wall to their right was the same construction as the outer city walls they'd passed through hours ago. They rose straight up, and at perhaps third-floor height above her head sloped steeply toward a distant ledge or parapet.

There was no place to turn, scarcely enough room for a man to walk either side of the wagon. Jennifer swallowed an evil taste, glanced at Dahven. His face was set and grim under the hood. Enardi on her other side was absolutely white, and she wondered if the boy was going to faint. She reached across with her good hand, squeezed his elbow, and

when he looked at her, she nodded. He managed a very thin
smile. She let her gaze go past him, up and around, casually
across her shoulder. Edrith was gone, and she'd never heard
him go. So, less quietly, were Chris and Lialla; she was
aware of the faint, distant clatter of hooves on stone, rapidly
receding.

Enardi drew the reins close to his chest, came partway
up. The two guards stood talking just in front of the mule,
one holding the bridle. "Sirs," Enardi said again, a little
louder. "Sirs, I might suggest this isn't a good way to get
ourselves and this wagon to the Street of the Blind Muse.
And I remember the street itself well enough to know this
is not it."

"No." The red-haired guard came back along the driver's
side of the wagon. "This, however, is where you were
going." He smiled, a cold flash of teeth below chill blue
eyes. "There are those who would have words with you,
Lord Dahven. And with those who travel with you." He
glanced into the bed of the wagon for the first time, swore,
and leaned across the bed to stare back the way they had
come. "Jessat, the other three! They're gone!"

"Cowards," Jessat snapped.

"They could have gone for aid—"

"Hah." The dark man let go his grip on the harness and
spat. "Aid from whom, Karadan? There's no guard this
time of day hereabouts; on a day like this, they're bunched
down by the temples anyway. Besides, aid against us? We're
guard, remember?" He looked at the three on the wagon
seat, passing over Enardi at once, his glance holding Jennifer's only briefly before it fastened on Dahven. He smiled,
a thin turning of lips, took two steps up the narrow alley
and drew his long knife to beat on the door there with the
hilt. He came back along the wagon then, to stop next to
the mule. Dahven looked down at him without expression.
Jennifer felt his hand slip from her shoulder to slide along
her back, down to the blade he'd fixed at the small of his
back. *Two of them*, she thought numbly. *Two against what?
I can hold the bo, I don't think I can use it. Enardi's—look
at him, poor boy, he's too afraid to move.*

Well, she could suddenly understand that; she was nearly
that frightened. But two of them against Dahven—Dahven
who'd stuffed his sword down under the seat so no one would
doubt the part he played, Dahven who only had a long dagger to face two men armed with something similar. No. Oh,

no. She shifted gingerly, carefully, slid her right hand into the sling. *I swore I wouldn't need this, I swore I wouldn't use it*—Well, bless Chris for insisting she put Edrith's spare knife and sheath inside the sling anyway.

Noise up ahead of them got her attention; three men had come out of the door Jessat knocked on. Two carried swords; the third had a throwing spear in one hand, and a bolos swung gently from his other. Jessat glanced over his shoulder, turned back and smiled. "There'll be no trouble, Lord Dahven."

"No trouble," Dahven replied quietly. Jennifer felt his left arm tense as he freed the knife from its sheath; her own fingers tightened on the dagger. She set her foot on Enardi's and when he glanced at her, she moved her eyes sharply back. She wasn't certain he'd understand that as an order to get out of the way but apparently he did. His own eyes slid back, he tightened his lips, blinked instead of nodding.

"Let go the weapon," Karadan ordered.

"Weapon?" Dahven asked.

"Now," the guard insisted flatly. "Or the lady will be the one who suffers. They say you're fond of her."

"They say," Dahven scoffed. His fingers pressed against her side, a signal to move, and he threw himself onto Jessat. Enardi rolled backwards off the seat as the red-haired guard snatched at his arm; Jennifer moved herself across to where Enardi had been, slashing in a hard arc. Karadan yelped as she touched the back of his hand, drawing blood in a thin line across the base of his fingers. He snatched the fingers back; Jennifer landed on the left-hand edge of the seat hard enough to jar her teeth and set her left arm throbbing furiously. A moment later, Karadan had her by the elbow, dragging her from the wagon. She shrieked in fury, drew a deep breath to project with an opera-singer's voice: "Thieves! Murderers! Let go of me, you bastards!"

"Shut her up!" the man with the throwing spear shouted. Karadan snarled wordlessly; he had his hands full and Jennifer still had the knife.

"Rapists! Robbers! Fire!" Jennifer bellowed. She screamed in pain as Karadan got a better grip on her left arm and squeezed; the man with the throwing spear dropped it and strode forward to wrest the knife from her fingers and hit her, hard, just under the ribs. Jennifer choked and bent double, fighting for breath. Dahven went down under three men, Jessat on top.

Karadan tore the scarf from her head and wrapped a hand in her hair, dragging her upright against him. "It didn't need to come to this kind of violence," he said against her ear. "No one wanted to hurt you—"

"Save it," Jennifer gasped. "Save the lies. No one believes you." She could feel his rather anxious, unhappy gaze on her; the man who'd hit her retrieved his spear and went past them to gaze around behind the wagon.

"Where's that boy who was driving? The other two?"

"In no place so unsanctified where such as thou mayst find him," Jennifer spat. "That's a quote," she added as he pushed back around her. "Which you'd be too stupid to recognize in *my* world." He reversed the spear and brought it up; Karadan swung her around, putting himself between the two.

"Don't, Miklan," he urged. "Their Honors didn't want the woman hurt—"

"Let them deal with her, then," the spearman said flatly. "For the other, though—" He gave her a nasty, gloating smile and stepped back. "No one said anything about him going home alive."

"No," she whispered and dragged against the armsman's grip; she hissed and went limp when his fingers dug into her biceps and the barely healed spear cut. They had Dahven on his feet again; there was blood on his forehead, a thin line of it running down his cheek. Two of them held his arms; the man Jessat stood a pace or so away, smiling grimly. He brought the knife up in an underhand grip. Jennifer shook her head. "No! Someone will hear, they'll come—"

"Shut her up, Karadan."

"Lady, please don't—" Karadan began unhappily. Jessat's knife touched Dahven's shoulder; the tip sliced through fabric. Jennifer spun into the red-haired boy and let her full weight hit him. Caught by surprise and thrown off balance, he staggered into the wall. She got a handful of shirt, went almost to her knee, pulling him forward with her, straightened at the last moment and got her right foot behind his leg. His head hit the wall, hard; Jennifer went down with him, tore loose from suddenly limp fingers and drew back, feeling cautiously for the man's dagger. He'd drawn it, earlier; she'd just heard it hit—there. She looked up, knife in her hand as someone yelled. "Dahven? Oh, God—" But it wasn't. Dahven has used the two men holding him for leverage and had thrown a tremendous kick; the man Jessat was doubled over, his face deeply purple, and as Jennifer scrambled between the mule's front and back feet, he fell onto his side and lay there, whimpering.

"Jennifer, look out—!" Dahven's voice cut off abruptly, as though someone had driven the air out of him. A foot slammed down across the blade of the long knife, pinning it and her hand. Miklan dropped his spear and reached down to grap her wrist and haul her upright; he'd dropped the bolos, too. The free hand cracked down hard across her left cheek and ear; she staggered into the mule and nearly fell. Miklan caught hold of both shoulders and shook her fiercely.

"Whatever their Honors want," he hissed, "no man with any sense would keep such a woman alive! First, however, you'll tell me who was the other with you: the boy who was driving the wagon. His name!" She shook her head, hard, set her lips in a tight line.

"Miklan." A hoarse voice from somewhere near their feet. The guard Jessat faltered to his feet, still bent nearly double, and clutched the mule's harness for balance. The animal danced nervously away from him, went still as the man swore and slammed a fist into the back of its head. "Miklan, there were three more—"

"Little warm sand gods, but you two were of no use at all, were you?"

"We couldn't do other than what we did," Jessat replied sullenly. "They'd have suspected—"

"Which they did anyway, apparently. Did you recognize any of them? The Zelharri?"

"There were a boy and girl on horses. I didn't know either of them; the boy might have been the outlander disguised. The girl—I never saw her before. The other—" He shrugged, winced and bent over coughing.

"Tell me who they are, when they left you—where they went. I might spare you." Jennifer set her lips in an even tighter line and just looked at him. His fingers dug into her left shoulder, hard, and for a moment everything swam. He eased the pressure. "Tell me."

"Go to hell," she said evenly. *God, idiot, what's the matter with you?* she thought in a sudden panic. But if he was going to kill her anyway, maybe it was better to provoke him into doing it quickly—*Oh, Lord, I can't believe this is me, even thinking that!* She gave him a flash of clenched teeth, looked over his shoulder. The two men still held Dahven but apparently hadn't done anything except to restrain him. She smiled at him; felt her heart lift slightly as he smiled back. She let her gaze move back past the wagon, then. Movement—? She felt her blood run cold. *Please God, don't let that be Chris, or Enardi, or Edrith! The two of us dying is going to be bad enough without them keeping us company.* One or two more—what possible difference could that make against men like these?

"What are you looking at?" Miklan demanded. She ignored him, even when his hand tightened on her bad arm; none of them had worn red coming into the city. Whoever was coming along this dead-end, narrow alley was mounted—and wore red and gold.

Jessat apparently had followed her gaze; one of the men holding Dahven shifted so he could look across his shoulder. He and his companion let go their prisoner so suddenly that Dahven fell back against the wagon. Jessat turned to scramble after them. Jennifer found herself dragged half a dozen paces past the mule, toward the open, sagging door in the left-hand wall; she dug in her heels then and dropped to the ground. Miklan yanked; Jennifer swore as her backside bumped into hard stone and then into a deep, wet hole between cobbles. Miklan swore in turn, spun back to hiss in her face, "It doesn't end here. Remember that!" He let her go, sprinted for the opening.

"Damn right it doesn't!" she shouted furiously after him. Dahven had her by the shoulders then, and he pulled her around, face into his rough brown shirt. He squatted down in the alley next to her.

"By all the gods there are, be still!" he said in a low, urgent voice, with a nervous glance across his shoulder. "You're going to get us both in terrible trouble."

"Trouble?" Jennifer sat back and wiped a hand across her forehead, dislodging what was left of Chris's taped piece of hair. "Trouble?" She scooted backwards out of the muddy hole, wrapped both arms around his waist and began to laugh.

13

E NARDI and Edrith were ahead of the guard by a few short
paces; they pushed by the mule to kneel at Jennifer's
side. "Are you all right?" Enardi asked aloud, adding in a
very low voice, "Let me talk as much as possible, I think
I can divert any suspicion."

Edrith laid a trembling hand against her forehead, nodded, and said in a voice that carried even less: "It's the
same men; be careful, both of you." Jennifer sighed wearily, let her eyes close and shifted her weight slightly so she
could curl into Dahven's arms.

"What trouble here?" a cold voice broke into a too-short,
welcome silence. It was the guard-master who'd interviewed
her at the inn. *It wanted only this,* she thought even more
wearily, but pried her eyes open and managed to lean away
from Dahven.

"I'm sorry you've had trouble with me twice," she said,
and offered him a tentative smile. She might as well have
been smiling at a brick wall; the guard-master leaned against
the wagon, one leg crossed over the other, arms folded, face
chill in its lack of expression. There were four others, one
just pressing past him; another knelt by the guard Karadan,
and two had gone on up the alley to begin testing the door.
Jennifer glanced that direction, nodded. "They went through
there—"

"We saw." The guard-master shrugged himself away
from the wagon, walked around Enardi, past Edrith to stand
behind Jennifer. He folded his arms again, stared down at
Dahven, who looked reluctantly up. "Why don't you simply
give us your real name, sir?" he went on abruptly.

Dahven shook his head. "I don't—"

"Before someone is hurt," the guard broke in flatly.
"Such as this lady has already been? Or before the lady is
killed? It's said Lord Dahven holds her high in his regard."

Dahven's shoulders sagged. *No!* Jennifer mouthed at him anxiously—too late. His eyes closed briefly; he nodded then.

"He does," Dahven said, and gave her a faint smile. "Though a man would never know it, seeing the way she's been used." He set her fingers aside and got to his feet. "I am Dahven, Dahmec's son. Not his murderer—but that's not for you to decide, is it?"

"No, Honor."

Dahven laughed. "Not Honor, you know. My brothers hold that title; they preface my name these days with 'the traitor,' or didn't you know?"

"The will has not yet been satisfactorily proven."

"Oh? How that must please my brothers." Dahven's smile vanished. "Never mind. If you must take me—"

"Then I go with him," Jennifer announced as she let Edrith help her up. Dahven opened his mouth; she closed the distance between them and set her hand on his lips, turned back to face the guard. "It is surely the man's right to be represented by counsel. I am his advocate." Behind her Dahven said something; Jennifer reached back to take hold of his fingers but held her ground.

For the first time, she saw something like an expression on the guard-master's face—it might have been the beginnings of a smile. "His advocate. Well. There is no law that prohibits me from escorting the man and his advocate."

"Jennifer, no—"

"Dahven," Jennifer said in a low voice, "your advocate suggests to you that you're going to prejudice your case. Shut up."

"I—oh, cold, yellow hells," Dahven gritted between his teeth and then did indeed fall silent. The guard-master had already turned away to fix Edrith with a cool eye.

"You came with this man from Sikkre?"

"No. I found him in Bezjeriad. It's a long story—"

"You will come also. There is plenty of time."

"I wouldn't have it any other way," Edrith said evenly. The guard-master gave him a sharp glance, shrugged and went on to Enardi. "And you—since we know now that these two are not from northern Andar Perigha, and that you did not in fact come from that direction with them— who are you?"

To Jennifer's surprise, Enardi fairly radiated practical good sense—what she thought of as the attitude of wealth and power toward mere power; she'd seen it now and again in the firm's clients back home, when one of them challenged a moving violation. "I am the son of Fedthyr, of the Street of Weavers in Bezjeriad. I had certain contractual matters to handle here for my father, and since this lady and her companions wished to travel overland, it was thought I might journey in their company."

"You knew who they were?"

Enardi shrugged. "Of course. But, sirs, no one has suggested to me or to my father that any of these people are criminals or others with whom an honest man should have no dealings—"

"That is not suggested now."

"Well. I wanted to come to Podhru, and since my father intends me to take his place one day, he prefers that I take over all such distant matters for him, rather than giving them to agents as so many do. I become ill when I travel by ship and my father does not like me traveling the road alone. And so—" He made a gesture that was Fedthyr at his finest, taking in his companions. The guard-master frowned and appeared to think this over while he glared at the nearest wall. After a moment, Enardi added tentatively, "Sirs, I truly am expected at the Street of the Blind Muse. This emergency has cost me hours, a thing I had not counted on since I sent messages from the inn; my host will begin to worry about me."

The guard-master transferred the frown to him; Enardi gave him a small smile, and waited until the man shrugged and sighed. "Ah, well. Another question or two, then, before we extract you and your wagon from this hole. On the way here, you saw no other outlanders?"

"Today?"

"At any time."

"Besides Jennifer? No."

"No other persons, not necessarily outlander but not Bez merchants? We particularly wish to speak with a young man with a lame leg, a woman who might be his sister—?"

"Ah." Enardi smiled and appeared to relax all at once. "That would be Duke Aletto and the sin-Duchess Lialla, wouldn't it?"

"It would?" The guard-master took a step toward him. "And why is that?"

"Well—Everyone knows about them, of course. There is rumor all up and down the Bez market, my cousins brought extremely wild gossip recently from Sikkre. But for my-self—I am sorry, sirs. I would not know where they are.''

''They are not with your company?''

''No. Just—myself, these three.'' Enardi glanced upward as though trying to determine how late the hour by the narrow strip of sky. The guard-master shook his head but turned to his followers. ''You—over there. Help the Bezanti get his wagon out of here and turned, direct him to the Street of the Blind Muse. It isn't far,'' he added to Enardi. ''Only a matter of two turnings back.'' He glanced over his shoulder as his other men came back through the now destroyed doorway, shutting what little was left of the door in a tooth-clenching shriek of unoiled metal hinge. They were alone: One shook his head, the other cast his eyes up.

Enardi looked at them anxiously as they came close, turned to gaze at the guard-master. ''Sir, if those ruffians have left—they knew my destination. You don't think—''

''Enardi, is it?'' The guard-master shook his head. ''Most likely they were after this man and the lady, not you.''

''They might think my father wealthy enough—''

''Not in Podhru,'' the guard-master said so flatly that Enardi fell silent at once and ducked his head, but he glanced sidelong at Jennifer, tipped her a very grave wink. ''I *would* suggest, however, young master, that you avoid such streets as this in future. There is no sense in actively seeking problems—is there?''

''No—oh, no, sir,'' Enardi replied in a very low and respectful tone.

Between them—three guardsmen and Enardi—they finally got the wagon backed free and turned, though Enardi had to unhook the mule and let Edrith lead him back separately when the little beast utterly refused to back more than two paces. The guard-master waited in silence while Enardi refastened the harness and climbed onto the seat. ''I won't insist you come with us now, young sir. But you had better come to the civil offices in the next day or so, to give your statement.''

Enardi nodded. ''If I weren't concerned about the hour—''

''We've enough to manage the rest of this day. You want the offices of the Emperor's Street Guard, remember that.''

''Sir. Thank you, sir.''

''Wait.'' Jennifer came alongside the wagon and climbed

awkwardly into the back. "I want my bag, my own clothing. If you don't mind."

"Whatever is yours, lady," the guard-master replied, and he sounded almost courteous. The courtesy held when he looked up at Dahven. "Honor, if you've any belongings there—"

"I've nothing but the horses," Dahven said. "Mine and hers." Edrith had already loosed them from the tailgate when they backed the wagon out of the alley. He handed Dahven his reins, accepted a hand up onto the back of Dahven's mount; he slid down again once it became clear Jennifer couldn't get the large purse—now fatter by a pair of jeans, a chambray shirt and a newly darned tee-shirt, a pair of high-tops with a wad of white socks protruding from one unlaced cuff—hooked into its usual place. Clearly she'd never get herself mounted without assistance, and Edrith finally knelt to catch hold of her left foot so he could lift her. She winced as her arm jarred on the saddlebow; again when her backside—unpleasantly wet and muddy as well as sore from at least one hard fall—touched the saddle. But she shook her head when the guard-master looked at her in inquiry.

"Nothing important," she said rather shortly, adding, "sir," as an afterthought. "Let's go, get this done. Enardi," she added as they turned away from the wagon, "take care of yourself, will you?"

He looked forlorn and very young—and perilously near tears. He nodded, ran a surreptitious finger under his nose, blinked hard. "I will." Jennifer managed a smile for him, then edged her horse nearer Dahven's; he freed a hand and took hold of her fingers. One of the red-and-gold-clad city guard edged in front of the wagon to escort Enardi; another—he had taken Edrith up behind his saddle—moved out ahead of them and set off the other way. Jennifer clenched her jaw and loosened her grip on the reins; her horse shook his head so his mane flew wildly, and followed.

A short distance away, down another dark side street, Chris held the two horses while Lialla crouched in an empty doorway, eyes closed, hands clutching at rough stone. He glanced at her, shrugged and turned away. *He* couldn't see anything, couldn't feel anything, either—she said she was going to Wield, so, fine. He suffered a momentary qualm, which he identified and dismissed a breath later: A city this big, there were bound to be plenty of people using magic. He'd been warned a dozen times to keep his mouth shut; no one had warned anyone else about using magic, though. Not something aboveboard like Night-Thread, anyway.

Chris wrapped reins around his fingers, neatly, concentrating on keeping the turns flat and even, and he swore under his breath, every word he knew in English, every word he'd picked up in Rhadazi since. *I think I'll murder Eddie,* he thought, but after a moment, he dismissed that thought, too: Jennifer had wanted them out of there, so they could get help. Chris still had to admit that at the moment when Edrith came back to warn them, it had made more sense for him to stick with Lialla. Jennifer was at least as capable as anyone else of taking care of herself; Dahven was good at it. Lialla—well, she wasn't half bad but the idea was to keep her out of sight and out of trouble, wasn't it? "Well," Chris mumbled gloomily, "I sure did that, didn't I?"

Who'd have figured those guys for Jadek's cheesy imitations of guards—who'd think Jadek would have the nerve to pull a stunt like that *here*? From the looks on those other guys' faces, the guys in the red, they hadn't been too thrilled. Chris finished winding reins around his fingers, shook them loose once more, glanced back at Lialla. "You know," he asked himself very quietly, "I wonder how come those guys were right there when Eddie went looking for them?" He could feel the blood draining from his face and if he hadn't been holding onto the horse, he'd probably have sat down right on the cobbles. "Oh, shit. You don't suppose those guys in red are Jadek's too?"

Lialla caught his attention as she got back to her feet and slipped on a pile of rubble, sending a cascade of small stones and bits of wood across his feet. He turned, caught hold of her. "You all right?" he whispered. Lialla shifted in his grip to look at up him, and he wasn't certain she knew him. She drew a gasping breath, nodded, pointed back in the direction they'd come.

"Moving," she whispered.

"Huh?"

"Oh, gods," Lialla murmured. "They have Jen, we can't—"

"No!" Chris dug his fingers into her shoulders as she would have edged around him and probably run right into the street.

"They have her, have Dahven!" Lialla insisted, her voice rising to a piercing whisper. "We can't—!"

He heard the wagon creaking very close by, heard it turn away from them, and, following it, horses. A mounted man in red and gold came first, braid decorating his shoulders and his horse. Another followed him—same colors, plain garb—and behind him . . . Lialla gasped and wriggled in Chris's hands. He drew a deep, steadying breath, expelled it in a gust, and with a muttered, "Well, *hell*," caught the sin-Duchess close and planted a kiss squarely on her mouth.

At first he thought she was going to protest; Lialla apparently thought so, too, but as the horses went by the narrow, dark alleyway, she suddenly leaned into him and—you couldn't call it contributed, really, Chris decided. Definitely cooperated, though. *Kind of nice.*

As soon as the sound of the horses passed and faded, though, she pressed both palms flat against his chest and twisted free. Her normally pale face was flushed across the cheekbones. Chris was annoyed to find himself blushing. "Um, hey, look," he began. Lialla waved a hand to silence him and grinned crookedly.

"Don't. I know what you did and why you did it."

"Well, you know? Maybe I really wanted to—"

Lialla's grin widened and she laughed, clapped a hand across her mouth as the sound filled the deserted little area. "Shhh," she urged him, but the laugh was still in her voice. "Don't. Leave it as it is, it's much nicer that way." Her eyes went grave over the hand, then, and she reached for his sleeve. "Chris, what are we going to *do*?"

"Um." He nodded, glanced all around them, scratched at his scalp until he remembered the hair was supposed to be flat. "Um, all right, we have options, we'd better go with them fast, though. Look, Ernie went the other direction; did you get a look at them? I don't think they did anything about him, I think that guy was pointing him in the right direction, sure looked that way to me. We could follow Enardi, catch up with him—but we can locate that street of his any time, if we can get back out of the city. Colin would know how to find it, wouldn't he?"

"Don't know," Lialla admitted. "Chris, I don't like to say so, but your young Bezanti friend—"

"Yeah, don't say it," Chris sighed. "Poor Ernie's not going to be much use in a tight spot and man, is that ever what we have right now. Besides, we don't know for certain he got turned loose, do we? Maybe they were tossing him out of town, or taking him some other place—I don't know. So, next idea, we find our way back out of the city, get the others, get Colin, make a plan—but I don't like that one, either. It would take time; our people may not have time.''

"Which leaves—?''

"We go after Jen and Dahven and Eddie. I—look, would you know real guards from fake?''

"Did I once today?'' Lialla asked gloomily. "But if you're worried about those men in red and gold, they're Emperor's Street Guard. There aren't so many of them, and they're terribly important. I don't think anyone would dare impersonate them; anyone who lives in Podhru would know at once.''

"Well, yeah. Like living in L.A. and passing yourself off as a Laker—never mind. Tell you later. Well, okay, maybe.'' Chris tugged at his earlobe, handed Lialla her reins and swung himself onto the horse. "All right. My decision, okay? We go after the guys in red, stay as far back as we can without losing them, so we don't get grabbed, and we at least know for sure where Jen and the guys got taken. And then: Well, we can figure it out from there. But I figure we'd better get back out to mom and your brother before they get mondo worried, maybe talk to Colin because he lives around here.''

"Go,'' Lialla said as she settled herself in the saddle and brushed back hair that had slipped from her plait. It was one of her crisp, precise orders—all he'd ever heard out of her for days, early on. Chris kneed his horse and went.

Except that Lialla had been the one, that second night, who'd offered him her share of the bread. "I remember how my stomach felt all the years I was growing, always empty.'' That had been unexpected, really nice. He cast her a side-long glance as she drew up even with him. *Hey, the chick's got a lot of hassle in her life, and she's still all right.* Too bad she was his aunt's age.

Aunt Jen. He couldn't see any of them, now that he was out in the open, but when he would have said so, Lialla drew him to a halt and laid a hand across his mouth. Listened, finally pointed. "Ahead of us,'' she murmured. "Go.''

Fortunately for Chris's peace of mind, they came upon the first of the five-way intersections just in time to see a glimpse of red and gold in the distance, before the horseman rounded the edge of a jutting building. Chris gave his horse a nudge to speed it up a little, drew back only as they came around the same building. There were three of the guard, one riding double—*God, that's Eddie up there, behind him,* he realized dismally. Just behind that horse, two more—Jen and Dahven, side by side, his hand on her leg. He knew her at once by the hair; it had fallen loose across her shoulders. The enormous handbag tied to the back of the saddle would have given her away if she'd been in full costume, though.

For some reason, the handbag reassured him, and he drew his first deep, comfortable breath since Edrith had come off the back of the wagon to warn them. "They let her grab her stuff, Li, lookit. Her jeans, her high-tops. Would they do that if they were just going to take her out and shoot her?"

"Take her—? Never mind, tell me later. The bag was under just about everything else; they must have given her permission to bring it, taken the time to free it." Lialla caught his hand and urged her horse on. "Hurry, we're losing them again!" She was quiet until they could see the last of the city guard once more. "It's very unlikely they'd have any sort of writ against *her* anyway."

"For helping you and Aletto—?"

"That's not a crime," Lialla said. "Even if there is a writ for Dahven—or for us," she added bleakly, "there wouldn't be one for Jen, or for either you or Robyn. You'd have to commit some crime that involved the Emperor."

"You forget about the minor matter of killing—" Chris began. But Lialla shook her head.

"That's Duchy business, not a matter for the Emperor. Unless someone murdered by Light, or murdered a member of the nobility, or royalty." She sagged momentarily. "Are they—? Oh, gods, there they are. That's why the Emperor might have writs of his own out for Dahven, or for Aletto or me."

"Because of this Carolan? Or Dahven's old man?"

"His father. Yes. Jadek could have sent a writ to Podhru because of Carolan, of course. But it would—he wouldn't, I don't think he would."

"Yeah," Chris said bitingly. "Who'd think he was still the nice guy if he did that?"

Lialla tilted her head to one side and studied him. "You know," she said finally, "you know more than anyone would think, looking at you."

"Hey. Someday I'll tell you all about life in the big city, and like that. Besides," he added as they neared yet another bend in the narrow street and slowed to check the way ahead before going on, "seventeen-year olds where I come from are a whole different kind of thing." He grinned, nudged the horse on. "But you knew that, right?"

Lialla smiled. "I knew that."

"Hey. Street's gone major wide, and those guys are—what's that thing, that big place they're heading for? Looks like a palace!"

"Oh." Lialla's smile vanished. "Unless I'm very mistaken, that's the government center, the clerks' building."

"Oh." Chris considered this, drew his horse and Lialla's to one side of the boulevard, where they could watch as the guard escorted their three prisoners across a stone plaza, between two long pools, and under an arch. "Do we dare go any farther?"

Lialla shook her head so hard the plait slapped across her thin shoulders. "Better not; we might not be recognized but we'd be known for outsiders at once. If the guard has actually put them under restraint, they might be looking for outsiders."

"Hey." Chris tugged at the side of her mount's bridle and leaned sideways to give her a quick, hard hug. "Lookit, in there at least they're safe from Jadek and the Sikkreni, right? Safer than they were out on the street, at least. And I don't think any of 'em got hurt, so that's something, too. So I think our job is to get back outside, get to that park, let mom and your brother know what's going on."

"I—" Lialla cast one last unhappy glance at the huge, efficient-looking rectangle of building, finally nodded. "All right. Let's go. But"—she tugged on his sleeve and held it until he turned back to face her—"you be careful! And watch everyone, will you?"

"With that last episode as a guide? Are you kidding?"

Once out on the boulevard, mixed in with so many people, Chris found it easier to pretend he was just part of the crowd. It was late enough in the afternoon and the street broad enough for him to make out shadow and get them oriented in the proper direction. The boulevard opened into another, similar street—busier, not quite so wide—and he heard Lialla sigh with relief. "I know where we are," she said quietly.

"Yeah. Me, too. Look, slow way down when we get

close to the gates, will you? Take a hard look around for anyone who might be trouble.''

''As if I'd know trouble,'' Lialla mumbled. Chris decided to pretend he hadn't heard that and just kept going.

The area around the gates was as crowded as it had been hours earlier but there was more haste among the people milling from stand to stand; more people seemed to have a definite destination that put them squarely in front of the horses. And the horses, Chris thought, had probably had enough of a bad day already; the one under him was growing restive and wanted to shy at loud noises. When it balked as a small child and a dog ran under its feet, Chris slid to the ground, hauled the reins forward over its head and held out his left to Lialla. ''Gimme,'' he said. ''Before the damn thing steps on a rug rat.'' She shook her head, clearly not quite understanding, but handed over the reins as he crooked the fingers at her. ''Don't want to get chilled by the local man, do you?''

''Possibly not.'' Lialla froze, staring out toward the west along the street. She came up in the stirrups, shaded her eyes with one hand. Chris stood on tiptoe, swore; all *he* could see was heads and the flanks of some damned large horses and camels. ''I—Chris, can you get through all this? Hurry, please; I think I just saw Enardi.''

''Oh, jeez, what's he doing—?'' Chris bit his lip as someone turned to look at him in mild curiosity, eased his way through the jumble of people and beasts. Some of the stands out here were closing up for the night, adding to the mess. But he finally broke through, handed Lialla her reins and climbed back on a now thoroughly displeased and nervous horse.

''There.'' Lialla pointed rather cautiously. ''Ahead of us—there must be ten people in the wagon, but isn't that him?''

''Can't—wait.'' Chris nodded and nudged the horse forward. ''I'm pretty sure that's him, and that could be the mule—but the wheel's a dead giveaway; it looks like a puzzle.''

They caught up to the wagon not far from the park; Chris had wanted to go after it flat out but Lialla had reminded him that two people galloping out of Podhru might rouse a number of questions. He'd drawn in, but the horse was nearly impossible for him to control; clearly it sensed his nervousness and impatience.

Enardi was on the seat but he'd given the reins over to Bi-yallan, who drew the wagon to a stop at once when she could see who they were. "You're all right! Enardi—Merson, please hold the mule steady for me." She edged over the wheel and jumped to the ground in a flurry of full blue skirts. "Are you coming with us? Is that safe?"

Chris opened his mouth; Lialla shook her head, stopping him. "No, now you're here. We'll wait somewhere around here—to make certain they're all right. Get them, take them in, we'll keep you in sight."

"Of course." Biyallan merely nodded and let two of her companions hand her into the wagon. "We'll sort it," she said over her shoulder, and brought the reins down hard across the mule's back. Chris's horse would have followed, and the reins wrenched at his shoulders. He tightened his grip, rotated his shoulders rather cautiously, managed to get the animal turned and following Lialla as she made for the shadow of a cluster of young trees. He wasn't certain he'd be able to dismount without shaming himself, but somehow he was down, still on his feet, not visibly clinging to the saddle. Lialla came around the horse, water bottle in her hand. She drank, held it out.

"Here. You need this."

"God. I feel like I know what mom means when she says she needs a drink."

"Oh." Lialla shook her head. "I never could see what Aletto found in the stuff; it only makes me ill and gives me a headache."

"Yeah." Chris managed a faint grin. "Me, too. And wine is really gross stuff. A beer, maybe—but it doesn't taste that great either." He sighed. "I'd just kill for a Coke, though."

"A coke—?" Lialla shook her head and as Chris began to speak she echoed him. "Tell—you—later."

"One of these days, I'll talk your leg off, explaining all this stuff. It's funny, though. The way mom drinks, everyone all through school that knew, all mom's—um, friends—everyone figured I probably started on booze before I could read. Not like she ever tried to keep it from me; mom's no hypocrite. I just—it doesn't taste good, and I got too many things I want to do without taking out the time for getting wasted." He shook his head. "Sorry. That probably doesn't make any sense, I'm just running my mouth, you know?"

"Worried," Lialla said. "I know, who wouldn't be? I

had the time, just no inclination for making myself ill. Aletto—well, he had nothing *but* time, after all. Now that he's got better things to occupy himself, he's quit.''

"Yeah. Don't just take that at face value,'' Chris said glumly. "So'd mom, and she's really serious about not doing anything to encourage your brother to hit the bottle again. But it's not that easy. I don't know how he's managing but I've seen *her* fighting it. Back at the inn, back when Fedthyr was pushing the stuff at her.'' He started when Lialla clutched his sleeve; her eyes were fixed across his left shoulder. When he turned rather cautiously to look, he could see the wagon, the mule moving at a trot, heading back east. "I didn't see them; did you see them?''

"Robyn—both of them,'' Lialla replied tersely as she stepped into the saddle and turned the horse toward the road once more. Chris dragged himself back up and followed.

Some distance away, in a pair of neatly if sparsely furnished rooms that fronted on an inner courtyard four floors below, Jennifer tucked the chambray shirt into her jeans and pulled the zipper up, ran fingers through her hair preparatory to going at the flattened and snarled mess with her pick. The city guard had turned them over to other men, old, bearded men dressed in unrelieved black, who in turn escorted them along hallways, up flights of stairs, and finally showed them through one plain door of many. The door closed quietly behind them; when she tried it, though, the latch didn't move.

Dahven was sitting on the edge of a deeply cushioned sofa, head in his hands, and so far as she could tell, he hadn't moved, not during the time she had used to shed Caro Ellaway's sweat-laden dress and sponge down in the deep bowl of clean water, not all the while it had taken her to get her clothes sorted out and on. She came across, socks on and high-tops dangling from her fingers, to kneel before him. "Dahven,'' she said gently. "Dahven, how bad is it? Tell me, before someone comes, please?''

"Bad—'' He sighed, removed one hand to let it fall limp across his leg. "It's surely bad enough. And with you here—''

"That's done, over with, past doing anything about,'' she said, as gently. "So you don't have to worry about that any more. Just tell me what to expect.''

"I—''

"No, wait. Let me get my shoes on. While I'm doing that, I want you to think, put your thoughts in order." He let the other hand fall, shook his head faintly. "Don't look at me like that. I'm your advocate, remember?"

"You weren't—"

"I was as serous as I've ever been about anything. And frankly, after the past few days, I begin to think I'd be *much* happier fighting with my mouth, the way I used to."

"Dear, beloved gods," Dahven said softly. "Your face is bruised—"

"Shhh. That's past, too. Worry about it later, if you must. It's not painful. It's not important. I'm your advocate, and I'm an outsider, I don't know anything near enough about your laws, your rules. Don't even say it, I know I can't learn all that in an hour or so. That's why I want you to think, so you can help me prepare. All right?"

"I—all right."

"Are they likely to come before I finish getting dressed?"

He considered this, glanced at the distant—barred—window, and shook his head. "Not at this hour. Not before morning, now."

"Good. Then think, will you? What charges they might bring, what the law is concerning such charges. What special rights you might have, or the Emperor might. I'll get my shoes on." She shoved her foot in one high-top, paused with a handful of laces, and bent over to wrap her hands around the back of his neck and kiss him. "If talk can get you out of this mess, somehow I'll do it. Believe that."

He bent down to pick up her other high-top and held it out to her. "I heard you talk my father to a standstill, remember?" He drew his eyebrows together. "Jennifer. Why are you laughing like that?"

14

To his credit, once Dahven had the opportunity to marshal his thoughts, he gave her a creditable synopsis of the events in Sikkre as he knew them—telling her dispassionately about his return to his rooms, finding his father and brothers already there. The waiting seamen.

"When I left Sikkre, my father was yet alive." He shook his head. "Whether any man chooses to believe that—"

"These Lasanachi," Jennifer said calmly. "Describe them." He glanced up at her, did so. "I find it difficult to believe that such men—visibly unlike most Sikkreni, dressed as you describe them—could enter or leave the Thukar's tower without someone seeing them. Someone," she added gently before he could say it himself, "besides those who freely gave their allegiance to your brothers. We know *they* would perjure themselves if your brothers asked it."

"We do?" Dahven glanced up hopefully and Jennifer managed a small smile.

"Your advocate intends to press that notion, and with conviction."

"Oh."

"I couldn't press it if it weren't already very likely. As things presently stand, I do believe we have a good chance of injecting doubt into the matter—as to your opportunity to murder your father."

"I could almost feel reassured, listening to you."

"Good. But that's only one side of the matter. Tell me what you can about the charges they might have against you."

He sat back and considered this. Jennifer drew one of her last yellow pads from the depths of the bag, set three ballpoint pens and a pencil across it, and waited—she hoped calmly. Dahven was already upset enough, without worrying that she didn't have a handle on matters. He leaned forward as she picked up one of the pens; his face lit up, then, and he reached for the pencil. "May I? This—the wizard Snake had three in a small bag he carried, with the paper I told you about, for music. He gave one each to Deehar and Dayher, not so long ago. They were pleased, and I thought it must be quite a sacrifice on the man's part, since his own was a piece no longer than my little finger by then."

"Pencil," Jennifer said, and closed his fingers over it. "Keep it, I have another—several, actually. That one's fairly new so the eraser's probably still good, they get hard after a while, don't work too well." She uncapped her stick ball-point pen, scribbled a couple of lines in one corner to get the ink flowing, made quick shorthand notes of what he'd already told her. Dahven got up and came around the table to watch over her shoulder. "All right. Tell me some more, we might well have the rest of the night, but I should think you'd like to sleep part of it."

He sighed, laid a hand on her hair. "Sleep. It may be my last night for that—"

"Don't." She captured his fingers, laid them on her right shoulder. "Tell me things instead, that's more useful, isn't it? A really good advocate should be able to spring a guilty client, I only have an innocent one to fight for, so it shouldn't be as difficult, should it?" Silence. She added, rather anxiously, "You were kidding about last possible night, weren't you? They wouldn't simply take you out and—and what? Execute you without even a trial?"

"Sword," Dahven replied briefly; his fingers tightened on her shoulder when she shuddered and closed her eyes. "Don't. It hasn't been done since Shesseran VIII let Po-dhru's nobles run wild, and then tried to settle matters overnight with extreme measures. I'm sorry, I shouldn't have said that."

"No, you shouldn't," Jennifer replied. "Come over here where I can see you, sit down, talk to me." She recaptured his hand briefly, released it as he sat back on the sofa and closed his eyes. "For a start: What would the difference be, legally, if your brothers swore a complaint for your father's death or if the Emperor stepped in and did it himself?" He shook his head, confused. "Would it require more proof in one case or the other? Or would the word of the swearer hold more weight in one way or the other? And in each case, what forms of defense are open to you?"

"You don't want much, do you?" Dahven asked mildly, and he flashed her a smile.

"Not much," she said, so quietly he had to lean forward to catch the words. "You alive, and returned to Sikkre where you belong." She leveled the pen at his nose. "If you dare laugh—!"

"I wouldn't dream of it," he assured her, but his eyes were alight as he leaned back. "After all, I can scarcely offer you half of Sikkre if I don't have it."

"Mmmm. You'll have to come up with something else to cover my fee, you know. Something additional. You already proffered half of Sikkre—before witnesses, as I recall—and my legal rates are pretty high."

Some distance away, the shops on the Street of the Blind Muse were dark and empty. Behind the storefront bearing a wooden cutout shape of a sheep clad in a bright red jacket, a number of young Bezanti merchants sat in the high-walled garden of Kamahl the weaver, eating fruit and cheese, drinking a sweet wine. The lighting was low, the voices quiet, but there was still an atmosphere of party. These, after all, were men and women whose parents held portions of the Bezjeriad market—and whose parents were still young and healthy enough not to wish to break up those shares of the market. It was unexpected and unforeseen fortune, to be twenty, or twenty-five, and have the opportunity to begin anew, to aid a man in search of his birthright—a man who had not only spoken freely of a good return on such aid but had signed papers at the house of Fedthyr promising various concessions in Sehfi's market.

It was some time before any of those gathered around Kamahl's braziers and lamps noticed that Fedthyr's heir Enardi, Enardi's strong-minded sister Biyallan—and the two Bez strangers they'd gone to ferry into Podhru during the late afternoon, as well as the fresh-faced twins who'd joined them, somewhere between the city gates and Kamahl's sign—were all gone.

In point of fact, the six had left only a very short time before.

Biyallan led them back through Kamahl's house and spoke briefly with the householder, waited then with the rest of them for the man to unbolt his door. Robyn swallowed and tried not to think about anything in particular as she stepped into the dark street, the door closed and the metal bolt slid into place behind them. Aletto wrapped an arm around her shoulder and gave her a brief squeeze. Biyallan touched his arm and then Robyn's on the way past them, and stepped into the empty street.

Some distance away, a blue light illuminated a narrow patch of cobble—at one of those godawful star-shaped intersections, Chris thought. They were everywhere, especially in this end of town. Lialla shivered down into her borrowed cloak—one of Biyallan's, very bright blue. Chris gripped her shoulder, and when she looked up, he winked. Reassuringly, he hoped. Biyallan looked toward the blue light, turned to set out in the other direction; she carried a partly shielded lantern that cast just enough light to keep her and anyone right behind her from tripping on the uneven pavement.

There was sound everywhere: voices raised behind walls or closed doors, a child crying. Dogs barking, and a distant noise of someone riding a shod horse at speed along one of the streets. *Better him than me,* Chris thought. After this day, he'd been truly relieved to leave the horses in Kamahl's stable, among his shearing materials, his milk goats and the motherless lambs he was hand-raising. Chris wasn't sure what the deal with this Evany was, but he was growing worried about the whole situation: Evany hadn't wanted them to bring the horses—well, maybe he didn't have room for eight horses; he and Robyn hadn't had a garage back in L.A., any of their apartments, and only once a carport that might have held a Volkswagen bug but nothing bigger.

All the same. Bits of things he'd heard, or thought he might have heard were coming back: This Evany was supposed to be a close friend of Aletto's dad, one of his close advisors; but someone had said some really rude things about him, one of those afternoons back in Bez, when they were all sitting around eating and chewing things over. Someone else had laughed, said something else even ruder— what, though? *I need multi-tracking,* Chris thought. *My brain's not up to all this kinda stuff.*

Didn't matter, if Evany was taking them in. Then again, there was that Casimaffi guy with the non-showing ship, wasn't there? Yeah, something about Lord Evany hating to stick his head up where anyone could see it and use it for a target? Something for sure about the guy not having the hair to say what he really thought, and living the last fifteen or so years scared someone was gonna do him just for having been Amarni's man? *Jeez*, Chris thought disgustedly, *talk about chicken-shittedness, how can anyone live like that?* Well, that wasn't his problem, so long as this guy wasn't actually living in Jadek's pocket, like old Chuffles supposedly was. *All this gossip and stuff, I feel like I spent the last six months watching all those afternoon talk shows and reading the Enquirer,* Chris thought in even deeper disgust.

Lialla tugged at his arm, getting his attention. Biyallan and Enardi were crossing a bridge; somehow he'd lost a few minutes and had no idea where they were. The air was downright cold above the skinny little stream, and it didn't smell too good, either. *I'll bet an ecologist would starve around here.* On the far side, Biyallan turned and went between two buildings, past shuttered, lit windows. Chris's ears and nose were assaulted as he passed them: wine and a large number of men talking, laughing, shouting and trading insults. Common room of an inn, fairly popular one. He hadn't eaten much dinner, too nervous, and the smell of the narrow alley, stale wine and some kind of meat threatened to make him sick. Lialla just ahead of him made an unhappy, wordless little noise and hurried past the second window; he was right behind her.

The alley opened into a courtyard; Biyallan gathered everyone around her and sent Enardi to the back door. He returned moments later with a skinny boy of perhaps ten, who glanced at them incuriously and led them back past stables, into another alley which emptied into a medium-sized, well-lit avenue. There were plenty of pedestrians here—mixed, laughing groups of young people in bright clothes, middle-aged men who moved from open shop to open shop with purpose; couples walking more slowly. It reminded Chris in an odd way of Westwood Village on a Friday night—*Except no movies, no video arcades,* he thought rather bleakly. Well, no one looked bored, anyway; they obviously didn't miss what they didn't have and didn't know about.

The boy moved at an easy pace across the avenue, along a narrow, raised stone walkway, back across the street and into a narrow little shop with a battered copper pot hanging above its door. The interior smelled like hot metal and there were copper pots and implements everywhere inside: hanging like onions from the ceiling, piled against the walls and upon shelves, spoons and like items strung on wires and draped swaglike from corner to corner. Chris stared in fascination until Lialla touched his arm and got his attention. The rest of their party was disappearing through a narrow opening in the back of the shop. The boy left them there, after turning them over to a girl not much older than he. The girl took them back into the shop, outside and back along the direction they'd come, turned at the next intersection and led them into an even busier street—this one narrow and uncomfortably crowded. There were cafes here— covered patios where families sat, or only men, or tables surrounded by young people who drank and laughed as though there were nothing serious anywhere in the world. Chris eyed them wistfully as they walked past, smiled at the girl who looked up from those she was talking with to meet his eyes.

The change in traffic was swift: One moment people everywhere, the next a quiet, broad street, a raised parklike area running down its center, with shrubs and trees and, by the fragrance, flowers. By the chill, there must be pools or fountains also; it was so dark, Chris couldn't make out anything but the darker shadowed outline against only slightly paler walls in the remains of light from the area behind them.

They stopped, so suddenly he ran into Robyn, who turned and gave him a little shove back. Their guide had stopped before a dark, shuttered shop. There was a sign above the door, a large dark square with a very pale sheep hanging by a strap from its middle. He couldn't make out anything else; it was too dark. The sign, though: *That's a fleece*, Chris realized. A genuine medieval heraldic symbol from his own world. *These people are gonna drive me nuts,* he thought in irritation. And then the rattle and scrape of a metal bolt brought his attention back to the moment and the darkened shop before them, their small and—he thought— nervous guide.

He couldn't see the person standing in the opening very clearly; he and Lialla were bringing up the rear and so he couldn't hear any of the low-voiced conversation, either. Biyallan and Enardi vanished inside; the child ran back down the street toward lights and safety. *Jeez, don't think that way,* Chris told himself hastily. Robyn turned a pale face toward him, hesitated, and let Aletto lead her into the shop. Chris sighed very quietly and followed Lialla. The bolt sounded as final as the one at Kamahl's had, except that one had only shut them out.

They stood for one brief moment in the dark before someone brought a light. This shop was as crowded as the copper seller's had been, but with fabric—thick bolts of it, just about any color he could imagine, stripes, fabric that sparkled in the lantern-light, everything else from a very matte black to an extremely bright red. A long bolt of various colored thin ribbon lay on a table, atop a thick piece of plush that felt like velvet.

The light was moving, and Chris could see their new guide: a girl or young woman with very long, coppery red hair that must have gone to her knees, worn loose over a flowing blue thing that fluttered around her ankles; she wore a wrapped band around her forehead made out of a similar blue with silvery thread in it. He couldn't yet see her face, but he felt better already.

In the room directly behind the main shop, the girl slowed to speak to two other women who were sitting amid a pile of cushions, one holding thick blue material while the other wound it onto a bolt. The two looked at their visitors with interest, and the woman holding the bolt—she looked like enough the girl in blue and old enough to Chris to be the girl's mother—set the fabric aside and got to her feet to push ahead of them all and vanish behind what appeared to be a blanket tacked to the wall. It covered a door opening; behind this, a dimly lit room redolent of lanolin and full of piled fleeces. There was a side door here and Chris could hear voices: a sleepy-sounding, rather cross child, a thin-voiced woman singing.

The girl in blue led them straight across the storage room and through a deserted, open area—floored and carpeted, roofed but without walls—that held three large looms, spinning wheels and other apparatus Chris didn't recognize. Beyond the roofed area, there was a brick-lined pit, a pile of wood, several large, blackened kettles set over a low, hot fire, several grouped lanterns and lines holding wadded-looking bundles of apparently fresh-dyed stuff.

There was a wall at the end of the loom area, a high, arched double door set in the wall. Beyond the door, a courtyard, with blue-lights surrounding a pool and set among an impressively landscaped garden. The girl paused by the doors, letting them precede her onto the graveled path. She held out the lantern to Chris as he slowed. "My father will come very shortly. There are other lanterns over there"—she pointed to the right of the pool—"if you desire more light. And there are rugs and pillows, for sitting." She was gone before Chris could think of anything to say; fortunately, he decided after he found his breath. The face didn't let down that wonderful hair one bit, and he'd probably have said something incredibly dumb.

Another girl came moments later, with a servant: a much younger girl, probably the age of Caro Ellaway's daughter, no more than thirteen, though. Chris bit back a sigh and wondered if he was fated to be saddled with the babies, while the babes stayed just out of hearing and sight. Biyallan was nice, but still a little too—*brisk* for his liking. And she had priorities, major ones; taking up with a guy was probably right at the bottom of her list.

The girl shepherded them over to the seating area and down among cushions while she lit lanterns; the serving-woman followed with a tray holding what looked like a bowl of dried fruit, and a pitcher of wine, cups. Robyn sniffed and sighed very quietly when one was handed to her; Chris cleared his throat. "Um. Is it possible, could we get water also? I can't drink wine myself, instant headache, you know?" The older woman looked at him as though he'd lost his mind—or, Chris decided later, as though a dog or Enardi's mule or something had spoken. Probably just like that woman in Bez; expected everyone to drink fermented grapes and like it. The girl gave him a cheerful smile, lots of neat, white teeth, and nodded, then turned to take the tray from the servant.

"Go on, get water," she urged in a very high and thin voice, before turning back to Chris. "My father does not often permit me wine yet, and when he does it makes *my* head ache, too." She settled the tray on the broad edge of the pool—a knee-high tiled ledge that ran around three sides of the shallow, rectangular water basin. The fourth sloped sharply uphill, vanishing into darkness. There was a tinkle of running water from up there somewhere, and Chris thought he could just make out a spill of water running into the far edge of the pool. *Jeez*, he thought rather sourly, *nice to be rich, isn't it?* The girl passed cups around, set the bowl in their midst and settled on the edge of the pool next to the empty tray, knees drawn up, eyes alight with interest and curiosity.

"I am Evany's fourth daughter, Roisan. He asked that we see to your comfort a few moments; he was detained by business. If there is anything we can obtain for you, any question we can answer?" *Yeah*, Chris thought, *who was that in blue and is she single?* Not that he'd dare ask—But the serving woman was back already, with a large pitcher and more cups together with a cut loaf. And just behind her, piled high with more cushions and several folded wraps, the other young woman. She distributed these while Roisan kept up a constant chatter. "This is the woman who cooks for us, Ehmat; the bread is hers, quite good. And my eldest sister, Meriyas."

"Hush, Roisan," Meriyas said in a low, resonant voice. "These people have come a long way; they are surely too tired to listen to so much pointless talk." She looked around the group, handed Robyn one of the wraps and Lialla another, cast Chris a glance from under long lashes and a warm smile that went right through him. He couldn't remember later if he smiled back. What he did remember was the sharp, warning look he intercepted from his mother. *Right. Don't mess with the local girls, especially not when Aletto needs folding green from the old man. But I can look, can't I? She* was sure looking, and he would've sworn she winked at him.

Aletto gathered himself together with a visible effort and did a proper job of introductions. He looked fairly worried, though, and Chris thought the fact of Evany not being right at the door to greet them wasn't helping. Well, it was about time Aletto grew some sense about trusting people; Chris himself was a little worried about this "business" stuff. What kind of business could be that important? It had better not be going off and getting more of those city guards together, to haul them all away. He, Chris, was going to be fairly unhappy if that happened.

Meriyas smiled again, rather generally, and went away with the cook. Roisan sat on the edge of the pool, watching them all, talking to Biyallan, who was apparently the only one of them able to put aside current worry enough to carry on a normal-sounding conversation.

God, Chris thought feelingly. *How are we gonna get Jen and Dahven out of that—what'd she call it?—civil service building? And Edrith?* That was the Emperor's guard, after all, the Emperor's civil service—and as Jennifer kept reminding him, this place was a far cry from a democracy. The guy could pretty much do what he wanted with anyone, then.

Except, maybe not. Historically, in his own world, major despots and dictators of the sort that did whatever they wanted, including wholesale murder, didn't usually have a contented middle class like this, there were a lot more armed guards everywhere—and they didn't ordinarily relinquish control of all but a postage-stamp corner of the whole country to others. Wrong scenario. Probably, like most monarchies, there were checks and balances on this Shesseran character. With such a huge civil service, and a reasonably small guard—there'd been a lot fewer uniformed men on the streets of Podhru today than cops in L.A.—that seemed likely.

It almost made him feel better.

Jennifer turned over another page of yellow pad, glanced over her shoulder as someone clomped down the hall beyond the locked door—the first sign she'd had in hours that there was anyone else in the building. Dahven was leaning forward on both elbows, one hand planted under his chin as though he needed the support, eyes half-closed. His other hand held the pencil she'd given him, and he was making marks—Rhadazi cursive handwriting, she supposed—on the two sheets she'd pulled free and given to him. She pushed hair from her forehead with the back of one hand and turned a page back, flipped forward to the blank sheet and began condensing what he'd been able to tell her—his testimony of events, what he knew of the law together with every possible witness and every single historical precedent she'd been able to get out of him.

It made a reasonably impressive sheaf of yellow pad, particularly since she'd used every single line, both sides, in order to conserve a resource that was dwindling even faster than her aspirins: paper. Paper, specifically, that was just this size, this thinness, this texture—yellow. She still had three legal pads with varying amounts of unused paper on them. Maybe by the time they were used up, she'd have adjusted to having to use something else, be able to think in a format that wasn't eight and one-half by eleven, blue-lined, yellow. There were enough law firms in L.A. already making their people shift to white pads because of recycling, anyway.

Unimportant, damnit, she told herself fiercely. Aloud, she said, "That's all you can tell me?"

He was still for a very long moment, thinking. "I can't recall another single thing." More silence, broken only by the scratch of his pencil, the more furtive noise of her ballpoint. "It won't be enough. Will it?"

She finished her note, set down the capital letter for the next point and dropped the pen so she could massage out her fingers. "I think it will. Remember we have Edrith, also; you know he won't let you down, don't you?"

"I know that. I'm simply thinking of his background, whether anyone would take the word of a known thief against that of two noblemen—"

"Combined with everything else, corroborated by my word—"

"You have a vested interest in me," Dahven said shrewdly.

"A possible one," Jennifer corrected him gently. She let him take her hand and massage the fingers.

"I—"

"Meaning, of course, that while many women might take up with a nobleman for half his birthright, obviously a lot of women haven't asked that much of you. There's no proof that I held out on you for that, is there? Or that you offered it? In any event, I don't think my testimony is that prejudiced, and since they've kept us apart from Edrith, they won't be able to assume we've matched stories—"

"Well, not since coming into Podhru," Dahven said gloomily.

"That's true. However," Jennifer hesitated, then reached to shove back his shirt sleeve. The pale, wide line where a Lasanachi manacle had been was still there, fainter now, slightly pink from too much sun. "You have other corroboration, of all of it. If you'll let me use it."

"Gods of my father." He tugged, freeing the hand, shoved the sleeve down with one hard yank against the table. "I can't—I can't do *that*."

"Not for your birthright? Your Duchy? For me—my life and your own?"

"I can't—"

"I won't ask it, not unless I must. Dahven, please, believe that I won't. I know how you feel about it."

"You can't."

"I can!" she said fiercely. "Oh, not personally, not all the way to the base of my guts, the way you do. From seeing Robyn beaten black and blue, her arm broken, her half silly from pain drugs—and trying to tell me, Chris, anyone who'd listen, that she'd tripped over something on the front step and fallen! Because her boyfriend got mad over something and knocked her around." Dahven brought his head up and stared at her. Jennifer nodded. "At first, I couldn't understand it. If anyone had hit me like that, I'd have killed them. If that wasn't possible—he was nearly twice her size, after all—I'd have called the cops, filed charges. He'd have been in jail so fast his head would've spun. She couldn't do that, she was so embarrassed, so ashamed that something that stupidly, dumbly violent had happened to her, that she lied about it. Hell, I don't know, by now maybe even she believes her own lie."

"But you know what was the worst thing about it?" Eyes never leaving hers, he shook his head slowly. "The absolutely worst part was, after Robyn got rid of him, he went on to get another girlfriend, beat up on her. And her kids, and her mother. He got away with it for so long, so many times, he didn't even worry any more about getting caught or stopped." Silence. Jennifer retrieved her pen, began writing next to the letter she'd set down, wrote another point, a sub-number, and stopped again to look up at him. "You wouldn't happen to see any parallels there, would you?" she asked.

"You think my brothers—?"

"Oh, Dahven, damnit! You know they were responsible for your father's death—whether he simply died of frustration and a heart attack, or they laced his evening wine with something! You talked to those men on the road here; you know damn well your brothers want you dead! Who or what's next after you? Anyone in Sikkre's market who dislikes their policies? Anyone who was your friend, your girlfriend, your ally, Aletto's?"

"They wouldn't—" He stopped, shook his head. "All right, maybe they would. But—"

"Trust your advocate," she overrode him firmly. "I'll do everything I can with argument. I told you I didn't understand Birdy's attitude, all that shame. Well, I'm older now, and I've been around a little more; I understand better about privacy. You have a right to it, to outsiders not knowing things about you. Things that would make them uncomfortable, or you. So I promise I won't ask you to show anyone your arm—or to take off your shirt and let them see what's left of the scars on your back—unless nothing else is going to save your life.'' She drew a deep breath, pen poised over yellow pad, and met his gaze squarely. ''But if it comes to that, I'll use anything I have, anything I can. I'd be a lousy advocate if I did anything else.''

Silence once more. She finished her synopsis and looked up to see he was still watching her, but now he was smiling. ''You're lying,'' he said lightly. ''A good advocate works within the laws; you said as much yourself.''

''A really good advocate wouldn't be in love with her client either,'' Jennifer said, and pointed the pen at his nose. ''That doesn't mean you're going to pull any of my strings, though, you got that?'' She stifled a yawn, capped the ballpoint and flipped the pages back so that the yellow pad lay flat. ''God, I think I'm dead. What time is it?'' She glanced at her watch and groaned. ''Too late. I think the sun's probably only four hours away. Any idea when they start work here?''

Dahven considered this, finally shrugged. ''Father's men began when sun entered the clerks' hall, about three hours past sunrise, in order to save on the cost and smoke of candles and lanterns. That may hold true here, it may not.''

''Well.'' She pushed away from the table, forced herself up onto dead, stiff legs and stretched hard. ''Four hours sleep is better than none, don't you agree?''

He got himself upright, turned away from the table, looked around the room, and through the arched entry to the next. There was a low, pallet bed in this room, another in the next. ''Four hours,'' he murmured, and when Jennifer brushed by him, he caught her fingers and brought them to his lips. ''I doubt there's any sleep in me, in all honesty.'' She leaned back against him, rubbing his chin with the top of her head; he pressed his cheek against dark curls and let his eyes close for a moment. ''Since my advocate demands strict honesty from me.''

She sighed faintly, but didn't pull away as he half expected; her fingers tightened on his. ''I'm not certain I'll sleep either. I should try, and so should you.'' She looked up from under a spill of hair. ''There's no reason for us to make the effort in separate bedding, though, is there?''

"Well—" He appeared to give this serious consideration, finally shook his head.

"Will they give you the courtesy of a knock in the morning, or simply come through that door?"

"Well—" He considered this in turn. "Given my rank, even if there are writs against me, even Shesseran's own writs—they were courteous enough when they brought us here, weren't they?" He reached down to slide a finger under her chin and looked at her consideringly. "Are there reasons for asking?"

Jennifer laughed quietly. "The look on your face!"

"What look?"

"Don't try and sound so innocent; it isn't working. Or so naively hopeful—or so confused. I'll bet you really are a hit with the girls back home."

"That's not fair," he protested mildly.

"Yes, that was my thought exactly," Jennifer replied dryly. "Yes, there are reasons, specifically that I'd like to at least be back in my shirt before anyone breaks the door down tomorrow. All right?" She turned and slid into his arms, resting her cheek against his shoulder.

He swallowed, his mouth suddenly much too dry. "All right." He swallowed a second time, leaned back to look down into dark and very serious eyes. "I meant what I said before, you know: that it wasn't likely this was my last night."

"Oh, I know that. This isn't desperation on my part, you know. Or prompted by fear." Her mouth quirked. "Or to seal the bargain on half of Sikkre, either." She took both his hands and began walking slowly backwards toward the second room, bringing him perforce with her. He stopped suddenly, shook his head.

"My arm band—"

"Your—oh, *that*." Jennifer laughed, then cleared her throat; her cheekbones were brightly pink. "Protection, right? Um. Thank you, I appreciate the reminder. Back by the window, in my bag—I think that's all—um—covered." She considered this, laughed again and went red right to her eyebrows.

"Jennifer?" Dahven asked in a quiet, baffled voice. She merely shook her head, took hold of his hands once more, and drew him across the main chamber and into the second with her.

* * *

A floor lower in the same building, and across the central courtyard, Edrith lay on a narrow raised platform, hands behind his head. He was contemplating the distant and not very visible ceiling; unlike Jennifer and Dahven, the guards hadn't offered him light beyond a single lantern, and whatever oil it had been filled with gave him a headache and made his eyes water. He had turned it down immediately after eating what was a surprisingly well-prepared meal (much better, Edrith thought, then anything he'd ever had in Sikkre's lockups), let the guard turn it up a short time later when the red-and-gold-clad guard-master came in with a long-nosed clerk. The guard-master had let him tell his own story first—again, surprisingly—about his discovery of Dahven in Bez, the subsequent journey to Podhru, and after had asked a series of highly intelligent and to-the-point questions. Not stupid at all, Edrith thought uncomfortably. He'd had enough time to think about things, to plan what he'd say about the whole state of affairs; it was difficult to keep to that with the guard-master snapping questions at him, that old man writing every word down. He'd come south with a number of people, yes, stayed off the road at their request, no, hadn't considered at the time they might be other than the innocuous travelers they said. Well, perhaps it had occurred to him after the first couple of attacks that it might be Zelharri's nera-Duke, but it wasn't his business to ask; he'd been hired to take care of the animals and to guide them to a certain house in Bezjeriad, and he'd done all that.

Yes, he had known Lord Dahven, several years' worth. No, he sincerely doubted the man was capable of anyone's murder. He'd felt the sweat on his forehead, running down from his armpits when he began describing the afternoon in the lower Bez markets, down by the docks, finding Dahven, blood on his hand, the rescue. By then he wasn't attempting to hedge the truth at all, knowing there was nothing in the story to reflect adversely on any of them—reasonably certain Jennifer would tell the same story.

He'd been frank and truthful about everything since—leaving out Aletto's name, and Lialla's. Now that he thought about it, it was curious that the guard hadn't asked any more about them. Maybe he was one of those only capable of concentrating on one point at a time—or maybe he'd been told not to bring up the nera-Duke. Edrith thought about this, shook his head and got himself settled a little more

197

comfortably on the pallet bed. That kind of thinking wasn't his forte, and he could second-guess the fancy-clad city guardsman all night and still only be guessing.

He'd turned the lamp all the way down as soon as he'd signed the clerk's written pages and they'd gone away, while he had gone in search of the last of the wine that had accompanied his meal and then this bed.

They'd been polite; he wondered if they'd somehow mistaken *his* rank, or if such men would be polite to anyone who might be under Dahven's protection. *Gods of my mother,* Edrith thought. *I hope they were as good to him, and to Jen.* Where, he wondered, in all this massive building had they placed those two? And how much longer before things were decided for all of them?

15

CHRIS didn't care at all for Lord Evany. The man—what he could only think of as a "little man"—came bustling into the patio after an hour or so, just percolating with self-importance. He wore silk, stripes that tried to make him look tall and slender and only succeeded in emphasizing the stretch of fabric over a discreet, round paunch. He was shorter than his youngest daughter, neatly combed and bearded, his hands soft as a girl's—or as the blue leather slippers he wore on fat little feet. *Soft*, Chris thought in mild disgust. *Middle-aged, upper-class, rich and soft. Swell.* He wondered how his mother was going to manage to suck up to this one; Ernie's dad Fedthyr had at least been a funny little duck. This guy was simply fussy, one of those who'd straighten the pillows behind you and empty ashtrays while you were using them—if, Chris corrected himself with a rather embarrassed glance at his mother, there had been ashtrays and cigarettes here. Fusspot. From the look on Robyn's face, she saw what her son saw: money, lots of old and conservative money, together with a corresponding lack of desire to take chances, or try anything new.

Aletto didn't seem to have any such worries, of course; this was the dude who'd pulled rabbits from a hat at the dinner table, or something like that. Chris had to admit, to himself anyway, that such a guy would be bound to make a lasting impression on a kid. All the same, Aletto wasn't exactly a kid any more, and a lot of lives depended on what he was doing. Wasn't as though he didn't know that, either. But he just didn't seem to catch on that you had to figure some years had gone by, you had to judge people by something besides a kid's impressions of them. *I learned that pretty early on, myself,* Chris thought sourly. *Not like it's impossible; should only take getting burned once.*

He brought his attention back to the moment with some difficulty; the headache was still there and his neck hurt, too, from being so tight so long. Evany was talking, quickly, his voice a little too high-pitched for a grown man's, and during the rare moments when he wasn't actually speaking his lips thinned against his teeth. *Yeah. Wants us gone, before we get him in trouble, cost him the fancy house and all.* Chris glanced over at Meriyas and mentally shrugged. Then again, the guy had a point; who'd want the Emperor getting pissed and kicking a chick like that out in the street? "My Lord—Honor Aletto," Evany corrected himself smoothly, "you are welcome to my house. How may I aid you?"

Aletto smiled; he had gotten on his feet as soon as the older man came into sight, and now he had Evany's hands in his. "Sir, you've scarcely changed since Sehfi. I've never forgotten your kindness in livening otherwise dull formal dinners for a boy. I understand from the Bezjeriad merchants who once bought and sold under father, particularly Fedthyr—he sends you his personal greeting, by the way—Fedthyr tells me there is a supply of coin to be put at my disposal—?"

"Yes," Evany said rather warily.

"And Father's old armsmaster is to meet me here?" Evany nodded. The smile hung on his lips as though he'd forgotten it, incongruous beneath the drawn brows and worried-looking eyes. Aletto smiled again, let the man's hands go. "I truly do not wish to rush you, please understand that, but I have been gone so long from Duke's Fort, and I hope to settle matters between myself and my uncle as quickly as possible. This indecision and uncertainty is not good for the Duchy, and," he added ruefully, "it is not particularly pleasant for me, either."

Evany's relief was almost comical; Aletto turned away and appeared not to notice. Chris bent forward to rub his nose and smother a laugh.

"Honor Aletto. You and your guests are welcome to my house. It is late now, of course; too late to accomplish anything of much import. Word is out, you understand, among our own kind. Gyrdan will doubtless come at first light, and there are others here in Podhru, men such as myself exiled when your uncle seized the Fort. They want to meet you, I know."

"Of course," Aletto said. He settled on the edge of the fountain, legs stretched out before him and crossed at the ankle. "Were any of that money mine, I should also like to see what manner of man intended to carry it north." Evany's smile faded briefly and his eyes widened, obviously surprised that Aletto was so sharp, Chris thought. A breath later, he had his face under control, and he laughed, spread his hands wide.

"Well, as you say, Honor, men such as myself understand the value of coin, and most of us dislike wasting money. A good cause, of course—" He let the sentence hang, gestured imperiously to his daughters. "The hour is late; tonight you may have my guest room—and such of you as wish may sleep here; the weather is quite warm, and most in Podhru sleep outside of the house when it is like this. The walls are high and I assure you that none will scale them to bother you." He waited while they discussed this—even Robyn preferred remaining outside. Evany smiled then and spread his arms again, taking them all in. "My daughters and my servants will bring more sleeping mats for you, coverings and more cushions. There is shade where you are in the morning; those trees block first sun. We will take tea together early, if it pleases you. Until then." He inclined his upper body, backed several paces, then turned and swept up the graveled walk and into the house, shooing his daughters before him.

It had been Biyallan's notion that she and Enardi should remain at Evany's for the night; that there wasn't much sense to the two of them going back to Kamahl's and possibly drawing someone's attention to either household. It occurred to Chris also that it would give her another opportunity to talk to Aletto—one the other Bezanti at Kamahl's wouldn't get. And of course a chance for Enardi to maybe finalize that deal Aletto'd already talked to him about. Chris dismissed Biyallan from his thoughts and sent a covert glance toward the house. Meriyas, on the other hand—*yeah, right, really cute. With my luck, she's got the brains of a poodle, or she was promised out by her old man when she was ten.* Well, a guy could *look*, though—if he was reasonably careful about it, he could. And Meriyas sure looked back at him, a lot. He sighed rather contentedly and picked carefully at his hair, washed out at Kamahl's and still too dark from the sage rinse but again clean and spiked with the least amount of hair spray he could get away with.

Lialla looked like she might already be asleep; she'd been nodding for most of the evening anyway, and now all he could see of her was a muddle of dark fabric tucked among a pile of light-colored cushions, one small hand that protruded from the Wielder Blacks to clutch at the fringed corner of one pillow.

Aletto was sitting against the fountain wall, pillows behind him and Robyn's head on his shoulder. She looked comfortable, even happy. She sighed, and Aletto turned to look at her. "That inn was really nice; I could envy Caro what she's got there." Aletto didn't say anything, but he moved, murmured something. Robyn pulled slightly away so she could look up at him and quietly demanded, "What?"

"Nothing."

She edged completely from under his arm and sat back on her heels, facing him. "Aletto, it's not nothing—what?" Silence. "Was it what I said?"

"Is that what *you* want?"

"I—what d'you mean, what I want?" Robyn ran a hand through her hair, dislodging pins and loosening the already unfastened braids. "Aletto—!"

He was looking down at his hands, talking in such a low voice Chris couldn't make out what he was saying; Robyn leaned close enough to apparently catch some of it and when she sat back on her heels again she was gazing at him in round-eyed astonishment. "Aletto! You know I don't want a choice like that! You think I plan on just—just dumping you and going off that way? What's wrong with you?" Silence. Robyn went on after a moment in a much lower voice. "Damnit, Aletto! Just because I couldn't commit to you the

last time we talked about all that doesn't mean I—oh, hell.''
She turned away. Aletto reached for her shoulder; she tore
it out of his grasp. "Did you listen to yourself? You just
knew I didn't care, you just knew I never meant to stay with
you—''

"You never said," Aletto began defensively.

"Why did I need *words*?" Robyn demanded. She spun
back around and came up onto one knee. "Look," she
added in a much softer voice. "Why are we fighting about
this? There's enough bad karma all around us without that."

"I don't want to fight," Aletto said stubbornly. "I just—
I want to know. I don't want to feel my stomach drop when
you say things like that."

"What, that I liked Caro Ellaway's inn? I did like it; I'd
like a home like that, all spacious, view of the ocean, light
and clean. That didn't mean I'm ready to go off on my own
and *get* one, does it?" She held out a hand, laid it against
his cheek; he wouldn't meet her eyes but his own hand came
up to hold it where it was. "Aletto—all right, then. You
want to hear it, want the words? I would like that kind of
home; I'm willing to take whatever Duke's Fort turns out to
be." Silence. "You aren't going to believe me, though, are
you? Not really?" She brought up her other hand to cup his
face, leaned forward and kissed him, sat back again. "All
right. Before we go any farther, before something else goes
wrong." She managed a shaky little laugh. "Before I open
my big mouth again and leave you feeling even more rotten
than you feel right now because Jen and Dahven got picked
up and you couldn't stop it happening—''

"I don't—''

"Aletto, I know you better than that, don't even say it.
Find Evany, get him to find us a priest or whatever it takes."

"I—you don't have to—''

"Don't you dare try and tell me I don't," Robyn said.
"It's called a life contract, isn't it? Unless *you're* having
second thoughts, you get that little man to set it up. Because
I'm not starting an heir for you without the contract." They
sat very still for what seemed forever; Aletto finally let his
head fall back and he laughed delightedly before jumping
to his feet.

Robyn sat staring at the cushions where he'd been. She
shook herself then, and sighed. "All right, kid," she said.
"You aren't invisible."

Chris shifted; the edge of the fountain was hard and cold.

"Wasn't trying to be," he replied. "Just came over to see if I couldn't help cheer up your boyfriend—sorry, your fiancé."

"Short engagement," Robyn said, and a brittle laugh ended whatever else she was about to say. After a moment, she slewed around to look up at him. "You mind, kid?"

"Not that it matters, greatly," Chris said. "But no, I don't really. He's got a lot more class than some people. Names unnamed, of course. Provided we get out of Podhru in one piece, he even has a reasonable future."

"Smart kid."

"Odd having a stepdad only a few years older than me— what, eleven? But, hey, I'm easy." He looked down at Robyn, who was eyeing him rather anxiously, and smiled. "Hey, Mom, don't sweat it, all right? I like the guy, you could do a lot worse—"

"I *have* done a lot worse," Robyn said somberly.

"Old business. So long as no one expects me to play babysitter for these heirs."

"I can't believe I told him that," Robyn said in a very small voice.

"I can't either; I never thought you cared about legit. Hey, before you say it, don't look at me that way, I don't care. Why should I? You never made a big deal out of it, none of my friends ever knew—so what?"

"Hey, kid—"

"Don't. Let it drop, okay? More old business."

"Yeah—well." Robyn let out a gusty sigh. "Yeah. In Aletto's case, though, it's the inheritance-thing."

"You been reading some of my history books?"

"No," Robyn replied dryly. "I actually read my own, back when. Aletto—what's he doing over there by the door?"

Chris turned and squinted. "Guess he ran into Evany."

"Can't stand that little man," Robyn said flatly, and her son laughed.

"Yeah, reminds me of the line from the French Revolution: 'A la lanterne!' Somebody like that could make a real Bolshevik out of you, couldn't he?"

"You're mixing your historical periods, kid."

"I know it. Hey, though." Chris tightened his shoe and balanced cross-legged on the edge of the pool. "Do I get to give away the bride?" Robyn laughed. "Maybe sing my own version of 'Here Comes the Bride'?"

"God. I'm afraid to ask what that would be."

"Easy." Chris considered this a moment, began to beat his hands against his thigh. "The lady with the long yellow hair is my mother/and if she wasn't, then I'd have another/her main squeeze is a guy named Aletto/who ought to be Duke but his uncle won't let go . . ."

"Chris, that's awful!" Robyn was laughing helplessly, hardly able to get the words out.

He lifted both hands and grinned cheerfully. "Hey, it scans, and I'm working on it, all right? This is off the cuff, I could do better if I had a couple hours. No, really, let me—" He picked up the beat again and went on. "But his uncle won't let go/of the Duchy Zelharri/but let's cut the chatter/and get on with the part that really matter./These two gonna marry, gonna make themselves an heir/So Aletto got a kid to/hand on the Duke's Chair. . . ."

"Stop," Robyn groaned. "Pax, time out, enough."

"Just trying to help. Beats the goopy 'Here Comes the Bride' thing they play at weddings, and you don't have an organ anyway, right?"

"Rotten kid." Robyn was still giggling; she waved a hand toward the darkened garden and a high wall, city lights visible beyond its top. "Main squeeze, my God. There has to be some traffic out there; why don't you go play?"

"Past my curfew, ma. Here come your *boy* friend," he added as he jumped to his feet. "I get the feeling I'm extraneous. All right if I go looking for trouble, then?"

"Don't you dare. And keep those fingers off Evany's girl, I saw the way you were looking at her."

"Yeah." Chris sighed. "All the fun for you, none for me. Hey, guy," he added as a rather abashedly happy Aletto came toward him, "just heard, congratulations, I can really recommend this lady."

"Kid," Robyn warned.

"Yeah, ma, scramming now."

Meriyas came out a short while later with a message for Aletto from her father. "He's sent word to the advocacy clerk he uses for contracts, the man will no doubt be here shortly." She gave Chris a shy smile on her way back into the house.

Robyn sat on the edge of the fountain, jaw sagging. "My God," she breathed finally. "A lawyer who makes house calls? Late *night* house calls? Now I know we aren't anywhere in our own world."

Chris laughed. "All it takes is money, right?"

Evany came out with the clerk—a very thin young man with a prominent Adam's apple and what must be the local equivalent of a briefcase: a short tube with documents and pens rolled inside. The actual signing was brief and low-key: The Advocate explained the printed form and its contents, spoke to each of them, and then Aletto signed the bottom, Robyn signed, the advocate signed. Another paper—apparently a duplicate—was produced for signature. The Advocate waved the second to dry the new ink, rerolled both separately and handed one to Aletto. Aletto turned to smile at Robyn, gave her the roll of thick paper and turned back to talk to the advocate, who produced another document. The two men talked over this briefly, the Advocate crossed out something, added something; Aletto beckoned then, drawing Enardi forward.

"This is something you will know more about than I; I asked Lord Evany to have his man bring a standard contract of delegation, and this is what he's given me. I still intend to ask your assistance here, as I said I would, and it seemed an excellent opportunity to deal with the matter. Especially since I hope to be able to leave Podhru within a day or so, as soon as we can collect the rest of our party." He held out the single sheet and Enardi took it. "Study it if you like while I finish my other business with the Advocate." Enardi looked a little dazed, but he nodded and drew off to one side, Biyallan at his shoulder so she could read it also. Chris edged forward and wrapped an arm around his mother's shoulders, gave her a quick, hard squeeze. She leaned into him.

"Beats a justice of the peace for speed," he whispered.

"Yeah. Lot less hassle. Aletto says he'll do the whole bit when he takes Duke's Fort back."

"When. Hey, guy's starting to think the right way. Good idea, though, people like a good show, you know?"

"I don't, if I have to be part of it," Robyn said, and sighed. "I don't know why I did that—"

"You got the guy's ego aligned right, and you like him, and he likes you. You need something else?"

"Yeah," Robyn said gloomily. "Reassurance I'm not gonna turn into the next Nancy Reagan."

"You won't," Chris said, "I'll kill you if you try. All

right? Besides, not everyone married to a governor—that's really what this guy is, isn't it?—not all of those turn out to be icky little white-glove girls. Think of all the power you'll have to do some good for people.''

"Yeah, sure," Robyn said, but he thought she brightened a little at the thought. She gave him a quick hug and went over to Aletto. Chris followed.

"I haven't heard of any writs," the Advocate was saying. "It doesn't mean much, though; I seldom deal with anything like that. But I can talk with men who do, to see if they know anything about the charges against either the woman Jenni—? Jen Cray, or the nera-Thukar. At least I will be able to tell you by midday whether such a writ was sent down by the Emperor, or by his brother. If Afronsan—well, it might be at least possible for a message to reach them if it is Afronsan who sent the guard. If the Emperor—I don't know what hope to hold out to you sir, because the Emperor has chosen to do nothing else until after his upcoming Festival; anyone charged under Shesseran's writ would be held until the Festival is over." He spread his hands, turned them palm up. "Lord Evany will know your whereabouts, if I have a message for you?"

"I—yes." Aletto dug down in the little leather bag on his belt and brought out a silver ceri. "This is for you—no, I know Lord Evany pays you for services, but this is for your time in coming tonight, and for your efforts tomorrow. Enardi?" The boy was waiting just behind him; he set the form on the table, signed it rather self-consciously. Aletto glanced through it again, signed it himself, handed it to the Advocate so the man could make his changes on the duplicate and countersign. Aletto took the completed original, held out a hand to the Advocate and then to Enardi. "We can settle specific points later, perhaps in the morning." He got up with only a whiteness to his knuckles to show that he was having any difficulty this particular night, and wrapped an arm around Robyn's shoulders. The Advocate quietly took his leave by inserting pens and documents in his carry-tube, sketching a bow in Aletto's direction and giving Evany one before the householder escorted him to the house door and turned him over to a servant.

"This is a propitious moment, Honor," he said on his return. "If you would like wine? Cakes? And the guests' chamber is yours—"

Chris could only see Aletto's back, and the tips of his

ears, which were very red. Robyn laughed, the bubbly little giggle that meant she was embarrassed. ''Um,'' she managed finally. ''That's really sweet of you.''

''But, please, it is no trouble at all,'' Evany purred. ''We will celebrate properly, if you permit, tomorrow. When the other Zelharri come.''

Aletto shifted uncomfortably and cleared his throat; Chris saw his mother's foot come down over the nera-Duke's and the arm around his back clamped his arm. Whatever he might have said—and all Chris's sympathies were with a guy in Aletto's position at the moment—he swallowed that with an audible gulp, and merely said, ''Thank you, sir.'' Robyn glanced back over her new husband's shoulder, met her son's eyes and cast her own up helplessly as Evany bowed them toward the house. Chris managed somehow to keep his own face straight until they were gone, then dropped onto the pile of cushions where Aletto and Robyn had been sitting. Lialla came and sat next to him, and he suddenly realized he hadn't noticed her at all, the whole time.

''Hey,'' he said. ''You get lost?''

''Oh, I was about,'' Lialla replied.

''Yeah, Invisible Lady, that's you. I'm trying to figure, does this make us cousins, or what? I mean, besides friends?''

Lialla smiled at him. ''You're a nice person, in case I hadn't said so, Chris. Let's see, my brother, your mother, so he's your stepfather—'' Her smile slipped briefly. ''So I'm a stepsister?''

''I think that tracks. Neat, you know? Mom never landed me with a sister before. Awfully fast, too.''

Lialla pulled back to look at him. ''You can't say you haven't expected it, can you?''

He rubbed a rather scratchy chin, finally shook his head. ''No, not really. You?''

''Aletto's been very taken with her for—almost since the beginning.''

''I know, she said as much. I figure if mom would coo over a goofy old duck like Fedthyr for Aletto, it must be love. I didn't figure tonight, but I guess once she opened her mouth and then he opened his it was either that or a complete split.'' He sighed. ''No, I wasn't surprised. Wish Jen'd been here, though; she never *has* seen mom get married, you know?''

''I just wish they were all three here,'' Lialla said somberly. "It's awful, not knowing what's happening, where they are." She stifled a yawn with the back of her hand. "You know, I was half-asleep before that whole stupid fight over Caro's inn, I think I'll see if I can't get back to sleep."

"Yeah, me too," Chris said. "If you're asleep you can't worry."

"Yes," Lialla said dryly. "Well." She yawned again, rolled onto hands and knees and crawled back into the nest of cushions and lightweight sleeping cloths she'd made for herself earlier. "Good night."

"G'night," Chris said absently. He sat for a while, staring at the pool, watching as a very light breeze rippled the surface and broke up moonlight, finally shook himself and went looking for a spare corner where he could stretch out. *Yeah*, he thought as he resolutely closed his eyes and settled the soft, cool fabric around his shoulders, *g'night, Jen. Eddie. Dahven.* It seemed forever before he slept, and the birds had him restlessly awake at first light.

Across the city, in the fourth-story rooms, Jennifer carefully untangled herself from Dahven's arms and slid from the bed. The room was cool, but not unbearable; she washed down quickly with the previous night's water, dried off even more quickly and fought damp legs into her jeans. She carried the large black bag into the other room, turned up the lantern and began unloading the things she needed: hair brush and pick; the deodorant stick, makeup. In the bottom of the makeup bag, her silver hoop earrings. Toothpaste and brush, hand cream.

It was difficult, working with the makeup; it almost felt as though it was a stranger's bag, unfamiliar contents, even though she'd used it in Bez just before Fedthyr's sprawl of a party. The face that looked out at her from the round metal mirror was too pale, which made her look anxious. At least makeup could help with that. Blush, liner, mascara—as she applied it, it began to feel right again. She ran the lipstick liner pencil deftly around her lips, filled the outline, gazed at the result and shook her head at the way her hair still looked. The hair spray she'd given Chris might have come in handy just now. She worked the brush through it, went into the back room for water to scrunch through it in hopes of bringing back the curl, set the pick and mirror aside and put everything else back in the bag, slid into the chambray shirt—thanks to Caro Ellaway only slightly rumpled and

208

still clean—tucked the shirttails in and fastened the cuff buttons.

Dahven was still asleep. She glanced down at him, smiled, went back into the main room making fists of hair, and drew up the chair where she'd sat the night before. A last opportunity to go through her case and get it in order, in case she was given the chance to speak for him.

Not a good way to think, Cray, she told herself and tugged at the fistful of hair she'd taken up over her left temple. *He's not a street beggar or a—some other commoner no one here might care about. They have to at least give the appearance of listening to his side of things, don't they?* She tugged at hair once more, released it and took up another handful in a tight fist. Of course they did.

Her only worry now was how long it might take. Conceivably, they could be in this room for weeks. Bad enough for them, but what would Aletto do? He'd have to cut his losses, go on without the two of them. But if Birdy chose not to leave without her sister—? Or if Chris decided to make a dust-up to get his aunt and his best friend out of the clink?

"You're just full of pleasant thoughts, this morning, aren't you?" she asked herself aloud, and bent back over the yellow pad.

16

₹

BY the time Dahven was on his feet and mumbling to himself over the bowl of washing water, she had eaten the breakfast they supplied, gone through her notes twice, made a few more additions to her outline, and was—she hoped—as ready as she was going to get.

A tap at the door had come just at sunrise, and it had been opened by two men in unrelieved black who brought a hot, thick pottery jug of tea and two cups, two enormous slices of dark bread. One set the tray on a bench just inside the door, closed it at once. She sniffed it cautiously, poured herself tea and sniffed again. Probably wasn't a drop of caffeine in it, but at least it didn't remind her of the worst excesses of the herb teas Robyn drank. No drinking water, though. And the bread, while filling, was very dry and there was nothing to go on it.

She measured the contents of the jug by eye as well as she could, poured herself another half-cup and left Dahven the rest, draping her tee-shirt over it to help retain the heat.

It was still steaming by the time Dahven got to it, and he ate and drank without comment, finally looked up at her from under a thatch of uncombed hair, and grinned. "You look wonderful."

Jennifer ruffled his head. "You look like hell and you still look wonderful."

"Oh." He considered this, brushed crumbs from his lap and grinned again. "I hope that was you talking, and not my advocate—I prefer better logic in my advocates." The grin slipped. "They said nothing when they brought this—feast?"

"Didn't even give me a chance to ask if I could get coffee and a Danish instead. I'd kill for coffee right now."

"I will make a note," Dahven said solemnly, "when I take you home to Sikkre, to make certain there is always coffee."

"Mmmm. Did I put that much of a twist on your psyche last night? You're abnormally optimistic."

"Something to do with a wonderful sleep," he replied and leaned toward her. "Do you know—?" But whatever he would have asked went unasked; with another of those warning taps, the door swung open, the two black-clad guards came just inside and stood aside for two men in the city guards' red and gold. Jennifer recognized neither.

"Lord Dahven? You and the advocate will come, please, with us." Jennifer gave Dahven's fingers a hard squeeze, caught up her yellow pad and pen, dropped the pad on top of the mess in her handbag and clipped it shut, shoved the pen down in her shirt pocket and slung the bag over her shoulder. Dahven gave her a look he no doubt meant to cheer her, but his eyes were suddenly bleak.

They went down three floors, down a narrow corridor like the one on the top floor, around a corner and through double doors.

A glance to her right through an open door showed what

looked like an empty courtroom consisting of a low table that might have served as a bench for two or three judges rather than the one she was used to, a few scattered chairs, a backless sitting bench along one pale wall. A black-clad boy was running a cloth across the table.

Business as usual? *Don't get too cocky, Cray,* she reminded herself sharply. *This isn't the Home of the Free, after all; they might be hauling you down here for sentencing.* Reserve judgment, she told herself as they came around a corner and stopped before another pair of doors blocking off the remainder of the corridor. One of the guards tugged on a rope, spoke through the square opened for him a moment later. He stepped back, the doors parted. Dahven reached to grip Jennifer's fingers; she squeezed back.

This was a small chamber, perhaps judge's chambers; there were windows on two walls, thick leather-bound books everywhere—in shelves, in stacks on a table against one wall, on a massive desk that could have been of any material: She could see nothing but black, sturdy legs; the rest was buried under loose papers, bundles of string-tied papers, open books. A thick, plain pottery mug was balanced on one corner, rather precariously. Jennifer was so fascinated by the desk—it reminded her very much of her own office desk, except that here there was no buried radio playing Mahler—she scarcely noticed the man sitting behind it until she was seated in the cushion-piled chair one of the city guard showed her to. Dahven stopped just short of the desk and remained standing. Jennifer drew the yellow pad onto her lap, let her handbag fall to the floor, shoved it behind her heels with one foot, uncapped the ball-point and leaned back.

The man behind the desk, she now saw, was probably somewhere around forty; he was dark, clean-shaven, his hair kept short—probably for practicality, she thought; he had the look of one of her old senior partners, every move planned to take the least amount of time, every possible activity graded and chosen according to need, possible returns later, importance to the firm. His eyes were a deep hazel and very direct. *Surely not Shesseran,* she thought.

"You are Dahmec's son," the man said abruptly as he came to his feet. "We have never met, but I knew Dahmec some years ago; you have something of his look." He moved his eyes to meet Jennifer's. "I am Afronsan, as you may have already guessed."

"Lord Afronsan," Dahven began. The older man shook his head.

"If we met elsewhere, other than this building, Lord Afronsan. Even my clerks leave the title aside; it wastes time and serves no purpose." He sat again and moved his cup to one side, bringing up a length of cream-colored, thick paper. "We all serve the cause of justice here," he added.

Jennifer swallowed, shifted her weight so she sat slightly forward. "Sir, I would like to see the writs, if any, against my client."

"Ah. Of course you would." He gave her a very brief smile. "There are no formal writs, at present. My brother, before you ask, has issued no orders regarding the present unresolved situation in Sikkre. However, he has given me considerable powers these past few years, and allowed me a free hand in setting up the inner workings of smooth government."

"Civil service," Jennifer murmured. "Of course. If there are no formal writs, then, may I ask what other charges there are against my client?"

"There are as yet no charges against anyone. There may yet be, and it is my hope you and the nera-Thukar will cooperate in what is still a very early investigation."

"Grand jury," Jennifer mumbled to herself, adding aloud, "Of course, I understand." She leaned forward to touch Dahven's knee and indicate another of the deep chairs with a nod, flipped over to the last page of her yellow pad and drew a deep breath.

Afronsan listened well—better than some of the judges she'd seen in the cases where she'd been allowed to assist at trial. He interrupted her remarks twice with questions, otherwise sat still, eyes fixed on her face. When she finished, he shifted that gaze to Dahven, listening with the same intense care as he spoke, this time asking no questions. When Dahven finished speaking, Afronsan sent one of the guards hovering at the back of the room for refreshment—tea for himself and Dahven, coffee and water for Jennifer when she asked if that were possible. The coffee was very thick, bitter, and needed a full packet of sugar from her bag plus half the drinking water to be palatable. She took a deep sip and sighed happily; it was still wonderful. She could almost feel the caffeine percolating her blood.

Afronsan set his cup aside—balancing it this time on a precarious stack of open volumes—and fished through papers in front of him. He came up with what he wanted, finally—a sheaf of several papers tied together across the top with thick blue string, bound to some kind of stiff backing—and beckoned to Dahven, holding it out for his inspection. Jennifer set her cup aside and got up to see. Dahven edged over so they could both look at it, turned the individual sheets as she looked.

Unfortunately, she couldn't read Rhadazi; but the document had a familiar sort of look, and Dahven confirmed this aloud. "Father's will. This is the will my brothers sent to be proved?"

"You have never seen this will before?"

Dahven shook his head. "One similar in form, of course. He still believed in having all his documents clerk-copied, instead of set in type; time-consuming for the clerks but he said it was his time in the long run, and his money." He turned another sheet to the last page, stared at the signatures there for a long time, shook his head again. "The signature might be Father's; it often varied and it was often erratic, the way this is—according to his mood, you know."

'Have you any way of proving a signature, sir?" Jennifer asked as Dahven handed the document over to her. She glanced up; Afronsan shook his head. "Then—" she prompted carefully.

"There are other things, however," Afronsan said. "The testimony of your servant, the man Edrith. I read it just before you were shown in here; it matches your statements in nearly every respect."

"Yes, well, it should," Dahven replied mildly. He had blinked when Afronsan labeled Edrith as his servant and Jennifer had to bite the corner of her mouth to keep back a smile.

"You could of course have planned matters that way, since there was time between Sikkre and Bez—had you come that way—or between Bezjeriad and Podhru."

Jennifer opened her mouth, closed it, finally nodded when Afronsan glanced her way. "Collusion. It's always possible, of course. In this case, it isn't true."

"When combined with other testimony, I tend—cautiously yet—to agree with you." He leaned back in his chair and pulled out several other sheets of paper—several of them folded and refolded and rather grubby. "When rumor began to appear everywhere, I sent men to learn what they could, firsthand. Here, the statement of a Zelharri common sol-

213

dier, who describes a certain encounter in the desert south of Sikkre.''

Jennifer felt for the edge of the desk, uncertain her knees would hold her. "His name is Garret," she said finally. "Son of a baker in Sehfi." She gave him the rest of the story as briefly as she could: the six men, Jadek's sphere and the dead man after, the kidnapping of Chris by Cholani nomads. The previous encounter with men who called themselves the Thukars'. Afronsan was staring at her when she finished, possibly through her.

He nodded once. "The statement matches his in sufficient particulars. I also have the unsolicited statement of a Sikkreni named Vey. He claims a close relationship with the streets of your market, and describes events of particular interest to me: that you were seen leaving Sikkre on the night certain outlanders went, on the same night the Red Hawk Caravan set out for Dro Pent. Some hours later, several men came through that same gate and went directly to the Thukar's tower. The Sikkreni states that he saw your return to Sikkre with first light, and that he saw the men leave by the east gate a short time later. Two rode, a third drove a wagon, he states, and in that wagon was a bundle of dark cloth that might have been a man. From that hour to the one when he put his mark on this, he claims not to have seen Dahmec's heir in Sikkre.''

He paused for remarks; Dahven was pale and beyond comment. Jennifer cleared her throat. "He made no—um, statement as to who those men might have been?"

"He could not be certain they were Lasanachi, if you mean that," Afronsan replied levelly. "Though by his description, they were not much like any Rhadazi, and were very like the Lasanachi in size and coloring." He produced another sheet. "This was obtained with some difficulty from a man who called himself Dighra." He looked up; Jennifer shook her head. The name meant nothing until Dahven, who was reading down the page, let his head fall back and he laughed.

"Little warm sand gods, it's the man who took me in below the Bez docks.''

Jennifer's eyes narrowed. "The boot thief," she said very quietly. She folded her arms, looked at the paper, and the writing she couldn't read, bit back a curse. "Tell me what he says." Dahven summarized as he went; Jennifer sighed, finally nodded. "Except that he left out the boots, it's the truth as I know it."

"Boots?"

"You don't remember that he stole your boots, ran off to sell them, leaving you sick and unwatched in that—that hovel?"

Dahven considered this very briefly, finally shrugged. "Doubtless he saw enough money in them to keep himself fed for some time to come; don't be hard on him. Besides, now I understand something Edrith said, after we'd left Bez. If that poor little wreck of a man hadn't been trying to sell my boots, Edrith might never have known I was there." He touched her hand. "Don't. Between you, you and Edrith and my brothers' men must have paid him for that act with a day and night of absolute terror."

Afronsan separated out three sheets this time. "The statements of a Bez market woman who lent her wagon, a physician brought to the house of a maker of spells and potions to heal a fevered man—the statement of the mistress of that house, describing the man. And—here, the last of them. The statement of her husband, who was present when the man was first brought from the docks, and who saw first-hand his condition before the woman who brought him utilized Night-Thread to heal his injuries." Afronsan glanced up at Jennifer curiously. "Unsubstantiated rumor says that the outland advocate who was originally brought into Zelharri is a Wielder of—let us say—unconventional style."

Jennifer shrugged. "If you're asking me—I do Wield. I doubt that what I do is so unconventional; I'm simply not bound by the narrow vision of one brought up to the talent."

"I'm not asking about any of that, beyond what you've told me. My only inquiry at this time is into the Sikkre problem, to settle the proving of this will and to determine what is to be done about conferring the title and Duke's Chair." He took back the sheaf of paper from Dahven, leaned back in his chair and finished what must by now be barely tepid tea. "There is no purpose in holding you— either you, Dahven, your advocate or your servant. There are no writs, no provable crimes which could be laid at your feet, and a good many incidents which would count as wrongs both against you and against the state.

"And so—" He paused. Dahven stirred, leaned against the desk.

"And so? Sir—I tell you quite frankly that it is my intention, once certain other obligations are behind me, to go directly to Sikkre and confront my brothers."

"We would prefer that you not contemplate such an action." Afronsan was watching him over a steeple of fingers.

Dahven shook his head, and Jennifer reached back to the chair for her yellow pad, to consult the first page. "Sir, it has been nearly fifty years since any man obtained a Duke's Chair by murder—I agree, sir, that no such case is proven here. However, in that case it was decreed by the Emperor that it was Duchy business." She looked up from the paper; Afronsan had transferred that mild look to her. She drew a deep breath. "And there is also the matter of the Duke's Chair of Zelharri, which has been left as Duchy business by lack of any action on the part of Podhru," she added.

"There has been no claim of any sort regarding Zelharri—either by the Regent Jadek to transfer title to himself, or by the nera-Duke, to claim his rights. Until one or the other event occurs, there is no matter there for the Emperor to investigate. And I," Afronsan said with a shrug, "am inclined to leave that matter entirely alone at present."

Something in his eyes, Jennifer thought. He knew damned well Aletto was with her, or had been all the way to the city gates. He had to be letting her know that; letting her know, too, that so long as no one came right out and mentioned Aletto or said where he was, Afronsan wasn't going to do anything about him. She cast Dahven a sidelong glance and changed the subject.

"Then let us leave it. The matter of Sikkre, however; if you have an alternative to my client walking into the grasp of men who to my certain knowledge have more than once attempted to murder him, then I personally would gladly hear it."

To her surprise, Afronsan laughed. "Yes. There is plenty of rumor as well as comment in the testimony about the temper of the woman advocate! No, don't apologize, I know you weren't intending rudeness. However, the matter is already in hand. Lord Dahven," he added, "the matter was Duchy business until the paper was signed and coin exhcanged and you were put in the hands of the Lasanachi. Your advocate may not be fully versed in Rhadazi law, but surely you know that flies in the face of law. The death of your father and the subsequent production of the will is suspicious, and we are so treating it, particularly in light of attacks upon yourself and upon innocent parties." Jennifer heard a faint tap and turned as one of the guard went to slide the peephole open. He slid the door open a crack, came across to the desk with another sheet of paper. Afronsan sighed faintly but took it. "I sometimes think they will find me buried under paper, when it finally slides from the desk."

"I know," Jennifer said feelingly, and when he glanced her way, "Some things are the same everywhere." She moved sideways a pace, took hold of Dahven's fingers while the Emperor's brother read what he'd just been handed.

"A last statement taken this morning, the boy who was driving the wagon yesterday. He confirms threats by armed men between Bez and Podhru, an attack by those same men not long after. He confirms your statements about the events after you were falsely led into the alley next to the north walls and attacked." Afronsan let the paper fall to his desk and was silent for a long, nerve-wracking moment. Jennifer felt cold fingers squeeze hers, returned the pressure.

"Having none of these men, we have more than half the story, but not all of it. All the same, there is no reason to hold any of you, though I would strongly suggest you avoid following strange men into traps for the remainder of your stay here." He smiled briefly, picked up his tea mug, stared into apparently empty depths, shrugged and set it aside.

"I suggest, again very strongly, that you complete whatever further—obligations, I believe you said?—that you have. In the meantime, there will be a full investigation into these matters. We will find and speak with men who were involved in the attacks, with persons in the Thukar's household, with members of the Red Hawk Clan. The market itself will be gone through carefully, since there is also rumor of dissatisfaction with new taxes and regulations. Your brothers will be asked for detailed statements regarding all of this." He smiled, very briefly, and Jennifer thought he looked rather smug, like a politician pulling a fast one—or, more to the point, a judge who's finally nailed someone who should have been in jail years before.

"The market," Dahven said finally. "You said new taxes and regulations; what, specifically?"

"I'll have copies of the relevant papers made for you, it will take a little while, but in the meantime I've eaten nothing yet today and you doubtless had only what they bring around to prisoners: filling but not exactly enjoyable. I'll have something brought—bread, cheese, fruit? Perhaps some wine?"

"Sounds wonderful," Jennifer said. "Perhaps more coffee?"

Chris had been watching people come into Evany's garden since ten o'clock by his watch; it was now noon and he was starting to get nervous. Enardi had gone to give his statement at the big clerk's building, but he'd promised to come back and pass on anything he'd been able to learn.

There was no word yet about Jen, Dahven or Edrith. Robyn, who looked as though she hadn't slept much, sat next to Aletto, who didn't look much better. Lack of sleep due to nerves, worrying about missing parties, Chris thought, rather than—than what all those old guys like Evany were kidding them about. *Tee hee, giggle, get it, get it?* he thought in disgust. *Wonder where Evany got his kids?*

Lialla was nervy, too, but she'd apparently managed to sleep. Chris decided what he needed was to find out how she worked that Thread she'd used on Ernie, see if he couldn't do it himself. Sounded better than sleeping pills.

Gyrdan had showed up somewhere just before noon, and gone straight to Aletto; he now sat cross-legged on the ground next to his Duke, a long, handwritten list in one hand, apparently running through who was going with them, what he had in mind for plans. Chris wandered by at one point to hear him say something about taking two routes at the vee just south of the pass, but at this point had enough on his mind that he couldn't find the least interest in his first real shot at military planning from the inside.

There were several men with Gyrdan—plain-clad, capable-looking guys. Chris glanced them over, was aware of thoughtful, interested looks in turn. None of them looked at him the way some of Evany's friends did, though. More like they were deciding whether he'd be useful in a tight spot, maybe even figuring it was possible he would.

Edrith came shouldering across the crowded patio then, and Chris forgot about Gyrdan, Evany, everyone and everything else. Edrith gripped his shoulders, let Chris throw a bear hug around him in turn. "Hey, guy, I wasn't gone that long!"

"Yeah," Chris said. He swallowed, looked past his friend's shoulder. "You aren't alone, are you?"

"Only cause *they* got asked to lunch with the big shots, and no one asks servants—"

"Servants? What—you? Says who?" Chris demanded rudely.

Edrith laughed. "It sounded better than drinking companion and sometime thief. They asked, I said that, they accepted it. As far as I know. I didn't rate an opportunity to meet the Emperor's heir at all, but they say he's quite unimpressive, dresses no better than I do and more interested in papers and books than anything else."

"You gotta watch out for those paper-pushers," Chris warned him cheerfully. "Jen's having lunch with—whatsisname? Afronsan?"

"Well—she and Dahven are waiting for some kind of clearance, or some papers or something, I didn't get that exactly straight. So the guard who walked me out said they were eating cheese and grapes in Afronsan's private chambers. Ernie went in, I saw him near the doors, talking to another of the city guards, the ones that came after us yesterday? They let me talk to him for a moment, he has to sign something once they create the copies, and the city guard said he may as well wait for the nera-Thukar and his advocate."

"He said—wait." Christ tugged at his hair. "He called Dahven that? Nera-Thukar? Like they really believe he's supposed to be heir instead of his jerk brothers?"

"Well," Edrith replied cautiously, "the *guard* said that. It might have been habit, you know, from when Dahmec was still alive." He gripped Chris's shoulders again. "I honestly wasn't certain I'd come out of that building alive. I can't tell you how glad I am to see you again."

"Hey. They can't kill people like you."

"Yeah. It would be, like, totally wrong. You know?" Edrith grinned, looked across the courtyard. "They said I missed the ceremony last night. Aletto actually persuaded your mother?"

"Caught her in a weak moment. Everybody's giving them a real bad time about spending the night in Evany's spare bedroom."

Edrith shrugged. "Not everyone, I'd wager. The old people, like Evany. They think that's funny." He lowered his voice. "D'you like that guy—*even* trust him?"

Chris lowered his in turn. "Frankly? Honestly? No. Not as far as I could spit him."

"Yeah, me too. Boy, did you see his daughter, though?"

Chris punched him. "Which one, Roisan? She's about your mental age." Edrith laughed.

"Yeah, well, I won't fight you for the other one; I don't want to go through Evany. She winked at me when I came in," he added in a confiding voice.

"Hey, she winked at *me* last night," Chris replied stiffly. He grinned then. "Maybe she's got a tic, you think?"

"Knows she's safe," Edrith growled. "You know—look all you want, dudes, just don't touch, Daddy wouldn't like it."

Chris sighed. "They make 'em like that here, too, eh?"

"Believe it," Edrith said. "You know?"

Edrith went over to give Robyn a hug of congratulations and passed on his news; she looked much less drawn and harassed after that, and Chris knew at once when she slipped the word on to Aletto. The nera-Duke suddenly was relaxed, smiling. Chris got Lialla's attention and told her. Lialla's shoulders sagged and her eyes closed; Chris caught her in case, but she straightened at once.

"I couldn't think how they'd believe those awful twins, how Shesseran could get away with holding a full noble—but all the same."

"All the same," Chris echoed. "I'll be a lot happier when they walk in here, but I feel pretty good right now."

The party atmosphere had faded a little late in the afternoon; many of Evany's friends had left, though Gyrdan was still over talking to Aletto and Chris had struck up an acquaintance with a couple of the younger men who'd come with him. Edrith was off with one of Evany's sons and two of Grydan's men, describing staff-fighting by the way he was moving his arms. Jennifer and Dahven came through the patio door arm in arm, almost unnoticed at first, until Enardi called out Chris's name.

Robyn was on her feet at once, arms around her sister's neck. Jennifer hugged back, hard, then tapped her arm. "Hey, Birdy, can't breathe. You look just fine; married life agreeing with you?"

"Smart mouth, kiddo," Robyn retorted; there were tears in her eyes and her voice. "Didn't think some of these people would ever let up." She shrugged rather helplessly. "Wasn't much else to do, was there? He was convinced I was heading back to set up shop with Caro Ellaway, and I couldn't just sleep with him."

"Says you," Jennifer replied quietly. "And since when?"

Robyn shrugged again, but managed a smile. "Well—since I ran out of pills about five weeks ago."

"Mmmm—gotcha. There are alternatives, you know—"

"Hey, girl, I taught you that stuff, remember? Would you really ask a man to wear one of *those*? If you had any? Jennifer? Why are you laughing?"

"Later. A lot later. He's looking for you, and I need to talk to Lialla."

Aletto was deep in conversation with Dahven, who was relating a truncated version of the hearing; Gyrdan sat between them and a little back, listening. "The bottom line, Aletto, is that they—Afronsan, actually—know full well you're here, but are choosing the ignore the fact. I don't know from anything Afronsan said whether that's because Jadek has said enough to warrant an Emperor's writ, whether Jadek has set one or threatened to; did Carolan have any other relatives?"

"None close—none who'd care what happened to Carolan, so long as they got his title and estates."

"Well, Afronsan made it pretty clear that he doesn't want to hear your name at all. I got the impression that you *could* file a petition of your own, and that it would probably sit on Shesseran's stack of unsigned petitions for the next two years, and you'd be stuck here.

"He also seems aware that I was on my way north with you; he's suggested that I keep to plan while his office hauls my brothers over the hot sands—"

"What can he do to them?" Aletto demanded. "After all, they're in—"

"He's not letting the will be proved, to begin with." Dahven grinned wickedly. "He's launching an investigation into illegal market control and unauthorized taxes, and until further notice, Sikkre's on gold standard." Aletto considered this in some confusion, shook his head. "Whatever goods they trade for outside of Sikkre, other than a personal deal between merchants, of course—*anything* my brothers wish to buy, they pay for at once, in gold. No credit, no currency. Afronsan says there's precedent from a long time ago for such an action; my brothers will be—somewhat distraught."

Aletto let his head fall back and he roared with laughter.

When he sat back straight, there were tears on his face. "He actually *did* that? To *your* brothers? Distraught?"

Dahven's grin widened. "Perhaps a little. A final matter, though: Afronsan says that since I will probably be in a position to come into Sikkre once my previous appointments are done—of which he knows nothing, of course—he has decided to send a handpicked guard along with me."

"He—" Aletto shook his head. "I'm sorry, Dahven, that must make sense but I'm not understanding it."

"Leaving out the spaces between lines? I agree, it's rather like learning a new language at first. He's sending observers, men who will join with Gyrdan as well as a pair of clerks loyal to him, personally. With the intention that whatever my brothers or your uncle set against us from the moment we leave Podhru, he'll have proof beyond a statement. Of course, I believe he's interested in seeing how you deal with your uncle—"

Aletto let his eyes close. "Gods," he whispered.

"But wouldn't you rather have his men *there*, when you go into Duke's Fort? So that should Jadek somehow speak out, or men loyal to him later say that you did or said a certain thing, they can put the rumor where it belongs?"

Aletto considered this in silence for a moment, finally and rather reluctantly nodded. "I suppose. If all else, they'll keep me honest to what I told that man south of Sikkre. That I'd talk only, that I wasn't bringing violence."

"Removal of the wrong sort of temptation," Dahven agreed cheerfully. "Never a bad idea, particularly now." He came partway up and looked around Evany's expansive walled garden. "The man's done quite well for himself, hasn't he? I should find my advocate and properly thank her for saving my throat. As well as wine, to drink your health." He gripped Robyn's hands and pulled her toward him so he could kiss her cheek. "He's a very nice fellow; I'm very pleased for you."

Jennifer and Lialla were in a quiet corner on the far side of the pool, by themselves, where Jennifer could fill Lialla in on developments. "He's sending his own men with us, ostensibly to keep Dahven safe."

"Really to watch and report," Lialla said shrewdly.

"Just so. He offered to make one of the clerks he sends a magician, one who's had experience in dealing with Triads.

I thought perhaps I should consult with you before agreeing to that.''

''I—why?''

''Because it might interfere with your Wielding; I don't know, and the best way to find out seemed to be to ask you. Or because you might know something about that. Whether, say, it would put your mother or Merrida in any danger, as Thread-Wielders—would something that stopped a Triad perhaps rebound on them?''

Lialla shook her head almost at once. ''I don't know that. What do you think?''

''I don't know, either, quite frankly. I personally don't want anyone around who might interfere with what I do, or might find fault with my style of Wielding and be able to stop me. I don't know that they could; I don't know that they couldn't.''

''If we don't take that kind of help,'' Lialla warned darkly, ''then it's only you and me—''

''No, it's all of us. And any charms we can get Edrith or Enardi—any of those kids from Bez, actually—to pick up for us.'' She folded her arms and waited. Lialla nodded.

''Then—all right. No outside magic. It would make me nervous, too; I'm having enough difficulty as it is.''

''You're not,'' Jennifer assured her firmly. ''Think about what you did with Enardi—''

''Think about your arm,'' Lialla said. Jennifer shook her head, unbuttoned the cuff of her chambray shirt and shoved the sleeve up past her elbow.

''I'm thinking about it. All right, I did the cosmetic work, so it doesn't look like hell. You put it back together for me when I couldn't even figure out which way was up—when I was too out of it, in fact, to be embarrassed at being in the middle of that room in my underwear.''

Lialla laughed at that. ''Your underwear,'' she scoffed cheerfully. ''It was as much covering as those things you wore when we ran!''

''It's different, trust me. Oh, no,'' Jennifer said in sudden despair.

''Oh, no? Oh, no—what?''

''Turn around and look; you'll see.''

Lialla obediently turned, and clapped a hand over her mouth. Aletto, Robyn, Dahven and Gyrdan had gone away from the reflecting pool and were in shade where there were several hammocks, some rose bushes, a number of low, poufy seats. She heard Dahven's voice, a burst of laughter—Dahven drinking a toast, apparently, and probably one of the more raucous ones he'd picked up in Sikkre's taverns. The pile of cushions in full sun were now occupied by Evany's daughters. Edrith was sitting with his back against a thick-trunked tree a little distance away, in shade. Enardi perched on the side edge of the fountain, rhythmically slapping his thighs. Chris was moon-walking—backwards, of course—across the narrow edge, and rapping as he went. He stopped as Edrith called out a warning, scooped up the almost empty tray someone had set there and walked on back with it, balanced it on his head and executed a neat one-footed one-eighty so he could moon-walk in the other direction. Roisan jumped to her feet and came close to him, intently watching his feet. A giggle escaped Lialla's fingers.

"He's got another one," Jennifer said and shook her head. "I don't know how he does it."

"No cause to worry," Lialla replied. "They're all babies."

"Like whatsername down there? In the blue? With the hair?"

"Evany's first daughter. Chris has kept his hands off, even without Robyn's warning."

"Boy, I hope so. She's a real little heartbreaker, isn't she?"

"Flirt," Lialla agreed. "What's he saying? I swear, he uses fewer Rhadazi words by the day!"

"Some things don't translate," Jennifer said after a moment.

Chris stopped just short of the far corner, set the tray down on the other side, and executed a full one-and-a-half spin before going back into his rap. Enardi probably understood less of it than Lialla did, Jennifer thought judiciously, but he was enjoying the whole process enormously, and it occurred to her she was going to miss Fedthyr's cheerfully naive son.

"This is singing?" Lialla demanded in a low voice.

Jennifer grinned and nodded her head. "Yeah, this is singing."

Chris looked up, glanced across the courtyard to make certain the rest of the company wasn't close enough to hear him, gave Jennifer a self-conscious grin and shifted into voice: "I'm the new D.J./with a brand new sound/and my rhymes aren't tight/but they're comin' around./

"Say I got no LP for my D.J./got no hi-tech at all, like back in L.A./got no fly girls, got no skateboard/no TV shows for when I get bored." He shifted down the ledge at an alarming—to Jennifer, anyway—speed, elbows and knees everywhere, slowed once again at the far end. "My D.J. is Ernie/and he's financially hot/gonna stay and do the deal/for a market spot." Roisan clapped her hands together in obvious delight; Enardi went red right to his hairline but the rhythm stayed constant. Chris went back down the ledge and came off it in a tightly tucked front flip, only just getting his feet all the way under him before he landed among pillows. He straightened up grinning. "Hey," he said mildly. "All right."

"Kid," Jennifer called over to him, "don't give the Advocate a heart attack, huh?"

"Hey, it's cool, it's all soft here, and I used to do that off my skateboard."

"You had a real emergency ward back then, too."

"Sure, here I got an old geek with stinky goo, look at Ernie walking all over the place already, you know?" Jennifer sighed, and he shrugged. "I learned that in gym, did it on a trampoline for weeks until they'd let me do it on padding. From a wall that high, I don't even have to think about it, you know?"

"That was nifty," Roisan exclaimed in her high, carrying voice. "Do another!" Meriyas said nothing but she was smiling at him. Jennifer sighed, cast her eyes up.

"Let me know if he finishes the next one on his head, will you?" she asked Lialla. "I can't watch." Dahven had stepped back into the sun and was looking for her anyway. She glanced around for her handbag, decided it was fine where it was, and started along the gravel path to meet him.

Chris's voice followed her. "Yo, the outland Advocate is my aunt Jen/she's tough with a bo and tougher with a pen/she got a boyfriend, a dude named Dahven/and I can't say if maybe she's havin'/"

"Chris," Jennifer spun around to yell over his next words, "wanna die young?"

"What?" he demanded, all injured innocence. "Gonna run me through with the pen?"

"I'll shove you in that pond, Mr. Mouth—"

He spread his arms in a wide shrug, laughed and looked

down at his very attentive audience of two. ''Hey, gotta chill, you know? Lady'll get me for slander—no, libel? She'll get me.'' He did a midair direction change, went back sideways down the ledge and stopped abruptly, crouched halfway into his flip. ''Hey, the thingie on this tray's glowing. Yo, guys, back off, something's wrong!'' He straightened his legs, and as Jennifer started to run back, flipped off the wall.

If he'd simply jumped, he might have gotten farther from the pool, but probably not far enough: Hell-Light boiled across the silver tray, shot skyward, and spilled like a glowing fog down the wall and across the ground. There was no sign of Chris.

17

''No!'' It burst from three throats at the same time: Jennifer's, Robyn's, and Lialla's. Half a breath later, an echo: Aletto, who had just caught Robyn and was struggling to restrain her—and Lord Evany, who came shrieking across the garden, arms flapping. He shoved Jennifer, hard enough to break her stride and send her to one knee, scooped both daughters close and encircled them, driving them before him toward the roofed weaving center.

The noise level was nearly unbearable—Enardi and Edrith both yelling in anger, surprise and fear; Robyn's anguished wail, Aletto trying to overshout her and keep her from either attempting to shapeshift or throwing herself headlong after Chris. But as Jennifer shook her head to clear it, she clearly heard Roisan's high, carrying—and at the moment bewildered—child's voice: ''But you didn't *say* not to bring it *out*! You said you wanted to present it, you didn't say to leave it alone!'' Jennifer decided she'd better shelve that; she felt Dahven's arms around her, hauling her to her feet.

''Thanks!'' She tossed that over her shoulder, already

running as soon as he let go of her. She could hear him right behind her.

Lialla stood for one very long moment, hand still over her mouth as though she'd forgotten it. Enardi scrambled away from the pool, Edrith struggled to his feet and backed up a pace, stopped uncertainly as the sin-Duchess took one forward. "Chris?" she called in a thin, frightened voice. Jennifer was still a good ten feet or more away, her ears full of shouting behind her and from the direction of the house, but Lialla must have heard something else. Hell-Light was lapping at her feet, and Edrith yelled: "Lialla! Get back, it's spreading!"

"But I can hear him!" she shouted back, and, dropping to hands and knees, she vanished into the glowing mass.

"No, damnit!" Jennifer threw herself forward, landing bruisingly on both knees. She caught Lialla's bare feet, edged both hands upward to fasten hard around the woman's ankles; she shifted her weight at once, settling on her backside, knees up and feet widespread to brace against a terrible pull. But then Dahven's arms were around her waist, holding her back. She tightened her grip on Lialla's ankles, and to her relief the woman didn't seem to be sliding away from her. When Edrith dropped down next to her, she shook her head. "Go, get out of here. I don't want it getting all of us."

"Not going," Edrith said flatly. "I'll help."

Jennifer shook her head furiously, checked the movement as sweat dripped down her hair to sting her eyes. "All right—fine, all right, in that case, make me a constant beat— like this," she added, and slapped down a three-beat with her feet. "And you'd better keep it going, because I have to have music, and if you can't help me concentrate on it, we might all get chewed up. Still want to stay?"

"Go," he replied. Jennifer merely nodded, then leaned forward against Dahven's grasp.

"Lialla? Can you hear me?"

"Hear—you." Lialla sounded breathless, the words muffled—mostly, Jennifer thought, by the protective circle of silver Thread the woman was trying to build around herself as she felt around for Chris. "Can you hear Chris?"

It wasn't easy, ignoring the hysteria behind her to concentrate on even Lialla's voice. "I—yeah, I hear him!" Jennifer shouted. Chris was rapping again, his voice suddenly strong, higher in pitch than usual and street-tough. As she listened, she could hear his hands slapping against something, setting a driving beat. "Hit it," she told Edrith, "just the way I showed you, got it?" He nodded, she cleared her throat and shut her eyes—shutting out everything, including the encroaching pool of Light that threatened to engulf Lialla's feet—and her hands—at any moment.

It later struck her as one of the stranger things of the entire episode, that Edrith's three-beat matched itself to Chris's beat, that *Stride La Vampa* should dovetail so neatly with Chris's angry rhymes. "Yo, my name is Chris/and I ain't scared/of you, jerk-faced Jadek/just because you dared/ to mess with Hell-Light/give us all some hard times/'cause the day's comin' soon/gonna pay for your crimes." She could only guess how the kid was doing—whether he was trying to keep his spirits up while Hell-Light gnawed at his soul, or if the rap was actually shielding him. She took comfort from the fact that he still sounded strong, and that he maintained the concentration to keep going—creating the rhymes as he went. Well as she knew the mad gypsy woman's aria, she had to really work to remember Italian words that told of a terrified old woman burned at the stake; she found herself wondering if such a song was a good idea.

Chris seemed to have no such reservations. "Don't you mess with me/don't go foolin' around/you gonna get me mad and/you'll be goin' down./Got yourself set up/for a nasty fall/gonna lose the Fort/and that ain't all./Say you gettin' me pissed/and when you do/you will not like what/ happens to you."

"Chris!" Lialla's shout was doubly muffled, by Light and the network of Thread surrounding her. "Don't stop, keep that up! I need the sound to find you!"

Chris's laugh came back at once. "Primo," he shouted, and shifted immediately back to voice. "Say, you got me pissed/got me thinkin' hard/when I get outa this mess/gonna pull your card./ Don't mess with me, dude/stay off my back/ 'cause I settle with you/and you don't wanna *see* that— ohshit-that-didn't-rhyme," he added rapidly. "Yo, I ain't fat an' ugly/like your cousin Carolan/ and your niece is real cute/so maybe we get it on/maybe do the Wild Thing/right on your front lawn!"

Jennifer ran through her aria, drew a deep breath and began the first verse once again. When she dared open her eyes, she found her inner sense hadn't deceived her at all; the Light was definitely shying away from her, leaving a half-circle in front of Edrith; Lialla's legs were visible for several inches above Jennifer's gripping hands. Chris had to be pausing for breath, though she couldn't really hear a break in what he was doing.

"Now don't go thinkin'/I'm pullin' your chain/gonna pull your plug/and send you down the drain./'"

Lialla suddenly edged herself forward and shouted, "Got him!"

"Hang on!" Dahven leaned over Jennifer's shoulder to yell back. "We'll pull you both!" And, to Jennifer, "Keep singing, I think you're helping." She nodded vigorously, let him edge her backwards, away from Hell-Light, more of Lialla coming into sight with each step.

Chris might not have been aware of any of them, for all the response he gave. "Yeah, my rhymes are violent/but you're the one started it/and when it's done, you'll be the body/and me the one who's carted it/off/so hey, Jadek, I mean what I say/I learned tough/way back in L. A./So what it's your 'hood/so what you're hard/so what you got a Triad/I'm gonna pull your card./So maybe you're tough/but I can be tougher/and we'll see when it's over/just who was the bluffer." Lialla was all the way out, now; Chris's high-top clutched in both hands; Jennifer let Aletto and Robyn catch hold of the sin-Duchess while she grabbed her nephew's ankle, hard.

For a moment, she wasn't sure she'd be able to move him, even with Dahven dragging at her; Chris came all at once, as though he'd been an overlarge stopper in a too-small bottle. He rolled over, sat up, and barked one last verse in the direction of the roil of Light that still blocked most of the fountain. "We're heading your way/and it won't be long/we gonna go off in your face/like a time bomb." He ran a hand across his eyes, shook his head. "Whoa, that was *weird*. Like a bad carnival ride or something." Robyn threw her arms around him and he held her close for a moment, patted her hair. "Hey, ma, it's all right, stuff didn't eat me." His hand froze in midair; he set his mother aside. "No, really, I'm fine. But—oh, *man*? Li?"

Aletto sat staring at his sister, eyes wide and frightened. She sat cross-legged on the gravel, head down, arms bracing her forehead. When he laid a tentative hand on her arm, she shoved it away. "Don't. Aletto, don't, I'm contaminated, don't—"

"She won't let me touch her," he whispered.

Chris caught a handful of Aletto's sleeve and tugged.

"Take mom, will you? It's okay, really." He crawled over, thumped down next to Lialla and when she jumped he wrapped both arms around her. "Don't; if you're contaminated, I gotta be really contaminated, so it's all right for me to hang onto you. And I'm gonna anyway, so chill, all right?" He tightened his grasp until she quit struggling. "Listen, you didn't have to do that, I just want you to know I'm grateful, and I'll pay you back, okay? Um, and I didn't really mean all that stuff I said about you, in there. All right?"

"Don't remember. Don't—"

"Nothing you got I didn't get more of, and I feel just fine. Forget the Wild Thing, bad joke, okay?" Chris rubbed her arms, scratched circles on her back with blunt fingertips. "You're shaking like a leaf, lady. You want a blanket or something?" Lialla fetched a sigh and whispered something against his shirt. He bent down to listen and when he straightened his face had gone grave, but he kept his voice determinedly light. "Hey, we can fix anything, remember? Hang on, I'll get you something to drink, bring over a blanket, all right?" He got halfway to his feet, seemed to decide this wasn't a good idea and crawled over to Jennifer. "Jen? I think we have a problem. Li says her eyes aren't working; like, she can't see anything."

"Oh, Lord," Jennifer whispered. She let her eyes close very briefly, let out a sigh and nodded. "Get her—hell, what it was you said. Stick with her, will you, kid? This—I've got to shut it down. Somehow. Wait, though; answer one thing: Wasn't there something—a box, something of the sort, on that tray?"

"A box, yeah. Rectangular, silver. Started glowing all of a sudden."

"Fine. Now I know what to look for. Back up, will you?"

"Hell, no," Chris said flatly. He glanced at the still very active-looking Hell-Light. "I'm gonna help. Because—No, listen, I don't know how your gargle-music works on this stuff but rap works: I had it held *way* away from me, like a foot away, all around. So, maybe between us—"

"Chris," Jennifer warned.

"Jen," he mimicked. "You gonna wait for it to eat us all, or can we cut the crap and do it?"

"Do it, then," she snapped. "Dahven—"

"You'd better not even *think* of telling me to back off so you can crawl into that—!"

"No. I'm telling you not to let go of me."

"I've got you." His hands were hard on her waist, and then he slipped one to hang onto her sash as she edged forward. Chris stood, slid his feet forward until they nearly touched Light, and he shifted back into voice: Outside of the trap, he sounded loud, arrogant and very challenging.

"Yo, my name is Chris/and I ain't scared/of Aletto's creep uncle/be he blond or black-haired./I'm chillin' in Podhru/'cause ol' Jadek's up in Sehfi/and he thinks he'll keep the Fort/but we know it's only ef-he/can pull Aletto's card/ and that's gonna be real hard—" Jennifer inched forward on elbows and knees, her own voice harsh and just a little too low as she began Alzucena's aria for the third time. *Too late to shift key,* she thought. Didn't matter anyway; either she or Chris—possibly both of them—was prevailing: Light shifted away from her on both sides, gave way before her. Grudgingly, it seemed; but as she shifted forward and her voice soared, Light retreated.

She was on solid paving now, a splintery mat under her. The reflecting pool wall had to be within reach, though she couldn't see it. The source of the Light spell: She couldn't see it, either, but she could sense *it*—just to her right, scarcely any distance at all. She began the last line of her aria—*Sinistra splenda, indeed!*—and lunged. Her hands sank into something that clutched like mud, or putty, something that clamped around her fingers and tried to suck her in. Her outstretched thumbs brushed against a hard-edged object; she latched onto it desperately, threw a misplaced pair of lines from later in *Il Trovatore* at the stuff that held her. It eased, just enough. She forced the open lid down with her thumbs, scrambled up and back onto her knees, and threw it into the water, where it landed with an explosive splash. Light vanished.

Jennifer drew a painful little sigh and forced herself to hold her hands where she could look at them. They were cold, a little too white. Stiff. They responded to her own chafing, and then to Dahven's when he wrapped himself close around her back and leaned over her shoulder to rub them.

Chris had already gone back over to Lialla, who sat cross-legged and stiffly unmoving where he had left her. Robyn sat close to the sin-Duchess, eyeing her worriedly but not attempting to touch her; by the look on his mother's face, Chris thought she had tried that and been fiercely rebuffed.

231

Well, that wasn't going to work with him. He nodded in Robyn's direction, blew her a kiss before putting his arms around Lialla once more. She tried to shove him aside; he tightened his grip. "Me again, lady; fellow leper, remember?"

"Chris, don't—"

"Shhh. Hey, don't worry about me. We got rid of the bad thing, me and Jen. Maybe fried your uncle when it hit the water, we should be so lucky, huh?" He took her shoulders between his hands and gave her a gentle shake. "You seeing any better yet?"

"Not seeing anything," she whispered, and her voice shook. Chris felt his heart drop. He swallowed, forced as much cheer into his voice as he could.

"Well, you know? That stuff was pretty bright; guy needed sunglasses in there. You know, I couldn't even tell which end was up, like I was floating or something." He drew her in close, began rubbing her back once more. *God, she's so thin it's spooky,* he thought. He cast a rather anxious glance in Jennifer's direction; she was bent over, head almost between her knees, Dahven bent over her, rubbing her hands. He looked at Robyn, who was dividing her attention between him, Lialla, Jennifer, and someone—probably Aletto—he couldn't see without turning clear around. He got his mother's attention, sent his eyes in Jennifer's direction, then glanced down at Lialla. Robyn nodded, got to her feet and went to bend over her sister.

Jennifer sat up, pushed hair back and let Dahven help her to her feet. She started across to where Lialla sat, then looked beyond the sin-Duchess and her nephew, slowed and beckoned to Dahven. "How much do you feel like a peacekeeper?" she asked, and gestured with her head.

He followed the motion: Aletto stood just outside the house, half a dozen stunned-looking armsmen to one side of him; he had Lord Evany backed against the wall. Dahven nodded, touched her shoulder and went around her.

Jennifer knelt at Lialla's side. "Li?"

"Jen? Get Chris away, please. I'm not safe after that—"

"Oh, hush, woman," Jennifer replied crisply. "If that's all you can say. I'd much rather you tell me exactly what you feel so we can see if we can deal with it."

"We can't! My father—"

"Your father wasn't a Wielder," Jennifer said. "He

232

wasn't even partially protected by a silver sphere when he hit Light; I'd be willing to wager he didn't have a decent Wielder to help him after—and don't you dare tell me he had Merrida, and prove my point.''

Very unwillingly, Lialla smiled, then laughed. ''Dear gods,'' she whispered. ''All right. What do you want?''

''Tell me what hurts, what's wrong.''

''What's wrong? *What's wrong?*''

''Without hysteria, please.''

''I—I can't see.''

''I don't know exactly what to do about that, but I'll try. What else?''

''I—'' Lialla swallowed. ''I can feel it. Like I drew it in, when I was breathing, brought it inside me.''

''Very possibly you did. No,'' she added sharply, ''don't let that panic you. Let's be sensible about this, and practical, can we? Is it a general feeling, something that's in your breathing passages?''

''It's—it *was* in my throat, then my chest. It's—I don't know, I can just feel it.''

''In the pit of your stomach?''

''That's just fear,'' Lialla whispered.

''Well, I can understand that, but I don't think you need to be afraid.''

''My father died of Light—''

''Don't let yourself think about that, Lialla,'' Jennifer interrupted her firmly. ''We all know it. But you've learned some things since then, haven't you? About Light? How about the men who used it to go from place to place? You know it can do more than simply waste a person away, remember that. Remember something else: about magic itself. It's just magic; whether it's good or evil depends on the person using it—not the magic itself.''

''I don't know that. You don't—''

''I know people like Merrida and Neri don't believe that. I've come in without the preconceived ideas Merrida fed you, or that Neri grew up with, I've seen a variety of magic, I've observed Light, and now I've touched it. Lialla, I simply can't believe Hell-Light is evil in and of itself—though I wouldn't say the same about the man who set it on you.'' She waited. Lialla shook her head but didn't say anything. ''All right, then. I can't ask you to agree with me, just think about it. Please. Now. I'm going to take your hands, feel them. See what I can tell, will you trust me that far?'' A nod. ''All right.''

Jennifer was vaguely aware of the shouting match going on over by the house: men's voices, the rather high one that was Evany's, Aletto's hard-edged voice topping Evany's. Dahven's now and again, as he tried to get a word in and settle the dispute. All that faded as she shifted into an awareness of Thread.

''I knew there would be trouble, I knew it, I knew I should have refused Gyrdan—!'' Evany's shrill voice was even shriller with fury and fear equally mixed. Aletto was simply furious clear through.

''There would have been no trouble, if you had not provided it!'' he shouted. ''What do you know of—of *that*?'' He gestured toward the fountain.

''I don't—''

''Don't you dare lie to me! I *heard* you and your daughter arguing over the box on the silver tray—the one she brought out? The one you were to have presented to me?''

''But I didn't—!''

''What—was it all right that my uncle send a box containing a Hell-Light spell to destroy me? And Chris? My sister! Look at her, Evany! She's blinded''—Aletto lowered his voice as he glanced over his shoulder—''and she may die! As my father died! Is that what you wanted? What did Jadek offer you for spilling Hell-Light in your garden?'' Evany stared at him blankly; his jaw was wabbling. ''Well?'' Aletto shouted. ''What? A place of honor, perhaps his cousin Carolan's estates? Or a separate—''

''Don't?'' Evany's voice rose, quavering, and broke. ''Don't. Do you really think—''

''I think?'' Aletto spun away from the man, slammed one fist into the other palm and stood very still, breathing deeply and heavily. ''What would you suggest I think?'' he demanded after a moment.

''He offered me Roisan, Meriyas—my two sons, my wife, my other daughters. Alive and healthy.'' Evany was blinking hard and his eyes were red-rimmed as Aletto turned back to gaze at him.

''He threatened—what?'' Dahven asked quietly.

''No threat.'' Evany swallowed several times, shook his

head. "No threat. Just—a suggestion, he called it. What he intended, if I didn't take the box—"

"He came here?" Dahven pursued.

"No." Evany was still shaking his head, as though he'd forgotten how to stop. "Sent a man—from Sehfi. A man I deal with on occasion, sells me heavy fleeces, gave me—a brooch. Plain bit of silver. I—wore it. And—not long before you came, I was sitting there, by the water, late at night. He—there was a ball of—of something, all around, I couldn't see anything beyond it, but I could hear him." Evany buried his face in his hands. "He'll know I failed, he'll—"

"He'll do nothing to you," Dahven said firmly.

"Nothing," Aletto said. He still looked very angry, but his voice was much less tight. "Because you're going to dispose of the brooch—"

"I don't dare, he'll know!"

"Perhaps so," Dahven said. "But knowing and being able to do anything about it are two different things. Jadek will be too busy in very short order to worry about *you*, or your family. But I suggest, if you really want to assure your safety, that you go to Afronsan, at once, and tell him—" Dahven paused, shrugged and went on. "Leaving out Aletto's presence in your house, tell him everything."

"But, I can't, I don't dare—!"

"The damage is already done, you know," Dahven said mildly. "None of us died, through no fault of yours *or* Jadek's. But he may choose to blame you for that. Now, unless you have another of those boxes up your sleeves, ready to spring on us—?" The older man shook his head wildly. "Well, then. Go to Afronsan, tell him the entire story— with the exception of the nera-Duke and his sister being here. He won't ask about them, he doesn't want to know anything about them, unless I'm gravely mistaken."

"He won't believe Jadek caused *that*," Evany gestured with a trembling hand in the direction of the reflecting pool; there was a smear of black, perhaps soot, all down the wall, and the water where Jennifer had thrown the box was bubbling.

"No? I think he will. He's more informed on matters than you might suspect, Lord Evany; I certainly was not aware of his interest in internal matters. Whether he believes Jadek responsible, he can arrange for someone to retrieve that thing and remove it from your garden—you'd like that, wouldn't you?"

"Dear gods," Evany whispered, and he looked truly terrified.

Dahven laughed; there wasn't any real humor in the sound. "Don't worry about Afronsan, or about your guests. He knows Jennifer and I came here; he appears to be notably blind and unhearing where matters involving Aletto are concerned."

"In any event, we will be gone from Podhru tomorrow," Aletto said. He had turned away to watch his sister and Jennifer. Chris had just stood to move away from the two women; stopping only briefly to pat his mother's shoulder, he came striding across the garden and shouldered past Aletto, around Dahven. He stopped just short of Lord Evany, who gazed up at him nervously. Chris folded his arms and stared back; his mouth twisted in distaste and he spun away and walked off. Dahven glanced at Evany, who was blotting his forehead on his sleeve—probably for the first time in his adult life unheedingly staining expensive silk. The man looked absolutely ill. Dahven touched Aletto's arm to get his attention.

"Why don't you send one of these men to get Evany's personal servant? He's near collapse." Aletto still looked angry but the fury left him all at once; he nodded, called to one of his new armsmen and sent him indoors. Once Evany was gone, he leaned against the wall, concentrating on the feel of cool, shaded and rough-surfaced brick against his hot face, oblivious of the men who stood around, watching him in silence, conversing in low, anxious murmurs, or staring at Jennifer and Lialla.

I don't think I can take much more of this, he thought in sudden despair. But then, surely, that was what Jadek wanted, wasn't it? And if he couldn't, what alternatives did he have?

Chris was still standing in the middle of the garden, fists clenched at his sides, ignoring the afternoon heat and humidity, when Dahven came up beside him. At first Dahven thought Chris might have been ignoring him, too. His eyes were fixed on Lialla or Jennifer—perhaps both. His voice was scratchy-sounding when he finally heaved a deep sigh and spoke. "She's been through enough, you know? She didn't need this."

"Lialla?"

"Yeah, who else? Mom's been through a lot but she's the kind that thinks everybody's really a lot better than they are, it lets her just—bounce back when most people couldn't. Jen—she's just plain strong, I don't know how she does it, but she does. But Li—she doesn't seem to think anyone's all right, she doesn't think she's any good—hell, *you* know that."

"I've gathered," Dahven said.

"Yeah, well. It's a dirty shame, she can be pretty neat, you can see what kind of person she could've been if that jerk Jadek hadn't messed with her head—sorry, bullied her and all that." Chris shrugged. "So all she really had was the Thread-magic. Except, she apparently can't find it because she *sees* what she does, and I think she thinks it's all gone because she can't see, and it's all gone anyway, because she's going to die—jeez, what a mess."

"Jennifer will fix it," Dahven said, but he sounded doubtful. Chris turned his head to give him a long, thoughtful look.

"Yeah. Me, too. Jen can do damn near anything, but what if she can't this time?"

It was Lialla's question, too—and a measure of her trust in her fellow Wielder that she was even able to ask it. Jennifer shook her head, realized Lialla couldn't see the movement. "Li, I don't know that I can't at least improve matters. If I can't, we'll find someone who can."

"Maybe that's what Jadek wants," Lialla mumbled fretfully. She could feel Light humming just behind her lowest ribs and it threatened to make her ill. "Find someone else, and it's someone Jadek paid to finish what that box began?"

"Sounds like second-guessing to me," Jennifer replied lightly. Lialla managed a very faint smile.

"I know," she whispered. "I said I'd try and stop that, didn't I? Jen, is Chris all right?"

"Just fine. Maybe you should learn how to rap before you jump into Hell-Light again."

"I don't have to now; I've got it with me."

Jennifer laughed. "Bad joke. No, Chris is all right. I—thanks for going after him. You didn't have to—"

"I did. Chris is—I like Chris. Aletto used to tease me like Chris does, before Father—before Father died."

"I know Chris likes you, too. Lialla, you won't die. Trust me."

Lialla's head drooped. "I have to, don't I?"

Jennifer emerged from Thread an hour or more later to find the afternoon nearly spent, the air almost unbearably muggy. She was deathly tired and the chambray shirt needed a good washing, as did her hair.

She hadn't been entirely successful, but Lialla could see again—well enough to distinguish individuals, if they weren't too far away. A tiny, dense knot of Light centered just above the sin-Duchess's diaphragm, between her lungs—and there, despite all Jennifer's tries, it had stubbornly remained. Finally, she had manipulated the soothing Thread Neri had taught Lialla to use, back in Bezjeriad. The woman slept on a pile of cushions deep in shade, Robyn and Aletto sitting close to her in case she woke, or in case she had bad dreams. After one doubtful look in the pool—the box lay quiescent on the bottom, in a far corner—Jennifer sat on the edge where Chris had moon-walked and splashed water across her face.

"If you'd like some washing water—" a high and rather frosty voice began. Jennifer looked up to see Meriyas standing a short distance away. "My father sent me to ask if there was anything you desired," she went on stiffly.

"I *would* like water," Jennifer said. "For washing and some to drink. And, Meriyas—" The girl had already turned away; she stopped and stood stiff-backed in the center of the path. "Don't try and attach blame, will you?"

"You should never have come here," Meriyas replied.

"Perhaps not. But how far back do you carry that? If Aletto never left home, if Lialla had married Carolan—if we had never been dragged from our own world into yours—if Jadek hadn't murdered his brother by Hell-Light and tried to take his place—and incidentally put your father out of work so that he had to leave Zelharri and come here—"

"Words. If you hadn't come here, Lord Jadek would never have forced that box upon Father. My sister might have died handling it!" she added fiercely.

"You might have died if you hadn't moved away from that wall so quickly," Jennifer said. "Chris nearly did. Lialla might yet die; she moved as quickly as you did, but then she went back, for Chris. If she dies because she braved Hell-Light for him, is that still only words?"

"Don't say that!"

"Why? It's true. I'm sorry things came out as they did,

238

Meriyas. All the same, there is no guarantee Jadek wouldn't have forced that box upon your father even if we hadn't come here, simply because of who he was. Perhaps Jadek knew where we were bound; perhaps he only assumed we would come here. It's entirely possible Jadek meant that box as much to harm your father as to kill Aletto; he was to present it himself, wasn't he? Think of that, if you need a direction to aim your anger. Maybe—oh, hell. Maybe anything. I'm just telling you there aren't any easy answers, and nothing is all black or all white. You're old enough to realize that, Meriyas.''

Meriyas stood very still for another moment. ''I'll bring your water,'' she said finally, and walked swiftly toward the house.

18

T HE remainder of the afternoon was mercifully short; the sun went down within an hour and darkness covered the garden. Evany sent servants with food and drink, with an offer of his spare room or the weaving area for Aletto and his people. The offer sounded stiff, even as delivered by Evany's man, and Aletto's refusal, though polite, was no less stiff.

The silver box was gone, though: Evany sent an elderly man out just before full dark to collect it. Jennifer sensed magic but was entirely too tired to care what sort of magician the man might have been, if instead he'd carried some sort of market protection—useful though that information might prove for them all in the days to come. *Later. Much later.* At the moment, it was an effort to force herself to eat anything. What little she'd been able to accomplish for Lialla had utterly drained her.

Lialla was extremely quiet—much too quiet for Jennifer's liking. She ate and drank whatever Chris put into her hands, replied when he spoke to her. She volunteered nothing, still would not let Aletto anywhere near her. Probably she would have refused Chris, too, if he'd shown the least uncertainty; Chris flatly refused to let her push him away and she finally had to give up.

He'd tucked her into a regular blanket and draped a silk-cloth over that, finally came over to where the rest of them were sitting—in the far corner of the garden, well away from the reflecting pool—and dropped heavily into piled cushions. "Jen? I think her eyes are getting worse."

"It could be because it's dark, you know."

"Yeah. Well—yeah." He ran a hand through his hair, swore mildly and began picking it into separate spikes. "So what do we do for her?"

Jennifer shrugged. "I wish I knew. I tried talking to her about Light before; she wouldn't really listen. It's—I don't know how well I can explain it, since you don't know any of it. Thread, you can hear and see *and* feel; Light—"

"I know about that stuff, okay?" Chris interrupted her gruffly.

"Not as a Wielder, you don't, kid. A dispassionate observer type of a Wielder; I hope I'm that, anyway. It's—Light deadens natural sound; it backs away from music. All right, I know you know about the music. Light, though: It was pretty damned quiet in there, wasn't it?"

"No fooling," Chris growled.

"Remember that hut, the first night we were attacked?"

"The deserted village. Sure I do."

"I studied the interior, trying to figure out how to shut it down. I got lucky that time, once I got rid of the device they'd use to confine the stuff in that building, it faded. But there was a wad of it—like, oh, hell." Jennifer ran a hand through her hair and snagged on a knot. She began carefully separating strands. "Say you had a ball of regular string, about the size of a basketball? And say you compressed that, somehow, so it was the size of a golf ball?"

Chris considered this, finally laughed. "Hey, you know? Nifty! Neutron Thread!"

"God knows what it *is*," Jennifer replied gloomily. She finished unsnarling one knot and began searching for others, cautiously combing through her hair with her left hand. "Ouch. I'm just trying to figure how to undo something like that."

"How?" Chris shook his head. "You mean, like, it's the same stuff? Really?"

"Don't know. It doesn't feel like it; it doesn't feel terribly alien, either. But basically, that was what Lialla did with your headache a while back—found an end and unraveled a ball of Thread.''

''Love these technical terms,'' Chris grinned.

''And,'' Jennifer overrode him with heavy patience, ''if it *is* related, I should be able to find a way to do the same thing. Or she should.''

''Yeah. Except I think she's too scared to even think about it.''

''I'm afraid you're right.'' Jennifer gave up on her hair, shook her head. ''We'll just have to do what we can for her, keep her spirits up.''

''Oh.'' Chris gave her a long look. ''Sure. And if it's taking her out like it did her old man? Then what?''

''*I* don't know! Look, kid, my hands are kind of tied at the moment, she won't let me get anyone in to try and help her, in case someone realizes who she is, figures she and Aletto are here, and hauls them in—or in case whatever healer came to help decided to kill her instead.''

''You mean, a healer in Jadek's pay? Yeah—hadn't occurred to me.''

''That—or one who saw profit in going to Jadek later, or even one like that old man who fixed Enardi's leg. Remember him?''

''*Ernie*. And the old guy—jeez, who could forget about *him*? Yeah, he'd probably freak bad over a combination like that, Night-Thread Wielder contaminated with Hell-Light. He'd figure she was better off dead and buried, like Caro's kid.'' He picked up a handful of pebbles from the nearby path and began dropping them one at a time. ''You don't make it any easier, do you?''

''Sure I do,'' Jennifer replied. ''I let you see the choices.''

''Choices? What choices?''

''Well—you seem to be doing a pretty good job of keeping her spirits up, kid. Don't give up, and don't let her see you're down, all right?''

''I *know* all that, okay?'' Chris tossed the last of his pebbles against a tree trunk. He sighed then, shook his head. ''Yeah, I'll do what I can. Don't you give up working on this, either, though.''

''You know me better than that,'' Jennifer replied acerbically.

''Yeah, guess so.'' Chris dropped his voice to a noncarrying murmur. "Listen, though: Aletto said we were getting out of here tomorrow. That right?"

"Think of a good reason to hang around, Chris?"

He grinned. "Hey. With our track record? What about supplies and stuff, though?"

"Aletto's got a small army of people out there right now; remember Gyrdan?"

"Oh. Yeah, right. Used to having to do all that stuff by ourselves. We aren't really going to just walk right up to Duke's Fort with all those guys in tow, though, are we?"

"Don't know." Jennifer shrugged. "Ask Aletto, or Gyrdan. I think Dahven got in on some of the planning session, too. I would have thought you'd be involved in it," she added mildly.

Chris shrugged. "Well—yeah. I felt kind of out of place, you know? I mean, a few years of gaming and stuff doesn't exactly match up to the kind of experience a guy like Gyrdan has."

"Oh?" Jennifer raised her eyebrows. "I don't know. Dahven tells me there hasn't been any real fighting in Rhadaz in several generations—leaving out Dro Pent, of course. Maybe Gyrdan was involved in that; but I'd be willing to bet most of those men are as virgin as you are—as far as fighting, of course," she added.

"Oh, *right*. You have the nastiest way of putting things, you know?"

"I learned it in law school."

"Yeah, sure, I know better. They can't teach *that*; you have to be born with it."

Jennifer laughed. "Well—all right. Maybe. You going?"

"I can take a hint." Chris was on his feet. "Think I'll take Eddie back over that way, talk to him for a while. *He* doesn't beat a guy over the head with—certain *words*," Chris finished darkly. He hunched his shoulders, strode off into the dark; Jennifer could hear the two conversing not far away, but they were talking too softly for her to make out what they were talking about.

She scooped up several of the pillows Chris had left behind, settled two under her head and a thin, matlike rectangle under her hips, curled up on one side and let her eyes close. Sleep wouldn't come, though: too many things happening, too quickly; her brain was chattering madly. She could hear Evany inside the house, his peevish voice raised in protest over something; Roisan's shrill, petulant voice as she argued with him. Too much trouble to try and sort that out. Behind her, Aletto and Dahven were discussing Evany; Robyn was either asleep or nearly so, because Jennifer couldn't recall having heard her voice in some time.

She finally rolled over, opened her eyes, edged herself and the mat a few paces into the open. Dahven glanced back, smiled and caught her hand in his. Jennifer settled her pillows next to his leg, squeezed his fingers and let her eyes close once more.

Aletto sighed very faintly. "I don't know. A part of me wants to murder the man—but how can you hate a man in that kind of position? How can you fault him for choosing between his children and a—the son of a man who was his Duke years ago, someone he hasn't seen in years?"

"He should have found a way to warn you," Dahven said flatly. "Oh, not overtly, not with Jadek possibly aware of whatever he said or did. Still, there are ways: He could have refused you lodging, he could have caused some difficulty to bring him to the attention of city guard—you'd have avoided him then, wouldn't you?"

"Gods," Aletto said bitterly. "I think about it, though; I put myself in his place—"

"Very kind of you," Dahven broke in. "And under other circumstances, I could accept that sort of thing. I'm prone to it myself, on occasion. But Aletto, there is a time and place for empathy, and this is simply not it!"

"I don't—"

"Don't understand? I'm not certain I can put it into words," Dahven said. "I'll try. You're responsible, not just for yourself, but for *everyone* who takes the risk of going against your uncle, anyone who supports you. If you come to harm, if you die—then it's not simply one man who dies, it's your sister, Gyrdan, Chris—Jennifer and myself—everyone here might pay because of you. Every last one of us will be at risk because there won't be any stopping Jadek: He already knows Shesseran won't interfere with him; even Afronsan is staying out of Zelharri business, though he's keeping a close eye on matters and I think Jadek's misfigured *him*. It's not only us, either; it's everyone in Zelharri who dislikes your uncle or who's ever said anything against him, anyone who suffers under his rule for whatever reason—Aletto, at the risk of sounding like one of the more

243

poorly written old tales, you aren't simply a man any longer. You're a symbol, a rallying point.''

Silence. Aletto finally sighed, shifted on the gravel and sighed again. ''I wish you hadn't put it that way.''

''You don't deny it, surely.''

''I suppose not. It makes me feel extremely foolish.''

''If it makes you feel foolish,'' Dahven replied somberly, ''then how do you think I feel? Why do you think I worked that particular problem out in the first place? Something to do with my brothers—?''

''Oh, Dahven.'' Aletto sounded stricken. ''I'm sorry.''

''No. That's not useful.'' Jennifer felt Dahven's fingers tighten on hers; she was too tired to respond. After a moment, he went on. ''At one time, I thought I'd simply go back to Sikkre, certain there was some mistake. *She* wouldn't let me. And then—then, I wanted to quit. After all, who could fight against an accomplished fact? My father dead, my brothers in power, everyone out for my head. Besides, I unfortunately know my brothers, I could understand them, how they must have thought and planned, until they finally took control of the Duchy. If I let myself—I almost *did* let myself accept it from their point of view, and I was ready to abandon everything, just—give it up, crawl into a hole. If they wanted it that badly, after all . . .

''I don't even remember what she said, what made me realize it wasn't just what I wanted, how *I* felt. It's everyone in Sikkre's market, the caravaners, people like Kosilla, her father with his inn—the people who go there. I'm Father's son, his heir, he raised me with an awareness of my duties. Oh, he tried with my brothers, of course; I'm not certain they ever understood anything about the duty end of matters, about the bargain between the Tower and those outside of it.'' Silence. ''Well, it took me long enough. But I finally realized I have to complete that bargain. And quite frankly, I dearly want to see my brothers pay for whatever they did to Father. I'm—look, Aletto, you know I'm not good at this kind of talk, I feel like, what is it Chris says?—a jerk, going on like this. Insufferable.''

''It's—no, don't,'' Aletto said slowly. ''It's all right. I don't feel that—that urge for vengeance. Not yet, at least. But that's a personal thing; it isn't that I think you're wrong.''

''I'm just telling you, is all. Those who turn against you: Casimaffi in Bez, Evany now. Understand it if you like, but don't let pity or misplaced empathy decide how you deal with them—or with Jadek, later.''

"Richard the Third and the Stanleys," Jennifer murmured drowsily. But when Dahven leaned close and asked what she'd said, she merely shook her head and somehow, between that moment and the next, slid into sleep.

They were dressed, packed and ready to go before the sun rose, the next morning. Evany stayed in his rooms, sending his man to offer Aletto food and other assistance—all of which Aletto refused. "Tell Lord Evany that while I am grateful for his offer, I cannot in good faith accept it, knowing my uncle might have made yet another test of his love for his family. He, and I may meet and discuss this matter at a time in the future, when I can view it without anger and he without distress. Until then, I give him thanks for the shelter and food—and I very strongly suggest that he speak at once with the Emperor's heir, as a means of protecting himself from any further attentions by my uncle."

Meriyas stood in the garden just outside of the weaving room as they filed past; Chris, who was supporting Lialla and guiding her footsteps so she didn't trip, ignored the girl. Jennifer slowed, considered saying something, but Meriyas had turned away to stare at Chris's squared, stiff shoulders. Jennifer shook her head, let it go. The girl would either sort it out on her own, or she wouldn't. *Not my problem, either way, for a change.*

They left Podhru in small groups—split up at Gyrdan's insistence, one or two of them riding from the city gates with two or more of Aletto's new guard, to meet up in a grove of young trees an hour beyond the north city boundary. Enardi came riding up last, with two of the younger guardsmen and Edrith. "Don't look so worried," he told Chris rather jokingly, though his own eyes were wide and somber. "I'm not going to try and go with you. I just wanted to say good-bye, I'll miss you guys. You know?"

Chris drew his horse near Enardi's and wrapped a long arm around the Bezanti's shoulders. "Hey. You're all right. But we aren't going that far, and I'll be back, you know? If nothing else, I figure I've got the inside track with Meriyas, if I can keep her off balance—"

"Chris!" Jennifer protested laughingly. He cast her an apologetic grin.

"Well—hey. She's really cute, you know? But a little

245

stuck-up; somebody needs to cut her down a bit. Anyway, guy—Ernie—you hang in there, okay?''

"You know it," Enardi said. "I'll keep Meriyas company for you, if you like—"

"Hah!"

"Sir—Aletto," Enardi went on as Aletto came riding up. "I'll keep in touch with you, through Kamahl, I suppose. I'll do my best not to let you down."

"You won't," Aletto said. "I won't worry about you at all, you know your way around a city better than I do."

Enardi turned away and nudged his horse, sending it back onto the road at a fast trot; he vanished from sight moments later.

Aletto sighed. "Well."

"Yeah," Chris said gloomily. "Here we go again, right?"

"Not quite as bad, this time," Dahven said. "There are a few more of us, for one thing."

There were: The little glade was crowded with perhaps three dozen armed men—everything from Gyrdan to several boys Chris's age, sons of men who had served with Gyrdan in Duke's Fort. There was a wagon, canopied like a caravaner's wagon and fitted with a bed, a wash basin, a long seat, storage for clothing and blankets. A second wagon carried supplies to feed the armsmen, a cook and his assistant driving it. This was followed by a small cart surrounded by half a dozen mounted men—these mostly of middle years or beyond. Afronsan's observers, these last. The cart was open except for a low-roofed wooden hut, a portable office that took up perhaps a fourth of it, a curtain blocking the open side that faced the rear: It held a postage-stamp-sized desk, paper, ink, pens—books. Jennifer suspected it also contained something that would allow Afronsan to directly observe whatever went on anywhere around the cart—possibly something the elderly clerks who used the miniscule hut could carry around with them, into Duke's Fort.

She couldn't actually sense anything; then, she'd never thus far been able to sense any form of charm-magic unless it was being activated around her—and not always then. She wasn't certain she liked the idea of being spied on; then again, Jadek wouldn't like it, either. And he had a lot more to lose.

Lialla was lying down in the lead wagon, Robyn riding on the seat with Gyrdan's driver so she could keep an eye on the sin-Duchess. Lialla had wakened calmer, but Jennifer privately thought this was because she was convinced she was going to die. Robyn said little or nothing, but Jennifer thought her sister probably thought that, too.

And what do I think? She drove a hand through freshly picked-out hair, shook her head and urged her horse forward as the caravan set out. *God knows what I think; I'm operating on conviction borne of blind and bloody-minded optimism right now.*

The day wore on slowly—rather boringly, after the event-filled past days. They stopped for water at a grove just off the road, where a well was kept for travelers; again to rest the horses and let them drink at a crossing where two small streams came together. Not long before dark, they halted for the night. Jennifer could see nothing ahead now but trees—fir and oak, mostly, surrounding an up-sloping road, and if she tilted her head back, the least sense of a ledge high above and well off in the distance. The air wasn't nearly as muggy as it had been, and once the sun went down and a breeze sprang up from the northeast, she found herself grateful for the leather jacket and for spare silkcloths.

Chris spent most of his day riding just behind the wagon, keeping an eye on Lialla; late in the afternoon, when she woke, he was able to persuade her to get into the saddle and ride next to him for a while. The sleep seemed to have done her some good; she had enough strength to mount and dismount without help. Chris stayed close in case she needed assistance, and to try and kid her into a better state of mind. Judging by the look on his face when she climbed back into the wagon, he hadn't been terribly successful. Jennifer pulled the silkcloth snugly around her shoulders, over the leather jacket and waylaid him as he came away from the wagon, shaking his head.

"How is she?"

He shrugged gloomily. "Hey. Thinks she's gonna die, you know? Aside from that—" He considered this, laughed without humor. "Yeah, right, other than that, Mrs. Lincoln, how'd you like the play? No, she's being pretty tough about it, but the bottom line is still, she just knows she's gonna die."

"I'll talk to her," Jennifer said.

"Yeah, well. Good luck." Chris found Edrith, and the

two of them went off into the woods. Some of the men had already built two fires—a warming fire and a cooking fire in a deep pit. Several others were working over this second fire, preparing food.

Robyn was walking stiffly, hands digging into her sides above the waistband of her jeans. Jennifer shivered. ''God, woman, aren't you freezing?''

''Not yet. I fell asleep sitting up on the wagon seat, had two of those silkcloth thingies wrapped around me, I think I must've sweated off ten pounds.'' She blotted her forehead with the back of one hand. ''Don't do that, by the way; I'm so stiff I think I'll *die*.''

''I'll keep that in mind. Where'd Lialla go?''

''Still in the wagon; she was after those legging thingies, I think.'' Robyn tested the air. ''Something smells good— besides the meat, I mean. Nice, having someone else along to cook.''

''Aletto warned them about you and meat,'' Jennifer said. She tucked her hands under her armpits and walked on toward the wagon. ''I'm turning blue just looking at you out here. Aletto should be down there by the rocks; Chris and Eddie went in search of the john. Tell them not to let that fire die out before I get a chance to thaw, okay?''

Robyn looked across her sister's shoulder. ''I don't think you have anything to worry about; they planning on burning down the whole forest?''

''It's in the rocks. See you there.'' Jennifer gathered up loose silkcloth and sprinted toward the wagon, now a darker shape against dark trees. Once she climbed inside the canvas cover, the wind fell to nothing, though she could feel it rocking the wagon now and again.

''Jen?'' Lialla's voice was muffled by cloth. ''Wait a moment, can you?''

''Sure.'' Jennifer waited. The rustle of fabric, the sound of fumbling and something hard hitting wood; a moment after, Lialla's hands and then her face were visible in the blue-light she'd unearthed from somewhere under the bed.

Blue light didn't do much for anyone—rather, in its own way, Jennifer thought, like fluorescent tube lights in public restrooms back home, or mercury vapor outdoor lights. Blue light left her feeling wan and faded; it pointed up every single fine line in Robyn's face, deepened the shadows under her eyes. At the moment, Lialla looked like a haggard old woman; blue light etching the long furrows from the corners of her nose to the corners of her mouth, others that ran down into her jawline; blackening the hollows under her cheekbones and beneath her eyes. "Just came to see how you're feeling," she said finally. Lialla set the light in a bowl on the low shelf opposite the bed, dropped down next to it. She laughed shortly, shook her head. "That bad?" Jennifer pursued.

"Oh—no worse," Lialla said. *Yet*, she might as well have added.

"Your eyes?"

"I can't decide. I think I could see better earlier, when I was riding. Now—well, I can still see, that's something, isn't it?"

"I think so," Jennifer said mildly. "I can tell you don't."

"I—well." Lialla forced anger out of her voice with a visible effort, shook herself. "Well. No. I don't. Jen, I know you're trying, I'm sorry I can't help you."

"Don't worry about it," Jennifer said. "You do what you can, that's all. Are you coming out to eat, or shall I have someone bring you something when it's cooked?"

"Send something," Lialla said.

"You'll eat?"

The sin-Duchess laughed briefly. "You and Chris. Yes. All right. I'll eat."

"The rest of it," Jennifer said as she paused with one foot on the step-down at the back of the wagon. "The sense of Light. Has that changed? Shifted? Moved around? Grown?"

"Same," Lialla said tersely. As Jennifer stepped onto the ground and turned away, Lialla leaned out and caught hold of her arm. "Jen—I'm sorry. Truly sorry."

"I understand conditioning," Jennifer said. "It's hard to break. I think if the alternative is letting your uncle win, though—"

"That isn't fair!"

"No. Life isn't. Nothing in this world has been, so far." Jennifer pivoted around, freed a hand and gripped Lialla's where it still rested on her arm. "That doesn't mean you simply give up. If you do, Aletto loses—in other words, he might well die, Lialla. Along with me, Chris, Robyn. Those men out there. Edrith—Eddie—who gave up a reasonably safe life in Sikkre to come help us."

"Don't—"

"I won't. I'll leave you alone. Think about something, though, after I'm gone. Think about your mother. If you give up, if Aletto loses everything, think what you'll do to her, beyond anything Jadek's already done to her."

"Mother—oh, *gods*." Lialla's voice broke; she tore her hand from under Jennifer's and vanished back inside the wagon. Jennifer shook her head and briefly closed her eyes, then drew the silkcloth close, got her hand back inside it and hurried back over to the fire.

"God, I should be a Jewish mother, I'm going to be so good at guilt," she muttered into her collar. Well, she'd planted the idea; whether Lialla was capable of acting on any of what she'd said might be another matter. She'd simply have to see.

Afronsan's men stayed to themselves, talking in a hushed group between the main fire and slabbed rock while they ate, retiring almost immediately after. Gyrdan himself ate with Aletto, but most of the men he'd brought were clearly uncertain how much leeway they were allowed, so far as talking to Aletto or mingling with the rest of them. Chris and Edrith ate together, then vanished into the woods for a long enough time that Robyn was beginning to grow visibly anxious about them. She stayed with Aletto while he and Dahven and Gyrdan talked, but only remained seated long enough to manage a bowl of soup—peppers, chicken and a heavily spiced, thick broth. Jennifer sniffed it cautiously, decided she might be safer with the plain meat that had been roasted in long strips on sticks. The bread was good, but not as good as Robyn's. Robyn ate some of it, dipping it in the soup, finally handed the bowl to Aletto to finish and curled up with her head on his leg, a silkcloth drawn up to her chin. Jennifer thought she was asleep almost at once.

She herself was tired, but too restless to even think of sleeping. The warming fire looked like a beacon, the smells of cooking meat and bread, soup and onions that had been set to roast in the coals—it was a wonder they hadn't already drawn someone's attention, or something's. The desert hadn't looked like bear country, but this, Jennifer thought, certainly did. She pushed to her feet, walked up and down the road to get her blood circulating a little.

A scuffling noise brought her around sharply, but it was Chris and Edrith, coming back from the woods. All she could see of them, with the fire behind them, was two dark outlines. "What're you two doing?" she demanded.

"Hey. Checking for bears and stuff, bad guys, you know?"

"Hey," Jennifer retorted. "You know what's scary? I can't even tell which one of you said that."

"Cool," one of them chuckled—Chris, she thought. "Hey, you all right out here, lady?"

"I was until you brought up bears," Jennifer said.

"Like that Who song says, 'No bears in there.' Nothing else, either. Real quiet around here. You talk to Lialla?"

"Yeah. Don't know how much good I did."

"Probably a lot, you talk a good line. Well, lookit," Chris added. "You might be warm enough, but we aren't."

"I know, all that exercise and fresh air isn't good for your boyish bodies, right?"

"Hey. The lady takes notes. You gonna sleep in the wagon?"

"No, don't think so. In fact," Jennifer said around a yawn, "maybe I'll walk back to the fire with you."

"Reminds me," Chris said as he moved over so she was between them. "I'd like to see if I can't learn how to wangle that one particular thread Li was talking about—you know, the stuff she used to knock Ernie out cold, so you could pull him out of that hole?"

"The calming Thread that Neri showed her?" Jennifer considered this, finally shrugged. "Well—why not?"

"Just not tonight," Chris added. "All these strange guys around, and I really don't think I want to zap myself tonight, just in case—but so one of us doesn't forget. Hey, know what? They got saws here after all." Chris nudged Edrith, who sighed heavily. "*He* says why would he have seen them before in Sikkre?"

"Well? Sounds logical. About the Thread thing; remind me later, will you?"

"You got it."

The road wound up almost from the first, the next day; at what Jennifer's watch told her was nine-thirty of a chilly, bright morning, Gyrdan brought them to a vee in the road and they stopped for a few moments, to walk out stiffness, to share water bottles, for Gyrdan to make his final selection of men who would remain with Aletto on the east pass road, while Gyrdan and the main body of Aletto's guard took the west road, and split up again several miles farther on, where the road came down across the Zelharri border and split into several smaller village tracks that eventually came back onto the east-west road that led to Sehfi and to Sikkre—the same road Jennifer, Chris and Robyn had stepped onto late one night two or more months before.

Gyrdan clasped Aletto's hand. "We'll come into Sehfi by various routes, but no later than three nights from now, at moonrise. With luck, we won't draw much attention, and might even have the gates secured when you ride in. If not, we can take them together." He glanced over the men ranged at Aletto's back—half a dozen men between Chris's age and perhaps fifty. "You'll be comfortable with only these? You're certain?"

"Gyr," Aletto smiled. "We had this out last night."

"Last night, the numbers sounded reasonable," the older man admitted. "Seen at your side, however—"

"They're more than we had coming from Bez, you know. Or from Sikkre. My uncle knows where I am, Gyrdan, even if he can't *watch* me. Isn't that one reason we're breaking up this far from the border? Fewer men at my back, and my uncle might continue to think me an easy mark and attack; more, he might see us as a threat to be eliminated." His smile faded, but only for a moment. "So long as each man knows the danger—well, but we had *that* out, as well, didn't we? Fare well, my friend, we'll meet in Sehfi, and with good fortune persuade my uncle without further violence to anyone." Gyrdan merely shook his head, turned aside and rode off, the main body of men, the cook's wagon, three of Afronsan's observers and one of the clerks behind him.

Jennifer didn't care at all for the east road: She'd traded her mount of the day before for one that didn't have quite as horsey an odor to it, and this one showed no tendency to ignore what she wanted of it. But it was slow, stupid even for a horse, she thought. And clumsy; twice since they'd parted ways at the vee, it had stumbled. Which was unpleasant enough to Jennifer's way of thinking, but the condition of the road was deteriorating as they climbed, and now there was a drop on her right side. Dahven rode on her right at first, but after an hour or so of very slow going, he left her to talk to Aletto. Robyn was already up front with Aletto; Chris and Edrith in front of them. Lialla had ridden for a short while, but she was back in the wagon once more, afraid to trust her blurred vision any further.

Jennifer had no idea if Lialla had even bothered to think

over what she'd said the night before; at the moment, she didn't much care, either. She was too busy concentrating on her horse's footing, on keeping the blundering animal away from holes, loose stones and the east edge of the road—and an increasingly steep drop—to worry about anything else.

Midafternoon; they'd kept moving, and she was beginning to wonder who had managed to fit an extra dozen hours in between that vee in the road and this point; but when she tipped her head back Jennifer could see the dark rocks that marked the top, see dark blue sky and a drift of fast-moving cloud beyond it. *Almost there.* She glanced at her watch: it read four-thirty, near enough. The sun was temporarily out of sight behind the top of the pass but it would probably be visible—and warm—once she came up the rest of the way. It wouldn't set for another—what, three hours? That at least. The wind up here was cool and constant, it flowed down from the heights.

She came out on top not long after; one final, absolutely hair-raising hairpin turn, followed by a steep and fortunately short washboard which ran between two black chunks of rough, lichen-covered rock. Something up here smelled pleasant—cedar, perhaps. Something clean and cool.

They'd apparently decided on a decent stop: Chris and Edrith were off their horses already and Aletto was in the act of sliding down from his. Dahven sat his mount still, facing back toward the south—waiting for her, apparently. He waved as she came across the ridge and onto open meadow. There were pale lavender flowers everywhere, dotted here and there with yellow dandelions; it would've been absolutely lovely, Jennifer thought, if she hadn't remained aware of the drop-off all along the east side, where grass and wildflowers came up against a low line of the black rock with its bright yellow-green coating of lichen. Not that she was going to ride over there to see just how far down it was; she could see the tops of several sparse, wind-driven and broken trees, down off the slope, enough to indicate how bad it might be.

She drew the horse to a stop, turned back to look behind her. Swallowed. The road looked even worse from this angle than it had the other way. Odd, though; she couldn't see the man with the lame horse, the one she had just passed on the east turn.

"Nothing wrong, is there?" Dahven had come up beside her; he held out his water bottle. Jennifer drank, shook her head, swallowed.

"Don't know. But there was a guy, the one with the beard? His horse was limping but he shouldn't have been that far behind me, not as slow as I came up."

Dahven turned his head and came part-way out of the saddle. "Odd. I don't hear anything. How far back was he?"

"Just beyond the last turn. Said he was going to check the hoof for rocks; would that take long?"

"No. Pulling one might, especially if the hoof was already tender, though. Maybe if I—"

"No." Jennifer caught his arm and gripped hard. "No, don't. I don't like it, don't like the feel—"

"You don't think already—" Dahven stopped speaking, held up a hand when she would have answered him. "Wait. Hear it? It's all right, he's coming."

"Are you—?" She could hear it too, then, the sound of shod hooves striking hard-packed dirt and an occasional stone. "All right. There—got him, he's walking, leading it."

"All right," Dahven said. He took back his water bottle, capped it, brought his horse halfway back around but drew it to a halt. "Jennifer? Come on, he can catch up, they're going to build a fire, brew tea."

"Go ahead, I'm coming," she said rather absently. Her eyes were fixed on the gray-haired man. His shoulders were bowed, his body bent forward with the steepness of the incline. His horse was still limping; hers took several paces forward, stopped. Jennifer tightened her grip on the reins and drew them in, hard. "Hold still, you rotten animal," she snarled. The horse flicked an ear at her, whickered nervously. "Hell with it," she muttered, "He can come on his own, he's fine."

Something below her shifted, as though a cloud had crossed the sun, as though she'd taken off yellow-tinted sunglasses and turned the world a bewildering variety of blues and greens. The horse danced back a little, turned itself sideways to the road. And then stood absolutely still. Out of the corner of her eye, she could see Dahven. *Oh, God, how'd he get that far away?* The armsman looked up, then, the movement catching her attention. And then his eyes

254

found hers, and for one horrible moment, they seemed to hold her pinned as still as her horse.

Dahven shouted something and spurred toward her, but the sound of his voice was muted, and he was moving at the wrong speed, the horse galloping almost in slow motion. The gray-beard, by contrast, flowed uphill like water, shifting smoothly toward her in a nightmare movement that stopped just out of reach. She wanted to yell; sound wouldn't come—anger or perhaps fear blocking her throat. *The bo*, she thought suddenly, but it was too late for anything now: The guard abandoned his lame horse at the top of the hill, sailed straight for her at a speed that badly mismatched the slow and deliberate movement of his legs. When he came to a halt, he could have touched her. She clutched the bo, dropped to the ground as Light burst from a point directly behind his head, spun around them, locking them together in a sphere—locking everyone else out.

19

JENNIFER drew a shuddering breath, tightened her grip on the bo and went into a crouch. *Jerk is the word for it! Let him try anything*—but he was somehow inside her tip before she could shift and bring the staff around. His hands slapped hers; hers went numb, and the bo dropped, vanishing silently into puddled Light and possibly the unseen meadow grass beneath it.

"Don't you *dare* threaten me." The face was the older armsman's; the voice, unmistakably Jadek's.

"Don't you even think you can intimidate me that way; I'm not your wife or your stepson," Jennifer replied stiffly. "And it's only a threat if I don't intend to make it good. After everything you've done since we last met like this—Mister, I wouldn't count on empty threats from *me*." Momentary silence. She folded her arms across her chest. "You're awfully damn hard on men. Was it really necessary to bother me again, or do you just like killing people this way?"

He used a broad swing of his arm to indicate the still-clear sphere. "I needn't kill; not now that I have a better understanding of how this works. Certainly not this near Duke's Fort." He smiled unpleasantly as he met her eyes again. "And of course it is not necessary to shield the ball. Unless you mind?"

Jennifer glanced up as he had; there was a bird well above them, moving in slow motion. She brought her eyes back down, shrugged and turned the corners of her mouth in a smile that fell far short of hard eyes. "Why should I mind? I've seen odder special effects in movies. Why don't you give up?"

"Why should I?"

"Because right is on Aletto's side."

"Do you think so?"

Jennifer shook her head. "What I think isn't that important. It's what others think, what the laws and the rules say.

Aletto is your brother's heir; holding onto the Fort and impregnating his mother with your heir doesn't change the fact that Aletto is Amarni's son, you're not.''

"Not to belabor the obvious," Jadek replied bitingly. "But if Aletto were no longer alive, or—as I have maintained all along, unfit to rule Zelharri—*and* if Lialla has no son, then I *am* Amarni's heir."

"Then you should have murdered Aletto years ago," Jennifer said coolly. She stuffed both hands under her arms to keep chilled and still-aching fingers from trembling where he could see them. "Instead you let him cross the country so people could see how obviously fit he really is." Silence. She gave him another dry smile. "Of course, that wasn't exactly intentional on your part, was it?"

"It doesn't really matter, you know. The Fort is properly mine."

She stared at him; he gazed back. "I really find it difficult to believe what I'm hearing," Jennifer said finally. "You're counting on a lot, aren't you? Shesseran's inaction—"

"That isn't so much to count on. What do you think—that a handful of merchants will come out of Bez and retake the Fort—on behalf of Aletto? Or his sister? That they'll petition the Emperor, demand I hand Zelharri over to my nephew? I think you badly misunderstand our ways here, outlander." He held up a hand as she strove to speak. "Oh, I know about the shipload of eager young Bez money-grubbers sitting in the clerks' hall in Podhru, waiting for an audience with Shesseran's paper-shifting brother—and shall we wager on how long they'll sit there? I do know which of their fathers offered Aletto support, back in Bez, beginning with my good friend Fedthyr. I will deal with them, in good time, once the matter of Aletto is settled."

"You're mad," Jennifer said flatly. Jadek laughed.

"Am I? Because I understand how to consolidate power, and how to keep hold of it? Something my nephew was incapable of learning, perhaps."

"What do you get out of it? No," she added as he laughed again and shook his head. "I'd really like to know. Money? There can't be that much in Zelharri. Power? As the Duke of a backwater Duchy, how much power can you have—or does it really give you a thrill, having goat-herders bowing to you and armsmen like that baker's son calling you 'Honor'?"

"If you have to ask, I doubt I could explain so you'd understand. I doubt *you* would understand anyway, woman; you've already shown a soft side like Aletto's."

"If that means I'm too nice to figure you out—or deal you out, if I get a chance—don't count on it," Jennifer replied mildly.

"I won't. You and that outlander boy—well!" Jadek drew a harsh, shuddering breath, expelled it loudly. When he went on, his voice was considerably less tense. "It was my chance, my only chance. Maybe I thought it out then; I don't recall. Doesn't matter. After Amarni died, Lizelle was mine. You can't say—no one can say—that I didn't maintain the Duchy," he added sharply. Jennifer freed a hand and waved him on. "Another man might have done otherwise, no one can say I wasn't a good administrator! I worked hard, long hours and years, always with an eye to how best to keep the Duchy, do you think Shesseran would've allowed me to maintain my place if I hadn't done the best possible job? And then, to simply deliver it—to that—that—drunken young lout!"

"I absolutely won't argue Aletto's purported flaws with you again," Jennifer said. "We did that, to no point. I do disagree about the Emperor intervening; after all this time in Rhadaz, I quite honestly believe you could have quietly murdered half the population without his intervention. All the same. By now, you know damn well Aletto's changed; you wouldn't be delivering all that hard work you claim over to a drunken lout. And he wouldn't be vindictive."

"No? You're more naive than I thought, woman." Jadek looked beyond her. "So he has a handful of guards now; is that to protect him once he enters Sehfi? Or as an honor guard for a returning hero?"

Jennifer glanced over her shoulder. Dahven was still riding toward the sphere, in agonizingly slow motion; she jerked her eyes away, wondering as she did so whether Jadek was trying an elaborate double-bluff, or if he really wasn't aware of the size of Aletto's full company. "You should know; you've been watching us all along, haven't you?"

"Oh, come now," he scoffed. Jennifer smiled.

"No closed-circuit TV, no short-wave, hmmm?" Hell, it might even be true.

"Explain," he demanded; she shook her head.

"I don't think so. You knew we were *here*, though."

"Aletto would come this way, as the shortest and easiest

between Podhru and Sehfi, of course." Jadek glanced overhead, back across her shoulder and he smiled now, an unpleasant twist of lips. "How lovely! You have the Sikkreni traitor with you—but that does not surprise me. You are fond of each other, I gather; I shall keep that in mind."

"You would do very damn well to keep it in mind. That, and what happened to anyone who's tried to come between us."

"A warning? Yes, I know what transpired in Bez. You killed a man—with his own knife, someone said. With your own, others tell me. Somehow, I don't feel as fearful as you might like."

"More fool you, then."

"Ah?" The smile widened; cold settled in the pit of her stomach. "You think so?" The sphere pulsed once, sending a low-grade shudder of current through her body. "You bear three marks against you: woman, outlander, Wielder. Incapable of understanding us Rhadazi and the way *our* world works; incapable of understanding how a man thinks, why his logic exceeds yours, or surpasses your emotional point of view. Worst of all, you Wielders, you are all alike: arrogant, narrow of vision—incapable of understanding anything that is not Night-Thread and its pitiful magics. The old woman—do you remember Merrida? You should, she was responsible for your being here, after all." He held up a hand before she could say anything. "Don't bother to deny that she did. I finally found a way to ask her that question and—well, let us say, she found it impractical to lie to me, about present events and her part in them. *She* had your attitude toward Light—evil, black, but somehow still not as powerful as the weak stuff she used."

"What did you do, kill her?"

"Why? You see, you do not understand at all, do you? Another time, we will discuss these things, believe that. But even here, time is growing short. My nephew's men are beginning to realize something is wrong; do you notice?"

"I'm hardly surprised," Jennifer replied. The man was shifting directions on her so quickly, it made her nearly as dizzy as the sphere itself. *Good cop/Bad cop in one body, really swell*, she thought dryly. The Chris-like thought steadied her for the moment. *Get rid of him*, she thought then. But how? Threats weren't working, she didn't seem to be able to anger him this time, either. Something else, though: Something occurred to her. *Show him up. Wait, give him a minute, a moment or two, a little rope to hang himself.* A quick glance over her shoulder showed Dahven, his horse dancing sideways away from the sphere, him trying to drag it back around—all in slow motion. Beyond him, though: Chris and Afronsan's men ranged in front of the wagon, Aletto standing with his arms around Robyn, a huddle of black at his feet—Lialla, sitting in the open, all of them surely watching. "Look, Jadek, we've chewed the same piece of meat half a dozen times. Why don't you just go away? I'm not particularly interested in listening to what a swell fellow you are; you apparently haven't heard a word I've said."

"I didn't come to talk."

"Oh, yeah? You sure could fool me." Jennifer let her arms fall to her sides and cautiously slid her right foot forward, feeling for the fallen bo. It slipped across her instep, and she left it balanced there. "If you have a threat to deliver, tell me; I'll pass it on, all right?"

"I didn't come to mouth empty threats, either. Now that you're so near Sehfi, I can deliver an ultimatum—you and the outland boy turn around, go back at once. Despite the things he said in Podhru, I'll spare his life. Take the guards with you, leave Aletto and his sister. And my nephew's new wife, of course." He smiled widely. "Perhaps you thought I didn't know of that—of her?"

"I don't think any of us particularly cared whether you knew or not," Jennifer said. She swallowed past a suddenly very dry throat.

"Foolish. And naive. People who don't understand the politics where they find themselves should not meddle in such politics. They might find themselves paying unforeseen consequences—such as a woman who might already carry my grand-nephew. I hope you understand me?"

"You'll kill her? As you have *anyone* involved in local politics, at whatever level?"

She had hoped to catch him off guard, but he merely shook his head. "I see. You assume then that I was responsible for Amarni's death?"

"I said nothing about that, did I?" Jennifer replied softly.

"You didn't have to. Advocates," he spat. "Always playing with words."

"Not always. Look, give it up; at this point Shesseran won't do anything to you if you back off, and Aletto won't impoverish you."

"I know that. Because Shesseran wouldn't interfere for anything short of overt murder, which I don't intend to commit. And Aletto—for the last time, understand that I am not handing my Duchy over to Aletto."

"A warning," Jennifer began.

He shook his head, held up a hand; somehow, she couldn't remember how she'd wanted to complete the thought. "No more warnings, outlander advocate woman. Not from you. You've begun to think of yourself as incapable of failure, haven't you? Well—" The twisted smile broadened to a flash of teeth, a nasty, positively evil smirk. He looked beyond her once again and raised a hand, fist clenched. "Let me show you what failure looks like. Beginning—now."

Lialla had let Robyn talk her into walking around a little on the shaded side of the wagon and under the young, slender trees; at the moment, she was rather sorry she'd come out, because her legs ached and her knees wanted to give way at every step. Her head ached fiercely. Robyn was undoubtedly trying to be cheerful and keep her spirits up, but now, she merely sounded desperately worried. Lialla managed to keep her temper in check, even managed a few monosyllabic responses to Robyn's anxious questions. Once they returned to the wagon, Lialla leaned against it gratefully, let Robyn think she was hungry and thirsty—she wasn't, but it got rid of the woman for a while, at least.

Where was Jennifer? She couldn't see very clearly and at the moment, it was particularly irritating. "Somebody?" she said in a low voice. "Someone—is anyone there? Chris?"

"Li?" She heard his voice a little distance away, felt his hand on her arm. "Hey, you all right out here?"

"Fine." She nodded, tried not to wince as the movement set her head pounding. "I—is Jen here? I need her."

"Not yet. Hey, that's kind of odd; I thought she and Dahven were right behind us. Hang on." His hand fell away and she sensed him moving away from her; heard the faint scuff of his high-tops against dirt. "Uh-oh."

"Chris?" Lialla squinted against glare reflected from the canvas, felt her way along the side of the wagon after him. "Chris, what?"

"I can see Dahven; he's sitting out there on his horse, fighting with it. What the *hell* is that thing, though?"

"Don't do this, tell me!" Lialla insisted.

"Sorry. There's—I think it's Hell-Light out there, big ball of it, don't see anything inside it really, except some kind of movement."

Lialla withdrew into herself, forcing contact with Thread. It momentarily threatened to make her ill, shifting her center of balance so she swayed back and forth. Chris wrapped an arm around her shoulders. "That *is* Light," she said. "Jadek—"

"Oh, jeez. Not another one of his fog-ball phone booths? Like out in the desert?"

"A—what you said," Lialla agreed tersely.

"Jen?"

"Inside. With Jadek—Chris, no, don't go that way, you can't help like that. Get Afronsan's man, get him out here where he can see this, go, do it fast! Go, I'm fine!" She could feel the doubtful look he gave her but he obediently let her down onto the ground and took off at a run.

Fortunately, he hadn't asked how she knew what was out there, and who: It would have scared him half silly. Lialla knew, and it scared her: She could feel the pull, Jadek's hand on the invasive Light that huddled just under her ribs; could still feel the almost overwhelming, horrifying desire she'd fought off, to snatch hold of Chris's dagger, to run it full into his belly—or now, to find her way back past the wagon, to find Aletto, draw the knife he wore against his backbone and drive it up, into his heart. To kill, rend, damage, to spill blood, run her fingers through it . . . Her jaw was trembling, despite the way she clamped her teeth together; her hands were sweating, and the moment she quit concentrating even the least bit, it broke over her like the waves she and Chris had dodged that wonderful, silly afternoon near Caro Ellaway's inn, outside Podhru. He'd taken her hunting shells, he'd shown her the bubbly air holes where crabs lurked under the sand, took her across rocks and persuaded her to touch the odd little things that closed around her fingers. She'd laughed, giggled like a girl—and Jadek wanted her to kill the boy who'd given her that?

Suddenly she was furious; to use *her* against her brother—against the boy who had become another brother. "He'll pay for that," she swore through clenched teeth. She came up onto her knees, closed her eyes and sought the Light that had inhabited her for two days and nights.

She wasn't afraid of it any longer, even knowing what

262

Jadek could do with it. Maybe knowing the worst helped, but at the moment there wasn't time for fear, wasn't any room left in her with so much anger spilling over and filling her. Someone shouted on the far side of the wagon, someone else's voice rose in a shriek. Robyn—Robyn had shifted. Jadek, unable to manipulate his niece to violence, had sought an easier mark. Lialla ignored the shrill cry of the enormous hunting bird, ignored too the chill and darkness as its shadow enveloped her and passed on. Light was a wad, like Thread—like the Thread that had marked Jadek's bruise on her face, where he'd struck her, the bruises he'd laid on her brother's back with his own stick. The strands were much finer, totally silent, bright enough to cast blood-red lines against the insides of her eyelids. *But not so different, after all,* she told herself repeatedly as she began working her way into the mass. Almost, it helped.

Light dulled Jennifer's hearing but she was aware of the shrill, spiraling cry that was surely Robyn. She wheeled around, clutching at the horse behind her as her knees threatened to give. Dahven, not far away, his face white, off his horse now but unable to force his way any closer; behind him and above, a slow-moving, broad-winged black shape: Robyn. She spun back. "Jadek, you bastard, you did that, didn't you?"

"Of course I did." He laughed shortly. "I warned you, woman, warned you all! Look at her," he added softly. "She doesn't do well under sunlight, does she? I could turn her human up there. But I don't really need to; all I need do is create wind at the proper moment; it will send her out beyond the ledge. She'll fall, and she'll die."

"If she does, you won't live much longer," Jennifer spat at him. "You can't control all of us—"

"Don't threaten *me*. I'm not here, remember? All you can do is kill this body I inhabit, but I can still accomplish whatever I choose. It's finished, here and now, for all of you. Because Lialla is mine, thanks to her foolish gesture in Podhru. Aletto will seek her comfort once his wife falls to her death and Lialla has my instruction how to deal with him. He'll die, too."

"No."

"No? How will you stop me? Once Aletto is dead, she will kill that outlander boy; Aletto's armsmen will have no choice but to stop her. You, arrogant outlander bitch, you and the Thukar's heir won't find life so short, *or* death so simple." Jennifer merely shook her head. *Kill the guard?* She couldn't kill an innocent man. But there were other ways. She slid her foot across the ground in search of her fallen bo. Jadek looked up once more. "Look at her. Such a shapeshifter can't compete long with the sun. She'll fall within another three wingstrokes."

Got it. She worked her toes under the bo, prayed she had it somewhere near the center so it would be balanced on her instep. Now, to distract him. "The men up there?" she said loudly. "Aletto's pitiful little guard, you called it? Some of it is Lord Afronsan's; he sent observers. I'd say you've given them a quite an eyeful."

Jadek stared at her for one very long moment, his eyes black and the smile hanging forgotten on his lips. He laughed then. "An excellent bluff—or it would be, if I didn't understand Shesseran and his paper-mounding brother better than that. You've lost, woman. Watch the shapeshifter," he added softly, and began fanning the air with his left hand. Robyn's shrill cry answered—it sounded frightened, and no longer entirely bird.

Jennifer stooped and sharply drew her right foot up at the same moment, tossing the bo into the air; she wrapped both hands around it, straightened her knees and slammed the long end up. Jadek ducked, but the tip hit his shoulder squarely. The sphere trembled, faded slightly. Jennifer whispered an apology to the man whose body Jadek had borrowed, swung the other end around in a short arc and cracked it across the man's upheld fingers. He yelped, cursed echoingly.

"Jennifer, duck!" She dropped to both knees and threw her arms over the back of her neck as something flashed past the horse's nose; the animal snorted and tramped nervously back. A howl burst from the man's throat and seemed to go on forever. Jennifer looked up to see the sphere vanish, the gray-bearded armsman swaying back and forth. Dahven's dagger was buried in his shoulder. The guard wailed again—a sound that now bore no trace whatever of Jadek—tottered forward a pace and fell.

Jennifer scrambled to her feet, shoving past her now frantic horse and let her head fall back, one forearm shading her eyes, the bo still clutched in white-knuckled fingers. Robyn was far overhead—much too high for the jerky fashion she was flying. And she didn't look entirely bird any longer. The cry was even less bird, more woman, entirely terrified. "Birdy!" she yelled. "Birdy, damnit! Concentrate, pay attention to me, and get—away—from—the—damn—ledge!"

"Help me!"

"Birdy, I can't do anything, you have to! Come on, turn toward the sun, do it, woman! Right into the sun—" For a long, dreadful moment, she couldn't remember how to breathe, her chest hurt and Robyn was hanging right over that hellish drop, blonde hair incongruously flung under the leading edge of both long, black wings, the way it so often hung down her chest, blowing back under the arms of her tee-shirt. And then somehow she managed to bank; two long sweeps and she was over open meadow. "Birdy! Remember how to circle? Do it, just like before!"

"Can't—just can't—!"

"Robyn, move your damn butt, get it down here!"

"Mom!" Chris was somehow with her, giving Jennifer something strong to lean against. Edrith stood beside her, gripping her fingers hard, and she couldn't even remember how or when he'd taken hold of them. "Mom," Chris yelled. "You pay attention to Jen, all right? Come on, you can do it!"

"Can't—"

"Robyn?" Where had Lialla come from? The sin-Duchess was right under Robyn, moving with her, and there was nothing weak or vacillating about her movements. "Robyn, concentrate on me, I'm going to lay down a sphere, you'll be able to see it, if you can't stay shifted the sphere will catch you. You'll have to stay right above me, though, can you manage that?"

"Can't—"

"You can!" Lialla insisted sharply. "Bring the wings in, start your spiral down, I'll hurry too! Come on, Robyn! Aletto's waiting for you, he's afraid to look, don't do this to him, Robyn!"

"Help—me—" But Lialla was hastily and deftly working Thread—Thread *and* Light, Jennifer realized dazedly—weaving something similar to a Wielder's silver-thread sphere, similar to Jadek's Light sphere—and yet, not really like either. Jennifer gave the sin-Duchess a sidelong glance, shifted into Thread, and felt it. Curious: It didn't affect her the way Lialla's straight use of Thread did—her shift and her contact with Lialla's work didn't distract Lialla, either.

She could almost feel the effort it took Robyn to draw in her wings, the horror that gripped her sister, the certainty that she was going to fall like a brick. But somehow she was descending, in an awkward but tight circle, directly above Lialla's sphere. Her head was fully hair, there were fingertips visible under the feathers; the sense of a human face under a superimposed bird's face growing by the moment. But she was down with a bounce as though she'd landed on an innerspring mattress.

Chris let go of his aunt and ran the few paces to where his mother was just sitting up, clinging to Lialla's arm. "Oh, jeez, kid, I think I'm *cured*," she said pantingly. "Never again!"

"During the day, I guess," Chris said anxiously. "Hey, here comes your old man." He gave her a hard, quick hug and got to his feet as Aletto came up, face white and his limp very obvious. "She's all right, scared is all." Aletto wrapped his arms around Robyn; Robyn buried her face against his shoulder.

Jennifer folded at the knees and sat hard, bringing Edrith down with her. The scent of fresh, bruised grass and flowers assaulted her nose, sending her into a sneezing fit. By the time she got that under control, Dahven was kneeling on her other side, eyeing her anxiously, one arm around her shoulders. She nodded before he could ask. "Yeah, fine, I'm all right. That guy, though—the guard."

"Lialla's taking care of him. I hope I didn't misread the situation."

"Situation—? Oh. You didn't, that was Jadek. Using someone once again. He's not—dead, is he?"

"I didn't kill him, no. He was still bleeding when I came away from him. I'm sorry; I tried to get to you and couldn't."

"I know." Jennifer laughed shortly. "I'm getting used to the damn things, I guess, I don't even find anything strange about being wrapped up in one any more. Funny: Three months ago, the extent of my experience with magic was rabbits out of hats. You did fine; I don't know that I would have tried throwing a knife through Light."

"Well, why not? I admit it didn't occur to me until after the thing started to fade."

"I'd have missed; I've got lousy aim."

"I admit I was fortunate; I seldom practiced throwing knives and I was never very good at it. And I didn't dare try until after you struck out, and I was certain the man was a threat."

"Was it obvious?" Jennifer asked rather anxiously. "Obvious enough for Afronsan's man?"

Edrith answered her. "Don't know; he doesn't say much, just looks at everything like it's giving him a stomachache."

"Just so." Dahven laughed. "Jen, why don't you get up so we can go ask him?"

"Good idea." She extended a hand to each. "Help me up. I want to check Aletto's new man first, though. Poor fellow."

Afronsan's man wasn't forthcoming about the incident, or about his reaction to it. Jennifer wasn't certain after talking to the clerk whether he'd seen anything, whether he was trying to remain impartial to both sides—whether perhaps Jadek had done something to his eyes, or even possibly bought the man off before they ever left Podhru. He did look dyspeptic, but then, he had the first time she'd seen him. Probably it wouldn't do her any good to push the issue; the man no doubt felt his opinions, if any, were Afronsan's property and none of her concern.

They rode on almost at once. Aletto was white and shaken, but now all the more insistent upon reaching Duke's Fort as soon as possible. Robyn, no less shaken, rode in the wagon for most of the afternoon and for part of the time Aletto stayed with her; later he went back to his horse and rode where she could see him.

The road, fortunately, remained fairly level for most of the afternoon, smooth-surfaced, and shaded.

The guard went back to his horse for a while. Lialla had healed the cut in his upper arm—Dahven's knife had only sliced skin, barely touched muscle and hung up in his sleeve. She'd also checked the horse's hoof, to discover that there was no foreign object and apparently no damage—the animal walked as well as any of them. He came out of the experience much better than his master: The guard swayed in the saddle rather alarmingly until Aletto found a way to convince him to take over driving the wagon.

Jennifer understood a little how the man felt; after even such a short confrontation with Jadek, she was finding it hard to keep up with the pace Aletto's guard was setting. Dahven watched her rather anxiously when he thought she didn't see, and stayed right next to her.

Lialla rode a little apart from all of them, and Jennifer could feel her touching Thread, rather as though she were enumerating the individual strands of it. It didn't vibrate through her as it normally did when another worked Thread so near to hand. Jennifer wondered what the sin-Duchess had done to overcome the effects of Light, or perhaps incorporate it—what the woman was working with or against at the moment. What she'd done to break through her own terror to confront Light. She was too tired to try and talk to her about any of it, though; and Lialla didn't seem to want conversation. Chris had tried when they set out, and he came away grumbling; he and Edrith moved out together for a while, just in front of the wagon, and it sounded as though they were working out more rap.

They reined in and dropped back to ride alongside Jennifer and Dahven as the sun edged off the road and up the trees. "Kind of nice here, you know?" Chris said. "Wouldn't mind having a cabin up here."

"With your usual?" Jennifer inquired. "A helipad and a copter for transportation back to civilization?"

He grinned. "Why not?" The grin faded. "Yeah, well. Always thought that was the way to do it. Guess I could still have a hang glider, though, couldn't I?"

"Big kite you strap yourself into," Jennifer translated for Dahven. Probably Edrith already knew. "Lets you fly, so long as there's wind. Well, sure. Why not a hang glider? If Caro Ellaway was right about the approximate dates outside of Rhadaz, maybe you can get hold of a hot air balloon."

"Yeah, the possibilities are just endless, aren't they?" Chris said sourly. "You know," he went on after a moment, "what honks me most? If we were gonna land in something like this, you know, big conflict and all, why *couldn't* it have been Middle Earth? Or one of the earlier games I used to play? Everything black and white, no one giving a damn if you just off the bad guys—"

"I thought you were all for offing the bad guys *before* Jadek's last little trick," Jennifer said.

"Sure I was. I still am. I wanna pull that guy's card so bad I can taste it. And then I listen to Aletto and mom—jeez, how can you be that way? You know?"

"What way?" Dahven asked. Chris shrugged; Edrith answered for him.

"Aletto should just flat hate his uncle, you know? Jadek murdered his dad, married his mother, Jadek is likely responsible for his marsh fever. Trying to marry poor Lialla to his cousin—and I can assure you there are plenty of hairraising stories in certain parts of Sikkre's markets about Carolan and certain of his less attractive tastes.''

"Well, even without that,'' Chris said. "I mean, all the crap he's pulled on *us*, right down to this last stunt with mom? And you know what they're doing up there, right now? Swear to God, Jen, they're coming up with all these reasons why the guy's doing it! Aletto actually said something, oh, hell,'' Chris said in disgust. "I forget just what and it doesn't matter, comes down to, he really thinks he can talk to the guy and Jadek will hand over Duke's Fort and go live on an island somewhere.''

"I'm not really surprised,'' Jennifer said. "I can't think why you would be.''

"Yeah—Jeez. You know, I can understand mom. She really does think that way—pacifist, no matter what, like no red meat, she doesn't just do it for convenience or when it's easy or the issues are black and white, she really means it. Says you don't kill people, period. Not for any reason.'' He brushed a fly from the back of his hand. "So she winds up doing in that wizard guy. Poor old mom, she sure has it tough.''

Jennifer nodded. "Couple of things, though, Chris: Birdy's tough in her own way; she's used to things going wrong. Think how much worse it would be right now if she weren't.''

"Hey. No, thanks.''

"And she's got a decent man for a change.''

"Yeah.'' Chris gave her a sidelong, rather abashed grin. "If you'd said that back before Sikkre, I'd've laughed at you, lady. There really was an okay dude under the dweeb exterior, though. I think his uncle has a *big* surprise coming.''

"No way!'' Edrith protested. "All those men of his we've fought? He knows—''

"Well, sure he knows. Knowing someone's changed that much and actually seeing it's pretty different, though; you wait.''

"I agree,'' Dahven said. "Remember I saw him outside Bez after about a month; Jadek last saw a weak, drunken, frightened boy and Aletto's learned more than simply how to use weapons these past days. He's in danger of becoming a decent ruler.''

"Yeah. If he doesn't just knuckle under and tell the guy to keep Zelharri—or offer to share or something else really dumb." Chris looked from Dahven to Jennifer to Edrith. "Look, I know he can't just take the guy out. The dudes down in Podhru wouldn't like it, and those guys they sent with us wouldn't like it, either."

"Glad you worked that out, kid," Jennifer said dryly.

"Hey. Remember who played the games, all right? Besides, Aletto might alienate people if he went in lopping heads like that. Starting with alienating mom, of course. And probably his own mother. Jeez. Eddie, now I'm starting to sound like both of them."

Edrith shook his head. "You're using logic on a hard problem, isn't that what you said before?"

Chris was silent for a long moment. "Tell you what. Right now, I don't know if I want logic, this whole thing just plain pisses me off. I don't want to hear about how the guy has his reasons, you know? *I* don't find it one damn bit useful knowing what Jadek's damn reasons are. He's the bad guy, damnit! If we're gonna land on him and make it count, that's how we gotta think of him, isn't it?"

He looked at all of them. Jennifer shrugged.

"I tend to agree with you," Dahven said. "When the Emperor sent men against the Lasanachi, when they tried to take Dro Pent, no one explained to those men what reasons the Lasanachi might have had for their actions. Ask Gyrdan some time, he knows, he was there; the Lasanachi were called barbarian invaders and men were encouraged to think of them in very black terms. That's necessary. I think even though Aletto hopes to retake the Fort without harming anyone, most of us—the fighting men particularly—need to see the Fort men at least as an active threat. Jadek as a particularly terrible threat, a source of wrong action, if not of evil. Once the Fort is in Aletto's hands, once Jadek is disarmed—let Aletto talk however he will to the man."

Chris frowned. "Yeah. And then Jadek sweet-talks his way out of everything, right?"

"I doubt that," Jennifer said calmly. "I don't have that much faith in Jadek's ability to maintain, as your mother would say, for very long. Afronsan already has a good deal of information against the man; his clerk has more now." She smiled and raised her eyebrows. "Personally, I doubt he can keep his temper in the same room with me for more than two minutes."

"Heh, heh." Chris considered this, shook his head and began to laugh. "Yeah. All we have to do then is worry about how to get your head back where it belongs, right?"

"I'll worry about my head, kid. And if it makes you feel better, I agree with you: You can understand someone like Jadek all you want—later. It's going to cost us lives if we go at him from your mother's way of thinking. Something else for you to think about, though: Remember what happens when you simply depose someone?"

"Edward the Second," he said readily. "Plantagenet England. They imprisoned him but some people wanted to put him back on the throne, so someone on the other side offed him." He sighed. "All this really reminds me more of Richard the Third, you know? Aletto puts so damn much trust in the wrong people. Except if he gets killed, he'll take mom with him."

"Richard the Third and Lord Stanley," Jennifer agreed. "Glad you remember some of the heavier reading I shoved down your throat last year."

"Hey, that was interesting stuff, Bosworth Field and all, you know?" Chris said. He glanced over at Edrith, who shrugged and shook his head, and at Dahven, who merely looked confused. "King who trusted the wrong guys too many times. This Stanley was one of his generals but he'd already defected. Only he didn't bother to tell the King until halfway through the fight, and then he just started fighting on the other side. The King died and wound up with his head on a pike."

Dahven looked at Jennifer. "I wondered what you were talking about in Evany's garden. Now it makes a little sense."

"I don't even remember. Must have been pretty tired."

They rode into a cool evening breeze. Chris broke what had become a long silence. "I'll tell you one thing. If Lialla has anything to say about it, Jadek is *toast*."

20

THEY stopped for the night at a place one of Gyrdan's men knew, where there was a firepit, a three-sided shelter for hunters or herders. Chris and Edrith set out toward a meadow they could see well above them and off to the west. Jennifer could hear Chris trying to explain wild strawberries to his companion, who, having grown up in the middle of the desert, had never eaten or even seen any kind of strawberries. Dahven was up talking to the guard driving the wagon—trying to find out what the man remembered from earlier in the day, perhaps, or possibly apologizing. Jennifer eased down from her horse, stretched out a stiff back and aching knees as well as she could, and went in search of Lialla.

At first, she couldn't find the woman at all, and no one seemed able to remember the last time they'd been aware of her. *If Jadek found a way to manipulate that wad of Light and take her*—Jennifer shut that thought off immediately, wrapped arms around herself and hugged hard. He hadn't done such a thing so far. Besides—there was Lialla, finally, her Wielder Blacks a dark blot against the bleached wood of the little shelter. Lialla was seated on a silkcloth, just inside the structure, eyes closed. As Jennifer came near, however, she looked up.

"I wondered when you'd come," she said finally.

"Took me a while to find you. But you looked preoccupied earlier."

Lialla considered this, nodded. "That would seem as good a word as any. You're curious, aren't you?"

Jennifer eased herself down, groaning faintly as her knees protested bending again. "I think that's as good a word as any. Do you object? To my curiosity? Because if you'd rather I wait a while—"

"What, with Duke's Fort just over the hill? And I don't object; I'd be wild with curiosity myself." Lialla managed a brief smile; her eyes were heavy-lidded, though, and she looked tired. "So. Tell you things, right?"

"She remembers," Jennifer said lightly. "What did you do, how?"

"Oh. If that's all," the sin-Duchess said dryly. But she obediently began talking, starting with leaving Podhru. "I could feel it even then, you know; not just the Light, but the sense that someone outside of me was trying to touch it. Or, trying might not be the proper word: Knowing Jadek, I think he could have gained as much control of me—of the Light—inside Podhru as he did on that ledge. But he knew I'd know what he was doing." She swallowed noisily, shrugged.

"And he thought you'd simply burst into tears and give up," Jennifer said crisply. "That about it?"

"Once I might have. Would have," Lialla amended honestly. "It worked against him this time; knowing upset me but not for myself—not because it was Light, or him. Believe it or not, I didn't even think for the longest time about that man he drained of life out in the desert. I was more worried what he might be able to make me do, if he could use that Light as a control." She made a tight, dispassionate story of Jadek's attack on her, his attempt at Chris and Aletto, through her. "Only Jadek could think of something so utterly foul, and I knew I couldn't simply fight him off, he'd try again, and again, and another time, I might not win. And then, I was so angry. I should have realized, you know: I *know* him, better than Aletto who still wants to find excuses for him. I know what he can do. But this! The idea that he'd make me kill Chris, or Aletto! I guess I always knew it, even before you talked to me in Podhru, but—" She shrugged. "I couldn't, until there wasn't anything else left except the Light. I was so scared, so furious, I didn't really care any more what happened to me."

Silence. "And?" Jennifer finally prompted.

"Remember what you said, out in the desert, about the nature of Light?"

"Don't remember." Jennifer shrugged.

"Something about it being like Thread—the thing you found in that hut. It seemed to me that the knot I carried was a little like the knot of Thread that marks a bruise. So I went after it that way."

"And it went?"

Lialla shook her head. "Oh, no. It broke up, and spread.

273

All through my body.'' She was laughing very quietly when she looked up. ''You didn't even recoil when I said that. Most would, you know.''

''I told you—''

''Ideas and reality,'' Lialla interrupted her. ''Belief in an idea doesn't always hold up well in daylight, you know. My first thought was that surely I had killed myself. But I didn't die and then I realized I felt better. Oh, I could feel it, rather like being warmed by a fire from the inside.

''It's—there was more instinct, more feeling with it: I knew at once there was nothing left in me for Jadek to catch hold of now. That it wouldn't harm me. All the same, it is very much like Thread. The longer I looked at it the more I could see the individual strands. And yet, it isn't like Thread—but I could still see and feel Thread.''

''That must have been reassuring.''

''Very. And it didn't interfere with Thread, except that it was more difficult to *hear*.''

''But you don't depend on hearing the way I do,'' Jennifer said.

''Fortunately. Once I was certain I wasn't going to immediately die, I decided I'd better cleanse the fog from my eyes. I went into Thread properly, caught hold of—the one Neri showed you, that yellow?''

''But *I* tried that yellow on you, in Podhru—''

''Wrong mix,'' Lialla said; her lips twisted. ''If you twist that yellow with Light—well, Neri might not approve, but it's quite effective. That man's arm should have given me a good deal of trouble; he doesn't even remember there was damage.''

Jennifer crossed her legs and began rubbing the insides of her knees. ''What you've done,'' she said finally. ''It's totally new, isn't it? I mean, a Triad wouldn't attempt to combine those two magics, would it? Would anyone?''

''*I* wouldn't have, unless I'd really needed to.''

''I wouldn't either,'' Jennifer said. ''But, how did it feel after? Forgive me, but you don't seem at all worried by it now.''

''Compared to before?'' Lialla grinned. ''Don't look so unsure of yourself, Jen; I know you're trying to be diplomatic. I wasn't only worried—I was terrified and being horrible to everyone because of it. In your place, I would have dumped me in Evany's pond and left me there. No, I'm not worried. It's—I don't know that anyone's combined the two before, I told you, history isn't a strong interest of mine. All the same, it feels right. As though they belong together.''

''I'm glad,'' Jennifer said. Lialla laid a hand over hers and gripped, hard.

''Thank you.''

''For what?''

''Because I wasn't afraid to talk to you about it. You don't judge things, the way I'm used to.'' Lialla sat up straight once more and folded her hands in her lap. ''It's curious, how things happen. I told Merrida so many times that I intended to devote my entire life to Wielding, and I wanted that Silver Sash so badly. Now—'' she shrugged. ''There isn't a Wielder in all of Rhadaz who'd stay in the same room with me, let alone give me instruction.''

''Not necessarily,'' Jennifer said. ''Neri, Merrida, anyone like them. There are plenty of Wielders out there, Lialla. I think you might find some, especially among the younger ones in Podhru, who wouldn't be afraid to look at things from a different perspective. Maybe later, when things are more settled, you can find people willing to help you work it out.''

''I doubt that,'' Lialla replied. ''All the same—I don't truly care about the Silver any more. Because this—there isn't a Wielder in all of Rhadaz who has what I have. Maybe it won't be as safe as Thread, or as easy to control. Maybe anything. It's mine. An entire new way to explore.''

''I'm glad you can look at it that way,'' Jennifer said. ''Think about the other. It might be something for you to do, once matters are settled for Aletto. You never struck me as someone who'd sit in her brother's court passing teacups.'' Lialla grinned, shook her head.

''There's some things I do know already,'' she said at last. ''Earlier, while we were riding—and just now? I found a new way to combine and use that red Thread, the finding Thread. I found Duke's Fort, and I'm reasonably certain of two things: Jadek's Triad is gone. And when you and Dahven forcibly ejected him from the guard, and broke that sphere, I think you hurt him. Keep that between us,'' she added flatly, ''because I'm not entirely sure.''

''I understand that. The Triad: You mean, there's no trace of it anywhere within or around Duke's Fort?''

''None. Not as far around Sehfi as I could reach, which

should have also included Carolan's estates, where it originally was kept.''

''Maybe he sent it away; there was a chance he was being watched, after all,'' Jennifer said. She enumerated on her fingers. ''And he might have known beforehand that Afronsan sent an envoy, though I thought I surprised him when I told him that.''

''Mmmm.'' Lialla pushed the black fabric off her hair and tugged at an earlobe thoughtfully. ''Possible, though I really feel it has been gone for more than a night or so. Also, remember that no one fully understands a Triad, except possibly another Triad.''

''You've said. You think a Triad could have scruples? That your uncle was playing too rough for them?''

Lialla laughed quietly. ''It all sounds like second-guessing to me. Including what I've done; I can't really be certain it worked as I thought it did.''

''You did say a Triad could conceal itself pretty well.''

''I did? I can tell where they *were*, though. And I can tell where my uncle is, because of his handling of Light. Say,'' Lialla added wryly, ''that I have an affinity for finding it now. Bad joke, right?''

Jennifer grinned. ''I'll laugh; it's not so bad. I won't say anything; no point in getting any of them overconfident, is there? What you actually did, though: Would you be willing to show me how you do it? Maybe see if I can make it work?''

''I don't know if I can,'' Lialla replied. She considered this, clapped her hands together and laughed. ''I'm sorry! I can't think how many times I've said that to you—''

Jennifer grinned. ''Well, at least you're not snarling it any more. But I *do* wish I had a silver ceri for every time you've said it. I'd be filthy rich.''

''Well, if I had a silver ceri for every time I've wondered where you came up with your questions—! Something out there smells simply wonderful. I have to admit, Jen, Robyn really is a good cook but I'm so glad to have real *meat* again.''

''Happens I agree. Honestly, *do* you mind trying to show me later what you've done? Maybe I can help you sort out your intelligence report—sorry, those words again, right?''

''That makes better sense than fog-ball phone booth.'' But Lialla chuckled. ''Chris tried to explain that this afternoon; if anything, it made less sense when he finished. As to showing you—no, I don't object, I'm not going to try and keep it all to myself. I don't know if there's a way for you to work it without infecting yourself with Light, like I was; I don't know if you'd want to. I think it could be interesting, the way you Wield—with so much music—to see if this combination would respond to you.''

"I'm willing to give it a try. Perhaps there's a way to use Light from outside; you do with Thread, after all. If it doesn't work, it doesn't," Jennifer said as she fought agonizingly aching knees and knotted thigh muscles, and got back to her feet. "Another thing, though: Want to help me show Chris how to use that thing Neri showed you for calming?''

"Chris?" Lialla got to her feet with an ease Jennifer both admired and cursed; her knees felt as though someone had lit matches just under the kneecaps. "Chris actually wants—? Well—but why not, after all?''

"You know Chris, interested in everything. Seems to think it would be good for the nights he can't sleep. I can't recall offhand when it's taken him more than thirty seconds to fall asleep, but—as you say, why not?''

"Seconds—never mind. I don't know what those are, but having been around Chris, I think I can guess."

Jennifer napped while food was being prepared; she woke long enough to eat, and afterward rubbed out Dahven's shoulders. When he reciprocated, she dozed off again.

Afrosan's men had already gone off somewhere to sleep when she woke, a short time later, and one of Gyrdan's men was walking slowly around the cooking fire, only occasionally visible in its dying light. Aletto was stretched out on a silkcloth on the far side of the fire, so Robyn could work out the kinks in his leg. It was some indication of his growing self-confidence that he was able to let her do that for him while he lay with his head propped up on crossed forearms, talking to Dahven and the man Gyrdan had left in charge of the small company. Jennifer bent her knees cautiously, found them still sore but not nearly as bad, and went around the fire to join them.

They were talking strategy and tactics once again, of course. She listened, hoping this time to possibly figure out what they intended to do, once they got near Duke's Fort. Some things made logical sense, like Aletto not wanting to throw a large number of men against a main gate reinforced against the possibility of attack (and why was it reinforced like that, she wondered, given Zelharri's remote location and the astonishingly low number of wars the country had faced?) Other things, like the way Gyrdan was breaking up his numbers, didn't make as much sense to her. Jadek probably knew how many were ranged against him, and he'd sure know once they came together in front of the Fort, after all.

She moved off into the night. A tense-sounding argument about the numbers and loyalties of Jadek's guards faded as she walked past the wagon and toward the shelter.

If Afronsan's men had taken it over—but apparently not, Lialla was there again or still. Chris and Edrith were with her now, and someone had brought out a blue light. It vaguely illuminated Edrith, flat on his back on a silkcloth some distance away, against the back wall, arms under the back of his head to elevate it; Chris was sitting behind Lialla, energetically rubbing out her shoulders and the sin-Duchess was bent forward over her crossed legs. Chris tugged and she came upright, head against the base of his throat, eyes closed and a look of pure bliss on her face.

"Yo, lady," Chris said as Jennifer leaned against the edge of the wall and looked down at them.

"Not interrupting anything, am I?" The words were out before Jennifer remembered Lialla; but the woman opened one eye, her smile briefly widened and she let the eye close again.

"If my uncle could see this," she murmured. She tapped Chris's arm. "Not *quite* so hard, please."

"Well, hey, you got steel bands for muscles, you know?" But he shifted to a more gentle kneading motion against both sides of her throat with his finger tips.

"Mmmm. Better. You're not interrupting anything, Jen," she added dryly. "No—what was it you said in Podhru, Chris—?"

"Oh, jeez," Chris implored, "forget that, will you? Honest, I was pulling the guy's chain, I wasn't trying to—well, you know." He leaned forward to eye her accusingly. "You're pulling mine, too, aren't you?"

Lialla laughed. "Got you. A question, though: I sorted out part of what you said, but a term evades me." Even in the blue light, Jennifer could see Chris's color mounting; his fingers went still. "What is a 'front lawn'?"

"Oh, *man*?" Chris freed a hand and tapped the end of

her nose. "You wait. You just wait. There's something else where I come from, called payback."

"Sure," Lialla replied with a grin. "If I were you, I wouldn't threaten the woman who's going to teach me how to use Thread. I could *really* pull your chain—"

"Yah," Chris scoffed as he went back to his massage. "Mess me up and who's gonna do your back for you? Who's gonna teach you the hip hop—?"

"You have to ask yourself," Jennifer said mildly, "if she wants to *learn* the hip hop."

"Hey, why not? But we already have a commitment on the hang glider, right, Li?" He grinned widely. "Yo, Jen, wanna sign up, you can be my second fly girl?"

"You have to ignore him," Lialla said. She was sluttering in an effort to stifle giggles.

"I think I'd really better. I don't believe I went through four years of college and three of law school to become somebody's fly girl. Sounds more like Meriyas's kind of thing. I mean, you know?" she added sarcastically. "On the other hand, if I get to watch you do the test flights, I'll tackle the glider."

"You know," Chris told Lialla seriously, "I like the woman in spite of herself. In spite of her deep and abiding trust in me, and my devotion to her better interests."

"Name once—" Jennifer began.

"Hey. Who separated the noble boy wonder from his blowsy barmaid so you could have a crack at him?"

"Got that on my own, kid. You going to sit here and mouth all night," Jennifer added, "or can we do some things here? If I understood any of that gabble around the fire, they want to be out of here at first light."

"Disgusting," Edrith said sleepily.

"Forgot you were there," Chris said.

"Yeah. My stock in trade, remember?"

"Not any more, it's not," Chris said vigorously. "We got a deal, remember?"

"Still might come in useful."

"Deal," Chris repeated firmly. "You still out on this Thread stuff?"

"You try, I'll watch," Edrith said. "It fries you, I'll know it wasn't a good idea."

"My friend," Chris replied sarcastically. Edrith rolled over onto his side and propped himself on one elbow.

"Deal?" Jennifer asked as she eased down onto the edge of Lialla's silkcloth.

"Got to keep all his fingers intact somehow, don't I? Keep him from looting the market out from under you and the noble boy wonder, too, right? So I figured it out, how to pay for the cabin up here, maybe another down by Podhru—the waves around Caro's place were absolutely primo, you know, and a surfboard wouldn't be too hard to come up with, either—and all like that. Now, all that would have to take money, even here. Even if I don't want to go Yup like Fedthyr and Evany and all those guys. So I figured, this place is a closed society, except Shesseran is starting to ease the gates open. Well, so there isn't much new outside stuff coming in yet. But there will be, don't you think? Just figuring how people are, why do things the hard way if there's a new and improved way?"

"Possibly," Jennifer allowed cautiously.

"Yeah, I know, it's not guaranteed, and I'm not trying for any kind of historical crossover any more, too damned confusing. All the same, just figuring people, and what stuff I got out of Caro. Now, I'll bet you the guys who first went into the Middle East and sold Cadillacs got *damn* rich, don't you?"

"Uh, Chris, I don't think Cadillacs—"

"No, I said no historical crossovers, right? Besides, if Caro has it pegged, it's way too early for any kinds of automobiles. Damn," Chris added feelingly. "But how about the guy who came in here with, say, the telegraph? Or steam engines? Or—I don't know. Whatever's out there that's useful." He came around from behind Lialla and sat, drawing his knees up and resting his chin on them. "For sure, I need to go find out, though. I can't just stay here and wait for it to come to me—whatever it is." He laughed quietly. "Hey, Jen. Remember a zillion years ago, back at that grungy antique shop in the desert, when you said I should get my own life, let mom do her own thing? Who'd have figured on this?" Before Jennifer could answer, he shook his head and turned to Lialla. "All right, let's try this. What do I have to do?"

It took time and all the patience Lialla and Jennifer could muster to deal with a frustrated Chris. He finally managed to access Thread, however, and once he'd done that, and learned how to regain a real perspective, he lost most of his reserve. He found the heavy, flat, broad and dully red Thread at once, which gave him confidence. To Jennifer's relief he handled the stuff with caution, and continued to listen to Lialla. When she tentatively suggested he try another, he nodded. The finding Thread was a little more difficult for him to separate from the rest until Jennifer gave him a vocal cue. He withdrew by himself some minutes later and sat, head and arms hanging between his knees, eyes closed.

He finally shook himself and looked around. "Totally awesome. All that *everywhere* and you just—walk through it, don't even see it. Amazing."

"Let me know if—when you want more of it," Lialla said. Chris nodded.

"Yeah. I might, if there's ever time. I just—you know, I watch you guys using it all the time, doing this stuff. Wanted to see what it was, mostly. Maybe you can show me how to do that rope, sometime. That could be useful." He got to his feet and stretched until his back popped. "Whoa, Stiff City. C'mon, Eddie, let's go walk around some before we crawl in?"

"Do I have a choice?" Edrith asked, but he was getting to his feet.

"No. Besides, if they're gonna haul us out at that kind of hour—you know mom's line," Chris added to Jennifer, "the only thing dawn's good for is starting wars and doing executions."

Jennifer laughed. "No argument."

Lialla turned to watch them go. "I know he'll need to eventually; I'll be sorry when he does go."

"I know."

"Well—about magic," Lialla went on briskly. "Ready?"

"New and Improved Thread?" Jennifer asked. "Sure. Try me."

She couldn't work it; after an hour, she finally gave up trying and emerged from Thread hot, sweaty and utterly frustrated. "I should've known," she said finally. "I can't *hear* anything. It's like—" She spread her hands in an angry shrug. "I can't work it at all. Maybe—oh, hell." She was silent for a moment, finally looked up with a rueful smile. "Now I know how you felt."

"Maddening," Lialla agreed easily. "But I won't let you give up, either."

"All right." Jennifer ran a sweaty hand over a slick forehead. "I can take a challenge; give me something to do later on."

"I have a feeling you won't lack for things," Lialla said. "I imagine Dahven has plans for your future—"

"Gathered that, did you?"

"You're not too obvious, after all, are you? I heard you threatening that man on the Bez Road; I heard Dahven after they got you in our room at that inn. You'll do an excellent job of guarding each other's backs, won't you?"

"I hope so. Even if Afronsan manages to oust the brothers from Sikkre, I don't know that that will be the end of things. There are some pretty raw feelings involved." Jennifer shrugged. "That's well in the future, though. One thing at a time, all right? Let's get Aletto set up first."

"When he is," Lialla said calmly, "he'll need advocates, I'd think. And it could take time to return Sikkre to Dahven, Afronsan's way. Aletto will have you up to your ears in paper."

"You're probably right," Jennifer said gloomily. "After a few days in Sehfi, I think I'm going to find myself lusting after a word processor the way Chris does after a car." And at Lialla's raised eyebrows, "Yeah, I know, those words again."

"You and Chris. I sometimes wonder how I ever managed, when I understood all the words I heard."

They rode well into Zelharri the next day, taking two short stops but only finishing for the day when it was nearly dark. Jennifer later remembered that day, and the following one, as blurs: an impression of blue sky occasionally crossed by thin, fast-moving clouds, warm air that seemed to drop to freezing as soon as the sun went down. Birds and small animals everywhere, once a deer standing motionless in shadow, watching as they passed.

By the next afternoon, they were only an hour from Duke's Fort. They stopped, waited for dark.

The early night hours were dark indeed: No moon, and most of the stars were muffled under thick cloud. It reminded Jennifer of their first night in Zelharri, walking in a line, hands outstretched so no one would run into a tree. Here, they led the horses, each person holding the tail of the animal before. It was an arrangement she didn't care for much; the hair was coarse, the smell of horse came straight back at her in reeking waves. Her own kept walking up almost on her heels, trying to nibble her shirt.

For the moment, she welcomed the diversion; fighting off a suddenly too-friendly horse while waiting to be crushed under its feet was considerably better than thinking about the immediate future.

She had been thinking of the confrontation with Jadek, though: She hadn't reckoned with the ride, once they found the road and set off to meet up with Gyrdan and his men. Galloping down a totally dark and—to her—unfamiliar road was one of the more terrifying experiences she'd ever gone through, and she was trembling all over when they finally stopped. Dahven, who'd stayed right beside her somehow, gripped her forearm and exclaimed aloud. Someone ahead shushed him with an urgent hiss.

"Your hands are like ice," Dahven whispered against her ear. "Are you all right?"

"After that ride? If I survived that I must be immortal," Jennifer whispered back. "Please tell me we're there."

"Nearly. It's all right, though. Even I know this road; it's flat and level and utterly straight for a tremendous distance both sides of Sehfi."

"God," Jennifer murmured devoutly. Dahven freed her hand from the reins, drew it up to his lips and kissed it, then chafed a little blood into it while they waited. Robyn was suddenly at her other side, looming up in the darkness.

"Everything all right?" she asked softly. "Aletto sent me back here, in case there's trouble at the gates. Do you mind?"

"Of course not, Birdy. Where's Chris? I haven't seen him."

Robyn sighed. "Where do *you* think? Right up front, of course. Lialla's up there, too, just behind some of the front men, Aletto couldn't convince her she'll just be in the way."

"Maybe she won't. I—"

"They're moving," Robyn said. A moment later, Jennifer could hear it, too, and a moment after that, her horse jerked its head forward, tugging at the reins. Dahven let go her fingers and they set out.

They went at a walk this time, fortunately for Jennifer's peace of mind. After a while, there were houses—a few in the trees to either side, then more right along the road. They passed a busy, well-lit inn from the opposite side of the road, moved back to the now wider and paved surface.

Houses and shops lined the road for a short distance on both sides, then vanished from the left; to the right, a wall rose. They came to a halt, and after a moment went on again; well to the left side of the road, off the pavement, hard against the trees. Jennifer felt as though someone had tightened steel bands down around her chest; the night air was chill and damp and tasted unpleasantly of wood smoke as it slid down her throat, but breathing was difficult anyway.

They stopped once more; people in front of her were dismounting. Jennifer swallowed, eased out of the saddle, held onto the stirrup for balance while she drew out her bo. Dahven came around, touched her shoulder and leaned close. "I have to go; Aletto needs me. Will you be all right?"

"I'm just fine." Fortunately, her whisper sounded fine; if he was out with Aletto, the last thing he needed was to worry about *her*. She squeezed his fingers. "Scram." He squeezed back and was gone.

Someone took the horse from her. She turned to say something to Robyn, but Robyn wasn't there any more. Strange men everywhere—she wondered briefly how she could be certain they were all Aletto's and promptly forced herself to think about something else. *Hands,* she thought desperately. *Boy, are they cold.* She cupped them before her face, alternately scrubbing them together and blowing on them.

"Jen?" The whisper could've been anyone; it startled her. Edrith leaned near enough that she could make out his features. "Li wants you. Can you?"

"Anything except stand here," she said.

"I know. Waiting's grim."

"You see Robyn?"

"Just now. She's with Afronsan's bunch."

"Good." That was one of them reasonably safe—so long as Birdy didn't shapeshift.

Edrith seemed to understand her worry. He patted her arm, kept his hand on it so he could lead her forward. "No one will bother her; Jadek will be too busy to think about her."

"Hope so," Jennifer said. Someone hissed a nervous, "Hush!" as they went by.

Lialla knelt at the very edge of the road, a little apart from the tight clutch of men that must include Aletto, Gyrdan, Chris and Dahven, though Jennifer couldn't make out any individuals. Edrith, to her surprise, stayed with her as she knelt at the sin-Duchess's side. "Jen? Good. They decided to listen to me after all; I wanted to see if I couldn't get into the family apartments, find Mother and Merrida, get them out of harm's way."

"All right, we can do that," Jennifer said.

"I wish I felt that confident," Lialla said rather sharply.

"Frankly, so do I," Jennifer muttered. Lialla gave her a quick, sidelong glance and then a flash of teeth.

"We stand a fair chance," Lialla said; she sounded a little less tense. "I know the corridors, we're both well protected. We have Eddie to get us in the gate Aletto and I went out—perhaps we can even get back out before they go in."

"We can do that," Jennifer repeated calmly. And all at once, she felt calm. There was something to do; something important to accomplish.

"Good. Let's go, then, get it done," Edrith said quietly. "They aren't going to delay long; once Aletto goes out to talk to the men on that curtain wall, it'll be no time at all."

"He's mad," Lialla said flatly, but she shook her head then and got to her feet. "The gate's this way." She went along the left edge of the road, hard against the trees for a distance, until there was a portion of wall opposite that jutted out toward the road. The parapet came out with it and also rose; there was no light visible above the edge, only reflected light from behind to show where the upper edge was. Jennifer glanced at that, at the bulk of building behind the wall. A blue-light burned in the one window she could see, a narrow slit near the top. Lialla tugged at her sleeve and whispered against her ear, "Family apartments. Come." She darted across the deserted road and along the base of the wall. Jennifer came right behind her, Edrith bringing up the rear.

Lialla stopped again finally, turned to shake her head and point upward. Jennifer nodded; she could see flickering, bright yellow light, could hear men talking and laughing right over her head. She suddenly felt highly visible and terribly vulnerable. *This isn't what I do,* she thought unhappily. A wrong step, those men would hear, they'd look over, discover the three crouched at the base of the wall— *No. Don't be totally stupid. They'd be looking into darkness because of the lanterns they've got up there. And they're making enough noise to cover anything I do—if I'm careful.*

Lialla tugged at her sleeve and started cautiously forward again. The wall took a step in, and she halted in the corner it created, took Jennifer's hand and guided it forward.

Wood. A door? Jennifer edged cautiously around Lialla, felt enough to assure herself it was some kind of door; larger than standard, probably to allow horses to pass through. Lialla slid around her, took her fingers again, and brought her hand down to touch the latch.

Jennifer nodded, but stepped back. Lialla would know if it creaked—or if it once had. What kind of lock was on the other side, or if it was locked. Edrith eased over to touch her shoulder and press his bo into her free hand, then crouched in front of the door to study the latch. Jennifer could just make out his near-motionless shape, not what he did. She concentrated on getting air into a painfully tight chest; two breaths later, the door swung into hay- and horse-scented blackness. Edrith came to his feet and went through it in one fluid, utterly silent movement. Lialla glanced over her shoulder and followed.

This is not what I do, Jennifer told herself again, despairingly this time. But she drew a deep breath, shifted Edrith's bo to the left hand along with her own, and went into the Duke of Zelharri's stables, silently closing the door behind her.

21

꤮

LIALLA waited for her just inside; in the dark, Jennifer nearly ran her down. The sin-Duchess was trembling violently and her hands were cold, the palms clammy. Jennifer wrapped an arm around her shoulder. *This is where Carolan died,* she realized suddenly. No wonder the woman was in such a state. "Come on," she breathed against Lialla's ear. "Let's get out of here; the smell of horse is going to kill me." She felt Lialla's energetic nod; she kept her arm around the woman as they started walking toward the faint gray square of light at the far end of the stable.

Edrith was waiting there for them, crouched by the opening, watching the wall to their right, looking up toward the men Jennifer could hear just above them. Lialla detached herself gently and moved to the other side of the doorway. Edrith took the staff Jennifer held out to him, edged back a little as she knelt next to him. She could hear the men up there clearly now; they seemed to be playing some kind of dice game, three different voices calling out numbers in rapid order, topping each other. Someone else was laughing, but the laughter sounded strained; in fact, they all sounded tense. Not surprising. They must surely know something was wrong in Duke's Fort, they must at least suspect Aletto was on his way home.

Edrith tugged on Jennifer's sleeve, drew her head close and leaned to speak against her ear. "Wait a moment."

She glanced out across the courtyard—it was entirely open and light from the walls spilled across it from two directions—and nodded. "Distraction," she replied softly, and he nodded in turn. Lialla looked across the open area, glanced up, and her shoulders sagged. But a few moments later, all sounds on the wall abruptly ceased. Someone beyond the road was shouting, though Jennifer couldn't make out who it was, or what he was saying. One of the wall guard shouted down, "The gate is shut for the night. Come after sunrise!"

Another spate of words from the other side of the wall. Directly above them, one man asked indignantly, "What fool is that? He must be from outside the Duchy, not to know better than to come here at such an hour!"

"Can't see," someone replied. "Get a lantern over here."

The light just above them was lifted up. Jennifer watched it move jerkily away from the inner side of the wall, then watched as the spill of light moved away from them, out across the courtyard; shadow replaced it all the way to the Fort wall. Edrith leaped to his feet and ran lightfooted across the open, staying right to remain in shade; the second lantern still threw light along the left side of the yard and all the way up the stable wall.

He gained the archway, Lialla right on his heels and Jennifer only a step or two behind. When she risked a glance over her shoulder, she could see the outlines of four men on the curtain wall, outlined by an upheld lantern, gazing out and down. Two were talking urgently to a third, and as

287

she watched, two more came down the wall from some-where above the stable. Edrith tugged at the end of her bo, then, and gestured sparingly with his head.

Lialla pressed past him and took the lead, but she stopped almost at once as another locked door loomed before them. Edrith put his bo into her hands and Jennifer noticed for the first time that the sin-Duchess wasn't armed. At least, not with a physical weapon. *If Jadek can block her, or somehow reach her—* No, she told herself firmly. She wasn't going to let herself think anything like that, not with her knees threatening to buckle at any moment. Edrith reclaimed his bo and gave the door a shove, held it for the two women, then pushed it closed behind him.

Down a long corridor, with open garden visible on one side and a variety of closed doors on the other. The air was chill, oddly scented with some herb Jennifer couldn't quite place. Lialla stopped before a very narrow opening that Jennifer at first thought must be an air vent, turned sideways and slipped through it. When her turn came, she found her-self in a blue-lit circular room, a stair leading up one side, a very faint light coming from somewhere high above. Lialla stood very still, eyes closed, swaying slightly, and Jennifer felt Thread vibrate ever so slightly all around them. Lialla shook her head and grimaced, visibly frustrated, caught up the blue-light and wrapped it in one of her scarves so that only the least gleam showed in front of her feet, and started up the stairs.

There was no railing. Jennifer held the bo out on her left side for counterbalance and clutched the wall with her right hand. Lialla's light was better than none, but not by much; she felt for steps with her toes and grew more and more aware as she climbed of the drop below her.

After maybe a hundred shallow steps, they came up through a floor and into a very small landing area. Lialla's blue-light showed a door; she passed it by and began climb-ing once again. This time there were walls on both sides, but the stair was narrower than ever. There was, fortunately, fresh air coming in from somewhere. It ruffled the hair back from Jennifer's forehead and the back of her neck, pleas-antly cool against sweaty skin.

Lialla paused before the next door, handed the sphere to Edrith, who passed it on to Jennifer. "Wait," the sin-Duchess whispered. "I'm not certain—just wait." She laid both hands against wood, closed her eyes and shifted into Thread.

Jennifer set her jaw and shifted herself, into a mental vocalization of Puccini, second act card game duet from *Fanciulla*, soprano and bass parts both. Trying to recall the sheriff's lyrics, in Italian, took enough thought to put distance between already jangled nerves and Lialla's extensive use of pure Thread in such an enclosed stone hallway. She made it all the way through the switched winning poker hand, "Tre Aci et un Paio!" before Lialla breached the door and pushed it into a darkened room.

It was cold, deserted. Lialla's shoulders sagged. "I knew better, but I still somehow hoped Merrida would be here," she said finally. "It's hers—this chamber. She said it was well protected against Jadek's finding. She never contemplated a Triad, though, not in Duke's Fort." She turned to look at them both and her face was very wan in the blue light. "You don't have to come any farther with me—"

"After coming this far?" Edrith demanded. "Rully, you know?"

"Don't be silly," Jennifer said acerbically. "Of course we do. Where from here?" Lialla gripped her arm and then his in silent thanks.

"The other door," she said, and turned to point it out. "It leads to the family rooms. Mother's apartments are down there. Jadek may be there, too."

"Can you sense Merrida or your mother at all?" Jennifer asked.

"I haven't dared try. Jadek might realize we're here if I do."

"I'll wager he has an idea already," Edrith said. Head tipped to one side, he was listening and he held up a hand for silence. "Hear that?"

"Dear gods," Lialla whispered. There were men shouting everywhere, suddenly, and even though the sound was muted by the thick walls of the tower, by the lack of windows, it was clear that an alarm had been given. "No time, no time at all, hurry!" she whispered, and, crossing the cold, dark chamber in two swift, long strides, she had the other door thrown open and was out into a long, dimly lit, carpeted hallway. Jennifer drew a deep breath, expelled it in a gust, and followed, with Edrith right on her heels.

* * *

There was no one in the hallway, either direction, though Jennifer could see a lot of light beyond the narrow window when she looked over her shoulder—possibly the same window they'd seen earlier from the road. Lialla was running now, the blue-light fully exposed—apparently forgotten—in her left hand. There wasn't much need of it here: There were glass-shades holding candles or oil lamps set at close intervals all down the walls. Perhaps every fourth lamp was lit, just enough to show the way down the hall, night-light fashion. It was still enough of a difference from the stable, the corridor and that dreadful, close tower, Jennifer felt utterly exposed.

Lialla hesitated only a moment before a double door to her left, then threw herself against it, slamming down a heavy latch as her shoulder struck wood. The doors split in the center and gave way silently.

The room beyond was a bedroom, furnished better and more richly than anything Jennifer had thus far seen in Rhadaz: sheer hangings draped in swags from tall, finely carved bedposts, thick, exquisite carpeting over a polished wooden floor. Windows with deep sills took most of two adjoining walls: These were large, with individual panes etched or beveled. A finely wrought gold candelabra sat on one sill, perhaps a dozen long tapers burning in its holders; lighting the sill, the bed, much of the room around it; light reflected from beveled windowpanes, casting shimmering prisms along white walls as the flames bent and flared. Lialla hesitated only a moment, glanced nervously over her shoulder and then ran to the bed. Empty. But across a low, dark chest at the bed's foot, a limp, pale form in swathing black scarves lay very still—so still that Jennifer, who reached her first, wasn't certain at first that she breathed.

The hair, the overall shape suggested woman, the face and hair said old, the clothing Wielder. But if Lialla had not spoken the name aloud, Jennifer would never have recognized Merrida.

The old woman had looked drawn and spent enough that night in the woods; now, she looked like death, and she'd lost enough weight that the bone structure of her face stood out in sharp relief; skin hung in grayish, crepey swags on her throat and forearms. She opened her eyes, stared at the two women unblinking. "Merrida, it's Lialla," the sin-Duchess whispered urgently. Merrida turned her gaze to Jennifer, let it touch briefly on Edrith and went back to Lialla.

"Know who you are." The old woman's voice sounded dry, as though it hadn't been used in a very long time. "What you are, though—*what have you done?*" she demanded in a furious whisper.

Lialla shook her head impatiently. "Merrida, please, there's no time for argument. We've come to take you and Mother to safety. Where is Mother?"

"With Jadek, below. Waiting." Merrida drew a breath that grated unpleasantly in her throat.

"Oh, Merrida." Lialla knelt to take hold of her old mentor's fingers. Merrida compressed her lips and snatched her hand back. "Merrida, what has he done to you?"

"He set Hell-Light against me, once his Triad discovered my safety. Hell-Light," Merrida repeated faintly. "He was particularly angry, something *you'd* done to thwart him, set his Triad to find—never mind. He did this—" She raised a hand, jerkily pulled it along her black robes with shaking fingers, touched herself just above where her sash should have been. It was gone, Jennifer realized suddenly. By the look on her face, it was clear Lialla had just seen that, too. "I'm infected. *He* did that, deliberately. I can't find Thread at all, it's gone, left me." Her voice had been fading; now she sighed, air whistling in her throat, and let her eyes close.

"I know," Lialla replied soothingly, her voice at odds with her eyes. "It's all right. Merrida, you'll be fine. I can deal with the Hell-Light."

She probably would have said more but Merrida began laughing; the laughter turned almost at once to a harsh, racking cough. The old woman fought her way onto one elbow, but when Lialla would have tried to support her, Merrida struck the hand away. "Don't *dare* to touch me! You'd help, you'd spread Hell-Light through me as you did for yourself, wouldn't you? Or did *she* do this to you? Either way, you've accepted it, haven't you? Let yourself fill with Hell-Light, and you've used it, too, haven't you?" She turned her head to fix Jennifer with an icy stare. "I overheard a thing or two about *you* a time since, below. Things you've dared with Thread. And you've convinced the girl, too, haven't you? Turned her back on the right and proper ways? Filthy, wretched outlander, I regret that I ever brought you here—!"

"You didn't," Jennifer interrupted flatly. "The music did, that and the magic, you said so yourself. If you wanted a certain code of behavior followed, you should have sent for an established Rhadazi Wielder to help them. Or you should have given me a dose of your ethics along with the language.''

"How dare you speak to me that way?''

"It's no thanks to you any of us is still alive,'' Jennifer replied evenly. "I owe you nothing.'' Silence. "I think you'd better pay heed; we haven't much time to spend on you just now. We can help you.''

"Help,'' Merrida muttered bitterly.

"Help,'' Jennifer agreed. "Look at Lialla: She's still alive, she can still Wield, Light hasn't harmed her. Are you going to let stupidity kill you or will you accept her offer?''

"I? You want me to accept *that*?'' Merrida turned back to glare at Lialla, her head jerking with the effort it took her to hold it upright, but she again slapped Lialla's supporting hand away. "Don't touch me, you evil, disgusting child!''

"Merrida,'' Lialla said in a low, desperate voice. "Merrida, please listen!''

"Filthy, dreadful girl! I knew if we must depend upon you we were all lost! I knew—''

"Shut up,'' Jennifer said evenly. Merrida's eyes went wide and slid sideways to meet hers. "If you can't say anything useful, just be quiet. If you want to die, that's your business. Exactly where is Lialla's mother? Where is Jadek?''

"In the main hall. Light,'' Merrida spat and turned back to Lialla. "There wasn't anything you wouldn't do for more magic, was there? Nothing!''

"Merrida, that isn't fair—!'' Lialla protested faintly. "I didn't—!''

"Lying brat!'' Merrida hissed and swung her hand; Lialla intercepted it just short of her cheek and gripped the old woman's wrist, hard.

"No,'' she said, and she sounded breathless, possibly afraid of standing up to Merrida even in her present condition. She drew a deep breath, then, and squared her shoulders; when she went on, there was no tremor in her voice. "No. It's enough. Don't you *ever* attempt to strike me again! Whatever I've done, it's my responsibility, my life, my person, not yours. I'm not your novice any longer, Merrida, and I'm adult by any Rhadazi standard.'' She released the stunned old Wielder's wrist and got to her feet. "I'm going down now, to do what I can to aid Mother.''

"She won't welcome you," Merrida snarled.

"Perhaps not. Aletto needs me, and Mother may listen, in time. Later, we can talk, you and I. My offer remains, if you'll have it."

"Unnatural, filthy, *evil*—" Merrida began in a harsh whisper. It faded; she slumped back on the chest. Lialla gave her one long, unfathomable look, then turned away and went from the room, back into the hall.

With the doors closed behind them, she hesitated, then turned to go on in the direction they'd been going. "Kitchens," she said softly over her shoulder. "We may get farther, going this way, than by attempting the gardens."

"Whatever works," Jennifer replied. "Let's go." *Before I lose my nerve,* she added to herself. *This is not what I do.*

There was another narrow staircase, this one only marginally better lit than the first, and the treads here were worn in the middle, damp in places. Jennifer set her jaw and went down them right on Lialla's heels, trusting to luck to get her to the ground in one piece. She heard Edrith's bo clatter against the wall, his muttered curses, a quick rush of steps as he regained his balance. Moments later they were in a large, open chamber lit by fires in two enormous hearths. There were a number of people—possibly cooks or kitchen boys—asleep between the hearths, visible only as tousled heads and mounded blankets. Lialla edged to the far side of the chamber and turned to hold a hand to her lips, then began threading a way between tables, stools, and past a long trestle with benches pushed just under its edge. Somehow they made it through without tripping over anything; Jennifer's nose wrinkled as dust rose from fresh, very dry straw underfoot, and she pressed a finger hard over her upper lip to keep from sneezing. Something in the darkness near the wall they were approaching smelled terrible —garbage or even an indoor compost heap, by the nearly overwhelming odor—but they were past it and through the door, into another hallway. It was unlit, bare stone, and cold. A distance away, they could see light through a partly open door—enough to guide them.

There were voices, too: As they neared the door, Jennifer realized at least one was familiar. Aletto's. The reply sent a shiver up her back: She'd never actually heard Jadek's voice before, but it was unmistakable.

Lialla hesitated at the end of the hall, turned back briefly and caught Edrith's hand in one of hers, Jennifer's in the other. "Luck," she whispered. Both nodded. Jennifer tightened her fingers around the bo and watched Lialla slip around the edge of the door, pause there; one hand came back in sight, a finger beckoned. Edrith gave her a long, grave look and gestured, letting her go ahead of him.

It was a good-sized room, though not as massive as she might have expected from what she'd seen of the overall size of the building itself, from vague recollections of grand halls in Ivanhoe-type movies. The walls were pale, the ceiling no more than ten feet high; there were windows along two walls flanked by heavy curtains, a parquet floor that looked like a giant chess board of two shades of polished wood. A long table ran nearly the length of one wall, a number of high-backed chairs along the other. The only thing that particularly marked it as a nobleman's hall was the low platform between paired windows. Two oversized armchairs of black wood stood there, upholstered on the seat, the center of the back and both arms in dark red plush; but there were no additional markings of rank on or behind them.

There were people everywhere; silent men, for the most part. A clutch of thirty or more in Jadek's colors, standing together and nervously watching those who'd come with Aletto. At first Jennifer couldn't see much beyond the two groups: She couldn't see anything of Chris, or Aletto. Or Dahven. Where Jadek was, certainly: But there was a break in the conversation as she edged into the room and she couldn't even be certain where he stood.

Lialla edged around the side of the room, away from the dais, neck craned, eyes searching as she worked her way around Jadek's men. She nodded once, beckoned. When Jennifer came up beside her, she could see a little farther into the room: a handful of civilian men—local citizens, perhaps, most showing signs of hasty dressing. These stood slightly apart from Jadek's guard but well away from Afronsan's two clerks and the men wearing the red and gold of Emperor's armsmen. Many of them whispered together, or stood in silence eyeing the observers; others peered in the direction of the dais, craning their necks—surely, that must be where Aletto was, Jennifer thought; she glanced at the observers and let out a sigh of relief as she spotted Robyn's blonde hair in their midst. Spread along the far wall and blocking a large double door, some of Gyrdan's men stood—

none of them held weapons but Jennifer doubted anyone would expect to simply ask and be let from the chamber. There were half-clad, sleepy-eyed household servants farther back, small huddles of them near the neatly set banquet chairs. She could see tense faces, saw lips moving as they whispered anxiously to one another; couldn't even hear the least sound. But Jadek's servants would be good at maintaining silence and a low profile, she thought.

Lialla drew in a sharp breath, touched Jennifer's sleeve and let her eyes indicate direction: a very slender woman stood at the edge of the dais, holding onto the back of one chair as though it was the only thing keeping her on her feet. She wore black, a full-skirted gown that might once have been attractive but now hung on a too-thin frame, exposing fragile-looking collarbones and even more fragile-seeming wrists; the narrow length of sheer black fabric that crossed her head and fell over both ears didn't conceal heavily grayed hair; a wide and impressive necklace of figured gold and dark stones seemed heavy enough to drag such a frail woman down. Her eyes were wide above a haggard mouth, and she gazed desperately straight before her. Lialla let her own eyes close briefly, then squared her shoulders with a visible effort and began working around the room once again. Edrith pressed past them both to clear a path; Lialla caught hold of his loosened shirttail and let herself be pulled along.

Aletto's voice, muted as it was by the room and the number of people in it, seemed overloud and all three jumped. "I said we would speak, Uncle, and I meant that. Concerning that chair, and my right to it.'

"I will not discuss anything with you, not in the face of such a threat as you bring into this house," Jadek replied with finality. Jennifer heard worried murmuring behind her. It was hushed abruptly.

"There is no threat, Uncle. But I have said before that I would not come here to discuss these matters with you unless I had an absolute guarantee of my right to leave this house thereafter if I so chose. These men—you know many of them, since they so were friends of my father; others are sons of those friends. They and these few men from the Emperor's household are my guarantee."

Another silence. "I am deeply offended that you feel I constitute a threat to you, after so many years in my care," Jadek said. He'd sounded angry at first; the anger was gone now—from his voice, at least, replaced by sorrow and heavy patience. A thin, tremulous alto voice broke the hush.

"Son, please, don't—"

"Hold your peace, Lizelle!" Jadek turned to hiss furiously. Jennifer, who had a brief line of vision between groups of huddled men, saw the woman close her eyes and take an involuntary step back. She could see the back of Aletto's head, and then all of him—Aletto: She'd seen the change coming in him, slowly, over so many long days and through so much adversity, and she wondered what these men thought, seeing it for the first time. He'd tossed aside the cloak and stood very straight—no sign of deformity and none of drink—no weapon. The knife he usually wore at the small of his back was gone as well. *Braver than I am,* she thought grimly. His clothing was plain and bore the mark of travel and hard use; his dark hair was ruffled.

Just behind him and a little to one side, Chris, who looked off indeed against a background of Rhadazi guardsmen with his spiked hair, his bulky denim jacket and blue jeans. Jennifer was relieved to see the tip of his bo sticking up above his head. Aletto probably was right not to come armed to speak to his uncle; Jadek would make a noise about *that.* But somebody up there should have a weapon to hand. Dahven—surely she could see his hair, just beyond Chris's shoulder? She thought so, but that was all she could make out. Gyrdan—there, at Aletto's back, arms folded.

And now she could see Jadek himself. Lialla came to a halt, clearly uncertain what to do next. Jennifer dropped a hand onto her shoulder and gave it a reassuring squeeze.

Jadek. He couldn't have not known they were so near; he must have had some warning. If so, he was doing an excellent job of pretending otherwise: Nearly black hair, only lightly touched at the temples with silver, was mussed as though he'd been pulled from sleep and his chin was shadowed with beard. He wore a loose, silky robe of deep blue that came to just below his knees; his bare feet had been shoved into soft, low shoes.

Lialla never mentioned his looks, Jennifer thought in surprise. No one had ever mentioned them. But she would have counted Jadek as handsome—actor or GQ-model attractive, if she hadn't known so much against him. His face was a little too wide across the cheekbones for her taste, his jaw very square, his lips a little full. He had powerful shoulders under the robe, which was belted to a narrow waist, the fabric itself thin enough to show off a lean body.

What a waste. She shook that aside; *don't be frivolous, Cray,* she ordered herself, and began to study his face closely. She couldn't see any sign whatever that Light had hit him after the fiasco in that meadow, certainly nothing like what Lialla had gone through in Podhru. Perhaps Lialla had misread. He *was* very pale—but in a world where tans weren't fashionable, that might be normal.

Just now, he was playing what he must count as a powerful card: his reputed charm. The smile was warm, a little sad. "Nephew. You've changed, visibly. If leaving Duke's Fort—and frightening your mother badly, incidentally—did this for you, then perhaps it was worth it."

"I think it was, Uncle," Aletto replied steadily. "And I would apologize to my mother, but I believe she understood my reasons. Surely, she knew there was no danger to me outside the Fort. After all, who would wish harm upon Amarni's son and heir?"

"Why, no one, of course," Jadek agreed. Aletto turned away briefly to exchange words with Gyrdan; Jennifer could see he was white to the lips. Gyrdan shook his head at first, finally nodded reluctantly, and went across the room. He spoke to the men who'd come from Podhru; they walked in a tight, stiff-backed group down the room, sending the whispering pack of servants farther toward the kitchen hallway door. Aletto now turned back and took two paces away from Chris, so that he stood nearer his uncle than his remaining two companions. Chris and Dahven exchanged glances that even halfway across the room looked grim. Jadek laughed very quietly as Aletto faced him once more: The charm was already wearing thin, the impatience beginning to show once more. "If you believe sending your hired thugs down the length of the chamber will serve, you clearly do not understand how things are done, boy."

"Oh, I understand well enough," Aletto said calmly. "Your men are between them and us, if you still think in terms of violence. If you choose not to take my word there will be nothing between us but words."

Jadek merely shook his head, the faint smile indicating to those around him that the notion wasn't worth an answer. Chris's voice cut through the whispers all around them. "Who're you trying to kid with the act, dude? No one's buying. And *you* know more about hired thugs than we do, anyway, don't you?''

Jadek tilted his head back and stared down the length of his nose in Chris's direction. ''I wasn't aware I'd given leave for you to speak. Or that the boy had.''

''Chill, man,'' Chris growled. ''I don't take off you.'' Aletto touched his arm, shook his head very faintly. Chris's shoulders tensed. He was still staring flatly at Jadek, who gazed back at him offensively.

The older man sighed elaborately and turned to his nephew. ''So far as Zelharri is concerned, we can discuss whatever you like, since you are here and I see I have little other choice. I do fail to see how your present and recent behavior would serve to show me that I should place you in power.''

The tone of voice was that of a loving elder chastising a foolish child. Jennifer felt Lialla's body tense and she realized after a moment she was holding her breath. Aletto merely folded his arms across his chest. ''Explain your meaning, please—to those here, not simply to me.''

''If you wish it. You have wandered throughout the land to stir up enmity against me, spreading rumor regarding my part in my own brother's death. You will have it that I have dealt in foul magic and ill-used your birthright, your mother, your sister and your own person. You have spread other rumors regarding the death of my cousin, a man I held dear—a man you yourself killed, deny it how you will. And now, you return home with force at your back, thinking to oust me from this place by threat of death or pain, overcoming my household with violence and violent men, counting upon whatever outrageous—and unsupportable—tales you've given to the Emperor to clear you of any act you contemplate against me. After your use of my poor cousin, you can't wonder that I choose to regard your arrival here, at this dreadful hour, as an active threat against Zelharri and my own person, can you?'' He smiled unpleasantly. ''Which does remind me—mention of lies and outrageous tales. Where is your sister?''

''She is not your business,'' Aletto said quietly. ''Nor does the matter between us at the moment concern her.''

Lizelle mumbled something, too quietly for Jennifer to hear. Jadek heard; he spun around to glare her into silence. Jennifer could see it in the set of his shoulders, the reddening of the back of his neck and his ears. He was slow to turn back to face his nephew—perhaps trying to gain control over his features first. Aletto shifted his weight and waited. Jennifer felt cloth sliding from under her fingers and clutched, but too late. Lialla was gone, pushing past men to reach Aletto's side. Jennifer swore under her breath, tugged at Edrith's sleeve to get his attention, and went after her.

"Why. Here *is* Lialla, after all." Jadek's face showed his surprise when he saw her. Jennifer, who had just come into the open, gave Lialla a worried look, then cast an anxious glance at the woman on the dais. Lialla was as pale as Jennifer had ever seen her and her fingers were twitching as though she longed to wrap them around her uncle's throat. Lizelle's eyes were fixed on her daughter and she was trembling; quite possibly she would have fallen if she hadn't the chair for support. Her hands were white with the effort of holding herself up. *God,* Jennifer thought; but Lizelle was going to have to look out for herself a little longer. *I don't dare leave Lialla, she just might murder the guy.*

She gave Lizelle one last look and her eye caught cautious movement off to the right: Robyn had eased herself away from Afronsan's men and was working slowly and quietly around the side of the chamber, now up behind the two chairs. Lizelle started violently as a strange woman came up behind her, but transferred her desperate grip to Robyn's fingers and allowed herself to be led around the side of the chair. She stumbled, sagged into the padded seat; Robyn eased down onto her knees beside the woman, largely out of Jadek's line of sight between the two chairs. She edged forward a little, her eyes on Aletto. Lizelle clung to Robyn's fingers desperately, but Jennifer thought she had forgotten her companion at once. Her eyes were open again, and they moved from Jadek to Lialla, to Aletto, back again, never still.

"Uncle," Lialla said, and her resonant voice filled the chamber. "You speak of lies and outrageous tales. If you accuse me of either, I deny it. If you claim proof of either, then bring it forth now, before all those here, and let me refute it."

Jadek was already shaking his head. "In my own time. I'd not shame you in public."

"No. Because you have no proof for any such charge." She took a step back so she stood just behind Aletto and a little to one side. "Since that is so, I agree with you, there is no need to discuss it now. Let us instead keep it a—personal matter—shall we say. Between the two of us. Brother, I am sorry, I did not mean to interrupt you.'' She turned her head away from her uncle; her gaze went to her mother and remained fixed there.

There was another long silence, broken only by faint whispering at the edges of the room, and then by Aletto. ''I, too, deny your accusations, Uncle. There were no lies or outrageous claims, as you named them. Whatever I said against you to any man, I knew for fact. Any violence I committed against any man was initiated by those ranged against me. I have made it clear almost from the first that I would return with sufficient men to see me safely into Sehfi's walls and then out again if that was my choice. Let *any* man come forth and say to my face I threatened to claim my birthright with violence, and I say that man lies.'' Another silence. Jadek simply stood, arms folded, and let him speak. The older man's face showed nothing at all of what he might be thinking. ''All the same, Uncle, since we seem unable to find a beginning point for discussion, I would be willing to set the matter before the Emperor by a formal petition. Let him decide, if you would rather, whether I am capable to accept from you what is by right mine.''

''By right,'' Jadek said so softly Jennifer could barely hear him, close as she now stood. ''By accident of birth only—''

''But that is all that was ever required,'' Aletto overrode him.

''Do not interrupt me,'' Jadek said, even more softly.

Aletto shook his head. ''When I was your ward, an underage boy, you had the right to command such obedience. No longer. You have lost, Uncle. I will have what is mine—and you can give it willingly now, or perforce when Shesseran comes to my side. Use sense, give over now.''

Jadek laughed. ''Do you honestly think me so soft and witless? But *you* are the fool if you hope to sway the Emperor with your outlandish tales, yours and your sister's. Oh, of course. Lest I forget: The lies of these outlanders the old woman obtained—to aid you, wasn't it?'' He turned to look at Jennifer and smiled, but his eyes were hard. She gazed into dark-rimmed pale blue eyes and kept her face expressionless. Beyond that first shock of hearing his voice and truly seeing him, she felt no fear of the man. *Foolish,* she chided herself. But something inside her had changed in the past hour.

"Not only our wild tales, Uncle," Aletto said, and Jennifer pushed aside her own thoughts to bring herself back to the moment. She wondered how the nera-Duke was managing to keep his temper—his cool—and actually face up to a man who'd been an overbearing parent to him for so many years. His voice was very calm, even; there was no indication he was afraid of his uncle, ever had been; no sign Jadek was getting to him in any fashion. He was, in fact, doing impressively under trying circumstances. "There are other people, other tales, plenty of both." He held up a hand and folded fingers down one at a time as he enumerated. "The armsmen you sent into the desert between Sikkre and Bez; others inside Bez itself and still others just before Podhru. Certain manifestations of Light and uses of a Triad—"

"Your accusations are outrageous. You cannot prove Light, and there is no Triad here," Jadek said flatly. "But even if I had one—Triads are not illegal."

"Nor immoral?" Lialla put in crisply. "Is that why yours departed—to avoid being involved in *your* use of Light? As to the substance itself, deny as much as you like, even the poorest of Wielders—anyone with any form of power at all could tell you've Shaped Light yourself, and recently. It's all around you, Uncle, it's become part of you. Odd I could never see it before I left Duke's Fort. Now, of course—but now, you're riddled with it." And as Jadek glared at her and compressed his lips in fury, Lialla smiled very faintly, a turning of lips that didn't lighten her own black eyes. "And it serves you truly fair," she added in a low, hard voice. "It came back against you, unexpectedly, didn't it? Before you could find a way to absorb the backlash, it ate through your defenses and it's gnawing at you still." He shook his head. "Don't bother to deny; anyone with the least power could tell. And I *know*, Uncle. Thanks to your kind lessons: a first at Lord Evany's fountain, the second in the mountains. I understand Light very well."

"You lie, Lialla, and it's a dangerous lie, don't you realize that? But I deny—"

"You'll die of it," Lialla said, flatly overriding him, "if you can't regain control." Jadek shook his head once more. "Deny you're dying, if you will. That anyway will remain true whatever you say."

He drew himself up and sighed in exasperation. "I had hoped for your mother's sake that you'd outgrow this. Let it go, Lialla." She merely shrugged and looked away from him. Jadek gave her one last black look and turned back to his nephew; his voice showed his anger now. "You listen to me, boy. I refuse, absolutely, to hand Duke's Fort to you. Whatever you think, however you've convinced these men to back you—by whatever promise of spoils or reward—I see nothing to assure me that you have learned anything which would give you the right to set aside my governance. I see less proof that I would survive the night. Oh," he scoffed and spread his arms wide, "these men you show me, *claiming* them to be Lord Afronsan's. Perhaps so, but I have no real proof and even so, they are few against your greater numbers and joined in your violent entry here to-night. I absolutely forbid you to petition the Emperor regarding a matter that is purely Duchy business! The Emperor is an elderly man with sufficient duties that I would feel shame to load upon him the burden of yet another which does not in fact concern him. *You* should feel shame for having even considered it."

"I?" Aletto asked mildly. "*My* conscience is clean, Uncle."

"Is it? But you have recently been in Podhru, while I was here overseeing Zelharri's many needs. What guarantee have I that you did not spread bribes among certain of the civil clerks to make certain that my papers would be mislaid while yours reached the Emperor—with money supplied by men who bear wrongful grudges against me?"

Aletto stepped back a pace and held up a hand for silence; Jennifer realized that the noise level in the chamber had been steadily growing over the past several minutes. She forced her fingers to ease their murderous grip on the bo, cautiously transferred it to her other hand and let the stiff one fall to her side where she could clench and unclench some circulation back into it. "Wait," Aletto said. "There is no point to becoming heated; I do not wish it, and I am certain neither of us wishes to distress my mother— or the others whose futures depend on whatever decision is made here. Speak with your men, if you choose, Uncle— or with Lord Afronsan's representatives, if that might ease your concerns." He turned away and went into a close huddle with Gyrdan and Dahven; Chris gave Jadek one last hard look before he joined the other men, and Jennifer could see his hand clenched into a hard fist at his side, his knee jiggling nervously, the way it did when he was truly furious. Edrith moved unobtrusively over to join his friend and leaned into the group when Chris glanced up and moved to give him room.

Lialla shifted under Jennifer's hand; her eyes went toward the dais. "Come with me, please," she whispered. Jennifer nodded. Jadek had walked away, and at the moment she couldn't see him. That was fine, so long as he wasn't anywhere near Lizelle or Robyn.

"Gladly. And we'd better hurry," Jennifer whispered back. But Lialla stood very still, staring toward the pair of plush-covered chairs, and Jennifer had to give her a shove to get her attention, and get her moving.

22

IZELLE's thin hands clutched at Lialla's; the younger woman went onto one knee and buried her face in her mother's lap. Her mother's anguished whisper scarcely carried any sound at all. "Oh, Lialla, oh, baby; precious, you're all right, you're alive. I didn't think—he said—"

Lialla's head came up; her face was as white as Lizelle's. "Oh, Mother, he surely didn't tell you I was *dead*?"

Lizelle shook her head. "No. But he let me think it." Lialla now looked utterly stricken, and her voice shook.

"I'm so sorry, Mother, I didn't realize—I never meant for that to happen." She swallowed. "I should have known he would do that."

"Lialla, it's all right, I knew you both had to go; don't, girl, don't look so." Lizelle touched her daughter's hair with shaking fingers. "It's all right."

"It's not all right! I hate him for that, for all that you had to go through!" Lialla whispered fiercely. She reclaimed her mother's fingers then and kissed them. "Oh, gods," she added drearily, "Mother, I can't stay here just now. Aletto needs me at his side. I had to make certain you were all right." Her eyes slid over the black dress, the thin form under it. "They said—he said you were—" The sin-Duchess blushed, shook her head.

"He claimed you were pregnant," Jennifer said quietly and deliberately. Someone had better defuse the emotion on this dais, she thought grimly, or Lialla wouldn't be any use to anyone. And poor Lizelle looked like she might collapse any moment.

"I was." Lizelle looked up at Jennifer curiously. "You're one of the outlanders Merrida got, aren't you? Thank you for helping my children."

"We all three helped where we could," Jennifer said. "Your children did fine themselves, though. You said— wait, you said you *were* pregnant?"

"I lost the baby, nights ago—I forget how many." The woman's eyes sagged closed. "He wanted it so badly; and he was so angry when he found out how I'd cheated him of an heir, I thought he'd—never mind. So when he insisted, I simply—" Her voice faded. She stared past Jennifer, finally blinked and gave her daughter a faint, tremulous smile. "At my age, though, and after so many years Thread-barren, I was afraid a child might not take, or it might be misformed. That—happens."

"You didn't warn him?" Jennifer asked; she bit her lip and when Lizelle looked up at her again with those smudgy, haunted eyes, merely shook her head.

"He—wanted it—a boy—so badly. If I'd said that, he'd have thought—thought I was trying to thwart him yet again. He was already so—" She swallowed, ran a pale tongue over her lips. "It was simpler to say nothing, and to hope. It was foolish, I suppose. Still, there was a chance I might have borne him the heir he wanted."

"Mother," Lialla said urgently. "You've had proper care, tell me you have!" Lizelle nodded once. "And Jadek doesn't blame you?"

Lizelle considered this vaguely, shrugged, then shook her head. "I can't tell, he's been so dreadfully upset—the baby, Aletto, something with his household but he wouldn't talk of it. Merrida said he brought a Triad to Duke's Fort, I made her hide from them, but—it didn't save her. The past days he's been even worse and—he hasn't spoken to me since I miscarried. Only when—the way he looks at me, *that* way— you know, Lialla, he won't speak, just stares as though he hates me, and I don't know what he wants, what to say or do. Perhaps he does blame me; he may think I did it for spite. But I didn't, I wouldn't have for such a reason, not ever, I swear it—!'' Her voice was spiraling toward hysteria; two of Jadek's men nearest the dais glanced toward the women curiously.

''Shhh,'' Lialla whispered urgently, and kissed her mother's hands in turn. ''No one in all Rhadaz would believe that, not of you, not even my uncle.'' She looked up as Jennifer touched her shoulder and nodded toward the room. ''Mother, I must leave you in a few more moments; Aletto needs me. You won't be alone, though. This, Mother, is Robyn; she's Aletto's wife, since Podhru.'' The older woman turned to gaze blankly down at Robyn, who offered her a shy, tentative smile. ''You'll like her, Mother.'' She transferred her mother's clinging fingers to Robyn's outstretched hands. Lizelle freed one and plucked at her daughter's sleeve; if possible, her face had gone even whiter and her eyes were wide and terrified.

''Lialla, promise you won't hurt him! Swear you won't!'' she whispered.

''Mother, don't—''

''Think of me, if not of him; please, swear you won't!''

''Lialla, go back to your brother,'' Jennifer said quietly. She caught hold of Lizelle's hand and eased it away from the younger woman's sleeve. Lialla opened her mouth, closed it again without saying anything, and fled back to the clutch of men around Aletto. Jennifer shook the older woman's hand to get her attention. ''Listen to me, please. Aletto does not want to harm your husband, and that's mostly for your sake. Listen to your son, to what he says. He's had a long time to think this through and he's doing everything he can to spare Jadek. God knows you'd be better off without a man like that; anyone can see what he's done to you. Right now, you're beyond realizing it, but never mind that. Aletto will not harm Jadek,'' she said, carefully spacing the words. ''Not if there's any way around it. But that will be up to Jadek.''

She wasn't certain if the woman had understood anything. Lizelle simply continued to gaze at her with those terrible, agonized eyes. Jennifer pressed the woman's hand into Robyn's once more, said, ''Take care of her, Birdy, and watch out for yourself.''

''We're all right,'' Robyn said firmly. Jennifer got back

to her feet and stepped off the dais. "Go help Aletto fix things; we'll be waiting right here."

The group around Aletto had broken up, and he was standing by himself once more, arms folded, patiently waiting. One of Afronsan's men came up and spoke to him; Aletto nodded curtly and the man went back to his companions. Jennifer watched curiously as the rest of the observers gathered around him. A moment later, they began working toward the dais.

Dahven's fingers caught hold of hers; she gave him a brief smile. He replied with a wink, squeezed and then released her hand. Jadek came away from the Sehfi onlookers and this time two large men wearing his colors moved with him. When he halted several paces away from his nephew, the two arranged themselves rather ostentatiously at his back. Dahven made a very faint shrug and cast his eyes up, then moved to stand behind Aletto; Chris took up the position at the nera-Duke's other shoulder. Edrith moved over next to him, turning at a right angle to face the merchants and the outer doors.

"Have you decided, Uncle?" Aletto finally asked.

Jadek spread his arms in a broad shrug, then folded them across his chest. His jaw was set, his eyes narrowed; and when he spoke his voice rang with anger. "There is nothing to decide, boy. I named you unfit to rule when marsh fever weakened both your body and your wit; I did as much a second time, when you murdered my cousin and fled Duke's Fort, and later when you confirmed my early judgment by spreading your vicious lies and conducting a campaign of violence wherever you went. How dare you come here in such a fashion, how dare you pretend before these men that I am a usurper and you the wronged heir, that I have kept back anything you could truly manage? Is this an outlander trick *they* have taught you, to attack your uncle and the man who kept you and cared for you after your father's death? Zelharri is mine, Aletto. While you were growing into a useless, wine-bibbing, whining, spineless weakling, I devoted all those years, all my energies to Zelharri. What have you done for this Duchy? Nothing! Not—one—thing!" His voice rose to a shout. He was breathing hard, red in the face, his dark-rimmed blue eyes were nearly black. After a moment he went on, not as loudly, but forcefully, clipping his words. "The decision is mine and mine alone. There is nothing else to say. If you are so foolish as to consider a petition to the Emperor, the door is there, the gates beyond, and Podhru—but you know how many days to the south Podhru lies, don't you, boy?''

"And we know how many obstacles a vindictive man can put in his path," Lialla said flatly.

Aletto glanced at her, shook his head, and she compressed her lips. "I am home, and I intend to stay," he said clearly. "Particularly since you insist this is Duchy business. Very well. I repeat, I am three years past age and sound."

"Sound," Jadek scoffed.

"Fit, if you prefer," Aletto said. "But that is a simple contention to remove. Let anyone who wishes examine me for fault—that is, for any fault," he corrected himself carefully, "that would preclude a man from ruling. I will have no man say a feeble man, or a cripple—or a drunkard—took what he could not control." He waited; Jadek simply stared at him. After a moment Aletto shrugged and went on. "Uncle, I realize you have not gutted Zelharri to line your own pockets, or willfully harmed her people; I know you worked hard all those years. I am not ungrateful.

"But now we have met once more, I know we could never live harmoniously in the same Duchy. And so—"

"And so you simply exile me? Am I given choice of place, or do you claim that right also?"

"Within reason, the choice is yours. If Mother chooses to go with you, that is between you and her."

Jadek laughed, very quietly. "But you hope, after all these years, that she'll toss me aside? Stupid, naive boy. Your mother will do whatever I ask of her; you don't understand that even yet, do you?" He lowered his voice even further. "I could laugh at you until I hurt; you're caught in a web of your own weaving. You don't dare kill me, not with Afronsan's men scrupulously taking note; you wouldn't keep Zelharri any longer than it took them to ride back to Podhru. Kill me, and you'll turn half the men in this room against you, at once; your mother will die cursing you." He grinned, a flash of teeth under dark, intense eyes. "But if you let me live? You'll never be quite certain of your safety ever again, will you? Or that of your sweet wife— and I wonder that you'll ever be certain any children she produces are *yours*. Your fever—" Aletto drew a deep breath, shook his head as Jadek paused and looked at him inquiringly. The younger man waved a hand for him to continue. "Kill me, and you'll always doubt the loyalty of the men around you who saw you murder your father's brother, the man who raised you.

"And your sister. If I am riddled with Light, what manner of creature is *she*?" His eyes strayed to Lialla, touched Jennifer, fixed on Aletto once again. "She could kill you at any time. And think about Lizelle—if somehow you could keep her here. Remember how many years she's been my wife.

"It's a pity, Aletto; but you're soft. Weak. Like your father, really. Whatever you do here, in the long run I win."

"You don't win if you're dead," Lialla spat at him.

"Be still, girl!" Jadek snarled; his hand was partway up but Lialla held her ground and it took him a visible effort to let the arm back down to his side. "*You* won't kill me, because you can't."

"Don't wager on that," Lialla whispered.

"I do, and with cause: Evany's courtyard bound you to me, more than you yet realize. Aletto won't kill me because he's too soft, too afraid of what people might think." His eyes went back and fixed on Jennifer. "As for you, woman; we have a score to settle, you and I."

She could almost have predicted what he was going to say before he said it. Jennifer shook her head very firmly and her voice was calm. "No."

"You said that the very first time we spoke. You've gainsaid me every time we've crossed paths. More than any other of that boy's allies, you've done damage to my reputation, my men, to my plans. It wasn't enough damage to matter, of course, you must see that. All the same, it is more than I'll let you get away with." He glared at her and whispered almost gently, "You're dead, woman, I swear it, whatever else happens. You and I—"

Dahven took a sidestep that put him at Jennifer's arm, and Chris shifted, ready to leave Aletto and protect her instead. *Bad idea, kid*, she thought, glancing sideways, and shaking her head minutely. To her relief he nodded and went back where he belonged. She brought up the bo and pressed it gently against Dahven's chest then. Jadek folded his arms across his chest; he looked satisfied as she took a step into the open. *God. I'll get myself killed; this isn't what I do!*

It wasn't. The realization flooded her all at once; this was what her subconscious had been trying to tell her since she'd gone into that stable. Perhaps why she'd been so frightened, for the first time truly frightened since she'd come into Rhadaz. *This has to stop. Someone has to stop it.* She raised her arm over her head and opened her fingers; the staff hit the hardwood floor with a loud, echoing clatter that immediately silenced the room. "No," she said clearly. "How dare you threaten me like this? How dare you threaten any of us? This is a civilized society with laws and government, not a barbaric hoard!

"And I'm an advocate—a woman who settles issues with law and precedent—not with lethal magic and weaponry! In all my life before this world of yours, I never physically harmed another human being, but now—thanks to you and men like you, I've killed a man, injured a score of others.

"I'm not proud of that, even though I tried hard never to strike a blow except in defense of myself or those with me. And that, let me tell you, isn't easy. After a while, everything looks like a threat if you're holding a weapon, every movement something to be countered by violence or death.

"I did oppose you; God help me, I'd do it again to keep myself or anyone else alive. I'm not foolish enough to hesitate to defend against a man like you. But the time for violence is over, it's done with, Jadek. I've had enough. I'm not fighting anyone—not you, not anyone. Not like that—" She shoved the bo hard with her foot, sending it rattling across the floor. "Not ever again, without dire cause. But absolutely, *not now.*"

She couldn't tell if people were whispering again, or if it was only the noise in her ears. Jadek gazed at her for what seemed forever, his face a blank. Dahven pulled her away then, out of the open, turning her so he was between her and Jadek; his face was unreadable, his eyes fixed on Aletto; but his arm was warm and reassuringly tight. Jennifer leaned into him and sighed. *I think I made an ass of myself,* she thought; at the moment, she really didn't care. It felt as though an enormous weight had fallen from her shoulders.

When she turned to look once more, she'd lost several moments: Jadek had gone over to speak with the merchants, and, whatever he was saying, it looked urgent. He stepped back from a number of very worried-looking men, strode across the room once more. Chris started and went into an alert crouch as the man reached inside the blue robe. Jadek freed a long dark cord with a rough silver sphere knotted onto it. He cast Chris a shrug and a faint smile, then turned to address the entire room.

"My niece was a very inferior novice Wielder when she left Duke's Fort; most here know how many years she toiled for no gain. And now, have you not heard the rumors? And you men who came with them from Podhru, have you not seen the attack she made upon one of your number? She Shapes Light! I doubted, for we all know Wielders hold Light to be anathema. But look at her, she not only Shapes but she has found a way to infect Thread with Light."

"Because you—!" Lialla began furiously, but Jadek over-rode her.

"I do not doubt she will try to lay that at my door also! Or perhaps she will deny it. But, she herself has said, any wielder of any magic can sense Light; and while I deny that I am such a man, I do wear a protective charm." He held up the knobby bit of silver. "Now, this was bought in Sehfi's market; its design and content are clearly known to the woman who constructed and imbued it. This charm tells me beyond doubt the sin-Duchess is contaminated with unspeakable power—one she actively sought, one she deliberately blended with what little clean magic she was able to learn.

"Even if I *dared* trust the boy, would any sane man feel safe around this girl?"

"You speak of dares—!" Lialla cried out in a shrill, furious voice as she strode forward; Chris grabbed for her sleeve, missed and swore loudly. "I do deny everything you have said!"

"Then I shall give you the proof," Jadek shouted, topping her with volume; for one moment, no one could understand what either said. Chris threw himself after Lialla and this time caught her by the waist, dragging her back from Jadek; Lialla swung wildly, furiously trying to hit him, to break his grip. All at once she froze, eyes fixed on her uncle, and then she screamed.

Jadek held the sphere between them and it began to glow: The two men behind him backed hastily away; others nearby dropped flat. Jennifer could hear people running across the floor at the far end of the room, the door they'd entered by slamming against the wall, the sound echoing down the long corridor. Lizelle staggered to her feet with a wild cry of her own, breaking Robyn's hold on her hands.

A dull, ruddy Light and a foul smell spiraled out from

the charm. Dahven tried to drag Jennifer away and tripped over someone's arm; both of them fell. When she got her breath back and her head from under his chest, she could see Lizelle moving unsteadily across the floor. "No, don't, please—!" Her voice was thin and high, hardly carrying any distance at all, but Lialla heard it. With a cry of her own, she closed the distance between them and spun around, placing herself squarely between her uncle's spell and her mother.

Robyn came running then, and threw her arms around Lizelle, pinning her arms at her sides and swinging her around, completely off her feet. Lizelle tried to fight her way free, but she wasn't any match for Robyn. The two women went staggering back and Robyn's heel caught on the edge of the dais. She sat with a thump and a grunt of forcibly expelled air. Lizelle fell on her face and didn't move.

Jadek's voice rose over the almost unbearable noise level: "I warned you all; look at her! See the charm's reaction!"

"You *lie!*" Lialla screamed back at him. "That's no simple market charm! Stay clear, all of you, it'll kill any of you on touch!" She needn't have worried, except for Chris, and Edrith who now guarded his back against any sneak attack by one of Jadek's men, no one came anywhere near her. Even Aletto had backed hastily away from the slowly advancing, spinning mass, though he hadn't gone very far. Lialla braced herself against Chris, brought up both hands, snatching at Thread, overlaying it with Light. She set her teeth, pushed sharply with her palms and blew, hard. Jadek's spiral flattened and spun back in on itself. Lialla shoved an elbow into Chris's ribs, sending him back a step and she pivoted against him, clapped her hands twice, hard. Something dark and glowing sped past her and across the chamber, across the corner of the dais. It went through the far window with a crash of breaking glass. Smoke rose from the broken pane; the wooden frame was smoldering.

Someone ran to deal with the fire, smothering it with cloths from the table. Jennifer let Dahven help her to her feet just as one of Afronsan's clerks pushed his way to the front of the room, followed by the red-and-gold-clad observers. The man's face was set in lines of outrage, and two of the observers now held drawn swords.

"Shame, sir, for shame!" The clerk's voice was thin and

high and it trembled with anger. "To unleash such violence!"

"I?" Jadek ran a hand across his forehead. Jennifer stared at him. He was even paler than he had been, and she wondered if he was going to faint or be sick. His face was slick with sweat; the blue robe was dark in patches under his arms, down his chest. His voice was rough, as though he was having trouble breathing. *Riddled with Light.* Lialla was right; the man might not yet be dead, but he was very ill—and he was only now beginning to realize it.

Afronsan's men came between Jadek and Lialla; she moved aside, Chris following her like a shadow, so that she could continue to watch the man. If she felt satisfaction—anything—it didn't show. She stood very still and watched. Chris glanced quickly around, met Jennifer's eyes meaningfully. Jennifer nodded, hoping she'd understood him. It wasn't difficult to figure anyway. *All that pretty speech I made, and all for nothing?* Lialla wasn't certain her uncle had been neutralized; Chris was suspicious. *Guess you don't get to turn pacifist yet, Cray,* she told herself. *Not until this guy's wrapped up in pretty paper and ribbon and gone.*

"That was unwise, Uncle," Aletto said. He held up a hand for silence and got it; the room was full and those in it utterly still. "To follow your earlier pattern in the presence of the Emperor's men?" He looked over at Afronsan's angry clerk. "Sir, I don't know your instructions—"

The old man turned his head to glare at him. "In the event of violence by either party? The Emperor does not countenance violence in matters of succession! This act has clearly removed your cause from the realm of Duchy business, Honor Aletto. You, Honor Jadek," he said crisply, "will accompany us to Podhru. There the entire matter will be thoroughly gone into, in detail." He paused for comment, but Jadek simply stood blinking at him as though dazed. Aletto nodded once and stepped back. Another of the observers came forward with fetters but the clerk waved them aside. "Honor Jadek will surrender such—market charms—as he possesses into our hands. Upon that, we will not consider him any threat, nor shame him with bonds." Jennifer caught hold of Dahven's arm and squeezed; when she glanced up he gave her a reassuring smile but he'd gone pale.

Jadek swallowed hard, wet his lips, finally nodded. "I deny any intent of harm on my part, here and now. And I call upon those who witnessed events to recall when I have need, that it was my niece who created a counterspell that rendered mine violent."

"Make note of Honor Jadek's statement," the old man said over his shoulder. The other clerk was walking slowly forward, eyes shifting from his comrades to the portable desk that hung from a shoulder strap and pressed into his hip; it was fitted with a thick, string-bound sheaf of paper, and he was busily writing as he walked. He nodded, dipped a fat pen into ink and went on scribbling. Jennifer set her teeth as the man paused next to her and his metal pen scraped unpleasantly across paper; she breathed a sigh of relief as he kept going. "We have already noted all previous statements, Honor. You will be permitted to instruct your personal servants to pack clothing for you, and whatever funds you require." Jadek nodded again and his shoulders sagged.

Jennifer eased herself into contact with Thread and, for want of a better idea, clutched at the red Lialla had first shown her. It throbbed in her grasp, numbing her fingertips, but there was no doubt which of those around her was Jadek. Light spilled from him in thin runnels; it all at once reminded her of the way blood had run from her cut arm and she shuddered, forcing herself back into reality. The stuff was bleeding out of him. Unless he found a way to stop it, he'd die, the way Merrida would die—if she wasn't already dead. Or unless he accepted Lialla's aid. Jennifer wondered if there was anything the sin-Duchess *could* do for him, though; whether she would. For her own account, certainly, Lialla would let him die and be glad. But her mother and Aletto had claims on her.

Lialla's face showed nothing; she stood several paces from Jadek, hands loose at her side, simply watching him. Chris still looked angry and frustrated but he stayed with Lialla.

"Uncle," Aletto said suddenly. Jadek slowly brought his head around and stared at him, as though wondering who he was. He laughed then, very quietly.

"Don't look so stricken, boy. You've won, it seems; you have what you wanted—at least, for now." He heaved a sigh and turned to Afronsan's clerk. "Sir, I'll go with you and gladly; I had wondered how else I might survive this night." He produced a wan smile. Aletto opened his mouth to protest, shut it again without saying anything.

"Watch him," Dahven murmured against Jennifer's ear.

She shook her head. "Can't you see it? I can, without Thread now; he's hemmorhaging Light. He'll be lucky to see the sun rise at this rate; it's sucking him dry, like it did his brother."

"No," Dahven insisted. "Even Amarni took days to die; he can't be so ill as all that!" She shook her head again, but studied the man more carefully. Jadek had stepped back to let all of Afronsan's men but the two armed guards pass; they stood behind him and to one side—near enough to remind him that he was under detention, but not so close as to serve as human shackles. Jadek was swaying very slightly and his lips had a bluish look to them.

The front of the room had by and large cleared out in the past moments: Most of the merchants had gone into a worried huddle a distance away; many of Jadek's men were nowhere in sight—somewhere in the rear of the chamber, behind Aletto's, perhaps. Near the dais, now, Jadek and his guards; Lialla and Chris. Edrith between Chris and Robyn, who knelt on the edge of the dais with Lizelle's head in her lap. Aletto and Gyrdan close together, almost within reach of Dahven and Jennifer. Dahven drew his breath in sharply, Jennifer uttered a little cry of protest as his fingers dug into her shoulders.

Jadek straightened all at once and Light flared, blinding and stunning Afronsan's guards; Jadek himself vanished in a roil of Hell-Light that shimmered from ceiling to floor and ran out in all directions. Merchants screamed and threw themselves at the outer doors. Jennifer caught the blast of power and it knocked her flat, onto Dahven, who landed hard, the breath driven from him. She scrambled onto her knees, back to her feet and ran forward, trying to shout above the uproar all around her: "Birdy! Get back, do it now! Li, where are you, you need me!"

"Yo, Jen!" Chris bellowed. She couldn't see, couldn't think. Fortunately, her ears still worked.

"Kid? Guide me, damnit!" She thought she heard Dahven somewhere behind her, shouting her name; she ignored that, shut her eyes against the sickening swirl of Hell-Light all around her and tried to concentrate on Chris's voice.

He shifted into voice, a furious tenor. "Yo, my name is Chris/and I still ain't scared/of a jerk named Jadek/just because he dared/to mess with Hell-Light/this stuff ain't so bad/we gonna clean it up/and everybody be glad."

"Keep it up!" Lialla shouted. Jennifer stumbled into her

314

outstretched hand and clamped onto it, dropped to one knee and clenched her teeth. *Stride La Vampa* still seemed like a poor idea—a worse one in the midst of Light than it had on the edge of pooled Light in Evany's courtyard—but it was all she *knew* that would fit with what Chris was doing. She slapped her free hand against her jeans for the three-beat and launched into it—her voice a dry whisper at first, growing in strength by the moment as Chris's rose and echoed.''

''Except for you/'cause you in for hard times/gonna chill down in Podhru/gonna pay for your crimes.'' His voice rose and ended on a startled squawk.

''Chris?'' Lialla demanded anxiously. She yelled herself then, a triumphant little shriek. Lights shivered all around them and began to fade at once. Jennifer remained where she found herself, blinking furiously and trying to focus on the elaborate square of flooring under her knee. It came and went through wheels of light and painfully bright flashes; those, too, faded, and Dahven enveloped her in a crushing embrace.

''Ever, ever again,'' he mumbled against her hair. She nodded, clutched at the front of his shirt and tried to remember how to breathe.

She pushed away from him finally and slewed around, still blinking catherine wheels from her eyes. Lialla leaned back into Chris, and Edrith was blotting her face with his sleeve, talking to her in a low, worried voice. Lialla nodded and he went into the crowd. When he returned he had a servant who carried a long, slender pitcher and several round mugs on a wooden tray. Edrith shoved one of the cups in Chris's hands for Lialla and brought another to Jennifer. ''Here. It's plain water, cold from the kitchen cisterns.'' She nodded her thanks, drained the cup and held it out for a refill, then got slowly and carefully to her feet.

There were men everywhere, milling around the room, some of the household servants who were tending to Lizelle. Robyn caught Jennifer's eye and nodded briefly; she was still holding the older woman's fingers. Afronsan's guards were being helped by their own and another of the household servants: an older woman still in her night robes and a plain, close-fitting cap who knelt next to a small wooden tray that held several boxes and bottles. Healer of some sort, clearly. Jennifer dismissed Afronsan's guards from her thoughts and looked for Aletto.

He knelt a short distance away, Gyrdan standing just behind him. Jadek lay there, very still, unnaturally white against the dark floor and the now totally sweat-soaked blue robe. At first she thought he might be dead, but as she watched his chest rose, fell again. As she came up, she was unsettled to see his eyes were partly open. She glanced sharply over her shoulder as something moved there, met Lialla's dark gaze. The sin-Duchess looked without expression at the fallen man, sighed as her gaze passed over her brother's bowed head. Jennifer followed when Lialla turned and walked off a few paces.

Lialla stared broodingly toward the dais, where her mother lay, watched as servants lifted the unconscious woman onto a litter and carried her from the room. "I would have left him alone, you know," she said abruptly.

"I know."

"Not for any—any *decent* reason, like the one you gave him when you threw down your bo." Lialla met her eyes, turned away once more. "I thought you'd gone mad when you did that."

"I must have, thinking I could get away with it."

"No. You were right. I wanted to kill him, worse than Chris did. I had more reason. Not just myself, but Aletto. Mother. And then, for both of them to ask me—" She shook her head. "Chris is right; things shouldn't be so complicated. But I'd have left him alone, if he'd permitted that."

Jennifer sighed. "Maybe we were all naive to presume it could be worked out. The one thing I said, though—someone with a weapon sees threats everywhere. He didn't leave himself any way out. He knew that would kill him—and he did it anyway."

"Stupid," Lialla said softly. "So stupid. In a way, he's won. Mother—and Aletto will let it gnaw him forever, wondering what he might have done to prevent this." She stared at this dais blankly, let her eyes follow Robyn, who had risen to her feet and now walked over to Aletto, to kneel beside him. "Maybe I'm mad, too: I think I'd save him if I could. No one deserves to die the way Father did, even I can't think it's a fair exchange."

"Yeah? Well, I can," Chris said flatly as he came up. "Li, I swear—will you save it until Eddie and I get out of hearing? Some people won't *let* you save them, don't you get that? He knew all that and he still went in a full flame-out!" He gripped her shoulder. "Chill with the dumb guilt stuff, all right? It won't get the dude back on his feet, and you be honest with yourself, you don't want that anyway.''

"Guess not. That doesn't seem—''

"It isn't *right*,'' Chris said. "It's what is, though. What is and what's right don't always meet up; even I know that.'' He squeezed her shoulder again and went down the room toward the outer doors, taking Edrith with him.

23

𝔷

THE weather had turned cool the past several days; not unusual in the high country for mid-September, Lialla assured her. Jennifer looked around the large room that had served her and Dahven for the past three months and sighed. She'd miss the room itself—the large bed, the airy, high ceilings, the enormous windows that let in north light and just a little pool of summer sun late in the afternoon. But the past two nights, her blankets had felt slightly damp, even with the fires lit, and she'd never properly warmed up.

The women who took care of the family apartments had offered to pack for her but she'd done it herself, taking inventory as she put things in the leather satchel. Chris had kept the Nike bag with him when he and Edrith left Zelharri a month earlier, but Aletto had had a near-copy made for her: Eyelets and ties instead of a zipper, but the craftsman had faithfully reproduced the shape and size—and the swoosh logo on both sides.

Her handbag was already packed: pads of local paper (a very pale yellow, unlined and tied with string), pens and pencils, the makeup bag—scarcely depleted at all—and the aspirin and vitamin tablets, now at a worrying low. She'd run out of toothpaste, and the brush was looking rather dreadful these days; Robyn had given her a tooth cloth and a corked little jug of paste that was at least partly mint. She carefully didn't inquire as to the rest of the ingredients. Robyn had also given her a box of loose willow-bark tea; it tasted dire but Robyn swore it was the natural forerunner of aspirin. Possibly it was; it seemed to dispose of headaches. Now, if only she could find something to take the taste out of her mouth. It reminded her of her introduction to the combination of stale drinking water in leather bottles, mealy apples and those oat cakes Lialla had been so fond of.

She had relatively few things to pack: Lialla had held to her promise of duplicates for her blue jeans—or tried to. Jennifer had finally managed to convey an alternative and now had three pairs of lightweight cottony pants, roomy affairs with drawstring waists, large pockets, snug ankles. Her socks were wearing thin, though she'd gone barefoot most of the summer, except when she ran.

To Jennifer's surprise, the running itself didn't cause that much excitement. After the first day, she couldn't bring herself to wear her shorts again, though. People stared; stood and stared, and called to other people, who also came and stood and stared. She'd felt like the only float in a parade after a while. Lialla joined her now and again; or Dahven did.

She hadn't really had much time to herself, other than the time she insisted upon for her runs: Aletto had made extensive use of her as an advocate, and she'd learned Rhadazi law as she went, made ridiculous and embarrassing mistakes at first, finally developed a feeling for what she did. Aletto's father had provided his own advocates a library— incomplete, but better than none.

She'd learned to read Rhadazi about the same way she picked up their law—by feel, by guess and by God, by learning from her mistakes. Aletto kept two of his uncle's advocates on—older men who were inclined at first to be stiff with her. They'd finally accepted her the way partners in her old office had accepted associates: someone to write the first drafts, carry the law books, make the small deals and take the flak when something went wrong. It was irksome but reassuringly familiar at the same time. Dahven spent most of early summer going back and forth between Sehfi and Podhru, anyway—she could soak up as much work and knowledge as she could handle in a single day without worrying about slighting him.

Lizelle had knit her stockings: pale blue wool, a little itchy, and the tops sagged out and worked down into her high-tops after a while. But Jennifer had been truly touched by the gesture. The woman had been crushed for weeks after Jadek's death, too weak to even appear at the burial ceremony. She'd kept to bed for a good deal of the summer and was still overly thin, brittle-looking. But she'd begun to take more interest in things recently: her own appearance, the herb gardens that had once been her pride, her needle-work. Jennifer had worried at first how Lizelle would feel about Robyn; a daughter-in-law only a few years younger than she, after all, and Robyn had been sprung on her. But Lizelle liked Robyn, a feeling Robyn reciprocated.

She had spent more time in Aletto's company than anyone else's the past few months, oddly enough. But Aletto had thrown himself into bringing Sehfi's miserable market back to strength, which necessitated numerous drafts of local contracts and even more drafts to be sent to Podhru—drafts which often came back as ink-stained messes, revisions and suggested re-visions tied to the back, long letters suggesting other revisions, new contracts—

Aletto had often simply sought her out to talk. "I can talk to Robyn," he said once. "Or Dahven. But not the same way. Robyn never believes me when I say I feel as though it's just around the corner, the mistake that will bring it all down on my head. Dahven laughs and says he feels the same way, and how can I believe that? You listen. And I like your advice." She wondered what he would do once she was gone; but those talks had grown less frequent of late. Maybe he was finally beginning to trust himself. God knew he'd better: He'd done a lot already, and there was a new atmosphere of optimism all around the Fort. But he had a very long way to go. And word had just come a few days earlier that Biyallan and some of her friends had filed petitions for the construction of a new road between Bez and Zelharri, another for certain new outside trade routes. Incorporating all that with existing business—simply final-izing all the paperwork—would keep the new Duke busy for a long time.

New pants, new shirts. Some weaver in the market had duplicated chambray very closely, if she remembered to be careful the first few wearings. Otherwise, the dye came off on her wrists. A handful of scarves. A new pair of soft leather boots and a pair of low shoes. Slippers for indoors, but she'd packed those nearly unworn: While the weather stayed warm, she went barefoot, the way Robyn did. Jen-nifer grinned; Chris had sworn his mother had to be tracked down and wrestled into shoes for the ceremony that named her Duchess. It was true Robyn hardly wore shoes of any kind other than for important occasions.

She dropped the small blackwood box Aletto had given her on top of her new shirts. It contained a silver filigree charm on a silk cord; *Protection against illness*, the charm was said to be. Eminently sensible of Aletto; but he was proving himself that, daily.

One last look around the room. There wasn't anything else, if something turned up beneath the bed, Robyn could have it sent on—or bring it, perhaps. It wasn't that far from Zelharri to Sikkre, after all. Especially if one could stay on the road. She tightened the lacing on the bag, double-knotted the bow and slung it over her shoulder, along with the handbag.

Robyn was sitting cross-legged in the sun down in her favorite small garden, weeding: There were roses here, a reflecting pool, plenty of brightly colored and scented things Jennifer didn't know; she hadn't ever recognized much beyond roses and marigolds back home, anyway.

"Hey, Duchess," Jennifer called out. Robyn looked up and grinned.

"Yeah, don't I look it, kiddo?" She sat back, blotted her forehead. "You look ready to shove off."

" 'Fraid so."

"You don't look that; I think Dahven must be driving you nuts wanting to get back now that he's got the go-ahead."

Jennifer laughed. "Just because you can hear him vibrating when he walks by. I don't think he really believed he'd prevail, whatever he said. He's been too hyper since he got that stack of documents from Afronsan."

"Well." Robyn sighed gustily. "You're not going to make me get up, are you?"

"You probably should; I don't know if that much cold, damp dirt is good for pregnant ladies."

"Sure it is. Remember where I lived when I was making Chris? So I'm a little older now." Jennifer laughed and knelt next to her sister, shed both bags and hugged her hard. "Hey, kiddo, you take care of that pretty guy, all right? And make him marry you before I get too fat to travel."

Jennifer sighed. "He's probably already got that date set; I'm the one holding back, remember?"

"Don't you *dare*," Robyn said severely and shook a finger at her. "He's not his father—or ours, come to think of it. You make an honest man of that boy, run his market for him and like that."

"Just the jitters, you know?" She considered this remark, laughed ruefully. "I mean, you know? Your kid ruined me."

"Which one?" Robyn demanded. "God, I miss those two!"

"They won't be long, this is supposed to be a shakedown cruise; remember? Down into Fahlia and into what should be Mexico. With an established trading company."

"Your idea, wasn't that?"

"Seemed better to me than jumping onto the first around-the-Horn ship heading for the Atlantic," Jennifer admitted. "And in our own world, there's a lot of good coffee that comes from that end of the world. Mexico, Central America—" She sighed deeply. "I have this vision of cornering the market here on Jamaica Blue Mountain—which of course wouldn't have gone down the tubes. It's coffee," she added, as Robyn stared at her blankly. "Wonderful, wonderful, expensive, *rare* coffee."

"Oh. Don't forget that tea I made up for you. Willow bark has that stuff that's the aspirin—"

"Got it with me."

"Good." Robyn looked at her for a long moment, then hugged her again and planted a kiss somewhere between her nose and her ear. "Take care of yourself. Write letters, damnit."

"I will." Jennifer got back to her feet, retrieved her bags and looked down at her sister. Robyn shoved long, straight loose hair behind her ears with a wrist. "Sure looks like a Duchess to me."

"We'll start a trend," Robyn said. She sat watching as Jennifer strode across the garden and out through the gates, waved as her sister turned to blow her a kiss; she adjusted the waistband on her jeans and after a cautious glance all around, eased the shirttails to the outside and released the button, let the zipper down an inch or so, and eased herself onto her knees with a gusty sigh of relief. They said there wouldn't be a lot more of the warm, sunny weather, and there were entirely too many dandelions in with the cornflowers.

* * *

Jennifer went back across the kitchen garden and down the long corridor toward the courtyard she, Edrith and Lialla had crossed that night three months earlier. Dahven had sent the wagon on ahead and was waiting with the horses. She wasn't looking forward to riding, not after avoiding horses as much as possible all summer—but Dahven liked to ride, was genuinely fond of his horses. If he'd realized she didn't care for them he wouldn't have insisted, of course; she thought it was a small enough sacrifice, under the circumstances. *If my hip sockets survive the first day, anyway.*

"Jen! Wait!" Lialla's voice echoed down the hall; she stopped at the door into the courtyard and turned back to wait. Lialla came flying after her, stopped panting just short of the doorway, where sun lay in a hot pool, and clung to the wall. "Wait, I've run—from—your rooms—"

"Take your time; you're saving me from a horse," Jennifer said. Lialla grinned, finally caught her breath and expelled one last pant in a loud gust.

Three months had done visible wonders for the sin-Duchess, though the change had been coming since the night she first left Sehfi: She walked with a confident stride, spoke with authority, Wielded with calm assurance. She was corresponding with several novice Wielders in Podhru and Bez; so far as Jennifer knew, she had been candid with all of them regarding her magic, and those who'd responded so far showed none of Merrida's narrowness, or Neri's.

Chris had contributed greatly to the most obvious change: Lialla had disposed of all but one set of Wielder Blacks; just now, she wore bright red trousers and a loose shirt patterned in red on white; that was belted to a narrow waist with a red-and-gold knotted rope belt of Chris's own design—a cross between macrame and sailor's knots and set with an enormous polished seashell: very like the belts that had been popular back in L.A. She wore her hair in a high braid, bright ribbons holding it at both ends. Jennifer found it increasingly difficult to remember the faded, insecure young woman in rusty black garments who hunched her shoulders, mumbled when she had to speak, who faded into the background with ease. Lialla looked easily ten years younger, buoyant, and if she wasn't fully in command of herself and her magic, she wasn't letting the whole world see it.

She held out both hands and gripped Jennifer's fingers. "I know it won't be very long until I'm in Sikkre but I didn't want you to go without saying good-bye."

"Good. I haven't given up on what you're doing yet," she added. Lialla laughed. It was a stock line between them any more; Jennifer had in fact long since given up on trying to master Lialla's meld of Light and Thread, and they both knew it. Of late, she hadn't even had that much time to work Thread, and she wondered how she'd ever fare if Dahven followed through his promise to present her with an a'lud and music lessons.

"You'd better not give up; I'm going to drill you like mad when I get to the Thukar's palace."

"Do that," Jennifer warned, "and you get the Tower room again."

Lialla wrinkled her nose and laughed again. "That wasn't such a bad room. It needs a new mattress, though; Robyn murdered the old one so I could make rope." She gave Jennifer a quick hug. "I will truly miss you. But I think Dahven got a better bargain in you."

"I think we'll do all right," Jennifer replied mildly. Lialla stepped back, waved vigorously and sprinted back the way she'd come, vanishing through the slit into the base of Merrida's old tower. Her tower, now, of course.

Jennifer shifted her load and walked across the courtyard; one of Aletto's men took the leather gym bag and ran ahead to call into the stable. By the time she reached the entry, Dahven was on his way out, leading the horses: his newly acquired and greatly prized matched grays. She hooked the handbag in its familiar place at the front of the saddle and managed to mount without any help. *All that running I've gotten away with here; more than I managed all my last year in L.A. Legs 're a lot stronger.* The smell of horse hadn't improved any at all, but it wasn't unbearable; the animal and its tack were all clean, at least. She gathered up the reins, let the stableboy shorten the stirrups, waited while he fastened her bag on behind the saddle. Dahven swung up and tossed a copper ceri down to the boy, another to the boy who held the gate open for them. They rode out onto the dusty road, turned right. Dahven turned to look back as the boy closed the double gates, peered down the road.

"It's an easy ride, if a warm one, and the sun will be in our eyes most of the way," he said. As they set out at a comfortable walk, he edged his gray over so he could take her fingers, then, and he smiled that wonderful, delighted, enchanting smile that had caught her off guard over his father's table. "Jennifer, let's go home."

Home. The word had such an odd ring to it; it had meant so many different things and for so long what it had meant most was pain—the place you can't go, any more. That might have been forever ago, like L.A., a cello, a red Honda, a dusty antique shop in the desert with Eisenhower—no, Stevenson—buttons in the window.

Old data. She shrugged, then smiled and brought his hand to her lips. "All right. Let's go home."